The Tale of the Missing Man

The Tale of the Missing Man

A Novel

Manzoor Ahtesham

Translated from the Hindi by
Jason Grunebaum and Ulrike Stark

NORTHWESTERN UNIVERSITY PRESS
EVANSTON, ILLINOIS

Northwestern University Press
www.nupress.northwestern.edu

Support for this publication came in part through the Global Humanities Initiative,
which is jointly supported by Northwestern University's Buffett Institute for Global
Studies and the Alice Kaplan Institute for the Humanities.

Printed in the United States of America

10 9 8 7 6 5 4 3 2 1

Library of Congress Cataloging-in-Publication Data

Names: Ehateśāma, Mañzūra, 1948– author. | Grunebaum, Jason, translator. | Stark,
   Ulrike, Dr. phil., translator.
Title: The tale of the missing man : a novel / Manzoor Ahtesham ; translated from the
   Hindi by Jason Grunebaum and Ulrike Stark.
Other titles: Dāstāna-e-lāpatā. English
Description: Evanston, Illinois : Northwestern University Press, 2018. | Winner of the
   Global Humanities Translation Prize.
Identifiers: LCCN 2018005644| ISBN 9780810137585 (pbk. : alk. paper) | ISBN
   9780810137592 (ebook)
Subjects: LCSH: Muslims—India—Bhopal—Social conditions—Fiction. | Bhopal
   (India)—Social conditions—Fiction.
Classification: LCC PK2200.E37 D3613 2018 | DDC 891.4337—dc23 LC record
   available at https://lccn.loc.gov/2018005644

For Gagan

The water roils, my shattered reflection quivers on it
The stone softens, and my dim words melt into oblivion.

—ZAFAR IQBAL

CONTENTS

Part One

Part Two

The Tale of the Missing Man

Part One

Doctor Crocodile

The doctor regarded him with curiosity. Gold teeth littered his mouth.

The doctor had just finished the same barrage of tests he'd done on several prior visits, tests he and many others had conducted. They called this nonsense "the checkup." Here was the same doctor he'd gone to see years ago when it all began, he remembered. The truth, however, was he hadn't so much gone to see the doctor as he'd been taken. That was at the beginning, only months after Father's death—ten years ago, now a full decade.

Did the doctor have as many gold teeth back then? He tried to remember. Had he also put on weight? It seemed this man had stealthily joined the ranks of the nation's helmsmen, steering toward progress and prosperity. Here was the embodiment of India's nouveau riche, doing quite well with his posh private clinic, cheerily vaccinating patients against death and other ailments. Even the waiting room now looked like a five-star hotel lobby, he thought, but then immediately felt embarrassed—the sad truth was that he'd been inside a five-star only once in his life, years ago. What gave him the right to compare anything to a luxury hotel?

The doctor's nostrils flared.

As for him, his thoughts broadcast on one channel while the other emitted nonstop chitchat with the doctor.

"I have an idea," he said to the doctor. "What you should do is stock a collection of all the world's holy books. When a Muslim like me comes in, have one of your assistants make him place his hand on the Quran right away and swear to tell Doctor Sahib the truth, the whole truth, and nothing but the truth. Just like in one of those courtroom dramas. So whoever comes in can swear on his holy book. Anyway, you don't believe what people tell you."

An understanding had developed over the years between doctor and patient that allowed for jokes and repartee. All doctors looked and acted about the same as far as he was concerned, but maybe in some sense this one was different.

"What, people don't lie through their teeth in court? Even after swearing an oath?" His jest was answered by a stern gaze. "But medicine has a cure for them, too."

"I can accept that. In fact, I have to accept it, I have no choice," he said, admitting defeat. " 'If you live in the river, don't tease the crocodile.' But, for god's sake, what about a cure for me? Please?"

The doctor didn't like to be called crocodile—he realized this instantly, and had only himself to blame for speaking without thinking. The doctor's face and wide-open mouth were just like a crocodile's. Any child would have noticed and said the same thing.

He cursed himself. How stupid can you be? Have you totally lost it? Who knows, maybe the doctor's own kids teased him by calling him crocodile. *See you later, alligator! In a while crocodile!*

"Everything looks good," the doctor said, showing no emotion. "You're fine. And if you stick to what I've been telling you, you'll be fine. Believe me, you are the picture of health."

You are the picture of health—the phrase echoed in his head like a kettledrum beating that drowned out all other instruments. Suddenly he was taken back to when he'd first met Doctor Crocodile.

The first time he'd seen the doctor, or had been taken to see him, by Bhai Miyan, his wife, Rehanna, and a few others, was ten years ago. They'd all been worried and anxious to do something. Bhai Miyan and the doctor were old friends, and the two men had a few words in private in the examination room before doctor and patient were introduced. Bhai Miyan came out and instructed him to go in.

"I know you're formal around me and cautious with what you say, but don't make the mistake of hiding anything from the doctor." Bhai Miyan counseled him as an elder. "Tell him everything. Don't leave anything out."

The doctor sat in a chair under a hundred-watt bulb, speaking to an acquaintance, surrounded by colorful advertisements on the wall. If there was any hint of the crocodile about him, he couldn't see it yet. The conversation was in English.

"I've turned in my resignation," the doctor said solemnly. "It's only a matter of time before my practice takes off. Besides, I wasn't working at the hospital for the money. I've got plenty, and now the government can't push me around and threaten to transfer me."

"That's all well and good," the other man said. "But what about me?"

Ignoring him, the doctor gave the patient a quick once-over, and told him to have a seat.

"So, what's the problem?" A friendly smile spread over his face: a resolve to ease the patient's pain. As he spoke, his office chair tilted back while his tiny eyes darted around the room.

He collected his thoughts and tried to put into words exactly what was the matter. One glance at the stranger in the room, though, and he couldn't summon his voice. The doctor sensed his unease.

"My friend here is also a doctor," he offered, but then, realizing the gravity of the situation, he cast a quick look to his friend, who got up and said he'd come back later.

"Now. Go ahead," the doctor said calmly, reassuringly, swiveling in his chair.

"Doctor Sahib," he began. But how could he describe with any clarity what he wanted to say? That when he's walking down the street or lying in bed or sitting in a chair, whether silent or in conversation, something shifts in his mind without warning, like when a cloud casts its shadow over a field or mountain. And when it shifts, he's not conscious of himself or anyone around him, as if his equilibrium were out of whack, and, if he doesn't gain hold of his senses right away, he feels as if he'd plunge into a deep chasm. It's like silence and a feeling of nonbeing are consuming him, and in order to regain his balance and stop the falling sensation, his body must strike just the right pose. How to explain this experience, so terrifying and painful? Was his body off balance, or his mind? Or was it an imbalance between body and mind? He imagined something shifting between body and soul, a slipping. Lasting only an instant, a second, a blink of an eye, this fraction of time is as fleeting as when film tears in a projector. Returning to his senses, he struggles to take in his surroundings, to recognize them again. He strains to remember the half-finished sentence, who he'd been speaking to, where he was. Snapping back, finally, he does what he can to pretend nothing happened. Somehow, he manages to regain control; it all happened so fast. By the time it's over, his mind is exhausted. Had it begun in childhood? As a teenager? He couldn't be sure, but remembered that it used to happen only once in a great while. Now it happened more frequently, to the point that it had become a daily occurrence, even several times a day, and each time the episodes grew longer. He wouldn't be surprised if he vanished right then and there talking to the doctor. He was at a total loss, ready to plead with the doctor: do *something*.

The doctor listened very closely to what he had to say, rocking back and forth in his chair, his not-yet-fat-encased eyes shifting.

"So, what do you do?"

The doctor asked this seemingly crucial question with a probing look, as if the cause of a person's illness were directly linked to his profession.

The doctor may have asked the question as casually as can be. But it didn't sit well. How are you supposed to explain to someone in ten seconds what it is you do? In his desperate state, though, he was so terror-stricken that he had no choice but to gain the doctor's trust. Even if it meant telling him everything he'd been through. What he wanted to do was to stand up, put his hands together in desperate supplication, and unburden himself fully. He wanted to say, "Doctor Sahib! What do I do? This is precisely the irony. I haven't been able to accomplish a single thing. Don't go by my looks, it's a double-faced joke the Almighty played on me. There's no proof at all that any illness or disease has resulted from my attempts to *do something*. Forget about extramarital bliss—in my twenty-eight years, I've never heard the song of a courtesan at a mehfil. I've never even seen the steps that lead up to her room, not even from a distance! I've laid eyes on a total of only one naked woman my whole life. Maybe one and a half, or, at most, one and three quarters, and one of them is my lawfully wedded wife. The other three quarters were spread out over a long period in installments. A little here, a little there. Look, Doctor Sahib, even though I've tried a thousand ways to abstain, it still happens. As a good citizen, I of course regret my missteps. Anyway, you're my doctor and I don't want to be my own worst enemy by hiding anything. I'm not talking about true love, but a few days of being crazy about someone was surely written in my book of fate. But it never lasted, it was never anything serious. So why would I stand on decorum with you? I won't hold back even the most trifling of details. You may be a professional through and through, but I'm sure there are questions even you hesitate to ask. Like whether a particular individual has a taste for members of his own sex. The name of our city comes up a lot in such conversations. You might like to know whether I take part in such activities. Even though I haven't yet, maybe somewhere deep down, the potential exists, with the right person. The truth is I've enjoyed an average kind of pleasure, within my capability, and with a woman, my wife. Though I sometimes meet someone of my own sex and fall under a different kind of spell. These kinds of contradictions are probably not uncommon at all. I studied engineering but dropped out midway because I didn't think anything would come of it. I wasn't the best student, but my brain did function. As a kid I wanted to play hockey, but played cricket instead, and a lot of badminton and table tennis. I playacted cinema, played cops and robbers. Cards and carrom. Collected stamps, took photos. I liked good movies, and bought records to play on Bhai Miyan's turntable. I bought film and sports magazines on a regular basis. I enjoyed reading novels and poetry, and I still read. I tried to write short stories. I still do, in secret. Up to a certain age, I kept a journal, and wrote in it regularly. I diligently corresponded with friends and family. Where did I go wrong? Or rather, where am I going wrong that this so-called disease has become my fate? I should add that I've never abandoned anything that I started—most of the things I started abandoned me. What's left is the drinking. And if you tell me to stop, I'll try to stop.

Looking into the doctor's eyes, though, he guessed the doctor was far more interested in what he did for a living than all he'd been through, and had no time for this tale of woe. He had a new clinic to launch, other patients to see.

"Business. I'm in business," he said, trying to summon a firm voice.

He was instructed to lie down on the table. The doctor's fingers commenced probing, touching, kneading, drumming on his body in every way imaginable, looking and listening, his bloodshot eyes squinting, darting around like red lights atop a speeding ambulance, spinning and flashing. It may have been a signal: *I'm in a hurry, get out of the way.* Then he took out all sorts of devices: a BP cuff, flashlight, reflex hammer, rubber tubes. The patient lay down, he sat up, he took a series of deep breaths and let them out slowly. Finally, as he put his clothes back on and sat down next to the doctor, he saw that the eagerness in the red eyes had drained away. Despair was written on the doctor's face in letters so clear there was no need to read: he was as certain as he was sorry that the exam had been a waste.

"Doctor Sahib," he cleared his throat and tried to muster some courage. "You don't think I may be suffering from manic depression . . . ?"

"Why don't you leave it to me to decide," the doctor interrupted, and continued brusquely. "Name?"

He didn't understand.

"Name? I am asking you your name. Oh, here it is. Z. A. Khan," the doctor read from a sheet of paper, a sarcastic edge returning to his voice. "May I ask you your full name?" The tone of his voice suggested an interest still piqued.

"Yes, of course. It's Zamir Ahmed Khan," he said obediently. "Why?"

"Just asking," the doctor said, aloof. "I'm making a list of tests you need, and the prescriptions you should take in the meantime. Three pills, one in the morning, one in the afternoon, and one right before bed. Don't worry, you're the picture of health, completely normal. And the medicine will make you feel even more normal. By the way, there's something very funny about your initials! The world goes from *A* to *Z*, but you go from *Z* to *A*. Fascinating!" The doctor let out a belly laugh, then said his good-byes. "Make another appointment in two weeks, bring your test results. Let me know how things go."

The tests all turned out normal. He dutifully took the medicine for two weeks, but his condition showed no improvement. The next time Zamir Ahmed Khan visited the doctor, he was summarily informed that he had developed the habit of thinking all wrong, that he liked to make mountains out of molehills, that he was so caught up in his obsessions that no drug in the world could cure him. From a medical standpoint, everything about him was normal. No need to take medicine. Ashamed and secretly doubting whether he really was sick, he got up and left, cursing the doctor under his breath.

But a few days later he was back again, list of complaints in hand. On the one hand was Zamir Ahmed Khan's condition. On the other, the doctor's diagnosis: normal.

Over the past ten years, all the doctor's predictions had come true. In no time at all, his practice had more than taken off, and government transfer policies hadn't intimidated him. Today he was a respected doctor, renowned throughout the city. And thanks to the money that came in, he was able to abandon the old shop and build an impressive new clinic, then opened a second office in the new part of town and built a lovely mansion for himself. He owned his own car, ran his own ambulance. All of it had gathered toward him over time as metal shards toward a magnet.

This time, Doctor Crocodile flashed his gold teeth with each yawn.

"So?" he turned to Zamir Ahmed Khan with a smile. "Have you submitted your claim form for the Union Carbide leak? Have you had your checkup?"

"Why bother?" he replied, smiling back. "That, too, by your blessing, will turn out as normal as can be."

"Ah, but you should still get a checkup," Crocodile replied gravely. "What's the harm? Wait, now I remember. You're in the carpet business, right? Synthetic? Wall-to-wall? I could use some new carpets at home."

"Just say the word," he said casually, avoiding the question. "Whenever you like. We would be honored by your presence in our store. Come pick out your color and whatever else you need. We'll have it installed. Just be sure to give me a call before you come."

"What else? Anything new?" Crocodile asked leisurely, as if he wanted to relax with a little gossip before seeing the next patient. "What's the latest?"

"Well, Doctor, here's the latest," Zamir Ahmed Khan said in a quiet, steady voice. "My wife left me."

"*No!*" The doctor shifted several gears at once in fluster and concern. "That's just awful! But when? How?" Crocodile was chomping at the bit and ready for some fun.

"She started leaving a long time ago, just after we got married," he said casually, pretending to be unfazed. "Each time she visited her family, she'd leave a little part of herself there. I'm not suggesting she stole stuff from her dower, or furniture, or pots and pans. All of that is still lying around the house. I'm talking about her soul. She transferred it bit by bit from our place to her parents'. This last time she left her entire body there. When both body and soul refused to come back, my two daughters stayed with her. They're closer to their mother. They've been living there for some time now, too."

Crocodile listened intently to Zamir Ahmed Khan, then burst out laughing. His mouth opened so wide and for so long that it would've been easy to count which teeth were gold and which were the ones for chewing. He was having fun. He picked up a pen to write.

"You're too much! You know, being able to poke fun at yourself is an art. And you do know how to tell a good joke. I ran into your missus just yesterday at the convent school, I was there for a parent-teacher conference for my daughter, and there was your wife, happy as a lark."

"Oh, so you're not only a doctor but also a mind reader now? When, my dear sir, did I indicate that my wife is, as we say in Hindi, 'deceased,' or, in Urdu, 'resting in peace'? What if staying alive really just means finding a bit of joy. I'm telling you that leaving me was her first step in finding it."

The doctor could hardly take it.

"You're killing me," he said again and again. He dried the tears from his eyes, wiped his face with a handkerchief, and took a sip of water. "But don't expect me to change my diagnosis just because of this. I'll say it one more time, there's nothing wrong with you. If anything's the matter it's because you keep seeing other doctors, against my advice, and take whatever they're prescribing."

Zamir Ahmed Khan wanted to ask, *Doctor Crocodile, do you mean to suggest that my wife hasn't left me?* But the doctor's eyes were telling him good-bye, so he kept his mouth shut. There was so much more he wanted to ask, but suddenly he felt very strange.

"Excuse me, please, Doctor Sahib!" he said, now a little afraid. As he stood, his limbs began to flail into all sorts of wild postures. He turned to the side, bent at the waist, and, like a gymnast, tried twisting his trunk and limbs into all kinds of contortions. He was drenched in sweat within seconds. He bowed his head, held still, took a deep breath, silent, eyes still shut, one moment more, snapped them open, head up, and there they were—the round, round eyes of Crocodile!

"Bravo, sir! Bravo!" Crocodile was ecstatic. "Now you've even taken up acting! Well done indeed, very well done!"

Ten years ago, his family members had decided he was an ill man. Not Crocodile. He'd stuck to his guns.

"Go to hell." The words involuntarily escaped from Zamir Ahmed Khan's mouth. He began to leave quickly but not without taking the visit report the doctor had slid across the table. Underneath the clinic's letterhead the doctor had written in English, "Mr. Z. A. Khan, age: 39. No treatment required."

Below was Doctor Crocodile's signature.

Out in the City

The world had witnessed countless changes over the past ten years, but doctors maintained consensus that Zamir Ahmed Khan needed no treatment. The joy of having two daughters, the night of the gas leak, his mother's death, and working with Junkman Sharafat at the Treasure Trove were the most significant events of Zamir Ahmed Khan's life. He had fallen in with some people and out with others. There were also experiences he'd rather forget. *Et tu*, Zamir Ahmed Khan? Someone wanted to point a finger at him, in surprise and dismay; Zamir Ahmed Khan wanted to pretend he hadn't heard and walk away.

As he walked down the street, words echoed in his head like a mantra: things were not as they should be. Not one bit.

On his left was the Bade Bagh cemetery, the largest in the city, and on his right, the tin shed where final prayers were performed before burial. Crocodile hadn't been stupid in opening his clinic in this area, where more than half the city's graveyards were located. Some convergences are indeed tragic, but it was pointless to think about it like this or argue. Since Bhopal was a city growing fast, at least half the new settlements were to be built on old graveyards. This made perfect sense because it is said that on the Day of Judgment seventy thousand dead souls will be resurrected from each grave. Settled or barren, the land, like mankind, has its own fate.

Just then, he passed the building on Hamidia Road where the hotel of Aziz, also known as Acchan, once stood, and where he used to spend a lot of time with him. The legal tenants, who had gone on to sublet the building to others, were now locked in a bizarre legal battle with the subletters, with the legal landlord relegated to the role of mere spectator. Different people had seized various parts of the building and had opened up shops and offices. The world would have changed beyond recall by the time the question of ownership was resolved.

The street was crowded. The movie at the nearby theater had just let out. Cars, motor scooters, three-wheelers, buses, trucks, bicycles, tongas, and pedestrians came at one another like enemy armies. So much dust and exhaust were in the air that it was hard to breathe.

13

The world has changed, Zamir Ahmed Khan thought, looking all around him, and change didn't necessarily mean for the worse. Those who refused to accept this fact would be counted among the ill. Not the physically, but the mentally ill. His own life circumstances contradicted this: in the name of change, things had gone from bad to worse. And to end this downward spiral as soon as possible, he would have to do something out of the ordinary, something meaningful. But what?

This sea of humanity moved with determination, as if each person had every single step plotted from the moment they'd left home. A world of difference lay between the Hamidia Road of yesterday, where he used to spend time with Acchan (or, even earlier, when he would go for evening walks with Vivek), and the Hamidia Road of today. He remembered the old road appearing much wider, when in fact it had been widened three times since then. Most of the old buildings had been replaced with multistories. Parks and green spaces had vanished. Countless stores had sprung up in their place.

Zamir Ahmed Khan often recalled something Acchan used to say back then. One winter evening while sitting in Aziz aka Acchan's room, he took a painkiller, Avil, and drinking for the first time, fell out of sorts with himself. It was an emotional moment at a delicate point in his life. Caught between wanting to drink and his body rejecting the liquid, Zamir Ahmed Khan had to summon everything he had to down a single gulp. And with it, he proclaimed to Acchan in English, "All I want is true love. Nothing more."

Acchan looked him in the eye and gave a little grunt. "Brother," he said, pausing to take a long drag on his cigarette. "If you want this wish to come true it might befit you to have a little money in your pocket. Better still, a lot, along with some common sense. In addition to all your other virtues and charms, of course."

Zamir Ahmed Khan bet Aziz aka Acchan that even without a single penny in his pocket, he'd be able to find true love, while Acchan, for his part, assured Zamir that if he managed to pull it off, no one would be happier than he.

What would Aziz say if he knew about his current condition? Thank god he wouldn't have to face him, as he had no clue as to Aziz's current whereabouts.

Something out of the ordinary had to be done, something meaningful. But what?

Sitting at home, twiddling his thumbs, more than six months had gone by. If he went out for some reason, no matter how small the task, why, as far as his family was concerned, he was a busy man! There was almost nothing left for him to do at the Treasure Trove. Also, he'd become a burden to Sharafat Miyan, the store's owner. These were the two reasons Zamir Ahmed Khan came up with, at any rate. Sharafat Miyan for his part had never said a word to this effect, nor had he told him to stop coming to work. True, Sharafat had questioned a couple of things he'd done, and he'd said words to the effect that he no longer seemed as interested in his work as he should be. But this Zamir could not accept.

"You asked me to work for you, and we had an agreement that it would be on my own terms," he said tersely to Sharafat Miyan. "It doesn't make sense for you to tell me this now. The way I see it, things'll run just fine without me."

Sharafat Miyan, who was somehow a distant relation, and who, when starting the business, had assured Zamir Ahmed Khan that he would be treated not as an employee but as a partner, was dumbstruck.

"Try not to take this the wrong way," he once said to Zamir Ahmed Khan. "When we first started out, you kept shop responsibly. Did anyone ever complain? If you're not coming in just let me know, no problem, it's okay, someone else can fill in. But we're expanding and we need to have someone responsible and reliable."

"I'm not in good health, Sharafat Miyan," he snapped. "At least try to understand."

"If you're not feeling well, go home and rest for a few days."

Sharafat Miyan was interrupted by a couple of customers coming into the store. Even though they were busy all day, Zamir found the time to count up all the favors he'd done for Sharafat Miyan. The higher he counted, the angrier he got. Junkman Sharafat and Salamat, his son, couldn't possibly have launched the business successfully without Zamir Ahmed Khan. What they'd needed most was a first-class salesman, and someone who spoke fluent English. Gaining the trust of a customer is an art. And at first, they'd never tired of singing his praises. "You and your words, they cast a spell on customers!" both father and son complimented him.

The Treasure Trove, with its carpets, chandeliers, expensive furniture, home furnishings, and high-priced knickknacks, was the kind of shop where the shopkeeper had to put up with attitude if the customer was willing to pay asking price, and where people went to buy things on a lark, not because they needed them. It was also also not the kind of place where customers could be easily sold on anything and everything. It was true that the initial capital had come from Sharafat Miyan, but everything after that, from the name of the store, to the interior design, to his own charming presence at the sales counter, and the way he pitched in with gusto and geniality, was entirely Zamir Ahmed Khan's doing. And he did it with such zeal and commitment, never once asking to be made a legal business partner. What's more, for the past nine years he'd cheerfully accepted whatever amount was placed in his hand every month, without Sharafat Miyan ever divulging how well the store was doing. When he first started, five hundred rupees was the monthly sum. This later increased to eight hundred, and then no more. True, Zamir Ahmed Khan did dip into the shop's till for his own expenses from time to time. Sharafat Miyan should've realized that supporting a family on eight hundred a month was impossible. But how much could he have really skimmed from the Treasure Trove? Working side by side with Zamir Ahmed Khan for who knows how many years, Salamat began to think he could run the store all by himself. And Zamir Ahmed Khan? No longer needed as he'd once been when the store first opened, nine years ago. Ungrateful son of a bitch, the father. A junkman by birth. And now the son, fruit of his life's labor, was just another piece of junk.

So the day after his conversation with Sharafat Miyan, Zamir stopped going to the Treasure Trove. Time passed, but Sharafat Miyan (forget about his son) never came to see how he was doing. His condition had worsened to the point that all he did was sit at home and do nothing. Sharafat Miyan continued to stuff eight hundred rupees into an envelope and send it to him for two more months. After that, it was as if he'd become a total stranger. They didn't talk, or get together in order to reach some kind of understanding. He sat at home waiting all the while, nine years of hard work stripped away.

What hard work? A little voice inside teased him whenever he feigned innocence. What happened to your moral compass, Zamir Ahmed Khan? What injustice have you suffered? Everyone was happy as long as your heart was in it. But then debauchery ruled your nights and you started sleeping during the day. What should Junkman Sharafat have done? How can you complain if Sharafat's son Salamat, by dedication and pluck, proved himself worthy of running the store? Then add up what you took legally and illegally, and be honest: you probably took far more than was your due. Partnership papers were never drawn up because you never developed a sense for business. And the money went where?

If you sat down and tried to do the math, it'd be pure guesswork: how much smoke, and how much water? The money didn't go to your wife and kids, but was used for your own pleasures. And how many pleasures have you chased? As if it matters.

The Treasure Trove with Junkman Sharafat wasn't such an honest outfit in any case. Sifting through junkyards and black markets, from small fiefdoms to big cities, he gathered whatever had value, including antiques illegal to buy or sell. He used his legal business of machine-made carpets, mass-produced chandeliers, vases, paintings, and lampshades as a front to sell real antiques to Indians and foreigners. He named the price, they paid. That was the real business. That's where he got the money he used for the shop's upkeep. And suppose all this was accepted fact? Would it make what Zamir Ahmed Khan had done any less illegal? And why take issue with it now, after he'd severed ties with the Treasure Trove? Hadn't all of this gone on while Zamir was still there?

Back when he worked at the store, he'd find customers for Sharafat Miyan's shady dealings (as he now termed them), and haggled with them over prices. It left a bad taste in his mouth, now that he was proclaiming Sharafat immoral and dishonest.

A saffron flag flew from a jeep on the road. The vehicle's loudspeaker blasted an announcement about a general meeting that night. On the other side of the road, some people argued with an auto rickshaw driver. Next to Zamir stood the empty building that a few years earlier had housed the city's only seventy-millimeter cinema. Bemoaning the growth of TV viewership, the owners had decided to knock down the theater and build a business center in its place. It was a part of a larger trend that spread its roots throughout the city and nation with each passing day—a transformation that seemed positive at first glance, but then grew perplexing. The roadside food shacks had changed their looks in the blink of an eye, and so had those of the proprietors. Prosperity reigned, it seemed to him, as he counted the growing number of things that enabled a life of luxury. But Zamir Ahmed still hadn't figured out the reason behind it all. No, not him, he wasn't participating in this collective affluence, even if he could understand what caused it. But how long could an entire society, country, nation go on making money and go on being prosperous, like Sharafat Miyan of the Treasure Trove?

He realized he'd pass out if he didn't find something to grab hold of right away, so intense was the flashing of light and shadow in his head. A passing auto rickshaw slowed down and stopped. The driver greeted him, asked how he was, gestured for him to get in. A few minutes later he arrived home, after passing by the city's now defunct ice cream factory, which used to make Dilkush Ice Cream: he remembered the cold road, slabs of ice, and scale hooks, and the counter of a distant childhood. Passing the Treasure Trove he noticed the dazzling window displays (truly magnificent), and Salamat, chatting with customers, sitting in the same chair that Zamir had occupied for years. It was fine. It was okay. He had been set free, he reassured himself as he paid the auto rickshaw driver. When the driver said good-bye and continued on his way, he was suddenly struck with the question, why had the driver shown so much courtesy? Did the driver know him? And if so, why hadn't Zamir recognized him?

Zamir Ahmed Khan racked his brain for a long time, but wouldn't remember that the auto rickshaw driver was Shaukat, who had worked in his father's sawmill for several years when he was younger. Back then, he was the one Zamir sent to buy *Sport and Pastime*, *Screen*, and other magazines from the old shop at the crossing.

It began to gnaw at him, so he stopped thinking about it.

Back at Home

All was quiet at home. His brother's wife must have been in the kitchen instructing the servant, while the children were probably doing their homework.

"Assalam alaikum wa rahmatullah," a shrieking voice greeted him. "Come in please! Come in please! Come in please! Mithu Miyan me and you!" The parrot screeched, then began his salaam and invitation to come in all over again.

The parrot had been Amma's pastime. She'd spent a good deal of time chatting with the creature, especially near the end. Whatever she may have tried to teach him, he hadn't progressed beyond greetings, welcomes, and the confession of faith.

"Mithu Miyan, how are you?" Zamir Ahmed Khan asked as he sat down next to the birdcage in the corridor. The parrot silently bobbed its head, beak quivering, and looked at him with eyes that had prompted proverbs about cunning and deceit the world over. Zamir had never been able to figure out what was so peculiar about the eyes of parrots that had earned them such a bad reputation. He had asked Amma, but all he got out of her was that maybe they don't get attached to their masters the same way dogs and cats do. Had anyone ever heard of a parrot returning after it had escaped from its cage?

Zamir Ahmed Khan couldn't understand how an entire species of bird could fall from grace for such a small act of ingratitude. And there was another expression—"to raise a parrot," meaning to feed a bad habit. But there wasn't anything special about the parrot Amma raised, good or bad, that would allow him to take the parrot species seriously as a whole. Amma had her own way of thinking, and taking care of animals was part of her basic faith right until the end. She'd raised her own children, helped look after and teach her grandchildren, and tried to share in the joys and sorrows of friends, family, and acquaintances alike.

Amma had never liked cats or dogs. The parrot had come into the house by chance from an old family servant who'd brought it from her village as a gift. Amma regarded the bird quizzically at first, but later became more and more interested in this strange green pigeon. The rest of the family members unanimously proclaimed that it was the result of a crossbreeding with another bird, that this flying creature could in no way be a purebred. Why? Even after a full year of trying to teach it to speak, the entire household, Amma included, couldn't make it utter a single word. But she wasn't bothered by the failure. She ordered an expensive brass cage with three swings, and busied herself with feeding the bird and keeping the cage clean. "So what if he doesn't say anything?" she said with a big smile. "Can you show me a birdcage in town lovelier than this? The real reason I'm raising this parrot is to bring out the beauty of the cage."

In the end, Amma's passion for raising living creatures found singular expression in the well-being of this lone bird. Then one day, people listened with a start as the parrot, between its whistles, repeated "Ammi Jaan— Ammi Jaan—Ammi Jaan." They were stupefied. The "come in please," the greetings, and the confession of faith were the fruit of her subsequent labor. The parrot, for its part, became so attuned to the timings of Amma's various tasks—when she should eat, pray, and get up, both mornings and afternoons—that she no longer required an alarm clock.

"So many stories allude to how evil spirits inhabit the body of parrots, Amma," Zamir Ahmed Khan had once said, teasing his mother. "How can that be?"

Amma laughed. "Look after the parrot however you like," she warbled. "When my time is up it's up. Its cage is not the one where *my* soul is kept locked up. *This* parrot is not that parrot. The angel of death knows exactly where to find that cage and that parrot. He's the one, and the only one, with the key."

And what timing! Right after her morning prayers, when the rest of the house wasn't up yet after a good night's sleep, Amma, as usual, stood beside the cage, and had the parrot recite the confession of faith, also heard by the half-awake. Soon thereafter, the parrot's uncontrollable squawking fully roused the entire household. They rushed to the cage and found Amma lying on the ground. They touched her and realized that it was all over; her body was already cold. By the time Rahat and Zamir Ahmed Khan had come down from the top floor, her body had been arranged on a bier at the entrance of the house. The whole numb family was standing in grief and in shock, like a discerning filmgoer unable to grasp the ending of a smash hit.

Zamir Ahmed Khan left the squawking bird behind and shuffled up the steps and toward his room with a heavy heart. An emptiness and void had opened up bag and baggage after Amma's death, in the house and in his life, and couldn't be filled with anything else. The stranger had come to stay, a guest who tightened its grip on the family. Amma's presence was likely the last bridge that competing family members and branches of the extended family could cross. As soon as it collapsed, all sorts of minor sultanates and fiefdoms declared autonomy. Rightly or wrongly, he had often argued with Amma when she was still alive. But unlike the rest of the world, he knew he could count on her protection. She stood by him no matter how much she complained. She'd be his last place of refuge, something he was acutely aware of even when she was alive. Abba's death had been a big shock, but hers was different. Now he had to come to terms with reality and live his life in a way he didn't when Amma was alive. It wasn't as if anyone had wanted to pull him aside and teach him the facts of life or explain that some things were not as they seemed. His own thinking had suddenly become so heavy and dense that Zamir Ahmed Khan found it nearly impossible to keep his balance beneath its weight.

One result of this was that Zamir Ahmed Khan cut ties with Sharafat Miyan and the Treasure Trove, and now cooped himself up at home. The other was the theatrical walkout of Rahat with the two girls.

"How long do you think we can manage with you moping around the house like this?"

This innocent sentence began the conversation that would end with Rahat's hegira to her parents.

It was the wrong moment for this conversation. One fortuitous word can sometimes slip out and set off a whole happy chain reaction. Here, the exact opposite occurred. As his wife articulated her important query, Zamir Ahmed Khan was lost in another world, far removed from simple questions of home and hearth. His mind was on last night's TV discussion about the forthcoming budget.

Rahat's questioning jerked him out of his reverie. Instead of worry or concern about his ill health, her voice now dripped with sarcasm.

"What are you talking about?" he said sharply, avoiding her gaze.

"I'm talking about how everyone in the world does *something*. Besides, who's completely healthy? Everyone has problems nowadays. Everyone has their own worries and anxieties."

His wife was speaking, but his mind had wandered off. He bored a hole straight through her words and descended into an underground filled with worry and vexation, emerging only to take a stroll along his favorite path: national progress, national development. The road that demanded the deepest of thought, the most elevated spirit, and one that defied common sense. If there had been a path made just for him, this was it. National progress and prosperity. Though invisible, the path was right there, even if it wasn't real. Progress and development. Or, peace and quiet. Or, the freedom to live your life as you please. Or, more money coming in, less going out. At least he'd never mixed up the real world with the memory of Phaphu Biya's bungalow or with his imagined paradise. More diseases could now be cured than ever before. Unprecedented ways to enjoy a life of luxury. Bicycles had made way for scooters and zippy motorcycles and shiny, low-cost, made-in-India Marutis. Yes sir, all on the path of national progress and prosperity! A double-wide, slick black shiny road built at the speed of lightning: Recondo Boulevard. The Third World has made you its leader just as the third-class carriages have been eliminated from the trains. And the din of the crowd roars in unison, "Our India, greatest country of all . . . Sare jahan se accha . . ."

He emerged from his underground humming, "Sare jahan se accha hindustan hamara . . . ," and Rahat was staring at him furiously, mouth agape.

"So what is it you want?" He tried to restrain his voice, but irritation crept in. "What do you suggest? Go out on the street and perform my, what do you call them, my Indian dances? Kathak or Bharatnatyam style?"

"What do you think everyone else does? Do that."

Rahat's words were a very tidy way to describe the state of things, he thought. But he no longer had to worry about her accusing stare or venomous tone.

"As if anyone's life adds up to more than a Kathak or Bharatnatyam dance!" she added.

Zamir Ahmed Khan couldn't help but be impressed with Rahat's metaphor for life. He relapsed into thought.

She continued, "You've weighed and measured everything that's possible to weigh and measure. You've looked into everything. But if there's anything you've missed, then by all means proceed with your investigation!"

It couldn't be clearer to Zamir Ahmed Khan that Rahat was taking advantage of Amma's no longer being there. This was one of the realities he had to face since Amma had left him behind.

"You think I'm just pretending?" he said, even more irritated.

"It doesn't matter. How long will this go on?" She'd decided it was time to end the argument. "Do you really think everything'll be okay if you sit at home all day, browse old books and magazines, stay out late?"

She wasn't that off the mark, but it's not as if he'd been pleased with himself sitting cooped up at home. He never thought in a million years he'd be stuck there, unable to make it through the door.

The balance sheet of their married life was then produced, tallying services rendered versus services received. In the end, the numbers didn't add up, and their matrimony was declared bankrupt. When Rahat had threatened to go to her parents, Zamir Ahmed Khan thought for a moment that he should try to talk her out of it. Like: Have you lost your mind? Did I ever say that this household could function without your help? You don't make much money, and you teach at a very small school. But don't forget it's your salary that allows the girls to get an education. It was your decision to not work when we got married. And after Amma passed away, did I get in the way when you decided to start teaching? Think of your husband's dilemma. He looks like a handsome, six-foot-tall walking advertisement of good health, right? But the truth is he's been struck with a fatal disease. No acting or pretending. I'm not saying that the doctors lie or got it wrong. It's possible my illness has yet to be described in medical journals. Every disease has its first victim. Don't you think it's possible I'm the first sufferer? A disease is nothing to shake a stick at. It chooses its first victim the same way that popular prophets or avatars are chosen. Just because doctors don't understand the condition now doesn't mean they might not later. I might make a full recovery in a few days' time. Try to understand what I'm going through. Hope makes the world go round.

The expression on Rahat's face made it clear that saying anything more was futile.

"If you say one more thing or give me any more advice I'll put the joke to song and will sing and sing!"

Rahat probably guessed that her words would lead to Zamir Ahmed committing an error—one enough, if it were hockey, to earn her a penalty shot. And then: she shoots! She scores! She wins!

It wasn't as if the girls, Sana and Saba, didn't love their father. But it was just as true that if he'd tried to stop them from going with their mother, they'd have gone anyway.

Zamir Ahmed Khan understood why she had to leave. When the carbon copy of his life replaced the original him, his wife had transformed into everything but a companion: she was now a laundress, cook, sweeper, private prostitute. How did this happen, and why hadn't the companion stayed? He'd counseled her about the advantages of keeping on good terms with the family, explaining that these were the people who would do good by her in the end. He'd assured her that she and the daughters would get his share of the house. Her dower had been set at fifty thousand when they were married, but she hadn't claimed the money in the first place. And even if she had—she wasn't stupid—where would it have come from?

The void in the room felt sharp, despite the sounds of the outside traffic trailing off. Dust on the furniture reminded him that it had been more than two weeks since Rahat had left. And she hadn't once tried to contact him.

"Ya Allah!"

The words slipped from his lips. "May you give Zamir Ahmed Khan the strength to wash the dark stain from his soul. Or give him enough strength to go to his in-laws and convince his wife to come back."

It seemed that his prayer had ascended to the highest reaches of the heavens, but once there . . .

The Underground, Upstairs

The room on the top floor of the house was immediately transformed into an underground den: his upstairs underground, where he could examine the dark recesses of his mind in private. More than once he had considered putting everything to paper in grand, meticulous detail, but follow-through proved elusive. Aspiring to be a writer and a scholar was one of Zamir Ahmed Khan's long-standing weaknesses. He clung to the notion that he'd now be leading a totally different life if he hadn't chosen his college classes so haphazardly and disastrously. Even as a boy he'd considered storytelling an art form. Instead of writing essays, he dazzled his teachers and classmates with stories. He religiously kept a journal until a certain age and wrote sprawling, epic letters, spurred on by talent and a sense of secret fun. Then moving away from all of this, under the occasional spell of various persons and events, he decided he wanted to be a poet, too. (Success eluded him here as well.) So he kept on writing stories. He submitted them for publication to various magazines, and most were accepted—but they weren't published under his real name. With each submission, he'd invent a new, fictive name that was pleasing to his ear. This would be the one he used to sign the work. So secretive was Zamir Ahmed Khan about his writing that he was the only person who knew it existed, even now. And his bent toward the literary was so enduring that the few people he still socialized with were poets or writers or journalists. Then there was the old crowd of movers and shakers whom he'd met a lifetime ago in Aziz aka Acchan's hotel, and whose names and faces had now become a blur. Also were the big spenders whom he'd gotten to know as customers at the Treasure Trove. Even before making the sale he knew his relationship with these types would never go far.

It was his literary-minded friends who had pushed him to write. They were impressed by what he had to say at a time when he was hard at work looking for something to do with his life (not at all unlike today), and particularly before he started working for Sharafat Miyan. Before he knew it, though, the Treasure Trove struck gold. He became so busy that his old friends thought he'd put his writing on the back burner, and there was only a glimmer of hope for him to break free from the hurried ways of the world.

All of them clung to the notion that even though Zamir Ahmed Khan was fully wheeling and dealing with the world, if he had a minute to spare, he'd come running to them. Or maybe they reasoned that his mother's death had been rough. *You know how it goes, he'll take it easy for a bit and then hop right back in the saddle. Aren't we all caught up with our own worries? What's the harm in calling a hill a hill and a spade a spade?*

They say that everyone has a book in them. If nothing else, then at least an autobiography. But then: will the writer dare stand in the crossfire of shame? Can he bear to pour out his thoughts on paper exactly as they pass through the mind, leaving out nothing? Can the images, sketches, equations, safely stored in the brain, plus all that's beyond the reach of any definition, ever be conveyed by words? Can the condition described alternatively as "mental illness" or "creative prowess" take shape in the assembling of word after word into lines of language? As the poet says, "Do I dare?"

If you think it, why not do it? Doers do.

But was Zamir Ahmed Khan among the doers?

When he was little, a Maulvi Sahib used to come to the house to teach the Quran and give religious lessons to Bhai Miyan and their older sister. Back then, the outer room, now cluttered with the flotsam and jetsam of life, used to be Abba's drawing room. Sofas had not yet come into fashion, and the room had a small platform with a large cushion on it, plus a few mismatched chairs with armrests lined up against the walls.

The Maulvi Sahib had once upon a time been Maulvi Muhammad Ahmed Khan, and Abba's teacher. As he settled into a certain age he began giving lessons to children so he could do good deeds, and not burden anyone financially. Abba had been one of Maulvi Sahib's favorite pupils, so Maulvi was given a free hand to teach the children as he saw fit. Zamir Ahmed Khan remembered his face: a large, radiant pearl with a white beard, white muslin cap, sharp, luminous eyes. He was jovial and always tried to find the bright side of otherwise ugly events, whether the partition of India, the dismal state of Muslims in the world, or the fast disappearance of Urdu, Arabic, and Persian culture in India, and with them the educational institutions that once sustained them.

Whenever Maulvi Sahib came to give lessons to Bhai Miyan and Aapa, Zamir Ahmed Khan's mother placed some paan on a fine Muradabadi plate, and sent in little Zamir to serve it. He was such a small creature that holding a plate with a single piece of paan while walking was no easy task. Mother gave him clear instructions: *First give your salaam to Maulvi Sahib, then put down the plate in front of him.* But each and every time he'd forget to offer his salaam; carrying the plate while simultaneously looking up at Maulvi Sahib's countenance proved too much, and he inevitably stumbled. A serene smile spread over the old man's face when little Zamir was reminded about the salaam by his older sister or Bhai Miyan. Maulvi said tenderly, "Why are you giving this poor child a hard time? Why even bother with salaaming or praying or schooling or learning? When this one grows up, he's only going to be a cow herder anyway. Wouldn't you say, little man? And if that doesn't work out, you can always learn half the alphabet and how to count to ten and become a muezzin. He'll count the rest of his days in some tiny cell at the back of a mosque."

The awful things people said with their ugly tongues! A cell in a mosque, now Zamir's homemade upstairs underground. What Maulvi Sahib had said to him in jest back then had now become an indisputable fact.

There was another memory, etched in his mind and linked to the image of the tiny cell in the mosque—the memory of blind Murshad, who used to live near the house in the masjid.

Murshad

"Really, what's the rush?"

Vivek was baffled when Zamir Ahmed Khan announced his decision to marry Rahat. "You should at least be able to stand on your own feet when you get married."

"Things are, well, moving," he said, trying to skirt the topic. "And something might come of it."

Even then he knew exactly what he was doing: lying to Vivek and himself. It was only a few months before the wedding. Everyone was astounded at his decision, aside from Abba and Amma, who put all their remaining resolve behind him. Maybe they thought the marriage was a last glimpse of hope to save their son Zamir.

"I just don't get it," Vivek said, sunk.

"Did I ever mention Murshad to you?" Zamir Ahmed Khan said to Vivek, as if trying to take him into his confidence. "Did I? Do you remember?"

Murshad, who was blind, lived in the neighborhood mosque. He had a dark complexion, a tall, broad frame, and his face was shaped like the pit of a Totapuri mango. A ring of hair circled an otherwise bald head, while the smattering of stubble on his chin, like the hair on his head, was more pepper than salt. Murshad swept and cleaned the mosque, was responsible for giving the call to prayer at the prescribed time, and, if the need arose, also led the start of prayer.

Every night after the evening prayer, Murshad left the mosque, supporting himself with his stick, and made his rounds through the neighborhood, dented tin bowl in hand. He called out in front of every house, "Spare a few crumbs for me, in the name of Allah. Allah will save you from rack and ruin. O Allah!" Though blind, Murshad still recognized each and every house. Doors opened, roti was placed into his sack, curry ladled into his bowl. For his part, he gave blessings during his walk back to the tiny room at the mosque. If his call received no response, he'd pause a moment before repeating in his most supplicating voice, "In the name of Allah, please spare a crumb." He'd linger a few moments more, and only then, and very gently at that, rap his stick against the ground: Murshad's announcement of departure. His voice then trailed off in prayer, feeling its way forward with his stick's tap-tap.

Lying alone in that little mosque cell—what did Murshad think about? As Zamir Ahmed Khan grew older, Murshad's existence had become a puzzle, but Murshad was no longer in this world to help solve it. The question grew more forceful and menacing every day. What did he do in that little cell, all alone? Prayer times were fixed, and how many prayers can an ordinary man pray anyway? Sooner or later, even prayer and worship grew tiresome and boring. And it wasn't as if Murshad was one of those spiritually elevated pirs or fakirs who day and night engross themselves in prayers or lose themselves in religious metaphysics. He didn't even know how to recite the call to prayer correctly—every day people complained. The poor man was illiterate, and the sum total of his prayer repertoire consisted of no more than a few memorized blessings and verses from the Quran. Many times he'd seen Murshad sitting in front of the gate of the masjid smoking bidis and talking to people as they filled water from the pump. What did he have to talk about? What was left for him to tell?

People thought of Murshad simply as Murshad—in other words, someone who came in handy to speak about, sometimes as a living marvel, sometimes as a good-for-nothing. It's not inconceivable that Murshad's life story was quite interesting, and it's possible that it wasn't at all. Either way, people would always think of Murshad as Murshad. His responsibilities included tending to the mosque's prayer rugs and caring for its lone wooden coffin, which resided in the same small room as he. People came to Murshad to ask for it whenever there was a death in the neighborhood.

Vivek remembered Murshad quite well.

Taking Vivek into confidence, Zamir Ahmed Khan announced, "I'm scared to death of ending up alone in my own little cell, like Murshad."

"But getting married is a huge responsibility," Vivek said, maintaining a somber tone. "It's not something you do just to take your mind off things."

"What I need to do the most is stay alive," he said, trying to change the topic in as few words as possible. "If I don't get married, I might commit suicide, or go off and live in the cell of some godforsaken mosque. But it's not so easy to find a deserted one nowadays, let alone a little cell."

Zamir Ahmed Khan wasn't lying. At the time he had decided to get married, he'd been going through a phase when his life was at a total standstill, even though he was mentally and physically healthy. He could have committed suicide without thinking twice.

Lying alone in that little mosque cell—what did Murshad think about? About the past, the present, the future? Or about that realm where people were dispatched every day inside the coffin that stood beside him? What did it taste like, the curry ladled in his bowl from so many different homes? What had brought him to the doorstep of the mosque near Zamir Ahmed Khan's house? What sensations did he experience with each mouthful of food? A kind of spiritual attainment, a mystical bliss? Or a feeling of being worthless? A sorrow and a sadness that the world had left him behind? Did he wish to do something with his life, or simply run away from an unpleasant truth?

What had imprisoned blind Murshad in the mosque's narrow cell? And what had so quickly transformed Zamir Ahmed Khan's rooms on the top floor into an underground? In spite of his marriage to Rahat?

Was it merely the ugly tongue of that Maulvi Sahib who had come to teach Bhai Miyan and their older sister?

What exactly had set the chain of events in motion? The possibility of success or the indifference to failure? Would he ever find the courage to write about Murshad? About Murshad, and the other two important people in his life at the time—Phaphu Biya and Dulhan Chachi? Was it possible to put his memories of them into words?

Phaphu Biya was Amma's real aunt, and her beautiful house was known simply as the bungalow. Could he as much as fashion a little story about the bungalow, to be published under a fictive name?

Phaphu Biya

Zamir Ahmed Khan's memory of Phaphu Biya and the bungalow was just as old as his memory of Murshad, but what he remembered most clearly was when the property of Abba's older brother, Bare Abba, was being divided up, all while he was still alive.

"What I don't want is any fighting or disharmony in the family after I'm gone," Bare Abba announced. His word was as good as law. He surveyed, he measured, he had walls raised, and soon the huge house was divided into five parts for the five families. All parties silently wiped tears from their eyes as the drama unfolded, but Bare Abba's irrefutable argument was that tears now were better than bad blood later.

To Zamir Ahmed Khan, the grand house was in many ways more important than his own house. He spent the greater part of his childhood either in the bungalow, where Bare Abba, Bhai Jaan, Abbas Bhai, Nasrat Bhai, and Kamal Bhai's family lived, just across the street from him and his parents, or playing in the fields and cemeteries nearby. His memories of the grand house and its inhabitants and the area around it covered such a wide swath of time that he couldn't accept that everything had changed so quickly. The outside world changed fast, as it must, whereas change within the house had seemed like outright betrayal. That sadness stuck until he remembered Phaphu Biya and the theatrics that had unfolded at her own place.

The memory of it flooded Zamir Ahmed Khan's mind and triggered images of the foundation, walls, and roof of Phaphu Biya's house, and of Phaphu Biya herself, as she came to sit down on her little stool, propped up with a pillow, coughing and wheezing, carrying her betel-nut pouch. She was Amma's aunt, but Zamir was so little when she died that he couldn't call her anything else but Phaphu Biya. Right in the city center, in Lakherapura, now dense with shops, stood her large, beautiful home, the bungalow. Phaphu Biya sat there alone with her tubercular cough. Her husband had been dead for a long time. She'd had one son. Some people said that he'd killed himself in the prime of his youth after quarreling with his father, while others tried to cover up the suicide by claiming he'd died in a hunting accident.

The yard of Phaphu Biya's house was large and spacious and had a beautiful garden where flowers and fruit grew—guava, bananas, pears, grapes, oranges, pomegranates, and figs, everything your heart could imagine. There were ponds, fountains, flower beds, and a crisscross of watercourses for the trees. When little Zamir Ahmed Khan was first taught the law of good and evil, including the importance of praying and the places called heaven and hell, he began to imagine heaven as Phaphu Biya's yard, only much bigger.

Something else in Phaphu Biya's bungalow captured his imagination and colored his imagined paradise: a swing on the veranda that hung from two thick cotton ropes. She'd sit on the swing in moments of respite from her coughing, supporting herself with her pillow, and then swing back and forth, gently, slowly, all the while gazing into the distance of her garden and yard. She rarely had the chance to do this, since she was mostly focused on spitting up phlegm into her spittoon, rocking back and forth, incanting, "Ya Allah, Ya Allah, Ya Allah!"

Then one day she died. Or if one wants to refer to her death in a more respectful manner: she passed away. The leaf of Phaphu simply fell off the tree of life; the rest of the family experienced an earthquake. Funeral formalities for the interment of the body and the weeping and wailing are unavoidable in every house where death has paid a visit. But here, wave after wave of family and caravan after caravan of interested parties all laid siege to Phaphu Biya's bungalow with their cots and beds and pots and pans. Mother and daughter and brother and sister quickly took up with opposing camps, ready to stake their claim and take their share of Zamir Ahmed Khan's paradise. When someone dies without an heir, just watch how even the good and the innocent are put to the test! Greedy eyes gazed longingly at the half-ripe guava in the garden as mouths watered eyeing the sour star fruit. The branches of the pomegranate tree hung low and heavy with fruit as the grapes on the vines began to wither and rot. But nobody would touch any of it, and nobody would let anyone else touch it until the estate was divided and settled. Amid this there was one detail Zamir Ahmed Khan understood only after he grew up. Even though Phaphu Biya wasn't related by marriage to any close relative in the greater family, she was Amma's paternal aunt, her father's sister. For another close part of the family, she was also a paternal aunt, some father's brother's wife. She was also some other father's younger sister for another part of the family, and another paternal aunt for still others. Each and every circle of the extended family began to overlap and jumble. Who was what to whom? Who was how close to whom? Who could even say?

And that's how Phaphu Biya's bungalow quickly became the Muslim's Karbala and the Hindu's Kurukshetra. Since they were close relatives, gunfire and hand-to-hand combat were ruled out (though it wouldn't have been surprising if these had erupted). Instead, a cold war was waged. The various factions adopted all sorts of guerrilla tactics. Zamir Ahmed Khan couldn't be sure, but sometimes he suspected that everything he remembered so vividly today could, god forbid, have been somehow connected with that guerrilla war.

But at the time he hadn't the courage or grasp to think like that.

He remembered the summer afternoons in Phaphu Biya's spacious yard with the swing; only a few days after her death, the yard's appearance had undergone a complete change. Sheets had been spread throughout the yard, and people propped themselves up on white pillows and cushions along the edges. The division between friend and foe no longer mattered because the business at hand was with the spirits, and the spirits were not of this world. A jinn had cast its shadow on one of the mourners, Tabassum Apa, and taken possession of her body. All waited with anticipation for the jinn, which came at a particular time during the day to enthrall her. The crowd parted to make room in the yard for Tabassum Apa, glancing at her with sidelong looks, fear and expectation in equal measure.

When the moment they were waiting for drew near, the crowd set aside notions of friend or foe and sat on their haunches as Tabassum Apa began speaking in tongues. Then came the seizure: she passed out, her limbs froze. She was immediately laid on the ground and left to rest a little while until her body unfroze. But she remained unconscious, eyes closed.

Then began the real show, with live action and surround sound. Tabassum Apa fluttered on the ground like a dying bird, writhed like a fish out of water, tumbled round and round like a rolling pin, all the while conversing with an unseen spirit. People said that Tabassum Apa's body, when possessed, had wondrous strength, and that nobody could hold her down. So much for the action. As for the sound, you never knew on any given evening the topic of her monologue. Sometimes she led the way through such an elaborate maze of philosophy and spirituality that people were left scratching their heads, understanding nothing. Other times she exuded laughter and gaiety, or she pleaded and beseeched, or simply whimpered and cried. Leaving aside those evenings when she perorated on the spiritual, Tabassum Apa's utterances could easily be understood at the level of word and sentence. Her audience carefully copied down her proclamations on the slates of their minds. It is said that people speak the truth when possessed by a jinn. Those who took Tabassum's dialogue with the jinn seriously tried to figure out how to interpret the words she uttered while unconscious. In particular, how to interpret them in respect to the question of the partition of the bungalow. An hour and a half into the show, after much rolling around on the ground, she began screaming and crying uncontrollably to signal the moment the jinn left her body. Tabassum Apa finally opened her eyes amid the dense crowd of onlookers as she came to. She was given water from a silver cup that had been graced by the sacred breath of a holy pir, and the people milling around returned to their respective encampments. The cold war resumed.

Back in their camps, people picked apart the words of the possessed Tabassum Apa, parsing and extracting and explaining to one another meanings that went far beyond common sense. Each interpretation served one goal: to assure people that truth had been spoken by the jinn via Tabassum Apa's tongue, proving once and for all that they were the sole and rightful owners of the bungalow.

After the battle had escalated into a full-scale war, its final outcome was determined by an additional factor, aside from the combatants. A significant number of individuals that had no claim to the bungalow were among those gathered. This group tirelessly twisted the facts under the guise of boosting morale for their own chosen side, resulting in the rise of such icy tension that people even stopped their hellos and good-byes. Tabassum Apa, in a noteworthy development, became the apple of everyone's eye, no matter what camp they belonged to. Those she visited tried to bribe the jinn in the hope of winning it over, always treating Tabassum Apa with the utmost hospitality. Tabassum Apa was blessed with a vigorous constitution. Though had she been a weak, sickly creature, the well-wishing and courteous treatment she received would certainly have assured her a full life of stellar health.

This drama continued for a long time. When Bare Abba divided the grand house and had walls erected, heedless of people's treasured memories, Zamir Ahmed Khan accepted his rationale, though he didn't fully agree. Once distance and discord were destined to happen, building a few walls wouldn't make a difference.

The bungalow? Zamir Ahmed Khan's imagined childhood paradise?

After the court decision, he immediately sold the part that had been allotted to him and returned home. None of his relatives lived there anymore, and he no longer owned any part of paradise. As for the jinn whose shadow had once fallen upon Tabassum Apa: it had been shooed away long ago by some pir. Today, she and her husband and children were contributing to the happiness and welfare of the country. A market now stood in place of the bungalow, a series of shops that sold everything from clothes to jewelry. All that remained now was Zamir Ahmed Khan's mind keeping safe the memory of Phaphu Biya swinging on her swing, and the melancholy of her life that grew more intense and profound every day.

He would leave something—he, too, would absolutely leave something behind. If nothing else, he would collect the ebb and flow of shadows in his upstairs underground. He would jot down a few details about Murshad, Phaphu Biya, Dulhan Chachi, and his own meaningless life. Definitely. If not today, then tomorrow.

Dulhan Chachi

I'm dervish, a *dervish*!

That was the first thing that echoed in his mind at the mention of Dulhan Chachi, even though Zamir Ahmed Khan himself had never heard her say it. Amma told the story that long before he was born, Dulhan Chachi, Amma's father's sister, had lost her mind while reciting her daily prayers, and stayed crazy for years. Saints, Sufis of high standing, and certain books can determine a particular person's spiritual rank and importance. Those who are truly elevated (and very few people can achieve such heights) would never proclaim themselves so. In her particular state, however, Dulhan Chachi sometimes laughed, sometimes wept and wailed, while "I'm a dervish!" was on her lips twenty-four hours a day. Following a failed series of treatments, charms, and amulets, she simply went somewhere, and her mind was mended. Though possibly cured, people still used the temporary spell of insanity as a ready excuse to call her crazy for the rest of her life. Ordinary people may feel the need to call someone crazy to keep them at arm's length from ordinary life and maintain their own claim to well-being. Dulhan Chachi, as long as she lived, didn't care about the world, and didn't hold it in high regard.

Zamir Ahmed Khan's first memory of Dulhan Chachi: her hair and even her eyebrows had already gone gray, but not one wrinkle blemished her face. Her complexion was a crimson-copper; her eyes, light green and bloodshot, as if she hadn't slept in years. People called her uncouth because of this. Even in her old age, when she wore plain, white garments, it wasn't difficult to imagine the kind of beauty she'd been when she was a real dulhan, a true bride. She was the old lady of the family and spoke without censoring herself, and that's why people were reluctant to enter in her presence. Zamir Ahmed Khan's earliest memory of her was from the period she lived in her ancestral village, Damkhera, leading the life of a recluse and coming to the city every once in a while for a wedding, or just to see people.

Dulhan Chachi's first stop was Amma's house whenever she came in from the village, quite possibly because it was the first she came across as she entered town. The moment she set foot inside, Amma and whoever else was present snapped to attention, including Abba, who used to keep his distance from almost everyone else. Dulhan Chachi had a rough voice, and when she began to laugh in the middle of a conversation, she'd work herself into a near fit. She'd lose control, unable to speak or listen, until tears streamed out of her eyes. Her face was flushed and she could hardly breathe. She'd laugh until the laughing tired her out, then became motionless. People gathered around her tried to go along with her merriment, but eventually gave up, cursed themselves, and fell silent. Sometimes it was hard to figure out what had set her off. Zamir Ahmed Khan still remembered vividly one particular incident when Dulhan Chachi had roped in Abba.

One day she came for a visit from the village with a special request for him, saying, "Look, I'm not one of those brainy scholars. I can barely speak Urdu. So give me the name of some book that'll teach me everything I need to know about our faith." Abba gave Amma a meaningful look; finding no objection, he proceeded to give Dulhan Chachi the name of a book that, in his estimation, contained all requisite information. The book was sent for from the market, and Dulhan Chachi returned to her village, happy as a lark—until her next visit.

She was back in no time. "Where's that so-called Maulvi Sahib," she questioned Amma. "I'm talking about *your husband*! Go get him. We've got some things to talk about that can't wait."

Abba was summoned.

"So, mister Maulvi Sahib!" A peal in her voice threatened to let loose a deep reserve of laughter. "What a delightful book you've given me to read, dear brother! There's more Satan than god in it! No matter what the poor human does, Satan gets him first. Satan's the one responsible for every last deed. So tell me this, if I'm supposed to believe that what's written in this book is true, then please explain to me, does our Allah Miyan do anything at all? Or is all the doing set aside for Satan? Well?"

Abba was surprised at her anguish and anger and stood silent for a moment. "Maybe I made a mistake?" he said sheepishly. "I'll buy you another book."

"No more stupid books!" she snapped. "This one will more than last me the rest of my life. But answer me this," she said, addressing more of an unseen force than Abba. "I get it that Satan's their little sacrificial goat. They blame Satan for anything they can't figure out. So someone go and tell those know-it-alls with the long beards, 'Hey! You know what Satan is? He is your tail, and you are the body!' Ha! They want to use Satan as an excuse and say that Satan and people are two different things, that when Satan casts doubt in my heart that I have sinned, I have strayed. Why not admit you don't have the backbone to fess up to what you've done and come clean with your mistakes? Who do they think they are, these brainy brains! Satan's teachers!"

Dulhan Chachi's heart held no extra mercy for strict, stupid mullahs, who she liked to call the tail of Satan. As for Abba, after this incident he went to great lengths to avoid talking with or even crossing Dulhan Chachi's path.

Often people listening to Dulhan Chachi observed her silently, snickering at most. But a few people deliberately teased and egged her on so much she'd swear up a blue streak. Take Satan: as soon as someone alluded to him, even the slightest hint, Dulhan Chachi was off, not to be stopped.

"Have you actually seen him?" she'd ask in anger or in jest, interrupting whoever was speaking. "I'm talking about the real world. Satan himself isn't real." When she was in the mood to enlighten others, she'd patiently explain, "The only thing that's black and white is a human being. If a person is good, he puts the angels to shame. But if he's bad," and here she began to laugh, "like our fine bearded friends who have one thing in their hearts and something else on their lips, then even Satan pales in comparison. If these people believe in their hearts that Satan really exists, God help us."

She'd repeat it again and again, giggling all the while, until she was too tired to go on.

She sold the house she had in the city, and decided to use the money for two things. First, to go on the hajj, the duty of every Muslim. Second, to have a well dug in the middle of her village. Dulhan Chachi would enjoy the fruits of the blessings of future generations who drank from her well until the Day of Judgment.

Dulhan Chachi's decision to have a well built was very much in character. But not going on the hajj. She held her own theory and interpretation of religion, according to which she calculated the relative importance of this deed or that. She hadn't given special status to regular worship in her own life, or to the many other things considered religiously significant that fell under the rubrics of duty and good conduct. Was the decision to go on the hajj the result of a feebleness related to her age? Or because of certain counsel given by her nearest and dearest? Or really and truly an expression of her heart's hidden desire? Who knows, but when Dulhan Chachi returned from the hajj, the family rolled out the red carpet in welcome.

"Lay off! So I did the hajj," she said, embracing everyone. "I'm back in one piece. No need for hullabaloo."

"People pray so that fate may ordain their death while on the sacred ground," someone chimed in, perhaps hoping that Dulhan Chachi would have undergone a change since the hajj. "It's a great blessing to die there."

"I'll keep praying," she snorted. "May you go on the hajj and earn that blessing. As for me, I'm a thousand times grateful to have come back in one piece so I can die at home. Is that any way to die? In the middle of strangers, no one to dig your grave?" Her temper had sharpened. "I don't need my paradise to be fancy. You can have your garden of paradise. For me, the garden variety is plenty."

As people gathered to hear Dulhan Chachi recount the epic of her hajj, they couldn't help but strike their foreheads in disbelief, cover their mouths to keep from laughing, and think to themselves, "Toba-toba, God forgive us!" From start to finish, the pilgrimage had turned out to be a torment beyond anything Dulhan Chachi could have imagined. It began the moment the ship left harbor in Bombay when she felt nauseous and began vomiting. She could barely sit or stand, eat or drink. The climate of Arabia didn't suit her, and the crush of pilgrims didn't either. But she'd decided to go, so tough luck, she'd have to go through with everything. If she'd had her way, she'd have left in the middle and come right back.

"The people kept coming, wave after wave!" she told Amma a few days later, wiping her tears between bouts of hysterics. "It was an explosion of people no matter where you went. They went crazy trying to get through all the rites, and if someone fell down, they walked right on top of them, those loons. You call this hajj? Everyone recited one or two prayers, trying to utter them while not understanding what they meant, but for the most part preoccupied with their own well-being. But enough about that! How can I describe all the obstacles they put in the way of salvation? They go crazy throwing stones at Satan thinking that's the real one. He must have really pulled the wool over the eyes of some prophet. But what kind of saint or prophet are you if Satan wastes his precious time on you? So everyone goes through the motions, but no one has the brains to get the hidden meaning behind. What can I say about right and wrong! Oh, they're mad about making the circuit around the Kaaba. Push and shove, jostle and wrestle, god help them! Then everyone's trying with all their might to kiss the stone, the Sang-e Aswad. Someone said that we're not going in for that part, but then see how fate works? A wave of people came along and the next thing I knew I opened my eyes and I was right in front of the Sang-e Aswad. When I lifted my head to kiss it," she said, with mad laughter, "What do I see? A big black stone slathered with every crazy person's spit. People were licking it, kissing it, and if they could have they might even have gnawed at it. My face was just a few inches away and I was about to plant a kiss when all the drool nearly made me sick and I turned away. People were so worked up with their smooches! I stepped aside and said, 'Go on, brother, kiss it with all that you've got!' Just imagine the scene."

Hearing her report, Amma's heart must have trembled with fear and she must have incanted God help her, God help her, while remembering that Allah forgave everyone equally, to which she could add her hope that Allah would remember and concede that Dulhan Chachi wasn't quite in her right mind.

Dulhan Chachi was no longer in this world, and god knows whether the well she'd had made still was. Did the drinkers from the well still think of the maker of the well, and bless her for it? Or had the passage of time filled it with dirt? Sometimes it's better not to know the whole story.

The Grand House and Apyaya

Zamir Ahmed Khan's memories didn't end with Murshad, Phaphu Biya, and Dulhan Chachi. His mind was like a beehive, where the mahua tree yielded the honey of memory, or the darkroom where Abbas Bhai developed his photographs in pitch-blackness. Bhai Jaan, his oldest cousin on his father's side, wearing a beret and a high-collared coat, driving a jeep with a searchlight and gun, the truck filled with the kill from the hunt. Bhai Jaan, with a gunpowder personality that erupted in a mix of sharp wit and rage. And Bhabhi Jaan, whose beauty was in a league of its own. Phaphu Amma, and her old Singer sewing machine, an existence full of tales and stories of the prophets, her pouch of paan and supari. Frail Phupha Miyan, bent at the waist, restlessly pacing through the house, peering and peeking everywhere, who used to talk to himself and sulk like a kid at the most trivial of things, shedding crocodile tears. Abbas Bhai, younger than Bhai Jaan, who loved photography and had a small darkroom built in the house. Aapa Jaan, whose monsoon wedding day coincided with the premiere of *Barsaat* at the Bharat Talkies across the street, with its songs "Jiya beqarar hai," "Tak dhina-dhin," and "Hava men urta hai mera lal dupatta malmal ka." Nasrat Bhai, who was fond of good food and good poetry, sport, song, and fine clothing. Kamal Miyan, older than him, but since they were so close, he didn't use "bhai" as he would with an elder, but simply called him Kamal Miyan. Kalim Bhai, a cousin from his mother's side, whom a cruel twist of fate had made mute.

And the crowd of childhood companions and contemporaries, offspring of various aunts and uncles from both sides of the family. In the expanse of his memory, they still sat cross-legged on the floor of the house, the one Bare Abba had divided into five sections by building five walls. Bare Abba knew all the children by name but didn't know them in any meaningful way.

Cops and robbers—Apyaya, the nickname for mute Kalim Bhai—teasing him—an outer room—playacting.

If he were to recall events in his life sequentially as an autobiography, which moment would his memory catch first? Before the fresh scents of childhood and boyhood, before his mind had given rise to the adult notion of doing things only for gain. Before the routine of getting up early, exercising, bathing, before schoolbooks and uniforms. Long before all of that, what was the one thing that set everything else in motion really and truly?

His memory of that moment was just like a memory of the world coming into existence might be. As when the wind first learned to gust, infant clouds began to waddle through the sky, and the sun and moon and stars and seasons had not yet a fixed routine. What else could account for the short days and long nights of winter, or the endless, sweltering days and listless nights of summer? Or for the rain that came whenever it pleased? A day would come when all the seasons of the year become one, and day and night won't differ. Then it could be said that the world has learned to walk. But even before the world had found its balance, Zamir Ahmed Khan had lost his own!

Because, god help him, he had been cursed by the innocent ones he'd teased and mocked as a child?

Like?

Like cursed by Kalim Bhai, nicknamed Apyaya.

A cold exhalation escaped from a frigid quadrant of his heart the moment Zamir Ahmed Khan thought of him, and he felt the room temperature drop a couple degrees.

Kalim Bhai earned his nickname because the only thing anyone ever heard come out of his mouth was "apyaya." It wasn't as if he didn't try to produce other sounds. Once he saw his chance he took it, and no one could stop him. He didn't waste time greeting his audience or asking for their indulgence, but bent down to sit on his knees, just like a poet. His hands traced majestic gestures through the air, as if he were a master vocalist, while his insides intoned the first notes of the Apyaya Raga. Unbeknownst to him, his singing eventually reached such a screeching pitch that a shocked family elder came running in, consoled Apyaya, and then admonished the children not to torture the poor boy; this was the moment Zamir Ahmed Khan understood the added virtue of being deaf as well as dumb.

Apyaya wasn't a separate person for Zamir Ahmed Khan, but so much a part of his own life that writing an autobiography without him in it wouldn't be meaningful, or even possible. Apyaya lived in a different part of town, but he was usually at the grand house with the other kids. Since he wasn't able to talk to others or hear what they said, all communication happened through gestures and signs.

As with any noteworthy topic, Apyaya's inability to speak was clouded with controversy. He was born deaf and dumb, according to one account, while other people insisted he had been quite talkative as a child. That's why they named him Kalim, they said, "the talker"—until the day he secretly swallowed a copper coin with a hole in the middle, and then the talking and hearing ceased.

Apyaya was only five or six years older than Zamir Ahmed Khan, but this age gap came at a time when even the smallest difference dictated that the older one lived fully in the world, whereas even the shadow of the younger one's existence didn't reach far. Only later did Zamir Ahmed Khan understand what the five-year difference had meant: Apyaya was a hundred, a thousand times older. Apyaya was well aware of his seniority and took it very seriously. When he became angry (it happened often), he unceremoniously twisted Zamir Ahmed Khan's ear, scolded him, pinched him, screaming "apyaya" all the while. When happy, he'd tell Zamir what a good boy he was, tenderly repeating "apyaya." His skin was jet-black, his face angular, and his eyes sparkled with the look of a wild animal, at once alert and morose. So much fun could be had teasing and making fun of Apyaya that most of the kids made him the butt of mean jokes. Since he couldn't go to a regular school, his elders had enrolled him in a government-run center to train tailors. Since the center was nearby, Apyaya stopped by the grand house every day on his way home. He spent his Sundays there, and made sure to spend time with Amma. Here was Apyaya, wearing white, coarse cotton pajamas that tapered at the feet, a long shirt that went down to his knees, a closed-neck vest, a muslin or velvet cap, and black leather shoes.

The grand house was grand not only because it was spacious but also because of the vast and open surrounding area. Bhai Jaan had taken over Bare Abba's job of managing forest land long ago; now, he was constantly going back and forth to Delhi to supervise wood supplies. Delhi meant halvah sohan, dried fruits, and chaat masala, goodies and spices that Bhai Jaan brought back with him in great abundance. Another of his profitable pastimes was to bring old jeeps from Delhi, refurbish and sell them. A small shed had been set up next to the grand house to keep the engine parts and do the mechanical work. The kill from the hunt was cleaned and dressed in the same shed. Bhai Jaan, sadly, was a man born before his time. Whether wood supply or forest work, car repair or furniture production, or the idea of opening Bhopal's first real dairy, Bhai Jaan was years ahead of his time and its opportunities. Being ahead of his time didn't end with his death. When Bhai Jaan passed away at the age of forty-seven only a few months after Abba's death, the family was deprived of the kind of impressive soul that is born once only every few generations.

But that was later, much later.

Next to the field and marsh behind the grand house was a large abandoned graveyard—abandoned because no new graves were being dug and no new bodies interred. Several thick, billowing tamarind trees grew there, along with other trees whose names nobody knew, though they were common. Countless makandi bushes that bore little black berries and looked like makois grew all over the sprawling, uneven grounds of the graveyard, as well as clusters of cheap flowers in Gevacolor, and god knows what else.

The graveyard was the place to play cops and robbers, everyone's favorite game back then. The gang of children gathered every Sunday at the entrance for the first order of business, the pregame assault on the fruit of the tamarind tree. The children struck chameleons with slingshots and cut their tails off, thereby securing the reward of making the reptiles Muslim. The children accepted without question the assertion of Hafiz Sahib, who recited the Quran in the mosque, and of other learned elders, that chameleons, since they changed colors, were infidels. Cutting a chameleon's tail off to make it Muslim brought spiritual merit. It was an easy way for the children to score religious points, not yet realizing the games of hatred that lay behind.

After harvesting the tamarind pods, they collected them on a stone in the shade of a neem tree that was part of a grave so large that it could have fit a whole family, no exaggeration. They then tried to find a slab of rock to crush the tamarind pods on the hard gravestone. Apyaya was assigned the delicate task of stealing salt and spices (and, if possible, some cumin) when the cook's wife wasn't looking. The children implored and beseeched him, in sign language. And in sign language, he refused, making clear the dangers the job entailed. When flattery went nowhere, only one way remained: threats and fear. Without a second thought, fists were produced for Apyaya to consider. The children stared him down, furrowed their eyebrows, told him what would happen if he didn't follow orders. It was as if he were just waiting for a good fright to use as an excuse to give in. Salt, spices, chili: right away! Tamarind pulao: on the double!

Everyone was dying to wolf down the pulao.

Mmm-mmm!

Yum-yum.

Too spiceee!

Dee-licious!

Any more?

All gone!

Next up? Cops and robbers!

The cops were armed with cheap tin cap guns used on Diwali. The robber had tied a bandana over his face as a disguise, kameez tucked into the waist of his pajamas, head shaved clean with clippers. For the final touch of verisimilitude, hidden behind eyeglasses made of tinfoil or plastic, you could barely make out Apyaya. After objecting a thousand different ways—*why did he always get the honor of playing the robber?*—Apyaya agreed, just like he agreed to everything else. But sometimes he didn't agree, and stomped off in a sulk. Or, failing all attempts to convince him, the kids gave in, and made him a cop. But in that case the real thrill of the game was lost. Apyaya was keenly aware of the importance of his expertise as the robber. If anyone but him attempted the role, Apyaya tried to explain through gestures the finer points that playing the robber entailed. Afterward, Apyaya would inevitably shake his head to express disappointment with the performance of the wannabe robber.

Once in character, Apyaya was given the order to hide in the bushes. The cops with their weapons split into smaller groups and began a mini combing operation over the area. Guns at the ready, proceeding with extreme caution, the cops went off in search of the bloodthirsty militant known as Apyaya. When the troops came so close to Apyaya's hiding place that he could smell the danger, he let out the kind of earsplitting "apyaya" that nearly shattered both earth and sky. Just like when some people listen to qawwali music they enter a state of rapture, Apyaya would rock back and forth, his hands tracing gestures in the air. As he fervently incanted the first notes of the Apyaya Raga, he stood up to take flight. Guns locked on his swaying body, cops' mouths issued a mighty "bang, bang, bang!" with the fire of guns.

After this, Apyaya could do as he pleased. Whether he fell into the hands of the police (dead, alive, wounded), or managed to give them the slip, there was simply no directing him. If in the mood, he'd die in the encounter with police, giving what he considered such a heartrending performance that his dying came decidedly alive. Or he might end up a martyr, or just plain wounded. But the most important element in the lively rendering of his performance was his aria of "apyaya, ooh, ahh, eee, apyaya, ooh, ahh, eee," whose crescendo and decrescendo and subtle coloring were unbelievable to the uninitiated. As for the cops, the days when Apyaya felt like playing the rebel were very difficult ones indeed. He'd find himself surrounded by policemen raining a hail of "bang, bang, bang!" Their serious expression said, "Enough! Die already, will you?" But the robber, unmindful, stood fast in his place, happy as a clam, and, in a soft voice, broadcast his internal recording of "apyaya, ooh, ahh, eee," swinging and swaying away, giggling to himself, the half smile on his face serving as a challenge and reminder to the police that they were no longer in charge. Taunting them further, Apyaya would toss away the eyewear, and unfasten the bandana from his face.

The game was suspended right then and there, and the oldest kid in the group would gesture at Apyaya. "Why did you go and do that?" Sometimes there was a good reason—a slight by one of the wee kids, or an excess perpetrated by one not so wee. Or sometimes the answer was that he did it just for fun. Whether it'd been the fault of a real wrongdoer, or Apyaya was just having fun, he'd receive threats to be shut out from future games.

The next round began anew.

Only now did Zamir Ahmed Khan realize that while the cops were fully armed, the robber, meaning Apyaya, was defenseless. He saw now that even though Apyaya was a blood relative, his family didn't have the financial means to indulge their kids' fondness for toys. Was that why Apyaya was the butt of all jokes, forced to be the robber among the gang of cops?

Apart from cops and robbers, another popular game at the time was playacting cinema in the outer room of the grand house. Here, too, Apyaya played a prominent role.

The room beneath Bhai Jaan's was called the outer room, next to where Abbas Bhai had set up his darkroom. It was there they received guests, anyone from Hafiz Sahib who came to recite the Quran to everyone else who might drop in unannounced—guests, friends, and acquaintances who had come to meet Bhai Jaan or other elders in the house, from whom the women in the family would remain in purdah. Bhai Jaan and Bhabhi Jaan lived in the room upstairs. Two doors in the outer room led to the front entrance. To the right of the door that opened up to the inner part of the house were stairs that led up to Bhai Jaan's room, whereas the grand house's courtyard could be reached by climbing down two stairs on the left and going through another door.

This part of the grand house—the outer room and Bhai Jaan's room above—had remained in its original place, even amid all the changes. The house looked like it was propped up between the huge hotel in front and the new brick houses and warehouses with big shutters on either side, as if it were waiting to be elbowed down with a thud.

One of the doors of the outer room was constructed in such a way that the upper bolt on the outside could be unlocked from the inside; to achieve this, a tiny window had been cut at the top. Apart from providing an opening to lock and unlock the bolt, it fulfilled the role that a projector would in a cinema, that is, projecting images onto the screen. The aperture permitted the shadow to be projected onto the wall behind it whenever someone walked past the outside of the door. Because there was no lens, or owing to some other phenomenon, the image was small, elongated, and topsy-turvy. As soon as someone came into the projector's range, their image was projected in inverse on the screen. The image moved left if the person walked right, and it remained visible as long as the person stayed within range of the projector.

This game of light and shadow held such magic that it never grew stale. Also, the family elders considered real movies to be an evil thing, and only rarely, by accident, did anyone get permission to see an actual film, so this outer-room cinema was a means of entertainment just as TV is now. No need to buy a ticket, and no fixed showtimes. Watch as long as you like, and leave when you've had enough. The children greatly anticipated the long summer afternoons when the sun was at just the right angle, and when the outer room was free for use as a cinema. But there were also unspeakable afternoons when some grown-up dropped by and dashed the children's most fervent prayers. He'd waste priceless hours talking about nothing, laughing at stupid things, chewing paan, spitting away, all the while the group of kids slouched in the corners, flashing one another quizzical glances, and grew despondent, thinking only of the approaching sunset.

His memory faltered when it came to those dreadful afternoons, but not when it came to the long, glorious days of playing cinema.

The matinee idol was, of course, Apyaya. Sitting in the room and waiting for people to walk by was boring, so the audience members themselves took turns going outside to create the necessary drama for those inside to sit and enjoy onscreen. Those summer afternoons were so sweltering that even the hawks in the sky couldn't hold on to their prey, so even the briefest performance was a heavy burden on the actors. Each one quickly played their part and returned to the dark, cool room. And then it was Apyaya's turn.

It was no lie that no one could hold a candle to his performance. Audiences were spellbound by the leaps and bounds of his body projected in mirror image on the wall. The sheer variety of poses and contortions and pirouettes compelled the audience to return Apyaya again and again to the hot sun. Though lacking sound or color, these short films were non-stop action, free from shallow, ephemeral questions like what happens next, plunging deeply into a sea at once spiritual and mysterious. When Apyaya guessed his turn was over (and his guess was usually right), he'd knock at the door to come back in, body drenched, wiping the sweat from his face. The group conspired against Apyaya by saying that according to the clock he still had time left, or chased him back out into the sun with a chorus of mesmerizing bravos and other praise that signaled they wanted more of his leaping and spinning and whirling. When he dug in his heels and refused, he did so knowing full well the children would take advantage of the darkness in the room to torment him so that he couldn't sit in peace.

If Doctor Crocodile didn't quite grasp Zamir Ahmed Khan's troubles, but laughed at them anyway, who could blame him? Or Rahat, when she compared life to mere theatricals, or smoky mirrors? You had the nerve to laugh at the world, so now find the courage to laugh at yourself. Even a mute still has a tongue. As if a curse never slipped from Apyaya's?

Pain and remorse bore down on Zamir Ahmed Khan when he thought of Apyaya.

And why wouldn't Apyaya have let slip a curse? There were hundreds of demons trapped inside him, taunting and teasing. A voice intoned, "Of course he did! And now look where you are!" He had a tongue, but was unable to speak. When he was angry, he couldn't lash out, compelled to adopt all sorts of dances and poses as he tried to find the right footing between heaven and earth, a place where he could develop what could be described by a bland term like "balance." There wasn't a sliver of doubt that the shadow of Apyaya, dancing and putting on a show in the outer room, was now trapped in his head and bent on revenge.

Was this it? Was Apyaya's mind tied in knots like his? (Though it was hard to imagine what language Apyaya thought in.) Did he ask questions, seek answers? Or was it enough to have been born? Was he content just to imitate others, like a monkey? How religiously Apyaya tried to follow the dictum of his elders and pray as much as possible! Apyaya ran his fingers over the verses of the Quran on the reading stand and energetically rocked back and forth as people did when they went into a trance. He had two greetings down pat: hands folded together in a "namaste" means Hindu, and right hand raised to the forehead in a "salaam" means Muslim. What was the difference between these two? The sum total of the differences for Apyaya in the rites and rituals of the two religions was the circumcision of Muslims, who prayed at the mosque, and the topknots of Hindus, who prayed at the temple. But did these artificial dividing lines have any real meaning for him? What stirred inside him and what remained dormant as he observed it all? He was beyond the illusory magic of words and language. His were virgin ears that had never heard the call to prayer, never heard the ringing of temple bells. Neither the profession of faith nor the gayatri mantra could mount his tongue. Would they have sounded any different to Apyaya? Meant different things?

Were they really different for him, either? Zamir Ahmed Khan, like Apyaya, had nothing to do with all that.

Sometimes it sounded like a thousand widows in mourning, beating their chests, covering their heads with ash, shattering glass bangles. Weeping and wailing, drowning out all else. Though this meant avoiding the main train of thought. Mourning what? Your existence is nothing but a reflection of your surroundings. But these were weak excuses. It went so far that even Apyaya, slowly but surely, found his way onto the country's path of progress and prosperity. Like the rest of the childhood gang, the older he got, the more it became clear he'd seen better days. But Apyaya accepted it all with great equanimity. After switching shops countless times, he still worked someplace as a tailor. He never became a master tailor and never made a name for himself in fashion. But he remained loyal to his needle and thread. He never expressed the desire to get married, and his family didn't push. Even his health was better than before, and he saved more than he spent.

What more can you wish for?

Truly, what?

White Lies

"All these tall buildings, stores filled with stuff, the crush of scooters and cars, none of it seems natural."

Zamir Ahmed Khan had said this to Vivek the last time they met, just a couple of days before Rahat's walkout.

"What do you mean 'natural'?" Vivek said, contemplating this.

"Not natural means that it's like gangrene spreading through all the razzle-dazzle. Everything's speeding up, going faster and faster. But the wealth seems hollow."

"Why?" Vivek asked pensively.

"How will society survive when the value of humans, even humanity itself, has sunk so low? You have no idea how much dirty money went into all these new buildings. How long can the game go on?"

"That may be true," Vivek said, a bit irritated. "But everyone's different."

"Everyone's a crook!" Zamir Ahmed Khan said cynically. "Whoever's rich must be a crook."

"And the poor?" Vivek asked. "D'you think they are where they are because they're so honest?"

Vivek's best quality was that he didn't lecture anyone. His pointing out a simple fact had stuck with Zamir Ahmed Khan. When he thought about what he'd done and seen in the days following their conversation, he felt stained with blood.

"White lies, on the other hand . . . ," he tried to say in defense, but stopped midsentence.

"Who decides whether a lie is white or not?" Vivek said steadily. "People are either honest or dishonest."

"And everyone has their own definition of honesty and dishonesty. A crook is free to consider himself an honest man." Zamir Ahmed Khan's agitation grew.

He didn't hide much from Vivek. At least eighty percent was on display.

"We're not talking about your Sharafat Miyan right now. Do you remember how much I was against your working with him?"

It was true that right from the start Vivek had been opposed to Zamir Ahmed Khan's working at the Treasure Trove.

"What should I have done?" Irritation gave way to anger. "You keep repeating the same thing even though you know everything I've been through. It's thanks to him I've managed all these years, for better or worse. You're the only one I told before I got married that things were so bad I could've committed suicide at any time. You were the only one who could've given me good advice."

"Didn't I say come work with me? My business was just starting to take off."

"For this I'll remain grateful to you for the rest of my life. And to myself for not taking your advice. I don't blame Sharafat, since it takes two to play the game, honest or dishonest. Those complaining about Sharafat Miyan had better have a clean past."

Vivek tried to laugh it off. "So why are you so obsessed about the country and the world coming to an end?"

"Because the world will end because of me and people like me. The disease is now beyond cure. Blaming and kicking yourself is going to be the next trend very soon. I'm not talking about the Treasure Trove or a scandal like Bofors. The display of wealth you see all around is one big lie. At least that's how it seems to me, since we don't deserve any of it."

Vivek, whose riches had not been carved out with lies, returned to his home and family and wife and children, leaving Zamir Ahmed Khan with his mendacity and the windfall of hardship. Facing these two things at once was like fighting a wounded water buffalo. No one could predict for sure who'd be killed in the end, the buffalo or Zamir Ahmed Khan.

When and how he'd first been infected with the mendacity virus was anyone's guess. But white lies had always been with him. Way back when, after plenty of discussion and counsel, Bhai Miyan's contribution being paramount, Abba had relented and decided to have Zamir Ahmed Khan educated in the ways of the world. Before Zamir was formally enrolled, Kamal Miyan took him to the school to show him what it was like. Kamal Miyan was studying in the fifth grade, Nasrat Bhai in the eighth. Nasrat Bhai was always making jokes, paid attention to what he wore, and loved sports. Kamal Miyan was quiet, serious, straightforward.

He rode to school on the handlebars of Kamal Miyan's bicycle. Most of the boys in the family had begun to sport an English haircut by then, while Zamir Ahmed Khan continued with the usual buzz. Father was more strict than others when it came to religious matters. Given that school was fast approaching, Zamir, too, had received permission for an English-style coif. It took time to grow, however, and he began going to school with Kamal Miyan with his hair in limbo. Kamal Miyan spoke with the teachers and dropped him off in a junior class. In addition to lunch hour, students were given a ten-minute break, when the kids went out to buy snacks. His first memory of not telling the truth was associated with one of these short breaks.

Across the street from the school on the stone walkway was an old man with poor eyesight whose shop sold peanuts, guava, ber fruit, and other sundries to schoolchildren. He knew Kamal Miyan, who introduced Zamir Ahmed Khan to him as his little brother. Following the first few days when he paid in cash, Zamir Ahmed Khan, slowly but surely, began to buy on credit. This was back when you could buy things for a few paisa or an anna; he couldn't remember anymore whether his debt had totaled one rupee, or one and a quarter. He stayed at that school for a couple of months before continuing with a home tutor to prepare him for enrolling into the third grade of an English-medium school. From there, he would graduate to middle school. It wasn't as if between all the other things that kept him busy he'd forgotten about the money he owed the old man. Maybe he felt that as long as he was able to get away without paying, why spend the one or one and a quarter rupees? His other concern was that the old man could die anytime, and it was his heartfelt wish to settle his account while he was still alive. But he never went looking for him, and he never paid back the money.

The more he thought, the more he was surprised by how many other ghosts roamed around his mind, aside from Amma's and Abba's. Zamir Ahmed Khan had made off with the money of a half-crippled old hawker. Which Zamir? The offspring of Maulvi Muhammad Ahmed Khan, a man so particular in maintaining the distinction between halal and haram that people entrusted him with their money, unconcerned, as if he'd kept it under ten locks and keys, even though they knew that his own economic condition was precarious? His lumber business, after years of toil and struggle, had finally reached the point where he was able to replace the old hand-held saws with machine ones. The family wasn't yet well-off, but the days of counting pennies were behind them. Then late one night someone came banging on the door and announced that the factory was on fire. When Amma, Bhai Miyan, Aapa, and Zamir Ahmed Khan heard the news, they panicked and froze, powerless to do a thing. Maulvi Muhammad Khan left the house and disappeared into the dark of night. By a stroke of luck, the fire was easily brought under control, and the factory suffered little damage. After the night of drama, people gathered in the mosque the next day and found Maulvi Sahib reciting his morning prayers as usual. As he gave his salaams to everyone, they told him that the fire had been put out and there was hardly any loss. He thanked god, joined the congregation in prayer, glanced toward the factory, and returned home.

That morning, at a time when the house still stood on its old foundation, along with its rickety walls and thatched roof, where the pomegranate tree, blossoming and fruiting, and the guava, its huge fruit nestled in red petals, stood safely inside the courtyard, the broad space partly paved with an eight-by-four-foot slab of flagstone, doused with buckets of cold water on hot summer nights to cool it down and wash it off, where the family sat and broke fast after sundowns during Ramadan, when Aapa still played with dolls but had also started lending Amma a hand with household chores, after Bhai Miyan had left the madrassa to start work with Abba at the factory—that morning, after breakfast, now drinking his tea, Father surveyed his offspring just as a farmer might glance over the crops in his field, pleased with the fruit of his hard labor.

"Well done!" Amma teased. "Instead of actually doing anything, he went and sat in the mosque!"

But Abba was lost in a sea of remembrance, memories of his childhood.

"Your grandfather was also in the lumber business," he informed the three of them. "He made a living selling firewood and wood for construction. He wasn't educated, of course, but he was a frugal man, a pious man, and prayed every day. Allah had blessed his work, so whatever he did was a complete success. And he had a big heart. He took care of our family and the relatives, and many others owe their welfare to him, too. He opened up shop in front of your Bare Abba's house and started his lumber business. There's no shortage of people who're jealous of good people, and members of the family were among those who set fire to your grandfather's shop. I won't name any names. Fire departments were not as common back then as they are today. Your grandfather was roused from sleep with the news of the fire, so he went straight to the mosque with inna lillahi on his lips and immersed himself in prayer. The next morning, he saw his shop had been reduced to ash. He scooped up all the ash by hand using clay shingles and sold it to the potters for however much they'd pay. And with this small sum, he began his lumber business anew. The lowly amount was a blessing. Abba's business grew steadily. Whatever we have today are the returns on the ashes from your grandfather's business."

And here he was, the offspring of a man like Maulvi Muhammad Ahmed Khan and someone who'd begun his relationship with the world through lies. By cheating an old, crippled hawker out of a couple of coins.

From there began the story of his schooling and the spoonfuls of deceit. Starting school was for him a healthy change and a welcome experience.

He met Vivek in class and the two were simply classmates for the first two years, but not yet friends.

The years went by.

His friendship with Vivek was based on a joke concerning their names. They were in seventh grade.

"What does Zamir mean?" Vivek asked one day. Answering a question like this came easily in an English-medium school since they'd just finished a lesson, in English, on Gandhiji, where this word had been introduced.

"Conscience," Zamir Ahmed Khan said confidently, as if he had known the English word forever. "What does Vivek mean?" he asked back.

"Don't you remember *Sanyam and Vivek*?" he laughed. "We read it in Hindi last year. Vivek also means something like conscience."

This coincidence formed the basis of a friendship that would endure through all the seasons, the hot, the cold, the rains.

The rains!

Monsoon, showers, clouds, water, lush green.

If he could shut out the lies for just a little while! Then the coming of the rains and the magical transformations they wrought would open the door to an unforgettable chapter in his life. One that sprang fresh and green and new with each passing monsoon, as if it were happening right now, this very second: meeting Akka.

He was in eighth grade.

A Very Short Three and a Half Minutes

In the rainy season the rains took on a distinctive mood. His personal deadline for the onset of the monsoon was the fifteenth of June, and the clouds, too, were faithful and probably stuck to their end of the bargain. Even if some days were deceptive, there was no reason for him to complain to the clouds, and it didn't affect his predetermined deadline. The rains did come, giving respite to the plants and trees and the sun-scorched earth. Before you knew it, fields, mountains, roofs, and walls had all turned green, and puddles were everywhere. The sun wouldn't grace the world for weeks on end as the town transformed into one big washbasin where everyone and everything was cleansed.

The downpour was incessant and merciless, and water collected into a raging river that raced toward the Patra runoff, while the neighborhood wood suppliers busied themselves tending to and securing their wood. The streets were deserted, no goods came in or went out, all work ground to a halt: it felt like a perfect holiday, and if any work was accomplished under these circumstances, it felt like a picnic. The yard behind the big house, where they used to prepare their tamarind pulao until some years ago, and the vast, tamarind tree–filled graveyard where they played cops and robbers had now transformed into a virgin verdant hue. It was as if hundreds of people had labored in the middle of the night greenwashing the ground. Small cracks in the earth overflowed with water and became like ponds. Sturdy planks of timber floated on the surface of the canals and were navigated like small watercrafts, but the game ended when the boat tipped over, casting its crew into the dank water. Eyes of tender green shoots peeked through from under dry brush and dead trees, choking the muddy waterways, as if they'd been lying in wait for the season's first rain. Roofs were a constant source of worry. Thatchers climbed high to fix leaks. Humidity and dampness from the rain descended on the body and settled deep down in the brain of people walking outside, putting everyone in a lazy and languorous mood. News spread overnight that the rivers bordering the city had crested, meaning that no one could enter or leave the city by road. The whole world was now restricted to an embroidered green island with its spectacular topography of hills and valleys, ponds, pools, and waterways, the quietly reveling residents forming its hem.

Another unforgettable memory of the rainy season was the red, downy insect that was allegedly born in paradise and now rained down from the sky, like Allah's mercy. It was called the red-velvet bug. These insects shot down from the heavens like pellets, while people collected them as a cure for various illnesses.

Everything visible and alive in that fragment of time was like the red-velvet bugs: born in paradise, and alighting from the sky with the rain.

School was canceled when it rained in the morning, and school buses remained idle. Sometimes the rain began after the children had reached school and recited morning prayers and sat down for their lessons. The torrent began without warning, and it felt like everything would be swept away. A willful rain washed over the entire school, into the corridors, up to the doors, through windowpanes. A strong wind twisted and bent sturdy trees' leaves and limbs into improbable gnarls. The children were already at school, and going home wasn't an option, so they huddled in classrooms and waited.

By a quarter past four in the afternoon, the school bus had meandered its way through the city and finally stopped at home.

The house was no longer its old self. Most of the thatched-roof side of the house had been torn down to make way for two floors of new white-walled rooms. Casualties of the renovation included the guava and pomegranate trees and the airy, stone-paved courtyard. Aapa had gone to live with her in-laws, Bhai Miyan had married and brought his wife to live with them, and Amma's hair was beginning to turn gray, a perfect match for Abba's beard.

Zamir changed out of his school uniform and into his house clothes the moment he came home, and went to the mosque for afternoon prayers—by Abba's decree, the first order of business. School and home were as different as heaven and earth. School was coed, with nearly all the teachers women, while at home, according to family custom, even young girls were kept in purdah. Abba had sent his progeny to an English-medium school against his own wishes. This was the compromise Abba had come to in his own way as he tried to locate the proper boundary between religion and the world. At first it wasn't so hard for Zamir Ahmed Khan to move back and forth between the two, but as time went by the antagonism and inequity between them sometimes made him feel as if the whole world were absurd and ridiculous. He came home from school, changed into his kameez and bottoms, and put on his muslin cap before going out to play. Of course, he'd fold it up and stuff it into his pocket the second he had a chance—and it still beat having a shaved head. More than a hundred years had passed since the

Mutiny of 1857, and some fifteen years since India's independence, yet his family's disdain for outward signs of Englishness remained as steadfast as it was superficial. As the present took shape, it went through god knows what kinds of trials between love and hate. As it found its own footing, reverence and scorn continued to test it.

He eventually arrived at the grand house that monsoon evening while looking for the old, favorite places from his past. The house, too, was a thing transformed. The greater part of it had been utterly remodeled. Most of the time he'd lived in the house had long since morphed into memories. Lodged in a deep, safe part of his mind.

When Zamir Ahmed Khan, lost in memory, peered into Bhai and Bhabhi Jaan's room that evening, he not only saw the things contained in it; his mind was now adept at questioning and searching for answers to what he saw. He'd arrived at this place after considerable clipping and pruning, making and breaking, coming together and falling apart—a semblance of structure had begun to manifest itself atop his own foundation. Attending school had naturally introduced some changes in his personality. He also realized that the world was bigger than home, the grand house, the neighborhood, Lakherapura, Damkhera, and the small number of relatives and people in the extended family. How big, he still couldn't guess, but no doubt huge!

There was a moment that monsoon evening that proved to be an important way station and focal point in the middle of the relentless flow of time. He went down the path with the towering guava trees of the grand house and alongside the sprawling flower beds and plants of the courtyard. At that moment, he wanted to reach somewhere, reach a place where he could step outside himself and see the past and present and future all at once. Where he could see himself from the outside. A birth of virescence, wet earth, the moisture of the first rain slowly drying from the roof tiles. Childhood card games, a faded memory of a passing train glimpsed through a window, and faces that, along with the rest of the world, had changed so quickly.

Bhabhi Jaan: sitting on a little stool on the inner veranda with an open box of paan, wearing her billowing chikan-embroidered kurta, green shawl loosely draped over her shoulders, green silk striped pajamas, countless green glass bangles on her ankles, sparkling diamond nose stud, a somber smile on her face. A cloud of smoke emerges from the kitchen and spreads through the courtyard, signaling that the aunt who has come to do the cooking has arrived. Bhabhi Jaan asks her something, but before she can respond, there's an ear-shattering peal of sound from an unknown, non-human voice, "SALAMLAYKUM!" Even before the sound reaches his ears it echoes and gently brushes against the trees and their leaves, flowerpots, pillars supporting the veranda, roof tiles, aimless clouds, smoke floating through the courtyard. He's unsure whether the voice first vibrated within him, then emerged, or whether it entered outside in, through his ears. He suddenly realizes to his creeping embarrassment that he's wearing his kameez and pajamas, cap folded inside his shirt pocket. The voice is a girl's—this he understands instinctively—and, Zamir being Zamir, he turns beet-red.

"Do you recognize him?" Bhabhi Jaan asks Miss Salamlaykum. He still can't bring himself to look up and see who it is.

"Sure I do!" replies a giggling voice. "He must be some uncle or other." A peal of laughter like pomegranate seeds bursting from the fruit disperses through the house. He has to look now, and the second he does, he's bewitched.

Zamir Ahmed Khan believed to his core that a gust of wind rushed in precisely at the moment his gaze met this much older, bespectacled girl standing before him. Leaves rustled, plants fluttered. A guava-tree branch swung around and said to another, "Salamlaykum!" Leaves twitched on twigs and branches stretched out on their tippy-toes while regarding her, restlessly, humming, "Salamlaykum!" in perfect harmony. The smoke whirled around the courtyard as it vanished with its own "Salamlaykum!" The clouds in the sky paused for a moment and mumbled, "Salamlaykum" as they looked down at the blushing boy standing on the veranda between Bhabhi Jaan and the mystery girl. He felt right then as if this moment in his life had been created in paradise and wasn't part of this world. It'd rained down from the sky, like the red-velvet bugs, and the funny thing was that as the years went by, this feeling solidified into belief.

It turned out that the mystery girl from Pakistan had guessed correctly that Zamir Ahmed Khan was her uncle by relation. A twelve-year-old uncle and twenty-year-old niece! The niece said, "It doesn't seem fitting to have such a young uncle." Why shouldn't she think of him as her little brother? She didn't have one anyway. He readily agreed, and they became friends. They agreed he would call her Akka, which is what a Marathi-speaking classmate of his called his older sister. There was no one like Akka in the whole world—he firmly believed this. None of the other girls knew how to talk like she did, and none had her sense of fashion. Akka was of the heavens, not the world, and the very incarnation of sanctity with a glow in her face a little like the rays of the morning sun or on a special moonlit night. Zamir Ahmed Khan knew that Akka's engagement to Kamal Miyan was right around the corner. On the one hand, it made him happy. On the other, he couldn't stand how differently Akka treated him when Kamal Miyan was around. His spirits sank, he sulked. Akka and Kamal Miyan made plans, went on many a picnic together, or walked in the shadow of sulking Zamir. A masked bandit living in the darkness of his heart knocked on the door, came in, and cut him off from the world of the living. Death and destruction were rampant as long as this monster remained at large. The bandit from the dark heart began his rampage, leaving marks from his whip every step of the way. As long as it roamed free, Zamir Ahmed Khan found himself at its mercy. Akka inquired what was the matter, as did Kamal Miyan. Others were sympathetic. But he was beyond their reach, vanished and lost in an imaginary world where a dim light shone, as if from a candle, but this light was merely incidental. The truth was that the candle burned only to kill the moth. The curfew outside was lifted the moment the masked bandit retreated into the darkness of his heart. Steel shutters on storefronts clanged open, hustle and bustle returned to the streets, and the bazaars were again a beehive of activity, while the amusement-starved crowds flocked to the cinemas, just as they often flock to the cities nowadays for political reasons.

Akka came back to India several times after her engagement ceremony, and before her marriage, and even after she was married. It wasn't until after the '65 war between India and Pakistan, when a degree of normalcy resumed between the two countries, that her marriage with Kamal Miyan actually took place, and this after a long delay. The memory of Akka most sturdily fixed in Zamir Ahmed Khan's mind was from the period before '65 and, in his mind's eye, came naturally with the title, The Age of 78 RPMs.

Bhai Miyan had an old record player at home, and Zamir Ahmed Khan used to buy records all the time. Back then, 33s and 45s hadn't really caught on yet, and no one could even imagine a cassette tape. The standard 78 was ten inches in diameter and could hold three and a half minutes of music on each side. Akka was a big fan of Indian film music, and Zamir's idea of a perfect day was listening to records with her or giving her the latest and greatest as a gift.

Some songs were so powerful back then that the first few notes were enough to set off a cyclone of sadness, leaving him feeling churned up inside. If he bought a record for Akka, he usually bought a copy for himself, too. Akka would later inform him by letter that on such-and-such date at such-and-such hour (Indian Standard Time) she was going to listen to a particular record. And he should do the same. The knowledge that somewhere out there, very far away, in a distant land and different country, Akka was listening to the same song gave him an odd sense of comfort.

"You know what?" Zamir Ahmed Khan said to Akka the last time they met. "My idea of a pretty girl is totally skewed because of you. I began to think that a girl can't be beautiful if she doesn't wear glasses."

"You still married Rahat. She doesn't wear glasses!" Akka laughed. The two women had become quite close.

"Just informing you about my idiotic behavior," he said, a little irritated. "What good-for-nothing decides on marriage based on looks? It just happens."

"You never used to be such a bore, yaar!" Akka pronounced with a hint of sarcasm and disbelief. "You used to be a real romantic, and quite the intriguing one."

"He became like that after we got married." Rahat found her opening to inject a little sneer. "One is of course influenced by the views and standards of those who live under the same roof, and therefore must respect them."

"My two girls are as sharp as they come," Zamir Ahmed Khan said to Rahat in an attempt to save himself from the verbal web being spun. "Why are you worried? Thanks to the gas leak you'll soon be wearing glasses, too, Allah willing!"

Who knows how much Akka did or didn't know about him anymore. Zamir Ahmed Khan, for his part, had never even dreamed of going to Pakistan. Kamal Miyan had settled in Karachi after the marriage. As the first clouds of the monsoon gathered, like the dance of a peacock, he had the thought that Akka had become a part of the fabric of life somewhere along the line—her coming to Bhopal, the films and outings, the stories of relatives settled in the mysterious land of Pakistan, all the poetry, joys, and sorrows. These thoughts still existed somewhere but were now seen through a stranger's eyes, in a stranger's slumber, through dreams on a stranger's pillow, with the certainty that never again in this life could he have the beatific glimpses of that lush green island of time.

It was baffling to think how centuries of Zamir Ahmed Khan's life could fit into a 78 RPM record that lasted for only three and a half minutes. Or to concede that the true length of endless time that spreads out from earth to sky like a dust storm may not be longer than that.

A very short three minutes and thirty seconds, and then—finis!

Bhai Miyan

"Zamir Miyan," Bhai Miyan called from outside.

"I'm coming." He shot a quick look at all the stuff scattered on the floor, stood up, lifted the curtain that hung over the door to his room, and respectfully welcomed Bhai Miyan.

"How are things, Khan?" Bhai Miyan asked formally, casting a cursory glance at the mess of papers, periodicals, and old files. Seeing Zamir Ahmed Khan in this state, an image must have taken shape in his mind—a roadside performer, full of hope, who'd set up his stall eager to start his show, while the audience takes no interest. People pass him by without stopping as he sits there, alone, with his bag, kettledrum, snake charmer's flute or monkey, cursing the newfangled entertainment under his breath.

"I'm well, thank you." Bhai Miyan had been formal, so he responded in kind. It's not easy to explain to outsiders the finer calibrations of the scales of behavior concerning people with whom one spends a large part of one's life and how they tip up or down of their own accord.

He brushed off dust from the sofa and tidied a space for Bhai Miyan to sit. Bhai Miyan rarely came upstairs. Zamir Ahmed Khan did not take his showing up as a good omen. His relationship with Bhai Miyan was marked by decorum and respect because of their age difference, but they did enjoy a certain degree of informality, particularly considering that back then an age difference of twelve or thirteen years often made two people total strangers to each other. The informality between them was precious, but there was little opportunity to express it. As for Rahat, Sana, and Saba, Bhai Miyan and Bhabhi loved them to no end, and particularly once the two of them became the elders of the household after Abba's and Amma's death.

What could be the reason behind his showing up like this? If it were about some job or errand, Bhai Miyan would have summoned Zamir Ahmed Khan downstairs. Something to do with Sharafat Miyan? Rahat? Or something else?

"It's beginning to get really hot." Bhai Miyan wiped the sweat off his face. "You still haven't turned on the cooler?"

"I have." He wanted to be done with the niceties as quickly as possible and get to the bottom of the visit. "The heat from the roof and humidity from the cooler turn this room into a real hammam. I don't dare use it during the day, but I turn it on at night."

"It's the same downstairs. You'd think the heat of the whole city is being created and distributed from our house. You're better off in the office or shop. At least you don't feel the heat as much there. It's Friday, so I have to spend the day at home. Your sister-in-law told me you were upstairs."

So that's what this was about! He heaved a long sigh, unsure whether it was one of ease or relief. Today was Bhai Miyan's day off from the factory, a day he usually spent at home. His mind had concocted all sorts of false assumptions! Crocodile, my dear doctor! The gist of your advice was: avoid jumbled thoughts. Don't use your brain in the same way a Bedouin dying of thirst uses his camel in the desert. It's true, he was bent on sinking his own ship! What to do? Once Bhai Miyan was gone, he'd say his prayers, and see. Perhaps find some peace of mind.

"Were you looking for something?" Stretching out on the sofa, Bhai Miyan gestured at the plunder that had fallen into Zamir's hands as a result of a life's jihad, and that now lay scattered around him on the floor.

"I was just looking at old photos, letters, and papers."

"How's your health?" Bhai Miyan's voice was full of tenderness.

"The usual." He let out a weak laugh and began to gather the envelopes into a file.

"This neighborhood? Where our house stands? It's no place to live anymore," Bhai Miyan carried on with the conversation, fanning himself with the flap of his kurta. "Even with a healthy and fine mind, you'll lose your wits. Take the traffic on the road. It takes fifteen or twenty minutes just to walk ten steps while crossing the street. And now with these zippy scooters and motorcycles, you can be run over at any time. The roads are bad enough as it is, but on top of that these idiots also install giant speed bumps wherever they like, without putting up any signs. I bet more people are killed than saved by them."

"Right. This is no longer a place to live." He seconded Bhai Miyan's opinion.

This was true, despite covering up hundreds of his own defects, wants, and weaknesses by living in the house his ancestors had built. Ideally he would have a house of his own, where he'd face life and find respite from the ever-looming shadow of his forebears. This had been the blueprint vision of his life once upon a time, but it never made it to carbon copy. For now, all he could do was be grateful to his ancestors for providing him with a means to hide.

"Miyan, my main concern is about the children. Just getting off the bus, coming home, even setting foot outside is like storming the fort on your own." It was as if Bhai Miyan had decided to devote his day off to complaining about traffic. "God knows what kind of awful people can afford to buy a car nowadays. A pedestrian's life means nothing to them. Hit and run! I see this all the time when I'm sitting in the shop. This neighborhood is incredibly dangerous for the children."

That Bhai Miyan kept returning to the children did not augur well. It not only made Zamir Ahmed Khan feel sad, he also felt an amorphous danger grip his heart.

"On top of it all, there's the problem with the slaughterhouse." Bhai Miyan moved on to the next headache. "It's been operating since we were little. They used to slaughter animals there, not just sell meat. Buffalo and goats, all halal. Nobody was much bothered by it. But even though they're only selling meat now, it's so bad you can hardly breathe. The stench is so awful you feel like your whole body's rotting. Head to toe. It's different during the day, but at night? Unbearable. And if it's this bad in our house, I can't imagine what it must be like for people who live even closer."

"I told you before," Zamir Ahmed Khan said, reminding Bhai Miyan of an earlier conversation. "The plot that sold for six thousand then you can't buy for even a hundred and fifty thousand now."

"What can I say?" Bhai Miyan slowly rubbed his head with his left hand. "Who knew that property prices would skyrocket? I've always operated with the assumption that you can get only what's written in your fate. It's all a matter of time and circumstance. Fifteen years ago, it was more dif-ficult for me to come up with six thousand than it is to collect a couple of lakhs now."

That was a fair assessment. Fifteen years ago, Bhai Miyan's bottom line was not what it was today. And did he have the same self-confidence and pluck back then? There were reasons for this that went all the way back to Bhai Miyan's childhood. Abba, against Bhai Miyan's will, had wanted to enroll him in a madrassa. The discord started from there. Bhai Miyan had not been able to complete any kind of education. Later, after entering the business with Abba, Bhai Miyan's fundamentally different nature came to the fore, and in the end he decided to start his own business. Bhai Miyan wanted to do things his way, while Abba stuck to his own.

Two major changes had taken place in the household by the time Abba died. Zamir Ahmed Khan's hopeful career was on its last legs, while Bhai Miyan stood firmly on his own two feet. Abba's despairing gaze had shifted from Bhai Miyan and come to rest on him. Bhai Miyan could claim, with relish or resentment, that he had not received any support from Abba. Zamir Ahmed Khan didn't have the luxury to make any such claim.

How would Abba have felt about Bhai Miyan's success? Would he have accepted it? It was strange to think about it. In Abba's reckoning, Bhai Miyan didn't follow the strictures of the business. He was unprincipled. True, Abba never denied that he was hardworking, despite his lack of principle. But disagreement remained between the two. It subsided only when Bhai Miyan's business succeeded, and perhaps only on account of this. Could any decision Abba might have made have brought him success in the end? What's more important in order to stay alive: chasing success, or abiding by your principles? Your principles! But the world has only meager means to judge principle. Was it just a whim of Abba's that made him misjudge Bhai Miyan? Possibly. That in his final days, he realized he had misjudged? Who knows how someone views the world when his eyes are about to close forever.

Bhai Miyan was busy talking. He had moved on from skyrocketing prices to a detailed account of his shop and all sorts of minutiae. Meanwhile, Zamir was lost within himself imagining how the world looked with closed eyes and how people came to terms with it: when the air feels liquid, and water dry to the touch. When the purpose of everything worldly that's passed before your eyes reveals itself, just like today when he remembered a day from his childhood, when he had gone to see a fair at the Bab-e Ali grounds with Amma and Mumani Jaan. He remembered the entrance, and then going inside, large grounds with countless stalls, where you could just look around, or buy whatever you liked, the faint sound of music wafting through the air—*The moon is gone, the stars have left, but you'll be always here and mine / na ye cand hoga na tare rahênge, magar ham hamesha tumhare rahênge.* There were amusement park rides and attractions like the Magic Mirror Pavilion, the Fun House, where each mirror distorted the way you look in a different way, the Live-Dancing-Shaking Song, where girls with pretty makeup danced and playacted to popular film songs, the Well of Death, where a man rode a motorbike around the inner wall of a well, almost reaching the top. Or the Leap of Death, another death-defying attraction held late at night as the final feature of the show that everyone could watch for free. A man, standing atop a tall ladder, douses himself with gasoline and then, to the sound of *Take heart, brave wayfarer of life / O zindagi ke rahi, himmat na har jana* and *Play with fire and don't be afraid / Khele ja to ag se khilari,* sets himself on fire. As the flames rise, he leaps, plunges downward, to be welcomed by a tank full of water. Also welcomed by hundreds of petrified spectators!

Then he remembered another door, the exit, similar to the entrance.

Zamir Ahmed Khan wanted to ask himself, did anything make sense? Anything at all?

One afternoon while having lunch with his two daughters, he'd told them, "Back in the old days, they used to have special measuring cups to weigh milk just like this one." He pointed to the small bucket-shaped spoon used for pouring ghee over the rice and lentils. His daughters had just returned from school and had sat down at the table with him, still in their uniforms.

"How do you know?"

"I used to sell milk when I was little."

"Where?" The two girls were baffled. Was their father pulling their leg?

"Right over there, my dears, where your uncle has his shops. Your grandfather's sawmill once stood there, where the sawyers used to saw wood by hand. Along with a cowshed, where he raised buffalo. Every morning I'd get up at the crack of dawn to milk the cows. When I was a bit older, they sometimes entrusted me to sell the milk. That was the time of old measurements like sers, pavs, and chatanks, this "Mister Liter" had not yet made his appearance. Open fields and meadows were all around. Sometimes Kundan, the buffalo herder, would take me with him. Behind the shed was a vegetable garden. The Patra flows out from the field and the railway line. We'd roam around all over."

He knew the two girls had been caught up in the magic of his words and transported to a different world. Good or bad, who cared? But it offered greenery, open fields, and the freedom to roam about as you please. Leisure, peace, quiet, tranquility, call it what you like, this is perhaps what everyone desires for himself at every stage of life.

"Abba!" After a prolonged silence the two girls called out in unison. "Abba, where did the buffalo go?"

"My dear daughters," he laughed softly, the words escaping his mouth, "where did your grandfather go?"

And the girls looked at him silently, lost, waiting for a voice to return from some other deep and silent well.

"One day your own father will go there, too . . ."

Bhai Miyan was calling out to him, worried.

The answer, the one he had once given his daughters and that had nothing to do with the present conversation, had escaped his lips. It was only natural that Bhai Miyan, who was already worried about Zamir Ahmed Khan's health, would be troubled by hearing a statement that had nothing to do with the weather, slaughterhouse, traffic, rise in prices, or business. He observed him warily.

"What's the matter?" he asked Bhai Miyan, trying to act casual. "Why the look?"

He felt anger, shame, and the impulse to laugh all at once, but he couldn't find the way to express any of this.

"I'm sorry," he lied, in an effort to reassure Bhai Miyan. "I was reading an Urdu translation of Maulana Rumi's *Masnavi* before you came in. I'm still under its spell."

This wasn't enough to dispel Bhai Miyan's concern. He suddenly appeared very solemn, and it seemed that a few moments had aged him by who knows how many years. Age enveloped Bhai Miyan in moments like these, who otherwise looked, and probably was, younger and healthier than most people his age.

"Have you been to see the doctor?" Bhai Miyan's anxiety broke through the dam of his facial expression and flooded his voice.

"Yes."

Bhai Miyan returned to fanning himself with the flap of his kurta. "And what did he say?" His nostrils flared.

"The same thing. That it's all my imagination, not a physical illness."

"But it could be psychological, right?" Displeasure crept into Bhai Miyan's voice.

"Who did you go to see this time?"

It was not surprising that on hearing Crocodile's name Bhai Miyan fell silent. If he had faith in one doctor in the world, it was Crocodile. For starters, he hardly fell ill himself, and if he did, Crocodile cured him. Doctor Crocodile was a man of many virtues in his opinion. He did not indicate superfluous and ineffective treatments, he prescribed few drugs, didn't think of his work as a business, regularly fasted during Ramadan (something Bhai Miyan never managed to do), had diligently treated Abba, and lent support to the family—and Amma had refused to take any other doctor's medicines while she was alive. In a way, Crocodile was an edifice more splendid and useful than Shah Jahan's Taj Mahal, and he was right here among us in our own town: it would not be inappropriate to call him a local treasure! That's why when it was first decided that Zamir Ahmed Khan would be taken to a doctor, the choice had fallen on Bhai Miyan's first and final favorite, Crocodile.

Still fanning himself, Bhai Miyan cleared his throat. He wanted to forbid him to think nasty thoughts about the good doctor.

"So, I was under the impression," he finally said, "that you had begun to take treatment from someone else?"

"Yes, that's right. And I still do."

Silence.

"Want my advice? Go to Bombay," Bhai Miyan said sternly. "The best of the best doctors are there, you can have tests done, receive proper treatment. In any case, it's better to get second and third opinions. It's possible that there's some small detail he doesn't understand, even though he's a first-rate doctor. But in Bombay . . ."

If it was Crocodile for doctors, it was Bombay for cities. Bhai Miyan felt the same kind of emotional attachment to both. Not that he hadn't seen and taken a liking to other places. He had crisscrossed the entire country several times, both for work and pleasure. But if his heart's compass pointed toward one place, it was Bombay. Some dreams, for some people, never die. Bombay was that kind of dream for Bhai Miyan. Whenever he thought about the bitterness, difficulties, and failures of the world, and the broken promises of life, he kept Bombay stowed away very safely, out of the reach of others. Zamir Ahmed Khan had never taken the trouble to understand why this was, nor had he felt the need to. He was jealous, however, of Bhai Miyan's luck of having his Bombay still intact, even at his age!

"Maybe it's just my imagination." He wanted to assuage Bhai Miyan's concern. "I'll keep an eye on what happens for a few more days."

Bhai Miyan was in a fix. He now fanned himself vigorously. The ceiling fan was on high, but it seemed the air was trapped in between the blades.

"How many months has it been?" he finally gathered his thoughts into words. "Day after day you've been shutting yourself in this house. It could be that this may also be affecting your mind. Have you met with Sharafat Miyan lately?" Bhai Miyan probed.

"What for?" Zamir Ahmed Khan replied casually, wanting to avoid the topic.

"Didn't he say you'd be a partner when the shop opened? There must be some record of this?" Bhai Miyan had become angry despite himself. He didn't like Sharafat Miyan, and Sharafat Miyan, unmindful of the family connection, had hurt Bhai Miyan's business at a time when it was going through its roughest and most critical patch. "If the son of a bitch keeps avoiding you, shouldn't we take him down a notch? What do you think?"

"Oh please let it go," he said in a near-supplicating voice, "I don't hold it against him. It was basically my fault."

"If only Abba had been alive," Bhai Miyan said, anger and grief combining in his voice. "He'd never have let you work with that man. I also told you not to, but then I kept quiet, because I thought you weren't cut out for the wood business anyway and you probably wouldn't like working with me. I needed someone to support me then. Luckily, your two nephews are capable of lending a hand now. I thought that working with that good-for-nothing would maybe put you on the right path. I don't want to talk badly about anyone, but that man is dishonesty personified!" Bhai Miyan had worn himself out. "And . . . ," he said with a tinge of envy, "look what a scammer that bastard is!"

"That's what he lives off of," he said, agreeing with Bhai Miyan. "As for his dishonesty, nowadays you can't be successful as a small-time crook without it. If you look at it that way, Sharafat Miyan's doing just fine. He'll keep building bungalows and buying new cars. The good life is his birthright."

"To hell with his good life, Miyan," Bhai Miyan said wearily. "People can still make ends meet and be honest."

"Absolutely," he said, trying to end the conversation. "Anyway, don't worry. As far as the shop's concerned, I'll deal with him."

Bhai Miyan sat thinking.

"One more thing . . . ," his tone softened when he spoke again. "Did you have a bit of a quarrel with Rahat?"

He stared at Bhai Miyan in silence. This, then, was the real reason for his visit, one he'd skillfully concealed. The family, Rahat, the girls. The things that gave shape to his existence. Not to mention Bhai Miyan's own love and sense of responsibility toward the family, especially since he had become the head after Amma's death.

"Not really," he said nonchalantly, standing up. Outside, the tiled roofs and the faded buildings held their breath in the scorching heat of the sun. "Can I bring you some water?"

"No thanks, Khan, I should leave now. Actually, it's been such a long time, so I stopped by Rahat's place on my way home after the Friday prayer today." Consciously or not, Bhai Miyan fell silent again. "She'd come home from school just as I arrived. I also saw Sana and Saba."

"I'm glad," he said, hiding his unease. "It was nothing major, don't worry."

"I don't think it's right for her to stay at her parents' place for such a long time." The intensity of Bhai Miyan's concern was tempered by the tenderness of his tone. "You haven't even been to visit them, and the girls were asking about you. It's not as if that house has enough room . . ." Bhai Miyan fell silent.

What could he say to Bhai Miyan? Nothing he wouldn't have guessed himself, at least to some extent. What kind of question was this, and what was the answer? Explanations, but of what? If Bhai Miyan had gone to Rahat's place, he'd have gone knowing the gravity of the situation, and had certainly given them some money to help with expenses. That's what he always did. The next thing coming out of his mouth would be the expenses for the trip to Bombay.

"I didn't send her away," he said softly. "She'll come back when the time is right for her, when she wants to. Don't worry."

If Bhai Miyan had expected more of an outpouring from Zamir Ahmed Khan, he was let down.

"Here's what I think," his voice sounded tired. "You should go to Bombay with Rahat and . . ."

"I think the first thing I'll do is have my eyes checked," he interrupted. "I have this friend whose symptoms are almost ninety percent identical with mine. He sought every treatment under the sun, but still felt the ground slipping from under his feet. He could fall any moment! When he finally had his eyes checked it turned out he needed glasses *badly*—he'd almost gone blind, stupid fool!"

The Railway Platform

It was only when he reached the station that Zamir Ahmed Khan began to guess how much his plan stood a chance to succeed. It wasn't like deciding whether to see one film or another, meet friend X or friend Y, or take the day off and laze around the house with your favorite book. It wasn't a simple choice of how to entertain himself. This was a path he'd conceived of as an attempt to be rescued, and with the hope that it would work. The only way to find out whether he was right or wrong was to go down the road. He couldn't handle travel by train; maybe this was the germ of the idea. Maybe he fought stubbornly with himself against this phobia. Or maybe the train phobia was just another way his fear of losing balance and falling down manifested itself, something Doctor Crocodile wasn't willing to honor with the word "disease."

There was a crush of people on the platform and the announcement had been made that the train was due. How quickly things revert to normal. Looking at the bustling crowds of people at this busy hour of night, who would believe that a mere two and a half years ago on a night just like this, the train station had been transformed into a place of death where countless coolies, railway workers, and travelers had been killed? Though the gas leak was a curse for the entire city, the most severely affected and the most casualties were in the station or among those living nearby. Two and a half years later, and the trains never stopped, not even for a single night. The city was in a state of mourning for a while, but soon everything returned to normal. There was once a time when people were unable to forget a single thing. Nowadays it's not easy to remember anything at all.

The train was about to arrive.

Soon the clanging line of cars will pass in front of him and grow quiet as the train slowly comes to a halt, then the crush of alighting versus boarding passengers. Let the standoff begin! The opponents give it their all to keep the status quo: disembarking passengers are prevented from getting off, and boarding passengers are prevented from getting on, knowing full well they are the biggest losers of the game. And such is the state of affairs across the entire country. People waste time fighting one another and looking for nonexistent, superficial, insignificant differences like religion and caste. Instead of elements common to all that make the country a country and the nation a nation.

The same scene can be witnessed on any railway platform in the country, where ordinary people invade the boarding train in droves.

People waiting for the train with their luggage, fidgety, nervous.

Zamir Ahmed Khan observed from a distance the surging sea of restless anticipation. He kept his distance for one reason: imagine he ran into an acquaintance who asked him where he was going. What would he say? He remembered an old joke. After showing his ticket to the train conductor, a passenger burst out laughing. Another passenger asked him what was so funny and he said, "I sure took him for a ride! I bought a return ticket, but the conductor can wait forever, ha! I'm not coming back."

Zamir Ahmed Khan didn't even have a platform ticket in his pocket.

Have you come to pick someone up?

No.

Dropping someone off?

No.

Going somewhere yourself?

No, no, a thousand times no!

So what are you doing on the platform this time of night?

Trying to take my mind off things. Probing my fear of riding trains.

So, what about this fear?

When I think of the moment the train begins to move, my heart begins to race, and I worry I won't find my seat, or even the right car.

Don't you make a reservation?

Even with a reservation. I imagine the train arriving clanging and departing banging. I'll wander around the station, lost, looking for the platform and train. Beseech conductor after conductor for help, show my ticket and reservation. One will lend a sympathetic ear, another will snap at me and shoo me off.

Did this actually ever happen?

No, but each time I feel like this time it will.

If you miss one train, you can always catch the next.

But it won't be my train! And then what do you do, left alone in the station with your luggage?

Wait for the next train.

Maybe I'll catch the next, maybe I won't. It'll be very late, all my plans messed up.

You're that busy?

No.

Really? Then messed up how? Need to go somewhere fast? Promised someone you'd be there? Expected at a wedding or a wake? Missing a connection?

No, no!

Sure, sure!

Who knows!

The crowd stood waiting, oblivious to itself. "Yoo-ur uh-tension puh-leez! Yoo-ur uh-tension puh-leez! Kripaya dhyan dijiye!" The voice over the loudspeaker continually urged people not to lose heart. The train is on its way, it's just about here, it's arriving any second now. Knowing full well that people have no choice, whether going somewhere or heading home. If the train comes on time, great. If not, they'll have to wait.

Zamir Ahmed Khan inspected his surroundings and tried to remember what the old station used to look like. It was considerably bigger now than it once was, with new platforms and additions. His memory of it was ensconced in his mind like an old, close friend who after many years one day disappeared without so much as a good-bye. When you meet him again after a long time, he's changed so much you can't even recognize him.

There didn't used to be a pedestrian bridge, just a gate to the station. There was forest on either side of the road with jungle jalebi and sheesham trees, and beyond that fruit and vegetable gardens. Past the station, past the power substation but before the textile mill was the dirt road that led to Damkhera, Dulhan Chachi's village. The shunting lines merged into a single main track. Coal locomotives traveled at a very leisurely pace back then, like clouds wafting through the sky, spitting out water and steam and smoke. Next to these tracks, the line to Bombay was where Apyaya had been made into the robber in the abandoned cemetery, where Kundan, Abba's herder, took the water buffalo to graze, and where Zamir himself wandered.

Another difference was that the signal for oncoming trains didn't look like a gun waving in the air, but gestured downward in the mode of a salaam. There were so few trains coming and going through the city that their rumbles and whistles came inside the house, just like the sound of today's traffic that whizzes past the front door. He used to sit with Kundan on the railroad tracks and wait for the signal to turn, then put his ear to the rail to see if he could hear the oncoming train. What was he listening for? Tension, noise, an angry rumble? A swirl of sounds he'd never hear again. Dream sounds. As soon as he caught a glimpse of the train, he and Kundan got off the tracks and stood at a safe distance. If it was a passenger train they'd wave good-bye to all the strangers. Farewell. As the train disappeared from sight, the flood of sound vanished into the air.

His experiment with a Gwalior state copper coin was another thing associated with these memories of trains. Kundan terrified Zamir Ahmed Khan with the story that if you put a coin on the tracks it'll derail the train. So one day he set off on his own and put a coin on the tracks and held his breath as he waited for the train to pass. As a precaution, he chose a freight train for his experiment so that when it derailed, not so many people would come to harm. He stood hands over ears, and watched, while the train merrily trundled along toward its destination. He approached the tracks and saw that the copper coin was flattened as thin as paper. That was the beginning of his hobby of collecting Gwalior coins and flattening them on the tracks, as if trains existed only to flatten coins.

The train passed by where he stood that night near the yellow sign with the thick black letters that spelled BHOPAL, continuing its way to Bombay, past the fields behind the grand house, then the old cemetery, and the Patra. A detailed map of all these places was locked in his head, but everything had changed so many times he couldn't keep track of the sequence. The field was no longer such an open space, despite the fact that it was still empty. The cemetery was no longer so silent, despite the fact that the houses built on the graves were as spacious for people as the graves had been for bodies. The Patra had dried up on its own, but people had also drained it to build houses, shops, factories. The only thing left was a trail of black sludge. Where once there was a handful of lumberyards were now dozens of sawmills. The land behind the grand house had gone through cycles of being settled and abandoned in a process unique unto itself.

If Zamir Ahmed Khan left the main road and walked alongside the railroad tracks, even now it'd take him no more than ten minutes to reach home. So what was it about the station and trains that had saddened his heart like a sunset, triggering the belief that darkness would never end, that never again would he be fortunate enough to see his shadow in the sunlight?

"Did you take the stairs?" a puzzled acquaintance once asked him in the hotel lounge on the seventh floor.

"Me, I prefer the stairs," Zamir Ahmed Khan said casually, or as casually as possible after climbing up seven flights.

"Didn't you see the lift?" the man asked, surprise undiminished. "Actually, there are two lifts."

"I did." Despite the cool weather and aware that he'd broken out in a sweat, he pulled out his handkerchief and wiped his forehead. "I sit all day long at work, so this is how I get a little exercise."

The man was so impressed he couldn't say a word.

Was it possible to tell anyone the truth?

If the man found out the truth, what would he think?

Terrified of riding an elevator in this day and age? What a useless guy! What a waste!

What'll happen in the elevator? At worst you die.

But I'm not afraid of dying!

So?

There's no elevator man, and pressing the button myself scares me.

Why?

Who knows what's going to happen.

What'll happen? At worst you die. So what?

I'm not afraid of dying. Riding a lift reminds me a bit of the danger I feel in trains. I can go up if there's someone else with me, but never alone.

Since he couldn't explain it, he lied to the man beside him in the lounge.

Really? That's all? Since when did he start speaking so much truth?

Who is it that claims to speak the truth? He cannot be proven a liar since he was the part of me that was both healthy and wise. The part that wasn't startled when certain secrets of life were revealed, didn't move on, but instinctively thought, so what? I don't suffer from the malady where you get dizzy and lose control over yourself when you look down from up high—what they call vertigo in English. I'm afraid of riding elevators or trains. As soon as I step into either one, the fear of losing my balance and falling into a hole turns into something that feels very real. A big part of the problem is solved if I find my assigned compartment and seat in a train. In an elevator, the problem begins as soon as the cage door closes and the lift begins to move. It simply feels like I'll never reach my destination. I'm unable to articulate exactly how I feel. On top of that, I can't even try to explain. Elevators and trains are so much a part of everyday life, so how can they be thought of as impediments? Here, the level ground and the difficulty he had walking on it had become his Waterloo and his Panipat. Was this the handiwork of the masked bandit hidden in his heart since childhood, or of the dishonest wanderer who had illegally taken hold of his valuable inner estates over time? Who knows?

It was in the hope of challenging, confronting, and finally defeating these burglars hidden inside that Zamir Ahmed Khan stood on the railway platform at this late hour waiting for a train whose passengers were all strangers. He had no idea where the train was coming from or where it was going, but its arrival had become urgent. If this game of hide-and-seek continues as before, Zamir Ahmed Khan stands only a remote chance of being saved. The masked bandit and dishonest wanderer will soon combine forces and seize the precious sultanate of his body. He should spend as much time as possible on railway platforms in the city. He'd watch each and every train come and go as if he were a railway department official or a coolie making his rounds carrying luggage. He'd make a list of the tallest buildings in town with elevators, and practice riding up and down the vacant ones every day for as long as he could. This was one way of fighting against the enemy within. You can succeed at anything if you try. As the fear that's gripped mind and body dissipates, the connection between feet and ground is reestablished, equilibrium restored, and the enemy within stumbles, its very being starts to falter. Why should this be so difficult? Here's the platform, the train is about to arrive. Passengers get off, passengers get on, and of course there'll be a little pushing and shoving. Even if the trains stop for a long time. Still. Even if someone gets caught up in the crush and doesn't make it onto the train, at worst he'll lose a little money after the refund. It's not the start of Armageddon. Or he'll have to postpone his journey. This won't start a revolution. To hell with it all, whether or not you take trains or lifts won't make the world come to a halt. Don't use these conveniences at all if you're not feeling up to it. What about phones, radio, TV? They're all different branches connected to the same tumult. Who told you to wander around the world, terrified of falling, crying out for help? Stay locked inside your house, your room. Be comfy. Go off to a quiet place and live like a hermit. Hand out amulets for a living, devote yourself to prayer at the grave of a fake saint. Forget about the dust and dirt of the world, woven around you like a spider's web.

Much later, Zamir Ahmed Khan, dejected, moved on from his spot. The station was empty. He hadn't even noticed when the train came and left. Or maybe he did have some inkling.

Preface: An Intervention

It is customary for the preface to come at the beginning of a novel. The author tells his readers a few words about what he's written. Usually the subject of these introductions is the novel in question (or whatever other genre of literature the book may be), but the introduction doesn't form an integral part of the work. If you feel like it, read it. If not, don't. In either case, it won't make a difference to the well-being of the text. The writing of this introduction here, however, has transgressed tradition. Possibly because it's an integral part of the book, even though these words are an outside intervention into the main story by the writer. In order to fulfill my responsibility as a writer, I would like to present my case in greater detail before the reader. I find myself morally obligated to do so, knowing full well what I'm capable of and what I'm not.

First of all, I'd like to state that this work is my attempt to write—whether successful or unsuccessful, the reader can decide at the end—the kind of novel whose characters, events, and setting in time are one hundred percent fictitious. It may be pure chance (or the writer's bad luck) that the characters and themes of this novel bring to mind a particular life or particular period, and reflect familiar faces and events therein. The writer is not obliged to accept responsibility of any kind for this. To clarify this position, I wish to say that the character in this novel known as "he" or "Zamir Ahmed Khan" is not I. I place so much emphasis on this fact because I know there may be people who find it difficult to accept. I also consider it my personal responsibility to point out that these people are not totally mistaken. Why? They've seen the shifting shadow of this fictive character and world I've tried to create in black and white, and they consider it a part of my persona. How could I ever prohibit anyone from this kind of assumption, especially when, most of the time, I myself don't know when imagination supplants reality and turns me into an imaginary being. I seem to breathe and see and hear and speak like a person who's never been born. The situation is doubly complicated since I'm not even sure whether this happens of my own free will, or whether someone compels me to do so. Whatever the case may be, if I taste sweetness in doing so, there's no release from the joy of bitterness either. If there's pain, there's also pleasure. If there's regret, there's also the experience of something gained. So, come and let me place before you some facts about this fictional Zamir Ahmed Khan that could not be fully revealed in the book so far. Because he's by nature an underground man. First, then, some details about the underground.

Regarding his looks, height, weight, and the way he carries himself, you can pretty much take him to be like me. The fictional city of Bhopal bears quite some resemblance to the real city of Bhopal, and the time is identical to a period that spans from the end of the 1940s to the final years of the '80s. Now that this has been settled, the rest is easy to understand.

Zamir Ahmed Khan is the kind of character who I'd be able to cure in a heartbeat (no offense to those fabulous doctors) if I spent even a second with him in real life. I believe that every human being in this world is compelled to live with a character born from his imagination. Telling the difference between the imagined and the person imagining the imagined turns out to be just as difficult as it is for Sufis and saints and the enlightened to distinguish between Ishvar and Allah. I call this character my missing man: even though it may be a flower that blooms from my own imagination, it is I who is most ignorant of its fragrance. Sometimes I also feel the exact opposite, that this missing man is not someone else, but my trusted alter ego. But this is not totally true either, as will be demonstrated later by the rest of the story. If I tried to simplify it even more, we all spend our lives in the company of such a missing man. Who, even though he is "us," is not "us." Another interesting thing is that in spite of the clearly noticeable differences among different individuals, everyone's "missing man" seems to closely resemble, or is even nearly identical to, the next. And to understand anyone's missing man is a good bit easier than understanding a human being made of flesh and blood.

So this novel is in fact *The Tale of the Missing Man*, whom we can distinguish from other missing men by calling him Zamir Ahmed Khan, the missing man of Bhopal, or the Lost Bhopali—Lapata Bhopali. Not only because he writes stories under pseudonyms from time to time and tries to have them published but also because he can't resist the temptation of writing doggerel in the name of poetry.

Here a confession is in order. I succumb to the spell of writing poetry or verse. Every now and then I have tried to test my ability to compose poetry, but in the end concluded that this difficult task is not within the means of a feeble individual like me. After reckoning with the limitations of myself and the world I know, I recused myself from writing, but not from reading, poetry. While I may have given it up, who will convince the Lost Bhopali? Free from constraints of verse and meter, unbound from the shackles of refrain and rhyme and mood, he's busy versifying, merrily secure in the belief that he's a real poet. However much a good poem may terrify me and stir awe in my mind for poets, as far as the Lost Bhopali is concerned, it simply steels his resolve and ushers his creative juices forth. It's practically the same when it comes to story writing. People and events I wish to hide behind seven veils only feed his enthusiasm to pen tall tales.

The problem with the Lost Bhopali, for better or worse, is that the more I want to love life, the more he becomes indifferent to it. In an attempt to steer a "Goodwill Express Train" between past and future, there are events I wish to forget and ignore. The Lost Bhopali counts the same events as milestones along the way, desirous to stop and rest at each and every one. People without whom life carried on nicely are now like scar tissue on his soul. I've committed faults, mistakes, and misdemeanors that no one in the world was around to witness. I have been largely successful in forgetting these, not to mention others, but for him, they seem like such a heavy weight on his shoulders that he loses balance. And then taking even a few steps becomes laborious. He's so guileless that he can't even grasp the cause of his illness. When he pours this paralysis into the mold of verse, he says, "This world is not without meaning / but what is it I await?" This is an example of poetry he didn't recite but rather refashioned after hearing a ghazal of a poet friend of mine.

The Lost Bhopali is an ant that has been feasting on the waste of my body, soul, and self. He shines as a candle of remorse, not love. He takes no pleasure in "what remains," precisely because it remains. But he feels grief for "what is not there" because this he can never recover. To put it simply: he's someone who, if his hut was destroyed and he was given a proper dwelling to live in, wouldn't stop dreaming of his old hut even though he now lived in a castle.

The Lost Bhopali has written a poem about his existence: *My life's a steady place / My chest a flowing boat / like Mecca is my heart / like Medina is my grief.*

What can you say to this? It's like holding a candle to the sun!

If I may say a few words about myself. I live an average life of calm, peace, and quiet. I keep track of the date and time, month and year, and worry about the future, and—god forbid—feel prepared to face disaster. People have always changed and will continue to change according to the demands of life at a given time and place. It's a fact that we—that is, we who are alive— have no alternative but to accept. Change is indifferent to people's wishes. Sometimes knowledge proves harmful, sometimes it's better to remain in the dark. Sometimes the past is a manacle and history a yoke, while sometimes change for the sake of change is no less harmful. A human being today has to take all these difficulties into account. And despite all of this, a healthy, happy life is still presumed. As for the present, the current state of political affairs in the country in no way points to a rosy future. But this doesn't mean that the thinking brain should stop thinking, or busy hands stop working, or walking feet stop moving. Newspapers and magazine headlines are no doubt deflating. Some of these spur debate among friends, but not to the extent that someone quits their job just to indulge in debate. Friends may talk well into the night, but that doesn't free you from reporting to work the next morning. I get up at a fixed time every morning, seven thirty, and at a fixed time reach my workplace. Lunch, afternoon tea, dinner, the wife, the kids, and other family responsibilities, seeing friends, weddings and funerals—a thin layer of chutney in the middle of two thick slices of busy busy. Not even enough free time to appear in someone's dream.

Hostility between Hindus and Muslims is nearing a frenzy throughout the land—you know it and I know it. Politicians quip that India has set its sight on the twenty-first century, so why object to such a lofty goal? The people talk and grow angry saying, true, the destination may be the twenty-first century, but temples and mosques and the Sikh state and personal law for different religions are stumbling blocks. And their anger isn't misguided. All the problems should be solved as quickly as possible so that our entry into the twenty-first century shall not remain a mere slogan or posture. If you look at it that way, our goal is indeed a good one: all we need to do to reach the twenty-first century with dignity is to awaken our willpower. Which is not such a difficult task.

When I speak of my average life of calm and quiet, it's clear that it encompasses the usual complications that fill up a day. Just think of all the things we can't obtain for ourselves and our families, despite our efforts. Looking at it one way, life hasn't turned out the way we thought it would. But who can we complain to? And why? If there are countless people who are better off than we are, there are no fewer who are forced to live in less-fortunate circumstances. Prices going through the roof every day, limited means of income. An inability, both mental and material, to cope with change, the growing intransigence of the majority community, and their hardening stance toward issues and problems facing the minority community. If you want to, you can drag this onto the witness stand for cross-examination. You can even decide the verdict: innocent or guilty. Perhaps I often do so myself. But taking a step back, the little I've been able to figure out so far has taught me that history, innocent or guilty, is beyond the reach of the witness stand. If this is criminal, it's only because millions of people have witnessed it for generations and have even been complicit. Despite the fact that their heads and hearts fill with remorse the moment they disengage and think about it disinterestedly. These moments and people are also a part of history, and their thinking, by all accounts, has its proper place. Be it Punjab or Kashmir, the Assam Compromise or the Ram Janmabhoomi–Babri Masjid controversy, or the demand for, and necessity of, a common civil code, and the backlash against it, or the stranglehold of terror in Sri Lanka, or the mujahideen-led campaign against the government of Afghanistan. Or taking it farther afield, the never-ending war between Iraq and Iran, the destruction and decimation of Lebanon, the fight between Israel and the Palestinians. It seems like one big tree battered by the same storm, canopy to root, while people keep on living under the same sky, on the same soil, subjected to the same whims of the weather.

All this I accept. But I want to tell you one thing: the real Bhopal of today is a mess, a victim of chaos and confusion.

I don't want to have to point a finger at the 1984 gas leak, even though that has also been the cause of a not insignificant amount of shame and embarrassment. This was truly the kind of disaster where, along with the immeasurable loss and damage, the city's inhabitants witnessed a miraculous side of humanity. Thousands died, innumerable people were affected in such a way that there seemed to be no hope for treatment or compensation, despite the fact that the city clung to every hope and desire for relief. The disagreements the Lost Bhopali and I have about other matters also extend to the disaster. Everything makes him weary of the world and dries up any wellsprings of love gushing forth. But the gas leak is prominent on the list of disagreements. As for me, what I'm referring to is the religious groups taking to the streets to instill fear of their unity and power in the hearts of other communities, and that have nowadays become a feature of the landscape in the cities and throughout the country. Sometimes it's to advocate for personal law, sometimes to demand to free the Janmabhoomi, sometimes to protect the Babri Masjid. How many times in the past few months has there been a situation that hunters would describe as a close shave? One community organizes an iftar gathering the last Friday of Ramadan to present its demands to the city, and the other sends out the call to keep their stores closed until the end of Eid as if to say, "Let's see where you'll do your Eid shopping now, son." It's the kind of sweet stuff that the Lost Bhopali's soul feeds on. But as far as the rest of the city is concerned it's observing a colorless Eid for the first time and every individual's missing self is suddenly visible. When children witness this change—children who have their own expectations and memories of holidays—their inner lost self is born, opens its eyes for the first time, and flourishes.

Piecing together these odd ramblings, what I would like to say, in short, is that the biggest difficulty regarding the character described in the novel as Zamir Ahmed Khan—the Lost Bhopali—is that even though he is one hundred percent imaginary, I as a writer attempt to make my character appear as a living, breathing character of the world around us. We don't know by whose hands, but suffered this character has. Quite possibly primarily by his own hands. How could such a good-for-nothing get married or have a relationship with anyone at all? All he does is exaggerate, distort, and mull over my marriage and relationship, and he keeps adding to or subtracting from everything that happens in my life.

And he will see it as part of my doings. I got sick, began to have spells, went to the doctor, was advised and medicated, and after all of this, today I feel fine. I fought with my wife, she left for her parents', a few days later I convinced her to come back. Abba, Amma, Bare Abba, Phaphu Amma, Bhai Jaan, Akka, Aisha, Anisa, Vivek, Aziz aka Acchan, Murshad, Dulhan Chachi—all these characters you've been introduced to, or will be. All of them are my principal capital investment from which the Lost Bhopali enjoys the profits.

Have I made myself clear?

No? Well, then, let me tell you a story.

A skeptical man once tied a red ribbon around his neck so that he could be recognized and wouldn't get lost in a crowd. A prankster found out about this silly idea. One night, he removed the ribbon from the sleeping man's neck and tied it around his own. The man woke up and saw that the mark of his identity was affixed to the other's neck. He said, "Miyan, if you are me, then who am I? Am I you, or are you me? Or are you you and am I me? Tell me, who am I?"

The relationship between me and Zamir Ahmed Khan, the Lost Bhopali, looks a bit like this. Sometimes telling who and who apart seems to be the most perplexing question in the world.

Part Two

The Cave

"Where do you live, yaar?"

"Where to? We're no mullah and can't take refuge in the mosque."

"With you, it's like 'the believer's hiding in secret, while the infidel is out in the open.'"

"They won't even let the kafir be a kafir! Before you know it, even the kafir's begun to sound like a true believer."

"How long do you expect them to keep quiet? After everything you've done?"

"The whole world's a wretched place, but the difference is that nobody seems to be affected by it."

"The Iran-Iraq War alone is a never-ending circus."

"Here in India, too, see how the situation has reversed our fortunes? And the reaction to it is the same as in the rest of the world, in the name of Islam."

"And what Gorbachev's doing?"

"In a way he's also a link in the chain."

"Iran somehow wants to lead Muslims."

"The main fight's between Sunnis and Shias."

"You think there is a lack of Shias in Iraq?"

"It makes more sense to call it a struggle between Arabs and non-Arabs."

"Absolutely. Iranians still proudly call themselves Aryans these days."

"Fire worshippers!"

"There used to be another one who prided himself on being descended from the pharaohs. General Nasser of Egypt."

"Didn't you learn anything from him?"

"Like what?"

"Fist in the air, *Say it with pride—We are Hindu!*"

"When in Rome, do as the Romans do."

"You do as the Romans do. Let us live with our socialist concerns."

"The day will come when even our homegrown communists will greet one another with Ram Ram."

"When?"

"Soon enough. Communism's being chased out of Russia and Europe."

"Like secondhand weapons and drugs?"

"We'll surely welcome it."

"In the state India's in now? With personal law and the Babri Masjid adding fuel to the fire?"

"Today even TV's not TV anymore. It's just become propaganda for the good old ancient times. Even the gods are gambling and placing bets!"

"So why don't you place your winning formula before your fellow countrymen?"

"Oh I have, time and again, but you gentlemen think it's a big joke."

"Do us the favor? Just one more time?"

"Okay. It's time that Muslims demand Greater India, an India that includes Pakistan, Afghanistan, Bangladesh, Nepal, and so on—all of it."

"And then what?"

"Then your being a nobody will be a thing of the past."

Evening proceedings in the Cave were in full swing. There were some unfamiliar faces, but it was mostly regulars who came together every night to sit around and drink. Conversation ranged from literature to politics to history to sports, and each individual in the Cave had full license and right to speak openly. A place where the successful and less successful from all walks of life could take their mind off life's sorrows: this was the Cave. It was Zamir Ahmed Khan who had christened the place, a name he thought fitting since everyone who came was in search of respite and repose from the tedium of daily existence.

The room resembled the catacombs of an old fort more than anything else. Thick limestone walls, termite-eaten beams, stone-slab ceiling, layers of whitewash peeling and flaking, the walls like the site of a prehistoric cave painting. A whirling fan fastened to a beam cut through the dank cigarette smoke and heavy air, as if it were breathing its last breaths.

The idea of a Greater India was a running joke, but one that had grown more serious over time. Zamir Ahmed Khan was back at the Cave after a long absence. He took great solace in the fact that nothing had changed: not the feeling of the place, not the faces, not what people talked about.

"Hey, listen," the conversation leader said in his "order, order!" voice. "The problem here is this. When someone starts to make a serious point, people stop listening."

"We're all extremely eager to hear the discourse on this matter," replied a second gentleman after downing his glass and banging it on the floor.

The conversation leader picked up on the other's tone, and objected. "What's that supposed to mean? Sir, he is banned from tomorrow on!" he instructed the "lord of the Cave," also known as the owner. "Two gulps and he turns into a drunken windbag."

"Oh, come on, yaar," said the gentleman, getting into the flow of the conversation. "How many times have we heard this before?"

"But listen you must," the conversation leader said with mock seriousness. "Your fate is this: whenever he says something, you listen. Am I right?" He wanted a wink of support from the others for his embellishment. After a chorus of "yes, yes, certainly!" he turned to the other gentleman and said, "All right, Khan—let's have it!"

People sat cross-legged on the damp sheet on the floor, with room for drinks, snacks, ashtrays. Here, no one was more important than the other. Whoever arrived first plopped down and took advantage of the back cushions. Broken glasses served as ashtrays, and an old pitcher was kept nearby for adding water to drinks. The rest of the room was filled with piles of old newspapers and magazines, and empty booze bottles of all shapes and sizes.

"So explain this to me," the evening's presenter began in a somber tone. "How has the creation of Pakistan served the Muslims of this country? Wasn't Pakistan created by adding or dividing all the districts that were majority Muslim anyway? Even in places where Pakistan wasn't created, Muslims still held political sway. If Partition hadn't happened, UP and even Bihar would have been saved from the mess they're in. What have Muslims gained in the name of Pakistan? A green flag with crescent moon and star that can be draped over a saint's grave to soothe the heart!"

"How did we get from 'Say it with pride, we are Hindu' to this totally different issue of better or worse for Muslims?"

"That's not what I'm saying," the leader said, a little excited. "It's just this situation that's being foisted on the heads of Indian Muslims. It's become quite fashionable. So, answer my question, what have Muslims gained from Partition?"

"The mistake, you know, was all Jinnah's," someone else said in order to move things along. "What could you or I have done about it?"

"So what you're saying"—now the leader became more animated—"is that you think Pakistan was entirely the creation of Muhammad Ali Jinnah?"

"Maybe there are many more! Now you're a history professor."

"But I swear to god, we weren't even there!" the esteemed conversation leader burst out, and everyone smiled.

"So, do you people accept the proposition that what happened in 1947 was a mistake?" the leader asked solemnly, coming to the point.

"What do we know, yaar!" someone said innocently. "It's not like we were adults doing adult stuff back then."

Another rumble of laughter.

More conversation. Conversation to delight, to pass time. The topics were real, but no one was inclined to take them on in earnest. Conversation those days in any case was confined to not being drawn into a spiral of criticizing reactionary religious views. The feeling of vulnerability grew with each day and permeated the air. Unfathomable worry and unease about what will come next. It wasn't just Zamir Ahmed Khan's private underground, it looked like a large part of the world was being divided and transformed into countless undergrounds.

His First Drink

What about the first time Zamir Ahmed Khan touched drink?

This, too, was now a memory of times long past, when he and Vivek were studying in tenth grade and had already become close friends.

They saw each other at school and also spent time at each other's homes. If a relative of Vivek's came to visit Bhopal, Zamir Ahmed Khan would be introduced to him. Vivek's favorite relative was Mamaji, who looked just like Pakistan's Sadar Ayub. Zamir Ahmed Khan, too, was very fond of Mamaji. Whenever the man visited Bhopal from Delhi he'd regale them with his stories, take them out, entertain them. First thing, however, he would pack all the boys into his jeep and set off for the barbershop. He'd point at their long hair and instruct the barber, "Khalifaji, please turn these shaggy kings of kings into human beings."

Mamaji was like a walking and talking festival of jokes, advice, remembrances, always playful and restless. In any gathering, he was invariably the star of the party. Whenever Mamaji came to Bhopal, a regular part of the program was a hunting trip.

So on that freezing cold winter night Mamaji and some others had been driving around in the forest in the open jeep for some time, looking for prey. They took sips from a bottle to keep the cold in check.

It was an open secret that the first person Zamir Ahmed Khan had ever seen drinking was Mamaji, sitting right there in Vivek's house, as casually as can be. First, he had never seen anyone drink before. Second, in his mind, he associated drinking with gambling, brawling, expensive hotels, and nightclubs. Therefore, Zamir Ahmed Khan was really surprised when he saw Mamaji enjoying his drink and telling funny, captivating stories, and the intimate atmosphere he created. Not that it lessened his own abhorrence of liquor.

On that cold winter night, Mamaji had insisted he take a sip from the bottle. Zamir Ahmed Khan had declined outright. But to win against Mamaji was impossible. And that was exactly what happened. Mamaji had secretly poured some alcohol (whiskey, no less!—this he found out later) into the soda bottle and placed it in his hands, insisting that he drink.

"Come on, Zamir, this won't do. Have at least some soda to keep us company. Here, cheers!"

The brief interval between the first sip and its running down his throat had gradually come to occupy thousands of acres of thought in his mind. Zamir Ahmed Khan had once experienced a similar feeling of foolishness when he had gone to the Hussainiwala checkpoint on the India-Pakistan border. On one side there were soldiers and onlookers, the tricolored flag, and then, just beyond, lay open territory, no-man's-land. On the other side of the open territory, more soldiers, more onlookers, and the green flag with the crescent moon and star. As he gazed curiously at the barren no-man's-land, he kept thinking what would happen if he decided to walk across. Would the hands of his wristwatch automatically jump forward by the half hour that separated the standard time of the two countries?

A similar borderline had been drawn in his existence, before and after taking the sip, and had crudely divided his life into two parts. Even though they lay beside each other they passed up no opportunity for hostility toward the other.

All this came from later reflection. In the moment, he had no sooner taken a sip than a strange, bad taste filled his mouth. Zamir Ahmed Khan felt like throwing up. Mamaji patted his back and consoled him. He felt oddly disappointed and sad without fully understanding why. To this day he'd never been able to suppress the nausea and making faces after taking the first sip of liquor. There was something about drinking liquor he didn't like, and maybe he could never completely get it out of his mind. And with it a thought whose effect overshadowed any question of enjoying it or not. As soon as the sip of liquor had run down his throat, Zamir Ahmed Khan's integrity had been lost, and irretrievably so. Something extremely serious and unexpected had happened and he could never make it right again. So intense was the onset of remorse that for a split second he even forgot how bad it had tasted. He sat in the jeep with the others, angry and ashamed at himself, longing to be swallowed whole by the darkness of the night and disappear. The jeep drove on. The beam of the searchlight continuously scanned for prey while the hunters sat waiting, guns and rifles in hand, eager to shoot.

If he put aside acts of dishonesty that he occasionally committed in the form of theft, and which he always hoped to redeem when the time came (by returning two or three times the sums taken), drinking alcohol was technically the first unlawful act in Zamir Ahmed Khan's life that could not be redeemed.

He became aware of the dividing line between lawful and unlawful only after it had already been drawn, and he found himself ashamed and embarrassed. But the line had been drawn, so to put a bold face on the matter he quickly gulped down some more "soda." He soon found himself in a state of heightened awareness he'd never experienced or imagined. Zamir Ahmed Khan could now see clearly in the dark. The stars in the sky shone brighter, had drawn closer to earth. His ears picked up sounds from afar. His body felt light, filled with a new power and energy, as if he could fly. Before he had the chance to mourn the loss of one side of the border, the joy of reaching the other had already taken over.

"Why would religion forbid drinking?" Zamir Ahmed had asked Aziz aka Acchan one time, already a little aglow. "I never feel as close to god when I'm sober as when I've had something to drink."

"And that's a good thing." Aziz took a long drag on his cigarette and exhaled slowly. "Some people behave as if they were god when they're drunk. Maybe it's because of those idiots religion forbids drinking."

Distinguishing Aziz's straight talk from his irony was particularly difficult.

"Don't you feel the same way?" Zamir got Aziz's sarcasm, but made the mistake of asking another question in the hope of who knows what.

"Yaar, I have to keep my wits about me," Aziz aka Acchan replied in the most natural manner. He was quite the miracle drinker since no matter how much he drank, nobody'd ever seen him drunk. "In fact, on the Day of Judgment, it is I who'll have to provide testimony for the deeds of guys like you."

This was said some years later.

His experience that night resulted in an allergy. The next morning he woke up with his body covered in red spots. Alarmed, he went to the doctor, who evinced no desire to know any details, but gave him a shot of Avil that made the spots on his skin disappear within hours. After that, Zamir Ahmed Khan always took an Avil pill before he began drinking, occasionally or regularly, for some time to come. His friends, especially Aziz, thought it was funny and told him to quit drinking, but Zamir Ahmed Khan didn't take anyone's words seriously. Eventually there was no more need for pills and the allergy subsided. He both celebrated and regretted that his character, on top of the dishonest refugee and masked bandit, harbored a third party that distinguished between halal and haram and was allergic to booze. This last one he had to fight and finally overcome with pills of Avil.

After receiving the shot he'd tearfully asked Allah for forgiveness, repented, and swore that he would never touch drink again. All solemnly and in good faith. But he also learned that during times of revolt, the attacker can be given intelligence about where to attack from the outside!

Where the fort's parapet had been repaired and which spot was most suited for breaking through.

Like: it had to happen quickly and without delay.

The Cave was alive with conversation.

The wine-soaked talk began to meander. In the idiom of the dastan, the discussion became like the magic satchel of Umar Ayyar with no beginning and no end. Nor any coherent sequence or order to what was being said. Despite countless speed bumps, the companions in the Cave were still going strong on the subject of Greater India. They were also engrossed in lamenting the country's sorry state and political decline. The conversation then expanded to include Bhopal's Iqbal Maidan and the eagle statue erected on its grounds.

"They proclaim their love for the environment and for trees and birds, and at the same time they change the name of our good old Khirniwala Maidan. Someone go and ask them what the poor innocent khirni tree ever did to them?"

"Besides," another voice confirmed, "it's outrageous that they name a park after Allamah Iqbal. As if he weren't a poet and philosopher but some star athlete."

"Well, wasn't he?" the leader said casually.

"What do you mean?" a few astonished voices chimed in.

"I mean that Allamah was really fast. Has anyone ever defeated him in Urdu till now?"

"And this statue of the golden goose they've put up right in the center of the Maidan? You think that's the divine bird Iqbal imagined?"

"Exactly, plus the bird of death. The artist killed two stones with one bird."

"Right, yaar! This golden goose of yours is also a symbol of the bird of death that hovered over Bhopal in the form of the gas leak!"

From the Iqbal Maidan to Iqbal, from Iqbal to Pakistan, from Pakistan to Iqbal's role in imagining Pakistan and on to Sir Sayyid and the Aligarh movement, the Shah Bano case and the government's appropriate or inappropriate interference in personal law, news of intensifying clashes over the Babri Masjid and Ram Janmabhoomi, the destruction of progressive values in daily life. And: we didn't expect this from Hindus, this doesn't put them in a good light, what can Muslims do, what should Muslims be doing?

Meandering wine-soaked talk.

A long seven years separated his first and second drink.

Love, Ten Weeks Long

Zamir Ahmed Khan eventually convinced himself that Allah Miyan must have forgiven that drink he'd had, and that by accident, too. He formally asked for forgiveness after the disaster, began to pray namaz regularly, and kept a more strict fast during Ramadan.

Zamir Ahmed Khan was now in eleventh grade. His subjects were math and science, and the plan was to go on for a degree in engineering after higher secondary. He was considered one of the most promising and hard-working students in the class. The exams for higher secondary were still a long way off when the second disaster struck.

And when it struck it seemed as minor as when a fully loaded truck has a blowout while passing someone walking all alone on a deserted road. If the passerby has rotten luck, the sound of the tire bursting may give him heart failure. If his luck is so-so, he may faint and collapse for a little while. The lucky one will smile to himself thinking about the truck and driver's bad luck, and continue on his way.

Zamir time and again tried to examine his own luck from every possible angle. In the end, he concluded that the blowout disaster was the real start-ing point in the dissolution of his personality—that is, if he wasn't deceiving himself, a possibility that couldn't be rejected out of hand. The first tower of the fortress of his person fell at the sound of the blowout in such a way that the fortress would never be picture-perfect again.

Today the affair seemed stupid and ridiculous, even if he just thought about it by himself, never mind discussing it with anyone else. A voice in his heart told him it was only a pretense, a fantasy for the sake of fantasy, which he had dressed up as the real thing in a whimsical way. Maybe the charge was true that he'd made too big or too little a deal out of it, but the fact of what had happened couldn't be denied. If rock-solid reality and a person's evident virtues and vices were the only criteria in life to draw any conclu-sion, would Laila and Majnun, Shirin and Farhad, Mumtaz and Shah Jahan be remembered the way they are?

Being a lover isn't as dangerous as having an amorous disposition. Since Zamir Ahmed Khan realized what this disposition was capable of, and because he was fearful of the masked bandit's rage lurking within, he maintained a measured distance from people as a matter of course. As he became closer with Vivek, he saw clearly that the greatest shareholder in his love and affection was none other than this masked bandit. The masked bandit couldn't bear Akka's association with any other, and now resented anyone becoming close or friendly with Vivek. And yet Zamir Ahmed Khan's first experience of the joy of love was utterly singular and distinct.

Aisha was her name, she'd just transferred into his class, and her family had just arrived in Bhopal from Bangalore. Before Aisha, he'd never felt this way when he first saw, met, or talked with a girl. True, meeting Akka had been a formative experience, but there was a subtle difference between the encounters with Akka and Aisha that he sensed without fully grasping. Besides, Akka was his cousin, while with Aisha, there was at least the possibility of love. He fell completely silent and sad when he saw her, as if sadness were the natural effect of her presence. Lines of poetry describing the vulnerability of the lover lost in sorrow came to his mind like moths to the flame. Or plots of tragic love stories, unusual situations he was dying to write, one stranger than the next. But his schoolwork and stress about exams prevented him from writing them. Aisha, Aisha, Aisha, he inscribed her name by pen wherever he could, in the backs of notebooks, in secret places in books on all topics where no one would find it, on the desk in class, a table in the library, in his various journals, on walls and lampposts on the side of the road, until, finally, he took a sharp knife and carved her name into the trunk of the huge shady gulmohar tree that stood in the zoo near his house, and which remained intact until a few years ago when it was cut down, roots and all, for the development of a new neighborhood. Thoughts of Aisha hovered over Zamir Ahmed Khan like a halo, but whether the halo was one of darkness or light he couldn't say. When he thought about it now, the feelings deep in his soul resembled how the world looked many years later during the full solar eclipse. Darkness had so fully enveloped earth and sky in the middle of the day, it seemed that it had emanated from another realm. Flustered birds in trees and crickets hiding in the corners of houses began to sing and chirp. Maybe there was as much romance as there was terror in this state of mind. An eerie silence spread far and wide, stranger than during curfew, since you didn't hear the sounds of police cars coming and going. Every single person during the eclipse, depending on their faith or beliefs, reminded themselves again and again of the unbreakable chain of life and death—and felt compelled to give more thought to death than life. Death is a part of life (this is a universally acknowledged truth) and maybe that's why, if you don't think of life at the same time, the thought of death is so frightening. It unbalances the established equation of common sense.

Death is the seasoning in the greens of life: it's accepted in every heart, and it doesn't surprise anyone. This misconception is shattered when someone in the prime of life finds themselves in a situation where they have a consuming experience or vision of death. When we don't patch over death with life, no difference remains between the two.

Zamir Ahmed Khan experienced this much later, during the solar eclipse. It was also what he felt after setting eyes on Aisha as he lived desperately through his first encounter with love. He was in the eleventh grade, it lasted for a few weeks, and he oscillated between joy and sorrow. And it was something he also finally understood with age, after sensing something take shape and solidify between his own skin and bone.

So even after he'd followed the time-honored tradition of falling head over heels in love with a stranger, Zamir Ahmed Khan, instead of a simple and straightforward declaration of love, emulated the great heroes of great love stories (which always have a sad ending), and decided to keep his love a secret deep in his heart of hearts. This impulse was fine for a little while, but he soon began to tire of physics, chemistry, and math. The pen in his hand turned into a bulbul and began to flutter as it remembered the rose. The girl had come from another city and was from an entirely different background. She was quick in her studies, had good taste in clothes, and was discerning in speech. But more important than these qualities, she was the proprietress of an exceedingly shapely, well-proportioned, attractive body that came with a face beguiling all by itself. The entire time he was in school with Aisha, Zamir Ahmed Khan found exactly two moments to approach her.

"Would you be able to lend me your Hindi workbook until tomorrow?" Aisha asked him one day after class in her singsong voice.

"Of course, but please take good care of it," Zamir Ahmed Khan said handing it to her, his voice implying that he was giving her more than a workbook.

A little ray of hope sprung up in his heart. Why not? Maybe lending and borrowing books and notes might be the start of something. Maybe there might be a love letter stuck inside when she returned his workbook. Even if that didn't happen, what difference would these mundane things make to his love? His hope remained firmer than the firmest belief. It was impossible now to hide his state from Vivek, who was actually fairly popular among the girls. Sometimes, Zamir Ahmed Khan feared she might tilt her favor toward him. One day he took Vivek into his confidence and poured out his heart.

"Bastard! So you've turned into a secret Rustom with his Sohrab," Vivek said, slapping him on the back. "She's quite an item, this Aisha. Should I put in a good word for you? You're Muslim, she's Muslim. Anyway, I'm just here as a bystander!"

He told Vivek in no uncertain terms not to do any such thing. What's the rush? He'd decided in his heart he'd marry Aisha and spend the rest of his life with her, so that was enough. It wasn't as if there was something lacking in Zamir Ahmed Khan that might give Aisha cause to reject him. He wasn't inferior to Aisha Sultana in any way. They'd complete their higher secondary. After that, he'd tell Amma and Abba to bring the proposal to Aisha's family, then the engagement, then five years later after finishing his engineering degree, the wedding. A house, family, happily ever after.

Zamir Ahmed Khan had plotted and decided all of this on his own. He never thought it necessary to communicate his wishes or ideas to Aisha. Who knows why?

And then what happened?

Just like always, the wicked world won the day.

The exams for higher secondary were still far away when Aisha Sultana disappeared for a week. Enemies spread ugly rumors during her absence and then Vivek gathered intelligence and reported that Aisha had been engaged from the beginning and would be married in a couple of days.

The palace of his dreams collapsed like a house of cards. But instantly he also solved the mystery of why Aisha had seemed so different from the other girls in class. She was older, and her body had already filled out in shape and form. This helped him understand the situation, but was hardly a consolation, and he wouldn't be able to share his pain with anyone except for Vivek. The maiden returned one week later, after her marriage, now a woman, and her going to school, attending classes, and flirting resumed. It was then that Zamir Ahmed Khan, looking for a second chance to talk to her, stopped her one day, took her aside, and said, "Aisha, you should have said something!"

After that, god knows why but Aisha stopped coming to school. Maybe her in-laws wanted her to finish her studies at a girls' school. She'd left, while Zamir Ahmed Khan was like smoldering kindling that sparks had fallen on by accident.

What difference did it make in the end? He came to his senses at just the right moment, sent his beloved to hell, and immersed himself again in his schoolwork. So much so that it was easy to get a high grade on the final exam. It may have been a foolish and adolescent thing to do, but boys going into higher secondary did think about getting married. From there began a long stage of life that required all one's skills and undivided attention, with no room left for compromise. And what did he really know about Aisha anyway, he who'd been hell-bent on making that big decision! He didn't even know whether she was married or not!

And yet these arguments and consolations were kept on the scrap heap in the back of Zamir Ahmed Khan's mind, and he sensed that this was the first battle he'd fought in his life where he'd conceded defeat without putting up a fight. This experience was the first patch sewn onto his soul and the first dent in his psyche. Just like when a fully loaded truck has a blowout while passing someone walking all alone on a deserted road. Fortunately the injury he suffered turned out to be no more than an internal one. Over time, he came to feel he'd been saved from great folly by the skin of his teeth. He didn't realize that the injury had been to his soul—a tiny, delicate opening that grew wider as he grew older. Until the day when only a chasm remained where Zamir Ahmed Khan had once been. A huge, deep hole that mocked him.

"I've got a joke." The companions in the Cave, bored with serious topics, turned to humor.

"Let's hear it."

"A guy comes in for a job interview, and asks, 'Sir! I will receive preference in the handicapped quota, won't I?' The interviewer doesn't know what to say and asks, 'But all your limbs are working just fine, no?' The guy's a little embarrassed, 'Sir! Actually, my name is Abdul Quddus. I am Muslim impaired.'"

A smattering of laughter and yawns.

"You'll be handicapped!" someone snorted. "I don't think I'm lesser to anyone."

"Easy, my dear! You're drunk, and it was just a joke."

"How about one more?"

"One more!"

"Have you heard of this good Sahib who suggested that they build a wall instead of barbed wire on the border of India and Pakistan? Just like the Wailing Wall in Jerusalem. Where all the people from the subcontinent can go whenever they want to hold on to it and cry, repent, lament, confess their sins, and ask for forgiveness."

"Enough! Pour me another one, yaar."

Leaving for Aligarh

On the surface, Zamir Ahmed Khan managed to recover quickly from his first big failure in life, and a failure in love at that.

Yes, the fortress of his psyche had been deprived of one or two towers in the mishap and was no longer picture-perfect. But it wasn't yet time for Zamir Ahmed Khan to take advantage of what he knew about the weak points of the mended ramparts, conspire with the enemy, and invite him to attack. This would come only after he suffered at the hands of Aisha, then Vivek, then Anisa. He received excellent grades in higher secondary and such a good ranking that he had no problem gaining admission to engineering college.

They would definitely continue their studies, Zamir Ahmed Khan and Vivek had decided together, just not in Bhopal.

Vivek went for biology and had to study for another year before applying to medical college. Zamir Ahmed Khan had applied to the local engineering college even though he'd decided not to stay in Bhopal. He was interviewed and admitted right away, another feather in his cap as his fame and import grew at home and among the extended family.

The year he passed his higher secondary exam was also a significant one for his family. Bhai Miyan had parted with Abba and was busy getting his business off the ground, while Abba, who had stayed away from business for years, was once again struggling to make ends meet. Zamir's success helped the two of them forget their bitterness for a while, and they unanimously supported his idea to go to Aligarh, where Kamal Miyan was doing his M.A. in economics. For years he'd heard Kamal Miyan sing the praises of Aligarh University, and it was on his advice that he'd decided to study there himself.

Several reasons lay behind his resolve to leave Bhopal. One of the many superficial reasons was that he could no longer live in the place that had separated him from his beloved. Despite all it had to offer, Bhopal suddenly appeared to be a place that tried a little too hard to be a provincial capital when it was really just a small town. A place where people frowned upon the friendship between Zamir and Vivek—two boys, never mind between a boy and a girl—and a place where everyone wanted to find out what was really going on, depending on their mental makeup. Bhopal, the stain of ill repute! The dumb Bhopali way of thinking and people with small minds! It was true that he was very close to Vivek, and every evening they strolled through the hills and along the shore of the lake to watch the sunset, arms slung around each other's shoulders. Sure, watching films together, they fought, they made up. So what does this add up to? Shame on you! Heaven forbid! This was the Bhopali mentality. If someone found them in a compromising situation, maybe the fault would lie in the eyes of the beholder or the mind of he who judged? A place and people like that? To hell with them! Living with these types was the biggest mistake of all.

Zamir Ahmed Khan had told Vivek in private, "Spending so much time together is a waste for both of us. Right now you should focus on your studies for a year to get into medical college."

"I agree," Vivek replied firmly, "I shouldn't stay in Bhopal."

"Where do you think you'll go?" He caught himself nearly telling Vivek to go to Aligarh.

"Maybe Delhi, where I can stay with Mamaji and study," Vivek said, reflectively. "Or I could live with Bare Bhai Sahib in Indore."

Knowing that Vivek, too, wouldn't stay in Bhopal filled Zamir Ahmed Khan's heart with relief. This conversation took place while they watched the sunset, sitting on a small bridge on the side of the road that led upward from the left side of the MLA rest house toward the jail. Patches of clouds were scattered across the summer sky, some set aflame, others red in the evening sun. The road that nowadays sees sixty cars pass by in a minute had lain in silent slumber for who knows how long. Their bicycles were propped up on their stands right next to the railing.

He'd sent his application to Aligarh and received an invitation for an interview.

In the middle of the high summer heat, he had gone to Aligarh for the interview along with Kamal Miyan, and had returned extremely impressed by the buildings, almost deserted during the holidays, the lawns, and the mysterious atmosphere of the campus. He'd stopped at Agra for awhile on the way back from the interview, and with Aisha on his mind saw the monument of eternal love with his own eyes, the Taj Mahal, also remembered as a tear left on the cheek of time. The sight of the Taj left him more despondent than impressed, who knows why.

"Did you see the Taj?" was the first question Amma asked after he came back, as if convinced that seeing the Taj Mahal had always been his heart's greatest desire.

"I did," he said casually, trying to change the topic.

"And how was it?"

"Just like in the calendars. Fresh and radiant. As if still waiting for the fortieth day after Mumtaz Mahal's death."

Amma laughed, a little surprised.

The letter had arrived: he'd been admitted to engineering college at Aligarh University.

His reputation at home and among his relatives grew, and a change occurred in the way people interacted with him. Zamir Ahmed Khan's domain was now no longer confined to Bhopal. He had joined a larger world, and one of note. Everyone assented to this notion and allowed him to feel his own importance. So now he was just a temporary guest at home and in town.

Preparations for his departure to Aligarh were in full swing: gathering the things he'd need, packing. Abba without words conveyed to him that the expense of studying and living away from home wasn't a burden to him, and that he shouldn't fret unnecessarily over the family's economic uncertainty. Bhai Miyan tried in various ways to cover up the pain of leaving family and was busy finding ways to comfort him. He took him to the tailor to have a black sherwani sewn, and to the market to buy other things he'd need. Amma was seen wiping her eyes with the end of her dupatta all the time now, and she spent more and more time each day after namaz praying for his well-being. Aapa and Bhabhi were busy preparing all sorts of halvah, pickles, and jams. A faceless gloom had settled over the household. When Abba approached him, it was with a new intimacy. Something changed in the way he spoke. A bridge of friendship now spanned over their conversations. If Abba ever invoked his age and experience as part of discussing some practical matter, he didn't lecture, but instead adopted the tone of an equal, a confidant.

"I'm no good when it comes to writing letters," Abba said as he sat Zamir Ahmed Khan down for a chat a few days before his departure for Aligarh. "If I have no choice, or if it's an urgent matter, I still barely manage a few words. But I promise you this, I shall write you a letter every week."

Zamir Ahmed Khan sensed a particular timbre and tone in Abba's voice that evening, and became lost in memories of how often he'd crossed the threshold of Abba's study and how much time had gone by. The field and its greenery, the mosque and Murshad, Dulhan Chachi, Phaphu Biya, the game of cops and robbers, the chutney, playacting cinema, and the end of his schooldays—everything would end up somewhere on those railroad tracks that in his mind were good only for flattening copper coins. Sitting next to Abba now, Zamir wanted to review the reel of his life before his eyes, the sum total from childhood to this moment. And it struck him that the source of light had receded into the distance with the focus now on him, sitting in this room, alone, listening to Abba's words. Words that were free from weakness or fatigue since he who spoke them was convinced that his life's labor had been rewarded with a worthy heir.

Before leaving Bhopal he went to visit with all the family elders. Bare Abba patted his back and gave his blessings, Bhai Jaan affectionately slipped him a hundred-rupee note, and Phaphu Amma placed her hand on his head and blessed him with the words, "May Allah bring you back safely." Amma gave him her prayer mat that she'd brought back from the hajj instructing him to say his prayers regularly and read the Quran whenever his heart was troubled. On the last day there was the kind of commotion in the house as if someone were simultaneously going on the hajj and being transported across the Black Waters on a life sentence. The elders pitched in for his travel expenses while the younger ones gave him presents. Some tears, some laughs. Things weren't as comical in the moment as when he remembered them now. This was how it was done in Bhopal back then.

The last time he saw Vivek before he left, he'd asked, "So it's decided? You're leaving as well?"

"I am," Vivek replied solemnly.

"To Delhi, right? When are you going?"

"Yes, soon."

"We'll get together during the holidays. Listen, don't come to the station to see me off. It wouldn't feel right."

Vivek had complied.

After Aisha, this was the second separation Zamir Ahmed Khan had to face. And all within a year's time!

A Mistake

After he arrived in Aligarh, it didn't take long to realize he'd made a mistake.

It was during a time when two distinct camps had formed at Aligarh Muslim University, one demanding to maintain the Muslim character of the university, and another demanding to change it. Whether they liked it or not, everyone found themselves in one or the other camp. The business of teaching and learning must have continued in the various departments, but it was the atmosphere of student politics that was heating up fast.

Victoria Gate, Jama Masjid, the Tomb of Sir Sayyid, Strachey Hall, the Bab-e Ishaq and Bab-e Rahmat gates, the university library, the canteen, Kennedy Hall, the huge M. F. Hussain mural in the Department of General Education, the labs and workshops and other buildings spread out in the Engineering College—all of these are preserved in his mind like a slowly fading blueprint. And the Ruby, the Novelty, the Tasveer Mahal, Tibbiya College, and just before it the old post office building where he opened his very first bank account. Shamshad market and its little dhaba-like hotels where they served fabulous chai in tea sets, and the Café de Phoos that looked right out of a dream, built out of thatch, and then the beautiful pond and mansion in Lal Diggi, the Kathpula bridge, and City Art Studio, where he went the first time to have his photo taken for his identity card and the second time for a group photo with his dorm mates. Uppercourt, the place to drink lassis, and the Gandhi Eye Hospital, the place people went for eye exams as part of the medical checkup.

In the evenings he strolled alone on the roof terrace of his hostel, watching others play cricket on the field behind the building and thought about Bhopal sadly, with a heavy heart. These memories were intensely disturbing and filled with unease.

Abba did write letters regularly. But Vivek neither wrote a single letter, nor stuck to the agreement they'd made in Bhopal. Instead of leaving, he'd continued his studies there. It was a betrayal Zamir Ahmed Khan wouldn't forgive Vivek for the rest of his life. Under no circumstances and no matter what. Aisha's behavior might have been explained by the pressure she was under. But Vivek?

Brava lover, Bravo friend!

The year spent in Aligarh was like Chinese water torture, with each day passing slowly, drop by drop.

But time does eventually pass, whether a long period of illness, or the recovery afterward. The academic year at Aligarh University was coming to an end. In the final months he'd tried to drop subtle hints to Abba in their correspondence that he wanted to continue his studies in his hometown. The reason? Aligarh just didn't suit him. And why not? He really missed Bhopal, and home. Despite this, Abba probably thought to himself, "Son! Aligarh doesn't suit you? You don't like it there? 'Not liking it' doesn't become an intelligent person like you. No sensitive person has ever been able to like the world, so how could you? You must look for excuses, you have to trick yourself into pretending you like it. Time is the great master, my dear son! When you come back to Bhopal, you'll find that life is no more agreeable for you here. That it makes no difference whether you're in your own city or getting settled in an unknown place. With strangers at least you can hope to become friends. But what else can you hope for with those you're close to other than run the risk of becoming estranged? When you come back this time you'll realize you've outgrown your city, and when the time comes you will return to Aligarh discarding the childish notions that you don't like it there or you miss home. Then this feeling won't be restricted to just Aligarh or Bhopal—wherever you live in the world you'll think despondently about this heart and memory. The basic demand of life is to keep moving. In order to achieve your goal you have to chase after it, no matter what your fate is or where it's written. Think about it, your ancestors were from what kind of tribe and clan in Afghanistan? And how many thousands of miles did they come to settle here in Bhopal? And for what? In order to watch the pretty sunsets? Take a stroll by the side of the lake and go on picnics? You may call it the exigencies of life or time, or the lure of the land that drew them here. But it wasn't nostalgia or trying to maintain family connections. Sardar Dost Muhammad Khan was not one of their acquaintances, and Rani Kamlapati didn't tie rakhis on their wrists. If you don't give up your cowardice, life will disencumber it from you. Everyone's like that at your age, and maybe I wasn't all that different."

All Abba's letters were peppered with these kinds of lessons. A reference to his life experiences, what he'd read in books, or just some straightforward advice. Oftentimes Abba's advice was to continue his daily prayers and worship. He tried to follow what Abba had to say as much as possible, but he wasn't able to detect any constructive effect of this on his thinking or daily life. He continued to stay in Aligarh simply waiting for the year to be over so that he could return to Bhopal. The only thing that was settled was he wouldn't live in Aligarh anymore but return to Bhopal.

Final exams had begun and Zamir Ahmed Khan pretended to study ever so diligently. He'd received a scholarship from the university he had to feign humble gratitude for, at least in front of his roommates. In the meantime, he unwillingly began to discover his real cognitive limitations, particularly in math, where he couldn't function very well outside the confines of rote memorization. He had only a slight inkling about these limitations then since he wasn't studying properly for exams anyway. He left the answer books completely blank for some subjects, getting up and leaving.

One Friday afternoon after his exams had finished he'd eaten lunch after praying namaz just like every Friday and returned to his room, where he was reading a novel—E. M. Forster's *A Passage to India*. Noticing his interest in reading, the senior hostel roommate had given him the book—emphasizing when he gave it to him that the author had dedicated the book to Ross Masood, the grandson of Sir Sayyid, who had once been the vice-chancellor of Aligarh Muslim University. That aside, Zamir Ahmed Khan became deeply engrossed in the book, for it tried to articulate important facts of life lost to the haze of history. Zamir Ahmed Khan wanted to talk about the book with the senior hostel roommate, but he asked Zamir for forgiveness and admitted he'd never read it and didn't plan on reading it in the future. His interest lay in a lighter fare of fiction and poetry. He then presented Zamir with a novel he'd written himself.

Student unrest had been growing steadily over the past weeks and months along with the demand not to meddle with the character of the university. The old vice-chancellor had left the university, and, according to student leaders, the administration had appointed the new one to push through changes of its own liking. Those opposing the proposed changes had facts and figures to prove that Muslim students in the university would have to deal with a whole host of new problems as a result of them. These leaders and their backers claimed that such developments would be a violation of the basic principles that the founder of the university, Sir Sayyid, had crusaded for when establishing the institution. They also claimed that this was part of a well-thought-out, deliberate, anti-Muslim policy being promulgated by the government. The educational backwardness of the Muslim community, their almost nonexistent representation in the government, and the administration's hypocritical policy were a heated topic of debate and flashpoint in every chai stall, hostel room, and department. Few may have taken part in the debate, but there were a number who spoke in favor of change, especially those connected to the representative of a progressive faction, who were able to answer numbers with numbers and had a slate of facts to refute the other side's.

The troubles were irrelevant to Zamir Ahmed Khan since his decision to leave was already final. It also seemed to him that the conduct of the anti-change faction was motivated more by emotion than conscience, whereas the proclamations of the reform group appeared more realistic and substantial. In a country that's fundamentally secular, and where secularism is the bedrock of the constitution, using religion to polarize people and institutions, or to favor or harm a particular community, was such a dubious undertaking that no argument in its favor could hold sway.

He didn't really go out of his way to talk with people about these issues or put forward his own views. If the topic came up when he was with friends, he'd say a sentence or two, and add that in light of his experience so far, he considered himself someone with firm secularist inclinations. Otherwise he'd say nothing. For the time being, he was trying to locate the characters from *A Passage to India* in faces scattered around him. Dr. Aziz, Barrister Hamidullah, Advocate Mahmoud Ali, Muhammad Latif, and the Nawab Bahadur on one side, Professor Godbole, Dr. Panna Lal, Mr. and Mrs. Bhattacharya, Magistrate Mr. Das, Mrs. Das, and Mr. Amritrao on the other. Their mutual suspicion and love and hate. The roots reached deep into history.

The writer had stressed the fundamental difference between Hindu and Muslim mentalities and illustrated them with telling details. This difference overshadowed all apparent similarities and dissimilarities, things that Zamir Ahmed Khan himself had never paid attention to. After the country's independence, the third group of characters in the book—Mr. Fielding, Mrs. Moore, Miss Quested, and so on—could no longer be seen in the same context as in the novel, but reading the book he felt the British had never fully left the country and that the people had never become truly independent. The portrait of Dr. Aziz was such an extraordinary depiction of an Indian Muslim that he seemed to live and breathe all Zamir's own misfortunes, complexes, biases, and sentimentalities. In Aligarh, he saw living, breathing, walking, talking versions of Dr. Aziz whose case was being dismissed from all the courts because of Independence and Partition. They had to learn how to live without complaints and protests, since there was no other cure except time. Reading the book, he was truly surprised at the author's knowledge and deep understanding of Indian society.

And why wouldn't he like it? Just like Dr. Aziz of the novel, he, too, enjoyed mosques, minarets, the call to prayer, formal greetings, poetry, and an atmosphere of manners and courtesy. How could life be imagined without Eid, Bakra Eid, Shab-e Barat? Also, there wasn't any chance for these things to be mixed up with politics. What did this atmosphere of doubt and suspicion mean in the country where Gandhi had sacrificed his life for the sake of brotherly harmony? And where Nehru had fought to the very end to build bridges between the hearts of his countrymen? This kind of thinking could only be the product of a diseased mind. True, from time to time things happened in the country that shouldn't happen—communal riots and arson and killing. But what was at its root? That same fundamental ignorance of people, which Sir Sayyid in his own way had played a part in eradicating and which the present government, for its part, was trying to mend. In the seventh decade of the twentieth century, the importance of religion had changed: this plain and simple fact that the so-called student leaders failed to understand. Maybe more time was needed for them to understand things as they truly were.

These and similar ideas, fully formed and half-baked, formed the capital, principal, and investment of the life he'd lived up until then.

One Friday afternoon after namaz and lunch, Zamir Ahmed Khan was reading the final pages of *A Passage to India* in his room, fan on high, when the ruckus outside seemed to enter right into the room and the sounds of people chanting slogans filled his ears. Someone knocked on the door and delivered a collective invitation instructing him to come outside armed with a rod from his mosquito net. Before he knew what was happening he found himself in the middle of an uncontrollable crowd besieging the quarters where some students were protecting the vice-chancellor, whom they'd taken pity on—the crowd threatening to kill the "coward," "traitor," "sellout."

Leaving the Cave

The Cave was lively that night.

A gentleman recited a ghazal to an appreciative audience. If someone lost their way inside a labyrinth of history and politics, poetry was the place of refuge. Poetry or witticisms. Poetry was stretched to the breaking point in that everyone was given a chance to recite their verse or opine about a verse recited. The last session of the night gave the poetry readers and the responsive audience ample opportunity to tie their shoelaces and look at their watches. Rather than bidding people farewell from the Cave, these last readings served the purpose of bringing them back the next night.

A void gradually grew in Zamir Ahmed Khan's mind where poetry had once been. Maybe it had to do with the poetry he'd been reading or listening to recently. But he feared that one day even the greats like Ghalib and Mir might seem insipid. It's not that his grasp of poetry was now more profound or that he'd developed a more critical and mature ear. He simply could not relish poetry anymore.

The evening at the Cave was drawing to a close. People stood up and bid one another farewell.

"You performed a miracle, yaar, today was really amazing."

"What can I say? It's the first time I've recited something from the heart in a long time."

The poet would receive this kind of praise as if he'd recited his own work.

"Don't play coy. More of this, please!"

"Very well!"

"Vaah, vaah, bravo, bravo."

"We're off." One gentleman took his leave.

"How are you getting home?"

"By scooter."

"Can you drop me off?"

"Let's go. What about him?" pointing in the direction of another gentleman.

"He lives just next door."

"So everything's set for tomorrow? Same time, same place?"

"Yes, yaar. Every day brings new change, and we have to keep tabs on how everyone's faring."

"What else is slated for change? We've had the gas leak, and the fight over the personal law has been averted at long last. The other worries will soon be a thing of the past."

"But what about this row over the temple and the mosque that's come up again? Think it can be resolved so easily?"

"And Bofors! I just can't figure out what's true and what's not."

"These problems aren't going anywhere as long as this country exists, and as long as both Hindus and Muslims live here. What's the gas leak and Bofors compared with those bad guys?"

"Tomorrow night?"

"Definitely."

"Good night."

"Good-bye."

A swell of good-byes before the sounds faded into the stillness of the night.

Something over the past few years had drawn a veil of alienation between Zamir Ahmed Khan and his city. The only connection that remained was during the lonely and deserted wee hours of the night, pregnant with the possibility of meeting someone. Meet who? Any face that could walk with him a few steps to indulge his old feelings for Bhopal.

Rahat was not at home. The thought hit him like a bolt of lightning and he stopped in his tracks.

With Rahat there it was easy to come home as late as he wanted and in whatever state. He didn't have to bang on the door or ring the bell, but simply wake up Rahat by calling out to her from the back of the house. She'd let him in, at the worst picking a fight, or a few angry words of reproach. This wouldn't happen anymore. He wasn't sure who would open the door if he rang the bell. Bhai Miyan, Bhabhi, or one of the kids. Zamir Ahmed Khan maintained a pretense about his drinking in the family, and he wanted to keep up appearances at all costs. What would he do tonight in this state? Even if he couldn't get dinner, he still had to spend the night somewhere. Having Bhai Miyan and Bhabhi worry about him for one night seemed a better alternative than going and making a fool of himself somewhere else. But where? Where could he go?

Zamir Ahmed Khan considered many doors he might knock on, but he couldn't think of a single one that would open for him this late.

It wasn't an easy decision to go and see Rahat at her parents' and try to placate her and make her see reason. The fault was all his, from beginning to end, but the way Rahat had left him and gone away felt like the transfer of some neighbor in a government colony. As if he didn't mean anything to her and wasn't important to her life. And she knew very well how alone and helpless he was in his current condition. Rahat's complaints did carry weight, but could she ever really complain that Zamir Ahmed Khan hadn't loved her in his own way? Set aside the question of fidelity for a moment. When husband and wife live together for a long time and are happy, they don't need to use words as crutches. A new language develops between them where words remain the same but take on fine, subtle shades of meaning. Maybe he and Rahat weren't all that happy, but they'd stuck together in spite of all the ups and downs, and that for a pretty long time. Maybe the thing called "infidelity" that stung him like a scorpion was another troublesome aspect of the disease that Crocodile and all the others still hadn't been able to figure out. The first time he'd been taken to Doctor Crocodile, no woman in the whole wide world, let alone Rahat, had ever touched him: he was untainted, a virgin. Later he was able to experiment with his body, during the time of Sharafat Miyan and the Treasure Trove. It was a part of life he couldn't expect Rahat to participate in, and Zamir Ahmed Khan didn't have the guts to risk approaching her. It was never an issue between the two of them, and Zamir Ahmed Khan hoped fervently and prayed to Allah that Rahat was totally ignorant of these practices. He was remorseful, he felt shame, but it wasn't going to kill him. How much of his life up to now was a consequence of things he desired and things brought about himself? How much was foisted on him by circumstance and because he had no choice? He wasn't able to sort out which parts of his life were caused by what. Having added some words and deeds to the accounting book of the masked bandit and dishonest refugee hidden inside, he concluded that he was still in the exact same spot as way back then, when a dividing line had been drawn between lawful and unlawful. Sometimes on this side of the line, sometimes on that. Crossing it again and again had become his life's goal, deliberately or not. Maybe it was wrong to live like this. Maybe he had no choice. But there was still enough left in his life associated with his Mr. Clean image, and he had to live through this incarnation before reaching the point he was at now. He hadn't even fled Aligarh yet when, in the words of the poet, there are worlds beyond Aligarh! Zamir Ahmed Khan couldn't go home at this hour, in this condition, so he endured another homeless, sleepless night in this city of his: Moti Masjid, Kamla Park, Hamidia College, Baan Ganga, the police headquarters on the banks of the Lower Lake, Pul Pukhta, where work to widen the bridge was in full swing those days, Ladies Hospital, home. If he got tired he could sit down somewhere and rest, even take a little nap before the light of dawn emerged and he'd be able to go home and knock on the door.

Back to Bhopal

Thinking about it now, the relationship between India and Pakistan after the 1965 war (and after his return to Bhopal) and the change in Zamir's relationship with Vivek were quite similar. First and foremost, it was a war or fight between two rivals who had once been very close.

Second, it was impossible for the two of them to keep away from each other for very long in spite of all the reasons for both open and hidden hostility. Third, though they'd been at odds for some time, their history of love and friendship was much older. And one of the greatest practical truths, ignoring all other superficial similarities, is that countries don't choose their neighbors and people don't choose their friends. They simply exist.

After the incident at Aligarh, Zamir Ahmed Khan's departure was very sudden. Even before the police and Provincial Armed Constabulary arrived, Kamal Miyan had told him to leave campus immediately. He'd wanted to go with him right away, but had to stay since he hadn't finished with exams. He packed up all his belongings in a fit of anger, assisted by Kamal Miyan and his roommates. As they loaded the luggage onto a cycle rickshaw, they heard the voice of the senior hostel roommate from UP call out to him.

"You're not short on money for your trip?" he asked with genuine concern.

He did have money, more than he even needed. But he had to honor the dictate of the dishonest refugee within, so a false gloom spread over his face, and he listened silently to the query.

"Here, take this," the roommate said, asserting his seniority and holding out a hundred-rupee bill. "Will this do?"

"Yes, certainly," he said happily.

"Perfect, now get going, Khuda Hafiz, be safe."

He traveled to the bus stand by cycle rickshaw and from there took the Agra bus. Then he bought a train ticket to Bhopal and the next morning arrived at the familiar station of his city. He convinced himself while riding home in a tonga that his time in Aligarh had been a bad dream. One he must try to erase from his mind completely and as soon as possible.

Zamir Ahmed Khan never thought about returning to Aligarh. When he thought of his time there, he was reminded of Mr. Fielding from *A Passage to*

India leaving India and his Indian friends behind. Mr. Fielding held on to his feelings for a while as he traveled farther, but then soon forgot as he became busy with other endeavors. Interesting, but not worth remembering.

It goes without saying that Zamir Ahmed Khan never wrote to his senior hostel roommate and never returned the hundred rupees.

Given the unrest at Aligarh, it wasn't hard to convince Abba and the other elders that staying in Aligarh would have been pointless. They probably even sympathized a little with the faction campaigning to preserve the minority character of the university. But having sympathy with a movement is one thing, and jeopardizing the future of one's offspring quite another.

"God only knows when things will calm down!" Amma said after hearing the report of Aligarh in a voice mixed with sadness and exasperation. "Even if they turned it into another Pakistan, they wouldn't be satisfied! Some of them want a Punjabi province, others are ready to give their lives to struggle against Hindi, and then there're the ones with their Hindi-Hindu-Hindustan slogan. China walks in, lops our head off, walks away. And grief-stricken India lets Nehru off the hook! What'll happen to the people here?"

Father listened very attentively to the whole story and then advised him that he alone should make a decision. Zamir Ahmed Khan sensed that his worth had diminished in Abba's eyes. Abba was the first, others would follow. The intimacy, friendship, and equality Abba had demonstrated the year before had begun to evaporate the night Zamir summoned all his arguments in favor of staying in Bhopal. This process continued at its own slow pace until Abba's death. No, he never refused Zamir Ahmed Khan support in any way. He didn't shy away from his duties as a father to his son. All this continued at the same sluggish pace as if it were an inalienable part of life. Like a scar on the face that becomes a permanent feature over time.

Zamir Ahmed Khan again applied for admission to the engineering college in Bhopal, and again was admitted, but he didn't notice the same joy in Father's behavior as the year before. He did see it once, after the student movement finally began in Bhopal, and the students set fire to the school principal's car and demanded his resignation, and then started fighting, when Abba grinned and said, "See how it goes, young Khan! So tell me again, why did you leave Aligarh?"

He doesn't remember how he answered. Anyway, most of his time back in Bhopal was spent settling accounts with Vivek.

"Zamir, can I ask you something?"

The question came up one night as Aziz and Zamir Ahmed Khan sat on the lawn of his hotel. By then he'd been back in Bhopal for two years.

Zamir Ahmed Khan had never seen anyone in his life quite as busy as Aziz aka Acchan, but his free time and his being busy were two sides of the same coin. Acchan was in fact one of those close relatives who—call it circumstances or poverty—remained strangers for a long time, sometimes for life. It would be like a breakthrough discovery for the family if anyone from that side actually amounted to anything. One evening in the New Market, Zamir Ahmed Khan bumped into Aziz, who was standing and talking in fluent English with some foreigners he was helping into a car. When Aziz saw him he flatly said, "Hiya," then resumed his conversation with the women. So that was all that happened, but the scene was enough to paralyze Zamir Ahmed Khan. He stepped away, waiting for Aziz aka Acchan to finish up. Actually, by that point he was sunk so deeply into his own muck he didn't have the luxury of time to figure out how to get out of it.

"Acchan!" he'd said while walking over to Acchan aka Aziz.

"Aziz," Aziz aka Acchan objected. "I may be called 'Acchan' with affection."

"Where have you been all this time?" Zamir Ahmed Khan asked with an apologetic smile.

"Have you ever been looking for me?" Aziz teased.

"No, and I'm sorry about that."

"How many times can you say you're sorry in one sitting?" Aziz said, taking his card out of his pocket and handing it to him. "Come over sometime. It's not far from your house. I hope your parents and everyone else in the family are fine?"

"Yes, but what have you been up to?"

"Struggling!" Aziz said with a little laugh and went along.

Following the address on the card, he went to Aziz's hotel and entered into an utterly new and alternative universe that would take time to understand, and where, on a cold winter's night, Aziz had said over a drink, "Zamir, can I ask you something?"

Back then, two shots got him so drunk that he'd have to keep himself from lifting off or slipping away all the time.

"Go ahead," Zamir Ahmed Khan said, absently trying to see his reflection in the bottom of the glass of golden-brown liquor.

"It's a little personal, so don't feel like you have to answer."

"Just ask, will you?"

"I've listened to everything you've told me about Anisa. But explain this other thing to me, this beloved friend of yours, who you refer to as your friend and enemy in the same breath, and who I know a little bit because of our card games and other diversions. What's up with you two?"

"What do you mean?"

Aziz aka Acchan kept staring at him.

"Does drinking and playing cards make you a bad person?" Zamir Ahmed Khan objected. "He's a fine, fine young man, my very close friend. I've already told you."

"I apologize," he said in the same sharp manner, still staring at him. "So you're not a samelingamist?"

"Huh?" Though he didn't understand the word, he felt like he was entering dangerous waters.

"A homosexual! Understand now?"

"Have you lost your mind?" he said, agitated.

"What does this have to do with me losing my mind?" Aziz said flatly. "You know that I rent out rooms here, both for drinking and gambling. And on top of that, if someone wants a girl, I'll get him one of his choosing. And if someone wants to sleep with a male, then who am I to stop him?"

"Is that what you think of me?" Zamir Ahmed Khan was angry now, and in his rage gulped down the rest of the golden liquid from the glass. "That's insulting!"

"Forget about it. Just a little question. Maybe you didn't want to answer it."

"Baba, you've got the wrong idea. What should I say?"

"Then why do you keep cursing him like he's some kind of unfaithful lover?"

"He's most certainly unfaithful. But not a lover."

"Okay, now you've found the right words."

"Acchan, sorry, Aziz! You should be ashamed of yourself."

"If I start in on the shame, life'll get a whole lot harder, brother! It already is for you. Let's move on. Allow me to give you some advice as a friend and elder, there's this suitable girl, just let me know, and I'll. . ."

"Enough!" Zamir Ahmed Khan rose up in anger from his seat. "So this is your big idea after everything I've told you?"

"And then what'll you do then?" Aziz continued, mocking. "The girl will give her soul to you and you'll make her commit suicide. Even if you're not interested in men, this pining after an unfaithful fairy will ruin your life, let alone your afterlife. You think life's only about breathing in and out?"

Zamir Ahmed Khan couldn't tolerate anyone calling Vivek such awful words like fairy for fee. Instead of letting the conversation go on, he got up and left Aziz's hotel in a huff, only to return the next night in order to kill some time.

Over time, Aziz came to think of him as a once-shining warship in stormy waters whose hull had been hit by a volley of cannon fire and that was bound to sink quietly to the bottom. He couldn't understand Zamir Ahmed Khan's behavior with Anisa, and couldn't understand his hot-and-cold relationship with Vivek.

Ikram Sahib

That Sunday afternoon was populated by nurses with stethoscopes around their necks, whirling through long corridors, apron- and white-scrub-clad, and patients wheeled around on gurneys, chloroform, tinctures, thermometers, and all the smells invariably associated with the city's big public hospital. When he'd found out through Nasrat Bhai that his friend Ikram Sahib had had an accident, he'd gone along with him to see the patient in the hospital. Ikram Sahib was a long-standing visitor of the grand house. Just like Nasrat Bhai, he was a good singer, but whenever a song was too difficult, he'd request Nasrat Bhai, who had a very supple voice, to sing it for him. His childhood and youth had been full of uncertainty, and because of this, and simply because he was who he was, Ikram Sahib was a very emotional soul. The accident, too, had been the dramatic climax to a failed love affair that'd prodded him to hoist himself up and out of the stretcher and jump from the third floor of the hospital. It was a miracle that all he broke were his legs.

On the ward, Ikram Sahib lay on a bed surrounded by green curtains. His scraggly, bearded face suggested he had not fully emerged from the influence of the chloroform. After giving Nasrat Bhai a hug, Ikram Sahib cried like a baby. His still-garbled speech mirrored his state of mind as he continually uttered nonsense followed by, again and again, "Nasrat! It's all over! Finished!"

Nasrat listened patiently to Ikram, patting his head, his chest, and then said very seriously, as an elder, "Over? Why would you say such a thing? Everything'll be fine."

"No!" Ikram Sahib started crying again. "Fine? What'll be fine? Nothing. It never was, is, or will be."

"Don't work yourself up," Nasrat Bhai again adopted the tone of an elder. "First focus on getting better, then everything will fall into place. There'll be a million others who'll come and go like her. Don't cry, it doesn't become you. You remember the poem by Iqbal, don't you?"

The empty, forlorn look once again returned to Ikram Sahib's eyes.

Nasrat Bhai knew about Ikram Sahib's love affair in inordinate detail, and, based on this knowledge, wanted to give him some friendly advice.

"A humble request, dear Nasrat, from your unfortunate friend. Promise you shall fulfill it," Ikram said looking Nasrat Bhai right in the eye. "Promise, won't you?"

"Yes, yes," Nasrat Bhai said, hesitating for a second. "Tell me, what is it?"

A wan smile slowly spread over Ikram Sahib's face, and the mad twinkle in his eyes grew exponentially.

"I hope you won't think I'm crazy," he said, forcing a laugh and relying on English, "like all those idiots. And you still haven't promised."

"I promise," Nasrat Bhai said, guessing his state of mind. "Tell me what to do."

"You, my friend, should do what no one else in the whole world is capable of doing. Sing me that song."

They held their breath.

"Which one?" If Nasrat Bhai breathed a sigh of relief, it didn't show. He kept up the suspense.

"What do you mean, yaar, which one?" Ikram Sahib was crestfallen. "How many songs are there I'd want you to sing? There's only one, my dear Nasrat! There's only one that truly reflects my life."

Ikram Sahib and Nasrat Bhai exchanged a knowing glance, and then Nasrat Bhai's intoned, "Alright, here it is!"

Would the people who witnessed the dramatic scene unfold that afternoon ever be able to forget it? First was a crazed countenance, body covered with countless bandages, staring into the void. Then the visitor clearing his throat, finding the right gear to drive the song. And the chorus, standing with hands clasped as if in reverential greeting. Finally the silence was broken by the spectral, whirling song issuing forth from Nasrat Bhai, "Why do you toy with my life again and again, mitti se khelte ho bar-bar kisliye."

People lead full lives and inhabit stories of their own. You might be acutely aware of their lives and stories, and even play a part in them from time to time. And then they arrive at the most critical juncture of their life, but all you remember them for is being the fork in the road that took you somewhere. Add that to the countless perplexities of life.

So that afternoon a sobbing Ikram Sahib was the center of attention in Hamidia Hospital, drawing the gazes of many tear-filled eyes as he drowned and then surfaced again and again in the eddy of the "Mitti se khelte ho" song that issued forth from Nasrat Bhai's lips. But for Zamir Ahmed Khan, notwithstanding the pain and suffering of Ikram's life, Ikram's only significance lay in being the fork in the road of the journey that half an hour later would take him to a girl named Anisa.

The story of Ikram Sahib's life after being discharged from the hospital: he never fully regained his mental composure. His well-wishers thought that the most straightforward remedy for his illness and suffering from his lover's betrayal was to get married as soon as possible. After getting married he spent twelve years cursing his illiterate, plain-faced wife, who wasn't on the same intellectual plane as him. Seven children were born to him during that time, who, god knows how, burnished his name with luster now that he was past his prime. Even though Zamir knew all these facts in great detail, they didn't add up to anything more than an interesting, made-up story. Like everyone else, he thought it wise to shun Ikram Sahib during the final years of this life whenever there might be the danger of a face-to-face encounter. Ikram was by then fed up with the world and despised just about everything, while he busied himself developing one theory and philosophy after the next with the idea of bringing revolutionary change. After a long process of contemplation, he arrived at the conclusion that sexual pleasure and producing offspring were the two fundamental aims of life. He began to accost strangers in the street to convince them of his idea, digging up arguments from religion and philosophy from god knows where.

That afternoon, Zamir and Nasrat Bhai abandoned the sleeping Ikram Sahib to his stupor, after he'd been given a sedative, and came outside into the ward.

"It's hard to believe," Nasrat Bhai said wearily in the hallway. By then his eyes had dried.

"Yes, simply awful," Zamir Ahmed Khan added after a deep sigh.

"Let's go," he said in an absent voice. "A friend of mine's been admitted in the student ward. Let's go sit with her for a while. You're not getting bored?"

"No, let's go see her," he said casually, and joined Nasrat Bhai as they advanced toward the other ward and the meeting with Anisa.

Anisa, Part I

"So *you* tell me, what should I have done?"

Soon after meeting Aziz he'd established enough rapport to talk freely with him. Zamir had been particularly encouraged by Aziz's having shared each and every secret with him using the choicest words. So, one evening, in between downing the golden liquor with Avil pills, he told Aziz about the Anisa affair from start to finish. He admitted to the whole tragedy and presented the question before him of what else he could have done. It was the last time anyone would hear Anisa's name from his lips.

Aziz had nothing to say after his long report.

"Tell me, did I do anything wrong?" he asked again, almost pleading.

"What do you want me to say," Aziz said, irritated. "Who the hell am I to tell anyone what to do? It's your life! Tear it to shreds if you want. It's not like I'm going to run after you with a sewing kit and patch it all up."

These days, whether he was asleep or awake, Anisa haunted him, trapped inside his head, roaming freely.

As for what happened, was Zamir Ahmed Khan the only one to blame?

When the human form lying on the bed covered from head to toe in a sheet heard the sound of their footsteps in the dark silence of the student ward, it stirred. Zamir stood silent behind Nasrat Bhai and allowed his eyes to adjust to the darkness. Nasrat Bhai cleared his throat and in a gentle voice said softly, "Anisa! Are you awake? It's me, Nasrat!"

The sheet slid down and revealed a head, and without any more details he guessed it was a girl's face. Now propped up against the pillow, this face gestured for Nasrat Bhai to sit down on the bench next to the bed, and the quizzical glance met Zamir Ahmed Khan's for the first time. There was intense attraction in her eyes—even a quick glimpse in the dim light revealed this.

"Won't you please have a seat?"

A languorous voice like that of a coddled child greeted Nasrat Bhai, stealing glances at Zamir Ahmed Khan all the while. "How come a busy man like you can wander in here this time of day? Nothing's wrong, is there?"

Nasrat Bhai, ignoring Zamir, began telling Anisa in great detail about the tragedy of Ikram Sahib. Anisa listened with half interest, all the while casting probing glances at Zamir Ahmed Khan. When the story of Ikram Sahib began to go on and on, she interrupted Nasrat Bhai in a voice that scarcely concealed her boredom. "He was born crazy, this friend of yours! Nothing he does surprises me!"

"Arré," Nasrat Bhai tried to object, but before he had a chance to, Anisa changed the topic and cocked her head toward Zamir Ahmed Khan. "And who is this? You haven't introduced us yet. He's been standing here the whole time. Please sit down, won't you?"

Nasrat Bhai returned from the world of imagination to the real one. "Oh, right, of course," he said apologetically. "You don't know him? He's my younger cousin, Zamir, an engineering student." And turning toward him, "This is Anisa, I've told you about her. She's a third-year medical student here, and tops in drama, dance, debate, singing, grades, you name it. When she was doing her B.Sc. in science college, she was stiff competition."

He greeted Anisa. He felt uneasy as he realized that Nasrat Bhai was growing uncomfortable by Anisa's interest in him, the gleam in her eyes, the way her gaze kept returning to him.

"You're studying here? In Bhopal?" she asked directly, without hiding her curiosity.

"Yep," Nasrat Bhai jumped in before Zamir had a chance to respond. "But he cut his teeth at Aligarh for a year first before coming back to Bhopal."

"Come, sit," Nasrat invited him to sit on the bench next to him. "Why are you standing? Sit."

"I'm okay standing," he said, wanting to escape both from these beautiful eyes probing him and from Nasrat Bhai's increasing unease. "You two keep talking, I'll meet you out in the hallway."

"Why?" Anisa firmly objected even before Nasrat Bhai could open his mouth. "Don't you like sitting here with me?" A sadness welled to the surface.

"I have some friends here at the college," he explained. "I'll go meet them in the meantime."

"No you won't!" she said in a bossy voice. "You have the rest of your life to meet your friends. Now that you're here, I'm more important. Have a seat already, yaar. What's your name again? Zamir . . . ?"

He looked at Nasrat Bhai, sheepishly, trapped, so Nasrat Bhai was compelled to repeat Anisa's request: come and sit down.

"Who are you friends with here?" Anisa asked personably. "I've never seen you with anyone."

"I'm friends with a few people," he said, briskly recounting the names of some people he'd studied with at school. "They're probably younger than you. Anyway, I mostly meet them off campus. It's amazing I've never seen you before."

"The names you just mentioned?" she said casually, stretching out and yawning. "As far as I'm concerned they're just little boys."

"That's right, my friend," Nasrat Bhai confirmed. "She's the college don! Not a leaf falls without her say-so."

"No kidding?" he said softly with fear and feigned interest. "But she looks so innocent and proper."

"Looks innocent?" she said, jokingly, taking no offense. "What do you mean? I *am* innocent. Right, Nasrat?"

"Uh, not exactly."

It was clear from Nasrat Bhai's voice that he didn't want to talk openly in front of Zamir Ahmed Khan. "Anyway, why don't you tell us how you're feeling? Any better?"

Anisa didn't respond, and in those few moments Zamir Ahmed Khan realized for the first time that with some people, even silence has weight. It wasn't as if up until then Anisa had been discussing a serious topic or speaking solemnly. Everything she'd said had been casual, funny, lighthearted. Yet as soon as she stopped talking, the room filled with heavy, uneasy silence, whose weight he felt increase by the second. In order to break free from the sense of suffocation, he wanted Anisa to say something, anything.

"I'm doing okay." She said this in an even voice, all the while gazing at Zamir Ahmed Khan. "Don't you have a girlfriend here at the medical college?" she inquired, ignoring Nasrat Bhai's presence.

"Whoa! Don't mind her, baba!" Nasrat Bhai said, interrupting, hands together in supplication.

"Well, I've just made friends with *you*!" Zamir Ahmed Khan said, trying to return banter with banter. "Isn't that enough?"

"So let's shake on it then!" Sitting cross-legged on the bed, wrapped in the sheet, Anisa offered her hand. "Why are you looking at Nasrat? Are you doing the friending, or is he? Let him, Nasrat, won't you? This brother of yours seems quite the obedient type."

She offered her hand quickly, and Zamir Ahmed Khan can still remember the first touch of Anisa as they shook hands. By no stretch of the imagination could her sweet touch be associated with illness. Touching her soft, feverish hand was like experiencing an unexpected power. As she leaned forward to shake his hand, the sheet she'd wrapped herself in slipped off. Even in the dim light, he sensed that the salwar kameez–clad body that emerged was shapely and attractive. Warmly shaking his hand, Anisa hadn't been able to fully express how glad she was—when suddenly everything switched gears. Her hand went limp, joy vanished from her face, her body slackened as if her soul itself were departing. Before registering the surprise on Zamir Ahmed Khan's face, she wrapped herself in the sheet again, assumed the pose of an ill girl, and lay down. He glanced at Nasrat Bhai, who was just as baffled by the theatrical change.

"What's the matter?" Nasrat Bhai asked, worried, standing up and pouring a glass of water from the thermos. He placed the glass in her hand. "Do you need to take a pill? Are you feeling all right? I'm so sorry we barged in and disturbed you. Lie down and get some rest now, please, we'll be on our way," he said in one breathless go.

While Nasrat Bhai expressed his concern in whatever way he could, Zamir sat there, feeling like a tongue-tied idiot. What could he say? The mood and atmosphere in the ward had changed so rapidly, as if by mysterious sleight of hand. He didn't understand. The figure wrapped in the sheet holding the glass in front of him was now a soulless body, eyes shut. He waited in the heavy silence for Nasrat Bhai to give the signal that they should leave, while Nasrat Bhai shifted nervously, waiting for Anisa to say the word.

It was the proverbial calm before the storm. Even before they could decide whether to stay or go, Anisa began to weep bitterly, choking on her tears. Zamir Ahmed Khan would never understand what it was in her voice that moved him so deeply. That he was ready to do anything to ensure the happiness of the girl sitting in front of him. In her voice he'd sensed the essence of the world's sorrows and pain, a concentration of grief and misfortune. So he went and sat down on the bed next to her without ceremony or hesitation, and wiped the tears off her moist cheeks tenderly, lovingly. Anisa took his hands into hers, still crying, and tightened her grip. "What's the matter, tell me what's wrong, where does it hurt, everything's going to be all right." Zamir Ahmed Khan's inner dialogue, soaked in emotion, spilled out in a gush from his lips. He felt as if he were sitting with Akka long ago after she and Kamal Miyan had a little spat, when she'd take off her glasses, sit and sulk, then burst out in tears at the tiniest pretext. He stroked the hair of the girl who had been so talkative and bold a few minutes ago, as she clung to his chest like a little child. Patting her back and wiping away her tears he didn't feel awkward, nor did he consider for a second that Anisa was a total stranger; a few minutes earlier he had thought about her in terms of body, curves, eyes, nose, and so on.

He was again sitting on the bench with Nasrat Bhai a few minutes later, staring with disbelief at Anisa, now under the sheet. Her crying had subsided and the look of sorrow and fatigue had begun to vanish. One of Nasrat Bhai's legs was shaking vigorously, an indication of the stress that had overcome him, while his gaze meandered between ceiling and wall. Touching Anisa, stroking her hair, and patting her back was a feeling still fresh and alive in Zamir's hands. He unfolded the handkerchief in his lap, still moist with Anisa's tears, and began to smooth out the wrinkles.

"Nasrat Bhai," Zamir Ahmed Khan said in an attempt to lessen the tension. "What was that poem about tears you recited for me that one time? It's one of your own, isn't it? *Eyes full of tears . . .*"

A smile of relief spread over Nasrat Bhai's face despite his anxiety.

"Want to hear a poem, Anisa?" he said, cheer returning.

"Sure," Anisa said in a muffled voice like someone with a cold who has to speak through their nose.

"It's a great one, you'll think about it for days. So, for your consideration! 'Do not regard me with tear-filled eyes, lest your tears then fill my own.'"

"You wrote that?" Anisa said a little surprised and began giggling like a child. "Arré, Nasrat, be careful reading lovey-dovey poetry to me in front of your little brother," she said, reproaching him gently between peals of laughter.

"Why are you blaming *him*? It wasn't his fault, he recited it because I asked him to. The sentiment may have been his, but the request came from me," Zamir Ahmed Khan said immediately, trying to take the blame.

"I don't know where to begin!" Anisa lovingly nudged him.

"Actually, it's not my poem at all," Nasrat Bhai said in order to exonerate himself. "I don't believe in this kind of light fare."

A nurse and some of Anisa's classmates came into the ward. They started chatting and Nasrat Bhai signaled it was time to leave.

"Nasrat!" Anisa sensed their impending departure and shifted to her bossy voice. "Don't go anywhere, I have something important to tell you."

After the others left, the two sat down again, watching over Anisa, a little uncomfortable.

Nasrat Bhai cleared his throat and said, "It's getting very late, I'll come visit you some other time . . ."

"Just a few more minutes," Anisa said, turning toward them. "I won't waste any more of your time. There's something I'd like to tell you and also a favor to ask, and then you're on your way. One thing you don't know, Nasrat, is that we were four brothers and sisters at home. Three sisters, I'm the oldest, and one brother, who's younger than me. We were still little kids when Mother died, and then Father, too. Different people and families took us in and brought us up. One of us went with an aunt, another with an uncle. My brother was the only one who went to live with our father's brother, and I can't even begin to tell you how much he loved his sisters, especially me. Him being the only brother of three sisters, of course we loved him to bits, and he would've given his life for us, too. His biggest regret was that we didn't have the chance to grow up together under the same roof. I don't want to sound overly sentimental, but, long story short, he died six years ago in an accident. The details aren't important. He was gone. Anyway, who has say over life and death? I'm telling you all of this because Zamir is the spitting image of my brother. They're so alike. If you'd ever met him, you'd be able to understand my surprise and pain and delight at meeting Zamir, which is a little like getting my brother back, as if he never died. Get what I'm saying?"

In the silence that returned to the ward, Zamir could hear the sound of his heart beating. The dramatic turn of events had also rendered Nasrat Bhai incapable of comment. He sat in silence, more vexed than surprised, trying to focus his thoughts.

So, of course! As soon as they left, Nasrat Bhai would share his suspicion that Anisa's story of her younger brother was less truth and more opportunistic fabrication, behind which lay some other game. To which Zamir would listen patiently, but not agree. He'd think that Nasrat Bhai was saying all of this out of jealousy. Nasrat Bhai would imply other things about Anisa that seemed motivated by the same feeling. Zamir tuned them out. But all this happened later. For now, as the sound of his pounding heart reached his ears, age-old ice began to melt in his mind and merged with the sea as a sweeping stream of dirt and detritus. This process was different from and beyond the reach of words like "pure" and "impure." The little brother of Akka in him was as overwhelmed with joy as he was surprised by the coincidence that the act of remembering Akka made him feel confident and certain that Anisa was his indeed. And that Anisa, too, saw and heard her brother in him. This was the truth, and he was fully convinced of it. The moment his eyes met Anisa's, he felt something extraordinary and unusual. Extraordinary in the sense that he generally never felt this way when meeting someone for the first time. No one can deny that a particular attraction can exist between two people that's meaningful and significant. He and Anisa were bound to each other in this kind of way. No matter what, he would never ever disappoint this girl before him, who at any rate seemed tormented by the world and who saw in him her little brother. Whatever expectations and hopes she might place in her little brother, he would fulfill them. He made a secret vow and summoned from his memory whatever was holy and venerable as witness.

"Now you've heard the tale!" Anisa said, emerging from her silence. "Now listen to the favor I want to ask. You, Zamir. And you, Nasrat, as his elder. My request is that you, Zamir, keep seeing me from time to time. Whenever you have time, no conditions. How can I put it . . . ?"

He didn't wait for Anisa to finish her sentence before he leapt up, clasped her hands, and sat down on the bed beside her. He assured her that she'd not been mistaken in her search for a brother, that no sister in the world would have a more loving or devoted brother, that he understood his brotherly duties and responsibilities fully and would never exhibit any deficiencies in fulfilling his tasks.

"And who has a lovelier sister than you," he said, overcome by emotion, patting Anisa's cheek. "Words can't describe how proud I am. Truly, I must thank god," he said, turning to Nasrat Bhai, who was twitching anxiously on the bench. "Without knowing the whole story, I couldn't help but fear that this would turn out to be some romantic setup, god forbid. As a brother, I can be very brave." He wanted to poke fun at himself as much as possible. "But as a lover? One thing's for sure, if I ever pursue love, I'll fail utterly."

Unfortunately, some people are able to speak with complete fluency and confidence—just as with a task well thought through—even if they don't understand the subtleties of language or the meaning of words. If this weren't true, then Zamir Ahmed Khan wouldn't have been so irritated looking back on his life subsequent to that afternoon. Who had given him the right to think or say big, heavy-duty words like "world," "despair," "tormented," "duty," "dignity," "bravery," "failure"? Really, what had actually happened? At most, a girl had seen the likeness of her deceased brother in another person. It had unsettled the girl, and she wanted this person to come and see her every now and again. What she hadn't requested was that he spend all his time with her, heart right by her side. Even if that's what she really wanted deep down, it's not as if he'd been waiting for her to request it.

The very next day, skipping most of his classes, he went right to the hospital carrying a huge bouquet of flowers, and a copy of André Gide's *Strait Is the Gate.*

He still felt ashamed when he thought about *Strait Is the Gate.* He'd only recently read the book, and the realization only came later that instead of actually comprehending its meaning, he'd merely been impressed by it. His failure to understand the novel was the reason he'd presented it to Anisa as a gift. Several days later the book would prompt a discussion that turned into a fight.

Confrontation with Vivek

Being close with Anisa was a great support and relief, especially during a period in his life that was full of trials and tribulations. It was the second year after returning from Aligarh, but he hadn't yet been able to adjust to the daily rhythm of college life, nor had he been able to figure out where his friendship with Vivek was heading. A third individual, by the name of Asim, had come between Vivek and Zamir—like a Mister Kashmir between India and Pakistan—and Zamir wasn't prepared to make any kind of compromise. As a result, even as he maintained his friendship with Vivek, jealousy and the desire to get even had set up shop in place of love. The cold war between the two kept going with great vigilance and the temperature fell dangerously day by day, but it was unclear when it would hit the freezing point. He'd stopped seeing Vivek almost altogether by then and spent most of this time with Anisa. But it never occurred to him that his motivation was more to settle old scores with Vivek by keeping his distance and less because of his budding love for Anisa.

The gulf that had opened between Vivek and Zamir, thanks to Asim aka Mister Kashmir, was replete with the full spectrum of emotions provoked when a third contestant intrudes between two lovers. Zamir didn't think it befitting to express his sorrow and anger in front of a stranger like Asim, but when Asim wasn't around he always reproached Vivek.

"Where have you disappeared to these days?" Vivek complained after a long absence.

"You sound just like Amma," he teased. "College takes up a lot of time."

"Since when do you go to classes regularly? I've been asking tons of people where you are."

"Where else would I be? If not at college, then in the hostel."

After he sealed his friendship with Anisa, their affair was the first thing he tried to hide from Vivek. A stubborn idea had entered his mind that he'd spend his life completely independent from Vivek.

"Amma was saying that you're also coming home late at night."

"So?"

"So I'm just asking."

"People in glass houses shouldn't throw stones," he repeated a famous line from a Hindi film in a dramatic fashion. "Get it, Chinoy Seth?"

"I don't get it. You're the film expert."

"To hell with movies, I've also been trying to ask you some questions. You haven't answered one of mine yet. So, no, I don't need any answers from you anymore. You can buzz off for all I care."

"You're so strange. I was just asking, and you're making a huge deal out of it. I was talking about Amma being worried . . ."

"No need for anyone to get worried. Since you have so much sympathy, go and explain to Amma. Ask Abba, too. And find out for yourself."

"I don't need your lies to find out. Get laid, have fun. But don't drag your family into it."

It stunned him for a moment that Vivek knew about his relations with a girl. And then it occurred to him he might even figure out the whole story.

"When I fall in love, the whole world will witness it," Zamir Ahmed Khan said defiantly, forgetting his calm introspection in a fervent anger, "Who do you think you are?"

"Is this medical girl the one treating your ills nowadays?"

"You should be ashamed for talking about her like that."

"Ah, so there is a girl!" Vivek said sarcastically. "Now tell me what I'm supposed to think about her."

There was no way around it. He cooled down, and told Vivek the truth about his relationship with Anisa. He didn't want to, but that's exactly what he did. Meeting Anisa, talking with her, spending most of his time with her: he told him everything in detail. Her mental turmoil, how she saw her younger brother in him, and how quickly Zamir Ahmed Khan had become so important to her.

He assumed that once Vivek learned the whole truth, he wouldn't exactly melt with shame, but he'd at least admit he was wrong. If nothing else, ask for forgiveness for his doubts and suspicions. Nothing like that happened. Vivek listened to the whole story so coolly it was as if there were nothing new or worth knowing. As if he were thoroughly familiar with the details of her life.

"I had no idea," Zamir fumed, "that Nasrat Bhai's a two-faced gossip. And that you can be so mean."

"When did Nasrat Bhai come up?" Vivek said in surprise mixed with sarcasm. "I hear from friends at the college and other people in town that she's a fast one and a fraud."

"So now you've taken an opinion poll about her?"

"What do I care? And would I dare explain anything to you? If you want to be friends with her no one's going to stop you. Go for it. But don't fall for this brother-sister charade, it doesn't look good on you."

"Our friendship should have ended long ago." When he said this to Vivek, his anger was at the boiling point. "You're the one person in the whole wide world who knows everything that's been going on in my life, all the ups and downs of my moods down to the last detail. And here you are, accusing me of lying. You're the lie, Vivek, and you need to answer for your share of what's happened to me over the years. So you decide we'll leave Bhopal together, and then you stay here, making me look like an idiot. You're the lie, you swear your allegiance to one friend, but then go out and make friends with buffoons from all over the place. You're the lie calling me a liar because you just can't face the truth. Listen, whatever people say about Anisa or will say about her in the future, I consider her as my sister. She is my sister. The truth is you're jealous and that's why you're spouting all this garbage. Why make up this thing about Amma and Abba being worried? And one more thing! This friendship of ours has gone to hell, and don't bring up Anisa ever again if you want to keep up a casual friendship, even if you go around talking about her. Understand?"

The result of this long angry conversation was that the chasm between Vivek and him grew wider and the merging of heart and soul with Anisa grew more intense and powerful. He kept spending most of his time with Anisa, ignoring his family's comments. It wasn't as if he'd stopped going to college altogether, but even when there he spent most of his time thinking and worrying about Anisa. Right after class, even skipping class, he'd go over to her place. She had her own schedule, and in order to make things easy for Zamir Ahmed Khan, she gave him a key so he could come and go as he pleased even if she wasn't at home.

Anisa, Part II

When it was all said and done, how much time had he spent in the company of Anisa? Five or six months at most. What he remembered as a prolonged series of events really happened in the blink of an eye. Like when people get stuck in an unforgettable dust storm that provides them with endless stories they tell again and again to their children: so was the beginning and the end of his affair with Anisa.

In the beginning, it absolutely felt as if they would be together for the rest of their lives, and that they were real brother and sister, or even something more than that. He explored all the quiet, empty, lonely places in the city with her, hiked in the hills, rowed a boat on the lake, talked about the pleasant things in life. The best thing about the quiet and clean part of town where Anisa lived was the wide streets that met one another at a ninety-degree angle, and the tall buildings with thick, whitewashed walls, entrances, balconies, windows, and arched doorways, that looked lost in the slumber of a bygone era. What passed as traffic was the occasional scooter, tonga, or a few bikes. On one side of the house a little ways away there was Golghar, a beautiful round building that back then housed the RTO offices, and behind it, a bit farther away, the new but desolate-looking law-court building—it was impossible to imagine that cases were being tried there and verdicts announced. The Barah Mahal, Stony Lake, the Pari Bazaar, all of these were in the vicinity, as was the slope leading up to the empty Idgah grounds, on which were only a few scattered houses. From the rooftop, the view of the domes of the Bhopal Taj Mahal covered with dry, dark lichens and moss, an unending expanse of old buildings, and in the distance the outline of the Taj ul-Masjid, not yet finished, looking like a ruin. And the same Bab-e Ali Maidan where as a kid he sometimes went with Amma and Mumani Jaan to see the exhibition put on once a year, where the song continuously blared from all the loudspeakers, "Na yah chand hoga na tare rahenge, magar ham hamesha tumhare rahenge," "The moon will disappear and stars no longer shine, but I'll stay yours forever more and you forever mine." He explored every nook and cranny of the neighborhood with Anisa, sometimes in the afternoon sun, sometimes under a moonlit

141

sky. He often went for walks with her to buy vegetables or other groceries from the neighborhood bazaar, and then they'd return via a circuitous, scenic route.

As time went on, he began to sense the problems that were to come. One was that spending so much time with Anisa had in effect cut him off from the rest of the world, and the other was that his innate indifference toward college had been allowed to grow and thrive. Another problem, the most significant at the time, manifested itself in the form of Anisa's personality. You never knew from one second to the next what her mood would be like. Sometimes happy-go-lucky, sometimes irritated and angry, and sometimes mournful and teary. When he thought about it now, it seemed that the changes in her personality accelerated day by day. On top of that were Anisa's close girlfriends who frequented her house and whose comments and insinuations he wanted to ignore, even if he couldn't. The sole purpose of their behavior was to demonstrate that they fully understood the nature of the relationship between Zamir Ahmed Khan and Anisa. It was understandable in hindsight that they had no choice but to think like that, since the ease of Anisa's behavior with Zamir could lead anyone to think anything. The way she put her arms around him when they sat together, how she kissed him on the forehead, head, cheek, and even on the lips no matter who was around, and the things she said that, even by his own standards, if said by a girl to a boy fell under the "too much!" category.

That night, he'd bought a set of UNICEF greeting cards and had gone to her place. It was only a couple of days until Akka's birthday, and he considered the tradition of writing letters and sending cards for New Year's, Eid, Diwali, and the birthdays of loved ones a sacred duty. Anisa wasn't at home, and as they'd agreed for whenever she had to go out without having let Zamir know, she'd left a note on the table. The note said that she'd gone out on some errand and would be back by 8:00 P.M. There was plenty of time, so he stretched out on the couch in the living room and began to browse through the book Anisa'd given him a few days ago with strict instructions to read it, a book about Freud's psychoanalytic theory. His taste in reading basically stopped at fiction, and he had a hard time reading anything to do with history, philosophy, psychology, and so on. So then instead of actually reading the book, he just leafed through the pages to pass the time.

Anisa came back around 8:30, looking tired and weary. Tussling up his hair she said, "I've completely ruined your day, haven't I!"

"Not at all," he said matter-of-factly. "I figured you were caught up somewhere. I would have waited a little longer before leaving."

"Don't make my mood any worse," she said, sitting down next to him. "There's plenty of trouble at college and elsewhere all happening at once."

"What happened?"

"My friend's sister's about to give birth, so I spent half the time in the Ladies Hospital taking care of that. Then I had to go to the girls' hostel to finish something for a class exercise I need to turn in. I'm half dead!"

"At least you got something done," he said encouragingly. "And it's good I had a chance to do some serious reading in the meantime."

Anisa cast a furtive glance at the Freud book. "How many times have I told you? Keep some of your course books here. You can study at my place, too."

"Let it be, yaar," he said, wary. "Now you've started pestering me, too? Which course, what studies?"

"That's the problem with you. No courage, no patience," she scolded him like an elder. "On top of everything else, you don't want to make the effort. What is it with you, you think you'll marry a wife who'll support you?"

"For the moment," he said, trying to stifle a yawn, "I am not thinking of anything. As the poet Firaq Sahib says . . ."

"Oh, please!" Anisa covered her ears as she stood up. "I'm sick and tired of this poetry of yours with its flames and moths and romantic crap. Go make someone else look stupid."

"Don't listen to it, then," he said with an irritated laugh.

Anisa disappeared into her room and when she came back a little later she had the stack of greeting cards in her hands.

"What are these, bhaiyya?" she asked.

"Huh? Oh, just some greeting cards."

"That I can see. But it's not Eid or Diwali, so why so many?"

"It's easier to buy the whole box. They come in handy," he explained. "Actually, Akka's birthday is coming up, and since the war the mail doesn't go straight to Pakistan anymore. I'll send the card to some friend in Kuwait, and he'll send it on to Karachi."

Anisa glared at him. Akka had become an issue. Whenever her name was brought up in conversation or in passing, Anisa didn't say anything, but her attitude made it clear she felt hostile.

"Really, yaar?" she complained. "You still haven't asked me when *my* birthday is!"

It was true. It wasn't because of any ill will, but simply by chance. An occasion to ask Anisa had never presented itself.

"It's my fault," he stood, pinching his ears, admitting guilt. "And I'm ready to beg forgiveness any way you see fit. How could your birthday escape my notice?"

"Maybe you already missed it," she said, raw, hurt. "It could've been yesterday, the day before, a week ago. What's it to you? But when someone means something to you, you remember them even if they're a thousand miles away."

"Anisa, please, don't talk like that. I admit I made a mistake, no need to be cruel. I already said I'm sorry."

"So which card did you choose?" Anisa abruptly changed the subject. "What's her name again? Akka? Does she have a normal name?"

"I haven't decided yet," he said, ignoring Anisa's question. "Any of them'll do, they're all nice."

Anisa opened the box of cards and began to leaf through. "Yeah, they're all nice enough," she said, keeping up the sarcasm. "But one must be special."

He didn't say a word. She picked one out and handed it to him. "What about this one?"

It was a gorgeous card. He still remembered. A night scene in the desert rendered in turquoise-blue colors, a star lighting the sky, while gazing upward and hands lifted in prayer were the Three Wise Men, who'd just learned of the birth of Jesus from the Star of Bethlehem. The sacred mystery of the moment was expressed in the muted tones and ambience of the illustration. It was truly the loveliest card in the box.

"It's nice," he said, confirming her choice.

"Then this is the one you should send," she said, observing how he would react.

"Is this really the right card for someone's birthday?" It was an objection rather than a question. "It seems to be more appropriate for Christmas or New Year's."

"No," she announced her verdict. "It's fine as a birthday card. Do you have a pen? Start writing."

"Huh?"

"Write, 'Many happy returns of the day.' "

He complied.

"Did you write that? Now, 'Many happy returns of the day, my dearmost, sweetmost Anisa!' "

He froze for a moment, glanced up at her, then silently wrote what she'd told him to write.

"Sign your name at the bottom, and write the date of my birthday. Now you know when it is, don't you? It's still a ways off, another two months. Good boy. Now come over here and give me a kiss, and a nice one. On my neck, my forehead, everywhere, and hold me tight."

Anisa curled up in his arms like a small child. Holding her tight he could hear the pounding of his heart. The sound of his heartbeat—*dhak dhak dharak, dhak dhak dharak*—reached Anisa and returned to him like an echo. The world around them became motionless and meaningless in the long silence. "See?" she murmured. "I've suffered so much. So don't you leave me, too."

He patted her back, petrified. Sometimes when someone goes through an experience of joy or pain, they think that they are not really happy or sad, but are merely enacting the feeling, putting on a show, according to the demands of the moment. That true joy and sorrow must be some kind of magical experience. Unfortunately they spend a lifetime waiting for that magical experience to happen, only to realize that it doesn't exist. Never did and never will. What they took for show and pretense—that maimed, meaningless, shallow experience—was in fact the real thing. Life is only show and pretense. Only much later did Zamir Ahmed Khan come to this precious realization. Holding Anisa in his arms that night he simply thought that for the sake of Anisa's happiness, he should be happy, too. And remind himself again and again that he was and ought to be happy.

"This was just a rehearsal," Anisa said, pulling herself away from him and sitting up. "But it was so much fun! Now start getting ready for my real birthday."

The expression on Anisa's face changed so quickly as she said this, it was as if she'd suddenly remembered something important. Her excitement and enthusiasm then vanished in an instant, replaced by a solemn, cold demeanor. "But first," she said abruptly, "it's the birthday of your dear Pakistani, isn't it?"

"It's not like I have to go there and celebrate with her," he said, wanting to steer the conversation away from Akka. "If I have to send a card, I'll send a card."

"Of *course* you will!" she snapped. "She looks for excuses every day to write you cards and send you letters, too."

He bit his tongue, and kept quiet.

"If she ever comes to India, you'll introduce us, right? What do you think?"

"Fair enough."

"You've made her sound so great, I want to see the real thing. Is she really, really pretty?"

"I already showed you her photo," he grew more irritated. "Let me know and I'll try to get special dispensation from the government to bring her here. Her fiancé is sick with worry about her just like you. We can kill two birds with one stone."

"Sick my foot!" she flared up. "Some fiancé. How many guys is she getting married to when it's all said and done?"

"What's that supposed to mean?" He tried as hard as he could but flew off the handle.

"So she's just playing with her little puppet then?"

"Anisa, pull yourself together before you open your mouth. What's that supposed to mean, this drivel." His anger had forced him to speak out. "How many times have I told you that I don't want to talk to you about Akka, I don't even want her name to pass your lips."

"So it's request hour for you now? I say exactly what I want to say."

"Well, Khuda Hafiz then. I'm leaving."

"Sit!" she said, grabbing his wrist. "There you go again, acting like a girl. You threaten to run away at the tiniest thing."

"It's what you're saying," he sat down, looking put out. They were silent. Anisa was staring at the greeting card he'd written a little while before. Zamir leaned against the cushion and again feigned interest in the well-being of his new friend Freud Sahib. The tension was thick.

"God knows when you'll grow up," she said, squeezing his hand, in the meek voice she could flip on like a switch.

"I'm old enough," he said sulking. "Don't you worry."

"Sure," she said, drawing in a sigh. "Your arms and legs have grown out nicely, but your brain got stuck somewhere. Okay, tell me one thing. Is this Pakistani of yours a sister to you just like I am? Seriously, don't lie. Tell me the god-honest truth."

Back then, it wasn't easy to distinguish between sister and not sister. His relationship with Akka had developed at an age when his mind hadn't yet been led astray. It consisted of a chain of events that had spread far and wide throughout his past, like a forest or mountain range or confluence of rivers that the earth creates so very naturally in its climate and geography. It wasn't like that with Anisa. Clearly, effort was required to make things happen. Instead of something that comes easy, it appeared that challenge was the hallmark of this relationship.

"Yes, she is," he made an effort to sound casual. "Exactly like you."

"That ruins everything!" she said, slapping her forehead. "She's my cowife then. I really want to marry you."

"All right, then, let's go and find a qazi right now!" he joked. "Tomorrow's too late. Let's get a move on! You shameless liar, haven't you heard that one before? The joke about the lie to end all lies?" He wanted to do whatever he could to change the topic, stop the conversation, run away.

"I've heard it, and I've heard it from you," Anisa's voice had again leveled off. "But what I said wasn't a joke. I was serious."

He stared at her, dumbfounded.

"No way," he said under his breath. "Not this."

"Why not?" she said angrily. "The fact that you reminded me of my brother when we first met or that you have some similarities with him doesn't actually make you my real brother."

"But that's what I thought all along."

"Well, you're wrong! The root of your stupidity is that you think of pure and impure love as two different things. Love is love, no matter what you call it or how you describe it. The most important thing for a relationship is attraction and true passion, the rest is just deceit, trick, pretense."

"So what you're saying is," he cleared his throat, "if attraction and true passion exist between a real brother and sister, there's no objection for them to get married?"

"Don't twist my words!" she said, sounding vulnerable. "And even if it did happen, you think it's the first time in the history of the world? Read your ancient history, the pharaohs of Egypt used to get married to their own sisters. And that was an exemplary culture that lasted for a long time. If there was something rotten in that custom, then why did people adopt it?"

"So that's why Allah had to bring Moses into the world, to end the rule of the pharaohs!" he said, unable to stop himself from making a joke. "You'll have to excuse me, but I had no idea that's what the pharaohs were up to. Even if that's what they did, they were pharaohs in Egypt and we're Indians in India. As far as I'm concerned, relationships are sacred, I can't imagine toying with them under any circumstances."

"Because you're so stuck on those relationships, because you're so myopic when you look at them, you can't even recognize a serious and objective opinion. Thinking about sex is such a dirty thing for you that the mere thought of associating it with your nearests and dearests seems a terrible sin. Is this a correct or scientific way of thinking? Aren't we putting our natural feelings into a needless straitjacket that spoils their true nature? You're reading Freud, don't you at least get a whiff of what's real from him?"

"I'm doing more reading than understanding." While saying this, a whirlwind of worry was creating havoc inside Zamir Ahmed Khan. "Sounds like some lawyer who manages to prove the guilty innocent and the innocent guilty on the mere strength of his clever arguments but at the expense of the truth. As far as Sigmund Freud is concerned, I can't say with confidence that he's right or wrong since I don't have enough information. But the one thing I can say is that either way, I don't agree with him. I also don't believe in this kind of quasi-scientific thinking."

"What kind of secular thought do you profess, then? Why do you criticize those who act according to their faith and call them ignorant and obstructing the path of humanity? Do you have faith or trust in anything at all?"

"I do!" Zamir Ahmed Khan said with rancor. "In whatever is done in the name of religion or faith, there's no room for any kind of integrity. It all seems like tricks and chicanery, for each religion to make its own set of fools. If I've ever said anything against religious people, it's from this point of view. But even if religion doesn't have the same high standing as science, it's just as wrong to cut off science from living, breathing truths and elevate it to the level of supreme holiness, just like religion. But believe me, I'm not a nihilist. True, I try to understand a nihilist the same way I try to understand someone who puts faith in religion."

"So what this basically means is that your head's a little off," she said flatly.

"Whatever," he said, giving in.

"And that's how queer-minded people normally turn out to be losers in this world."

Not at all. Zamir Ahmed Khan didn't mind in the least what Anisa was saying in the moment, and it didn't occur to him for a second that she wasn't just speaking words but in fact making a prophecy, uttering a curse. A curse and a prophecy that would come true to the very letter. Back then, the possibilities for success were very much alive. True, many targets had been missed, but it seemed he still had plenty of arrows left in his quiver. He had only covered a short distance in a long race. Like an experienced runner, he'd saved his best breaths for the final rounds when victory or defeat was decided.

"You, Zamir," Anisa was looking at him with an expression as if she'd finally reached the heart of the matter, and was now going to announce what she'd been putting off. "You can't even be truthful to yourself, forget about me. On top of that, you're resorting to this highfalutin language to hide your lies. In order to live, you need a courageous soul, not just a blabbering mind. As soon as you hear what I'm about to tell you, you'll say, God forbid! God forbid! But I'm asking you what's the meaning of this body of mine if I don't know how to use it? If all you need to exist is a brain, the body could have lived and died as weedy underbrush. Why waste money on the trunk of a body? Whoever makes the world go round has a little edge to them and isn't a mushy flour ball like you and your thinking."

Anisa would have gone on if not for the sound of a motorcycle pulling up outside. Trying to figure out who it was, she fell quiet. After a few silent seconds, someone rang the bell. Zamir wanted to get up and see who it was, but Anisa gestured him to stop, stood up, and in a controlled voice asked, "Who is it?"

"It's me, Anisa, open up," a whisper came from outside.

Relieved, Anisa opened the door and addressed the individual standing outside. "Mamu, what are you doing here so late?" There wasn't a hint of surprise or caution in her voice. She neither invited the person to come in, nor did she step aside so that he might enter on his own.

The man standing outside said something about some aunt who had suddenly fallen ill and needed to be admitted to the hospital, but all efforts had been unsuccessful, and she was at this moment lying on the veranda of the hospital. Even dropping Anisa's name hadn't worked. The man told his tale of woe in great detail, while Anisa, without saying a word, stood there listening.

The man requested that Anisa go to the hospital and try to help: seeing Anisa, some of her acquaintances might have a change of heart and take pity on the woman.

"Come in," Anisa finally said, stepping aside to let him in.

A middle-aged man entered and sat down in the chair next to the drawing room door. Worry about his wife's illness was written all over his face. Anisa didn't deem it necessary to make introductions. After thinking it over, she said, "I tell you what, you go to the hospital. I'll meet you there in a little bit. I know my way around, I'll be there in half an hour or so."

"How will you get there? So late at night?" the uncle asked with concern. She ignored it.

"Please go on ahead," she said, standing up and seeing him to the door.

"Do take care on your way," he said entreatingly before starting his motorbike. Anisa stood and stared, without giving a reply. The motorbike finally started after a couple of tries, and the chugging sound of the bike slowly faded into the distance. Anisa closed the door and sat down in the chair.

"Who was that?" Zamir Ahmed Khan asked after some time.

"Weren't you listening? That was my uncle. After my parents died, he was the one who raised me and took care of my education. Listen, yaar," she said, standing up and changing the subject. "Will I get a taxi at this hour? Why don't you be a dear and check. Just down the road a little. You can go straight home in the taxi after dropping me off. Unless you're in the mood to spend the night?" She teased him and went inside. "Ha, as if you'd even consider it!"

He found a taxi a short ways away and returned with it. Anisa was ready. Before getting out at the hospital, she put something in Zamir Ahmed Khan's hand. "You forgot your cards, here they are. I've kept one for myself. Go on, and good night."

A Disclosure

The following days were difficult.

After that night, he went to Anisa's place a few times to check in, but she wasn't there. No note for him at her place, and he couldn't figure out why she was suddenly so busy. He surmised that either she was caught up in studying for an exam, or something had happened to Mumani, her aunt, at the hospital. He'd wait alone at her house for hours, and always left a note when he left. But she never replied. Getting the cold shoulder and her indifference seemed even odder to him. Just a few days ago he'd been the one who wanted to avoid her, but now being apart from her, and like this, didn't feel right. If she'd wanted to she could have easily dashed off a quick note. But she didn't. After a week of running in circles, he decided that this back-and-forth to her house every day was a waste of time, and tried to return to his neglected studies. Another week went by when one afternoon somebody delivered a short note from Anisa: "Meet me if you can, Anisa."

He arrived at Anisa's house per her invitation that evening and again she wasn't home. The rivulets of resentment that had gathered in his soul now coalesced into anger. But he calmed himself, unlocked the door, went in to wait. He was startled to find Anisa sprawled on her bed, sound asleep. The blank look on her face was of an innocent little child lost in the crowd at a fair. He went up and tickled her ribs. As soon as he touched her, or maybe even a split second before, she opened her eyes as if she hadn't been sleeping but only pretending to sleep. She grabbed his hand, smiled as she sat up, and in a voice still drowsy with sleep said, "Come." He sat beside her on the bed, and stared at her face, unblinking.

"Where've you been for so long?" she mumbled, trying to cross the threshold from fatigue and sleep, then without waiting for an answer immediately asked another question. "God, what time is it, yaar? Do you know I've been out for three days straight, as if I were paid to sleep! I don't know when was the last time I wound my watch, but it's not working."

"Where were *you*?" he said tenderly, caressing her hand. As he gazed at her, all the resentment welling inside and the doubts he'd harbored instantly vanished like a fairy from a magical tale. And then he felt his solitude in the world with full intensity and violence. "Why did you keep the door locked from the outside?"

"I should have locked it from the inside?"

"What I mean is why did you hide yourself away?"

"That was exactly the point. I was incredibly tired, and wasn't in the mood to see anyone. And I thought that the one I want to see has the key anyway! That if he came to the house he'd also take the trouble of actually coming in. Hey, can you grab the cigarettes and lighter? Do you want one? Good boys don't smoke, ah, that's a good boy! I waited for you for a couple of days and then this morning I gave Bua the note I wrote and asked her to deliver it to you. She assured me she'd get it to you, but my hopes weren't high that she'd find a certain gentleman's residence." As she spoke, Anisa continuously inhaled and exhaled cigarette smoke through her mouth and nose.

He was suddenly again enveloped in the haze of doubt. It was the first time he'd seen her smoke, and her skill and nonchalant handling of the cigarette suggested that this habit of hers wasn't a new one.

"Hello? Did I lose you?" Anisa asked, sensing he'd slipped away.

"Mind you, losing yourself is a serious business!" he said solemnly. "I was caught up in the same worries. I can't count the number of times I came here looking for you, leaving a message each time. You weren't here, and no note either. What could I do? At least tell me where you'd disappeared to."

"My dear, dear, dear!" Anisa took a long drag, and slowly blew out the smoke. "So there's Qais, who would've combed the Sahara looking for Laila. And then there's you, who can't even make it to the hospital. Oh the times, oh the world we live in!"

"So you're starting this again?" He let go of Anisa's hand and edged away. "I most certainly went to the hospital, I can't even tell you how many times I went!" he said in a bald-faced lie.

"False!" she said, wagging her finger at him. "One hundred percent false! Where did you look for me in the hospital? Tell me. Did you ask for me in the ward where you dropped me off that night?"

"No, not there, I walked all around the college and then came straight out."

"If you'd talked to anyone at the college, they would have told you, or if someone'd seen you I most certainly would've found out about it. Going to class doesn't seem like a decent thing to do when Mumani is dying in the hospital. She was going to die anyway, but only after struggling in vain for days. God knows what holds people fast to this world, the thing they've bound their soul to."

"What, Mumani has passed away?" he said, trying to summon condolence into his voice. "I'm so sorry."

"It's fine, yaar. Sorrow and concern are better saved for the living," Anisa replied, trying to brush it off. "The thing is I've been spinning like a top nonstop for days."

It seemed that this resolved the issue about the troubling new development, Anisa's smoking. Mumani's death, or the news of the death of someone so close, would raise anyone's blood pressure. On top of that Anisa must have looked after her in the hospital day and night for so long. Under the circumstances, it was understandable if she smoked in order to distract herself. He had no right to get so worked up.

"When did she pass away?" This time, the sympathy in Zamir Ahmed Khan's voice was more genuine.

"One week ago today," Anisa said as if she were referring to the opening and closing dates of some film. "They took her body to Sehore, it's a matter of burying her and doing the rituals in the ancestral cemetery, you know. As if she'd be denied her chance of going to heaven or hell if she wasn't buried in ancestral. But what can you say to people?"

"You'll have to forgive me, I hadn't heard the news." He transformed into an embodiment of remorse. "So when did you come back from Sehore?"

"Who, me?" Anisa said with some surprise. "Why would I have gone to Sehore? Those people took her body there. And what would you have done if you'd received word? Whatever time she was given, she lived, good or bad. Though it's true that seeing you would have given me strength during her illness."

"Unbelievable!" Zamir Ahmed Khan said, rubbing his hands in grief. "Exactly one week ago was the last time I came here looking for you, and that must have been the very day when Mumani . . ." He stopped mid-sentence and observed silence for a few moments. His mind wandered aimlessly, like drifting clouds seen from above. Then he picked up his train of thought again. "So all this time you haven't left the house?"

"I've been holed up here for three days straight," Anisa explained. "Mumani was dead. But what about me, the living? What should I do? So there's this classmate of mine who has a jeep, and five of us drove out to this unbelievably beautiful place way out in the countryside, right on the Narmada, where we stayed in a government guesthouse. The place has a lovely name—it'll come to me. We stayed for three nights. If I'd run into you, I would've asked you to come along. You can't believe what a gorgeous spot this place is, you'd really like it."

"What, me?" he said, cutting her short. "I don't know your friends and wouldn't even recognize them. They would have felt uncomfortable, and I would have been bored."

"No, not at all!" Anisa stood up from the bed and recounted the names of the people she'd spent three days with in the countryside—three girls, including Anisa, and two boys. "I think you know all of them?"

"What do you mean, know them?" he said, glumly. The truth was it felt as if a nail were being driven into his head. The other two girls Anisa mentioned were decent girls, but the boys were among the fast, spoiled, rich kids in the city. "We've said 'hi' a few times, but that's it," he said, finishing his sentence.

Anisa left to shower while he took charge of making tea.

"Anisa," he asked, sipping his tea, "do you drink?"

Anisa gave him a penetrating look. She silently took a sip of tea, got up, went into her room, returned with an open bottle of whiskey, and placed it before him.

"Want some?" she asked, matter-of-factly. "Any other questions?"

He sat limply, eyes downcast.

"Oh, I just thought of a line from some poet," Anisa said brightly, leisurely sipping her tea. "Forget about meter and rhyme, the meaning of the line is that there are always more answers than questions. But maybe I just read it for the meter."

He knew the poem. He'd read it himself. The poem was probably by Jan Nisar Akhtar. He also liked it, as a poem.

"You haven't told me yet what *you've* been doing all this time," Anisa said, changing the subject. "Your tea is getting cold," she reminded him. Trying to end his drawn-out silence, she sweetly offered her half-smoked cigarette. "Have a puff or two, yaar. Every once in awhile, it won't kill you."

"No, I don't like to smoke," he said, prickly and irritable.

"C'mon, take one drag for me!" she said, sweet honey in her voice.

He took the cigarette and had one, and then another drag. It wasn't just pretense, it was true that he didn't like either the taste or smell of cigarettes at all.

"But," he said, as if to himself, handing the cigarette back to Anisa, "why all of this?"

"Why what?" Anisa asked, intrigued. "All of this what?"

"The smoking, the liquor—what's the point of it all?"

Exhaling the cigarette smoke through her nose, a smile spread over Anisa's face.

"The point?" she said, slowly, spelling it out for him, "the point is that I like it, that's it."

He again fell silent, gloomy.

"What's gotten into that head of yours!" she said, exasperated. "Is there something wrong? What are you getting at?"

"I can't say whether it's good or bad, but normally it's frowned upon. People who drink and smoke aren't seen in a good light."

"There you go again, talking about what people think!" Anisa said, irritated. "I don't care what other people think, I want to know about you."

"If the whole world says something's bad, there must be something wrong with it."

"The world! People!" Anisa lashed out. "I have no idea what to do with you!" Then the next second, her voice again exuded tenderness. "Zamir, my dear! Tell me, yaar, when will you grow up? Let's hope this entire life of yours isn't spent waiting for you to do so. When will the glorious day come when you let people be people and start living on your own terms. I'm not saying that drinking or smoking in and of itself will be the proof. If it doesn't become you and if you don't like it, don't do it. But for god's sake, enough with the advice!"

There was a truth in what Anisa was saying that, deep down, he fully agreed with. No one in the whole world had the right to give advice or compel you to change your ways. In fact, he didn't even view drinking or not drinking through a strict religious lens. And yet his mentality was such that somehow certain things were forever clothed in the garb of moral or immoral.

"But why?" he asked again, irritated.

Anisa didn't respond.

"And if that's the case," he continued in a wounded voice, "then why did you hide from me for days on end?"

Anisa waited a long time before responding, but then, when she did, her voice was dripping with sarcasm.

"All these questions," she said. "Tell me, in what capacity are you asking them—as a friend or a brother?"

"Can't a brother also be a friend?" In his mind, Zamir Ahmed Khan thought this to be a very original answer in that it also contained a question.

Anisa was still irritated. "That kind of brother should at least have enough common sense and mental dexterity to know to what extent he takes her as a sister and to what degree he may question her. After a certain point this whole business becomes ugly and vulgar."

"I'm sorry. That's not what I meant."

"Not a problem. I know what you meant. Anyway, a friend has the freedom to make or break the friendship as he wishes. But the bond of brother and sister is a lifelong obligation. Questioning this achieves what? Aside from making things more complicated. Don't you think so?"

He was silent.

"All the things I've said are just a reflection of your perception of me," she said, taking a swipe at him, with a smile, "a perception I consider untrue and unacceptable. It's fine if you remind me of my brother, but I've always thought of you in terms of a friend. And one I would like to know as a man."

Completely helpless, he appealed to her, "So, you should have stopped me right then and there on the first day in the hospital when I declared I would love you as a sister and fulfill my duty as a brother. You should have told me you think of me as a friend, not as a brother. Then I would have seen things differently right from the start. Why did you start this mess?"

"I didn't do it on purpose," she explained. "It eventually happened by itself. If you hadn't given me so much attention, looked after me, and kept coming to my house all the time, there wouldn't have been any confusion. Think of all the people who you meet for the first time and feel this might be a lifelong connection, but the next time you see them you realize your first impression was wrong. And sometimes the next time never happens. So think about it. How could I have known from the start what fate had in store?"

"But I've been calling you my sister in front of the whole world!" he lamented. "And I've indeed considered myself your brother. So what now? Not that, not anything?"

Anisa smiled at him as if he were a small child.

"Well, actually, I thought about telling you something, when the time is right, and we're more relaxed." Anisa reflected for a few moments and continued, somberly, "A few things about me. But it seems like there won't be a better moment than now. I would never have told you these things, but since here we are, it's probably not a bad idea to give you some clues about how the world works based on what I've gone through. What am I going to do about you? You're like an overgrown child at times, despite your wits. Sure, I didn't hide my drinking and smoking from you. I do so to relax, sometimes when I'm happy, sometimes when I'm sad, sometimes when I'm tired. I've never felt the urge in front of you, so that's why you haven't seen me smoke or drink. In any case, it's completely unnecessary to go into detail about this."

The Beginning of an End

Anisa had declared that she was going to tell him some things about herself, but it was late in the evening, and she still hadn't broached the subject. She was hungry and hadn't had any food for who knows how long, so Zamir Ahmed Khan borrowed a bike from a neighbor, cycled to the Coffee House, and returned with some samosas and cutlets. After returning the bike, he found Anisa's door locked from the inside. He knocked and she answered.

"You're back," she said, letting him in. "There's a real chill in the air tonight. Would you like a shawl?"

He declined. Anisa took the food into the kitchen, put it on plates, and returned. "Come, eat," she said going into the room where she usually slept, studied, and changed.

He followed Anisa into the room and saw a glass on a stool with a little liquor left in it.

"I know what you're thinking," she said, sitting down cross-legged on the bed, pointing to the glass. "Now she's starting with the drinking as well. Actually, the thing is that number one it's gotten much colder, and number two, as you know, your humble servant had to wash herself in cold water, which she usually doesn't do until the hot season." She finished what was left in the glass, lit a cigarette, refilled the glass with whiskey, and continued, "And the third thing is that it's easier to talk about certain things if I have a drink."

Watching her sip the whiskey, Zamir Ahmed Khan suddenly blurted out an idiotic question, "Don't you mix that with water?"

"It's good like this," Anisa reassured him, smiling. "Yaar, excuse me. I forgot to ask if you wanted any. Go bring a glass, since, hey, you said it yourself, your integrity's already down the drain. But not because of anything I did! As for your allergies, we can take care of that, too. What do you say?"

"No, Anisa, please!" he whimpered. "I won't."

"As you like," Anisa said with a little smile. "Anyway, a couple of drops, it'll really hit the spot!"

"No!" he said, folding his hands in supplication, "I can't handle it. And listen, I've been thinking, I don't need to hear all the details and whatnot.

You put it best, the bond of brother and sister is a lifelong, intentional companionship. I'll never ask about it again!"

"Listen to me," she said, patting his hand. "It's not that you have the sole right to decide things. Do I also have a little bit of say and sway in the matter, yes or no? Look, life's not some kind of board game you play until you're not having fun anymore and then start all over. Since we've come to this point, at least hear me out with a little patience and courage. It's not like some weird tale you wouldn't be able to cook up on your own. You saw my uncle that night, didn't you? Remember?"

Though it had been only a few days since he'd seen her Mamu, he probably wouldn't be able to recognize him again in a crowd.

"Yes," he nodded, and then Anisa began to recount the details of her life. He already had a rough understanding of the main events.

"My father," she began, "was a man of modest means, but he did have a little farmland in a village near Ashta. Even though the land wasn't particularly good, it was enough to provide for everyone, no hardship. Abba was educated in the sense that he did take his intermediate exams at the time, but wasn't able to pass. Mother couldn't read or write, but she was a very skilled housewife, and she and Abba got along very well. As far as I remember, I never saw them fight. Then suddenly we were hit by two unexpected tragedies. Amma died of a heart attack. Maybe he couldn't bear the pain of losing her, and Abba soon followed. That monstrous year was 1953, when one blow of misfortune left us three sisters and one brother orphaned and with no support in this big wide world. I was ten years old then, and my sisters and brother were all younger. It was clear I couldn't look after them on my own, and there was no relative who could manage taking in all four of us. They were all middle class, and assuming the burden of four new family members was really beyond what they could manage. We were split up. An aunt from Amma's side took in one sister. The other went with another aunt from Abba's. My little brother went to live with an uncle who was a lifelong bachelor, and began to help out in the fields. This uncle of mine who you've met was childless, he took me with him to Sehore, where he was a teacher at a government primary school. And it's the result of living with him that, even though my studies were delayed, I was still able to complete them in the expected fashion, and that's why I'm studying at the medical college today."

Anisa took sips of whiskey and drags from her cigarette as she told the story.

"I don't want to romanticize things," she said. "I hate this kind of attitude and posturing, though it's exactly what you've been doing. Maybe it's just a matter of our different temperaments. Sometimes I think this flaw of yours is actually a strength. But I'd never be capable of it."

"So, my uncle, who you saw that night, was my mother's younger, and only, brother, and was a favorite of hers when she was alive. Even his wedding to Mumani, who died last week, had been arranged by my parents. It's a different matter that much later it turned out that there was no worse union than the one between Mumani and Mamu. In the beginning when I was still at my parents' house, I only heard about their fights, and even found them to be interesting. But then I had to go live with them, and witness all the back-and-forth with my very own eyes, and finally even became part of it myself. Fights between husband and wife may take one form or another as they drag on, but ninety percent of the time the basic reason is some imbalance in one or more aspects of their relationship. So here, too, Mumani wasn't able to satisfy my uncle's sexual appetite. But it didn't end there. Eventually she couldn't even stand the mention of sex, and couldn't bear to be touched by him. Meanwhile, Mamu went poking around into anything he could to satisfy his appetite. Even a ten-year-old girl is able to catch a strong whiff of this kind of affair. I also kept hearing and sensing what was going on around me. Time and experience had made Mumani very bitter. She recounted the sins of my uncle, first in a roundabout way, and then quite openly, and advised me to be on my guard. She kept warning me about his frightful plans. I understood some of it, other things went over my head. But after a while, her words began to get through. Mumani kept expressing the unease that consumed her, while my uncle for his part truly began to cultivate me according to his plan. And then one day when he had the chance he did with me what he wanted to do."

Anisa took another swig and laughed apropos of nothing. "What can I say when I think about what happened? Disgust, hate, sin—these are only just words that come to mind when you want to make yourself feel better or convince others. The first thing is how it felt in the moment. Even now, I don't want to give it a particular label. The experience had its own thrill, but in any case I wasn't the one who decided what happened. Even if the distinction between right and wrong had entered my mind, what could I have done in the situation? I was being reared on the scraps of my uncle, he was covering the expenses for my education, clothing, shoes, so it was also his right to exploit me. It wasn't like it happened just once, no, and then afterward Mamu wouldn't look at me or I wouldn't look at Mamu out of shame. Not at all! I lived with my uncle for a full thirteen years, and whenever he summoned me to fulfill my obligations, I went straight to him without so much as a peep."

Zamir Ahmed Khan, after being plunged into deep water, returned to the surface. The undulating shadows from the world beneath were seared in his eyes. Along with it, he was now able to see with these eyes the familiar world where he'd been alive and breathing all along.

"So that's my tale of the world," Anisa said, standing up with a smile, "and the true story of an uncle and a niece." She asked to be excused for a minute and went to the bathroom.

Even though it wasn't long before she came back, it seemed to him as if he'd been sitting there alone for ages. He had no idea what he should say to Anisa. Show sympathy? Praise her, and commend her resolve for living life with such courage? He was paralyzed. Could he truly and openheartedly support the way Anisa lived her life? Is adopting the path of least resistance the best way to stay alive? Is this the ultimate truth? He wrestled with it in his mind, and felt there was something a little fishy in the account he'd just heard from Anisa. Something wrong, something false, but he couldn't put his finger on exactly what. And if the entire story had been fabricated by Anisa, a lie? Words that had been delivered as a blow in order to convince him of her way of thinking, in which an uncle had been made the sacrificial goat to serve her designs? What a mess he'd landed in! Zamir Ahmed Khan felt for himself.

She returned, sat on the bed beside him, clasped his hand, pulled him close. "I feel like I shouldn't have told you my story like that," she said, laying her head on his chest.

"Really, you mustn't worry," he said with the kindness of an elder. "You didn't do anything wrong. No one in the whole world will come to know this secret through me. I understand what you're going through. A brother and sister, as you said, are forced to stick together for life, and as long as we're alive there's no escaping it . . ."

In Zamir Ahmed Khan's estimation, everything he was saying was exactly what the moment called for, and what he ought to say. But as Anisa listened, the softness and tenderness in her body evaporated, replaced by a growing rigidity. Even before he was finished, she'd withdrawn her head from his chest, shifted away, and uttered a searing epithet.

He was flabbergasted.

"You dare comfort me?" she hissed like a wasp and stood up. "Now listen to me! The mistake wasn't me telling you, it's you knowing about it! Get out! Go and scream from the rooftops what happened to me! I didn't tell you all this just to make you my secret keeper. Brother, sister, forced to stick together, ugh!" Another nasty expletive. "I was describing the real situation of real family members. And you, once again, even though you have no place in it, want to be family? How much time have I spent with you, trying to tell you that we're friends, or more? But maybe you wouldn't be able to enjoy that. So go ahead and be on your way! I can't be your sister and you're not ready for a real relationship."

On his way out, Anisa threw the Sigmund Freud book at him. "Don't forget this. It might come in handy someday. Out!"

An End

A house: humming, full of life. Someone who loves him, who cares for him, sees him off with joy or in anger. A second house: someone in similar circumstances waits for him to arrive. And the distance between the two he travels all alone, forsaken. He perfectly understands that obstacles can hinder him at each and every step, cause unwanted delays, postpone his arrival at the place he's expected. It's also possible he will never arrive. The one who arrives there, bearing his features and physical appearance, has lost his innermost soul. So much so that the people waiting, instead of happy to see him, are despondent. This was what Zamir Ahmed Khan was thinking as he returned from Anisa's house to his own that night, each step driving a nail into the road. He didn't even feel the cold while covering the long distance between the two houses. A door had been closed behind him, probably forever. Another door, still far away. He'd arrive and knock, without hope for a warm welcome. Lines from Walter de la Mare's poem "The Listeners" came to his mind from who knows where. "'Tell them I came, and no one answered, that I kept my word.'" The traveler calls out to the shadows, an echo of his voice in the dark void then returns to envelop him. When he doesn't get a response, a perplexed look comes over the traveler's face. Finally the sound of his foot placed in the horse's stirrups, then the receding sound of the horse's footsteps as it trots away. The entire scene once again plunges into deep silence.

Morning arrived and he made a big decision: he would never see Anisa again. He'd come up with several reasons to prove that this was the right thing to do. He didn't deny for even a second that Anisa possessed several unusual qualities. He'd taken a vow to fulfill his duty and had had every intention to do so. If he wasn't able to do so, oh well! According to Anisa, just saying he was her brother had hardly made him so! It's not as if anyone could alter someone else's destiny. Besides, he should worry more about himself, and not about the chapter called "Anisa," now that he'd closed the whole book and tossed it in a well.

Zamir Ahmed Khan carried out his resolve with a seriousness of purpose and peace in his heart as if it were an act of truth-embracing satyagraha.

163

To sever ties with Anisa necessitated getting rid of everything that might remind him of her. In a short span of time, he'd assembled innumerable items, mostly gifts from Anisa, and some things they'd bought together. Ties, cufflinks, a handkerchief, cologne, shirts, a pair of shoes, a pair of sunglasses, a few books, including the Freud, some photos with their negatives, and a few short notes written by Anisa. One dark night he filled an old bag with all these things and walked some distance behind his house to the well that'd once been functional but was now partially covered with a concrete slab since the road was being widened. Now water was pumped in a little ways away. Standing at the well, he felt the weight of the bag in his hand, then consigned it to the water as a sacrifice, and was done with the whole affair. A splashing sound, then silence. With that, Zamir Ahmed Khan had freed himself of a significant burden.

But this is an oversimplification. Suddenly he felt as if a vacuum had appeared between day and night that, for the sake of his health, had to be filled at all costs and as soon as possible. His mind again and again returned to Anisa, so he scolded it, and forbade it from doing so. The challenge was to accept someone with their own inherent flaws, but she'd demanded that he become her unwilling partner in crime. Maybe he could have accepted what she was doing, but not his taking part in it. The girl was a big sham, no question. And he was the jackass who didn't see what was really going on! This conviction grew stronger over the course of days. He'd completely misjudged her. Anisa was a phantom and a lie.

Now that he'd broken up with her, who would he be with!

College was just like attending a private club, no more. Still, he began trying to go to classes more regularly. Patching things up with Vivek wasn't easy, but he threw his heart into it and at the same time tried to revive the friendship with Mister Kashmir, Asim. One night he expressed his desire to Vivek to have a drink so he might unburden himself from the tension building in his mind. This would be his first drink after the drink in the jungle. They spent two days straight: Avil, drink, talk. Asim was there at the beginning, and they passed the time in conversation and having fun without getting into too much personal detail. The next time it was just he and Vivek. He'd sensed that Vivek had been reserved the first night, but this time the conversation was relaxed and they talked about everything under the sun, and Zamir's fears abated. So little time had passed since Anisa he couldn't decide what to tell and not tell Vivek. Generally there'd been no secrets between the two of them, but talking about Anisa was different and more complicated.

"And how's that sister of yours?" Vivek made the mistake of asking in a sharp tone before they'd even finished their first drink. Zamir Ahmed Khan stared at Vivek bitter and dispirited.

"She's fine," he replied in a steady voice, wanting to move on. "Since you and I are here together, let's talk about things of common interest. Why should my sister—her name is Anisa, by the way—come between us?"

Bitterness infused the liquor, and after that they didn't meet for a few days.

One day he ran into one of Anisa's classmates who wanted to know why he'd been quarreling with Anisa. He tried to dodge the conversation, but she told him to go and see Anisa immediately. "She's very upset," she said. He didn't go see her, but bumped into Anisa's classmate again. She asked him even more emphatically this time to go and see Anisa right away—a request clearly contrary to the decision he'd made. He did not go.

That morning he remembered a little bitterly that it was Anisa's birthday. He regretted that he'd given her the card beforehand, but pushed it out of his mind and went on with his daily routine. The next day, an item appeared in the newspaper. Anisa had taken her life the day before. "Medico Commits Suicide." He read the news and sat in silence. A silence that was to only become deeper with time and age, that was to throw him off balance and make living life difficult. That would drive him out to wander the streets, disturbed, incurable. That silence . . .

How could Zamir Ahmed Khan have been so cruel and insensitive? His bewilderment grew the more he thought. How could he have regarded a human being just like a thing he'd bought from the market that didn't work properly and could be cast aside? And why did he feel Anisa was trapped in his head day and night swirling around and haunting him? Sometimes with an ironic smile, sometimes with her empathetic laugh as if she wanted to say, "Zamir, when are you going to grow up?" Sometimes explaining something, sometimes as if warning him, or trying to say, "Look! The road leading 'there' is very narrow and restricted. *Strait Is the Gate*. Now all your book learning makes sense! Now it's your turn to experience the pain!"

A meek and helpless voice inside him was impatient to ask, but where is "there?" Where do we intend do go? What's our destiny? Anisa would burst out laughing at his useless questions and then recede in the darkness of his mind. He was surprised that Anisa wasn't in the likeness of a sister when she entered his mind. She appeared as a girl, a girl whom he'd lost because of his own stupidity. The doubts he'd harbored about Anisa and his accusations against her slowly hardened into a cross that he must bear, he had no choice. If only! If she were alive today and would share his pain. Then he wouldn't be having hushed conversations with his inner evil twin bent on his downfall. He wouldn't have lost his balance, sending him out to skulk through by-lanes of the city that were more unfamiliar day by day, oblivious to the difference between day and night, afraid of himself. It occurred to him then that he'd never been wronged by anyone in his whole life. Abba, Amma, his brother, sister, wife, kids, family, and friends—everyone had been very accommodating with him and had tried to do him well. And what guarantee was there that he'd be saved from this downward spiral if Anisa were alive today? She, too, would have left him long ago in frustration. Suddenly a different idea came to him that gave comfort. No, Anisa would never have done that! She never would have let things reach a point where someone would get fed up with Zamir Ahmed Khan.

After Anisa's death, Vivek's behavior toward Zamir Ahmed Khan had taken a dramatic turn. Without bringing up what happened he once again tried to meet with him in the spirit of the same old intimacy. Even after pretending to be cool about it, Zamir Ahmed Khan was still shaken to his core. On top of that the prejudice he harbored against Vivek still hadn't subsided. So things didn't work out.

Those were the days when he began to hang out with Aziz aka Acchan.

One More Intervention:
A Reintroduction

To fulfill my responsibility as a writer, I have already intervened once in the novel's main story, and now in order for me to be able to fully say what I want to say, another intervention is not only relevant but also mandatory. When we look back on our life while caught up in the unfolding of a particular event, some important things that shaped or spoiled the face of the future are overlooked. Major changes and crises, the deaths of national politicians, a significant shift in the country's postelection politics, a drought or flood that set a new record for death and destruction, or a war fought with another country: people easily remember these things. But insignificant things like a particular medicine or disease—things that play a decisive role in determining a patient's health and fate for the foreseeable future—fade from memory. This, then, may be the state of people's memories concerning the changes our country underwent in the 1960s that, slowly but surely, gave birth to the times in which we now live and breathe. The period when Zamir Ahmed Khan, the Lost Bhopali, who is a product of my imagination, meets another imaginary character, a girl named Anisa, and spends time in her company. Zamir Ahmed Khan is the kind of character who is compelled to observe and remember his own face's evolution or devolution in the ever-shifting mirror of time and change. He has been given life on the page primarily with this in mind. He is of course modeled on a living human being. We're fully cognizant of the fact that whether you call him a mortal or a man, he is by all counts the embodiment of weakness. So engrossed was he in the emotional details of splitting up with Anisa that he neglected to take the pulse of other exterior events. Let's forgive him this shortcoming, and allow him to err in the dark of night through the once-familiar, now progressively less-familiar by-lanes and streets and along the edge of the lake in his very own city, Bhopal, as he curses himself and mourns Anisa. He is doing what the lovely Punjabi word "syapa" implies: lament. To wander and lament is the destiny of some; the Lost Bhopali looks for each and every excuse to mourn. Leaving him aside for a moment, let's take

167

a cursory glance at the country and the prevailing winds at the time through the prism of other events that, according to this humble writer's understanding of the preceding period, generated the mood and determined the country's future. Zamir Ahmed Khan may have gone missing a thousand times over, but there's nowhere he can hide from our gaze. After this brief reintroduction we will retrieve him at the time and place of our choosing.

In my estimation, the 1960s remain the most important decade in India's postindependence history. Like it or not, we still must reap the crop from seeds planted back then, and for god knows how long. The country's independence was a dream. When it came true, the fact that its citizens had to interpret this dream in the face of unpleasant realities led to disillusionment. First, enemies cast the evil eye on the dream of freedom, while Jinnah Sahib and his followers, by way of Partition, were successful at creating what they called a "moth-eaten" Pakistan. Seasoned politicians would bear this kind of shock, but honest and idealistic people couldn't stomach it. According to the poet, "These tarnished rays, this night-smudged light / This is not that dawn." In the name of the dawn of freedom, tarnished rays were accepted as preferable to servitude. It's not as if I regarded the actors from this period with needless suspicion. Rather, I believe that this was our first and fundamental mistake. The attitude of trying to make room for compromise within ourselves turned the entire postindependence history into a long list of compromises, good and bad. The 1960s contributed to this state of affairs in a significant way. The country was partitioned, Mahatma Gandhi was murdered, the Indo-Chinese war and twice an Indo-Pakistani war were fought, the death of Nehru and Shastri, the Kamaraj Plan, the reign of Indira Gandhi, the opposition parties heeding Ram Manohar Lohia's call to stand together for elections for the first time, and as a result, the Congress Party's grip on power was a little shaken for the first time since independence, then the period of flourishing ragtag political coalitions, then the Congress government taking steps that appeared major, but were not as effective as they purported to be, in order to get themselves out of check, such as the removal of the privy purses of the rajas and maharajas, the nationalization of the banks, or in 1971 Indira Gandhi running the risk of midterm elections and emerging as the avatar of the goddess Kali, then a resurgence in the declining popularity of the Congress Party, and, again the return of Congress to power in various states in 1972 and the support of its policies—all of this is on my list. The commercialization of opportunistic politics had already started quietly, cunningly. So as a result we're forced to live and breathe today in an environment that has put a big question mark on our basic identity. The problem didn't stop at party politics: Congress, the biggest party in the country, had itself exploited political issues as an excuse to split into factions to serve various leaders' egos. Today's generation of politicians maintain the division of Congress into "indicate" and "syndicate" factions the same way as earlier generations were divided into progressives and moderates. Most of the principal characters from this important drama have long since been forgotten. But back when Zamir Ahmed Khan took Anisa's hand and the two wandered the streets and hills of Bhopal, rowed little rowboats on the lake, went to the movies, listened to songs on the radio or blaring on loudspeakers in the streets, songs like "Qasamen vade pyar wafa sab, baaten hain baaton ka kya," "Ham-tum, yug-yug se yah geet milan ke, gate rahe hain, gate rahenge," "Rula ke gaya sapna mera," "Tum agar sath dene ka vada karo, main yun hi mast nagme sunata rahun," and so on, these politicians were a larger part of the national psyche and more important to daily life than these songs. The names that are generally remembered are those of Indira Gandhi, Jagjivan Ram, Yashwantrao Chavan, K. Kamaraj, Maharani Gayatri Devi, Morarji Desai, Atal Bihari Vajpayee, Rajmata Vijaya Raje Scindia, or George Fernandez—people who played a political game by placing their bets on V. V. Giri and Sanjiva Reddy, while Mrs. Gandhi, in the business of dead consciences, had asked for a "call of conscience" vote, and fully succeeded in this game of smoke and mirrors. For some time then the Indira Congress went by the name of Congress (R), to prevent other leaders from splitting off and pursuing their own interest—how to win the greatest number of votes given the changing political landscape—and then the remaining Congress continued under the banner of Congress (I). A few such incarnations of Congress remain today, but they haven't gained any real traction on the national political scene.

Congress's continual internal fracturing didn't mean that other parties were far behind. As some vanished, others were born as new brands, or came back with a fresh look. The Communist Party, the Swatantra Party, the Praja Socialist Party, the Samajwadi Party, the Hindu Mahasabha, the Jan Sangh were national parties that lost their relevance over time and were subsumed by others, while a few more, feeling the pulse of the people, chose to reinvent themselves with a new design or packaging. The prime example of this compromise-making mentality was after the 1969 presidential election, when in 1977 "Loknayak" Jayprakash Narayan called others to join forces, so king and slave and everyone in between united against Indira Gandhi under the banner of the Janata Party. By all means, after the excesses of the Emergency, this effort should have had something to show for itself, and it was likely with this in mind that voters had handed such a robust mandate to the Janata Party. But the Janata Party lost no time to split into the Bharatiya Janata Party and the Janta Dal. So speedy was the splintering it set a new record, one party breaking away in the hope of merging with a more expedient group. There's a law on the books that forbids switching parties, but it has absolutely no effect on political horse trading.

But I think I'm getting ahead of myself. Right now the time is 1967, before all the rot seen so clearly later had fully taken shape. We find ourselves at the beginning of the decline when, instead of the demand for the creation of Khalistan, a separate province was founded for Punjabi speakers. In the south, the anti-Hindi maelstrom has been quieted after reassurances that English wouldn't be chased out of the country. In Kashmir, after countless maneuvers launched from Delhi, Sheikh Abdullah is released from jail, then again detained. In Uttar Pradesh and Bihar those who support or oppose Urdu hold nonstop rallies and demonstrations. The idealists are growing old and weary, and the group of freedom fighters hold the reins on most matters of the country. They sacrificed little but have earned great names for themselves. And now, so many years after India's independence, seem bent on bilking the country. Agreements are struck, and an attempt made to pawn off problems onto an unknown tomorrow. Ambitions grow, and the reflex to demean one another has become deeply ingrained. Obtaining a comfortable lifestyle is taking the place of fighting for ideals. Ram Manohar Lohia is still alive, as is Jayprakash Narayan, and various other important figures who grasp the quickly deteriorating state of the country and identify the weakness in the foundation of independent India's structures. Each of them in their own ways tries to rectify this, but without any real success. The reason: a dire lack of people who consider politics as a means to protect ideas and the welfare of the nation rather than to advance the welfare of their brothers and nephews at the expense of the miserable, the poor, and the needy.

If you ignore my cynicism and see things in light of facts that have come before our eyes and do the math, it'll be as clear as the light of day that "prosperity" in our country has come at the expense of basic principles. Gains have been made, no doubt, but a large part of these gains was achieved through lying and fraud, shady dealings and scams.

Does the individual exist because of society, or society because of the individual? It's hard to say, but each is a reflection of the other. It's also hard to say whether the conditions Zamir Ahmed Khan encountered in 1967 or what he went through later were the outer manifestation of his inner world, or what was going on in his head was a miniature inner replica of the outside world. And it's not only bad things that are happening in India. Dams are being built, five-year plans are successfully being implemented, we are seeing signs of self-sufficiency in agriculture, railway lines are being laid stretching to the most far-flung corners of the country, roads are being built, industrialization is growing rapidly. The promise of oil exploration in our very own country is being fulfilled, and our scientists, ready to take off and explore the cosmos, are prepared to meet the world's most developed countries eye to eye. Countless accomplishments like these were achieved in the twenty years after independence. Even more have been recorded into the ledger of the country from that point to the present day. But it's too bad that no reflection or glimmer or light of these achievements is perceptible in the personality of this Lost Bhopali. And why is that? Maybe this question is the root cause of Zamir Ahmed Khan's illness, the one doctors are incapable of treating. Maybe it's the imbalance between losses and gains since independence that's inscribed into his psyche. He abhors the establishment of statues in the country, especially those of individuals. He argues that aside from tearing down all the old ones after 1947 and putting up new ones in their places, there hasn't been any substantial working toward change. Edward, George, and Victoria have all been replaced by homegrown heroes.

This is the logic of my imaginary character. Despite his cynicism, I am unable to entirely disagree with him. Zamir Ahmed Khan was an emotional, hypersensitive soul who didn't get with the program or put his best foot forward in a smart, deliberate way. Instead, he stumbled. Once harmony between head and heart was lost, the spiral simply continued. Even when he did something after thinking it through, and even when he compromised—the kinds of actions that often lead to peace of mind, spiritual calm, and a successful life—he did it in such a way as if he were taking revenge on himself for something. This created a great likelihood of damage being done, and that's exactly what came to pass. To state this in simpler terms, I'm going to open a chapter from my own life and go into it with some detail, despite my reluctance to do so, so that I can underscore the difference between my and Zamir Ahmed Khan's attitudes toward life.

Case Study: The Anisa Affair.

Zamir Ahmed Khan and Anisa are two characters that may be peculiar and odd but who, in my opinion, cannot be labeled abnormal. Neither can the fact that they exist be viewed suspiciously, apart from the way their relationship ended. How many people do we meet in life in whom we see a glimpse of our intimates—parents, siblings, a leading lady from a failed love affair? We grow attached to many of them, sometimes for life. Eventually we even forget what it was that attracted us to that person in the first place. Was it the likeness to Mother's face, the way of thinking seriously like Father's, or the sweet behavior like a sister's? These relationships then take on a life of their own, and live their own lives. Are there not a significant number of people who see a brother or sister in one another when they meet for the first time, and then go on to get married and live happily ever after? This unavoidable understanding is arrived at so we may live in good health. Who would behave as Zamir Ahmed Khan did in these circumstances, and how many girls could imagine an ending like Anisa's?

It's all lies, fabrication, horse manure. A meaningless authorial flight of fancy!

In my own life, many things have happened that are indeed similar to events in Zamir Ahmed Khan's life. A girl from the medical college I met for the first time said to me in that same hospital ward that she saw a trace of her dead brother in me. She was an extremely lovely girl with an unusual personality, and all the best fellows at the time pined for her attention. Our age difference and the period when we met also approximately mirror those of Zamir and Anisa. We became acquainted, spent time together, and this eventually led to a close friendship. One day, without having passed through the winding by-lanes of love and courtship, our relationship changed into that of woman and man. While we continued our sibling-like relationship, at least as far as the world was concerned, both of us were all too aware that it could never lead to marriage. I experienced this phase of life in the capacity of her lover. An unforgettable, once-in-a-lifetime experience. So what's the point of having experiences? To learn and to move on. In the end, she decided to marry a doctor colleague. My heart ached and I wanted to ask a thousand questions, but I didn't display any of it, and fulfilled my responsibilities at her wedding as a brother, without having taken an oath as Zamir Ahmed Khan did. As a result, I gained a place in her husband's heart. In my estimation, it's easy to understand these three roles. When I met her by chance, I wasn't harboring any scheme to dupe or deceive her, but I didn't really view her as my sister. The desire to look at and touch such a sexy, attractive woman was a completely natural urge at that age. I wasn't the one who initiated it, though it's hard to say at that age who does. But once it did happen, it had its own special thrill. I wasn't carried away by the tide of pleasure, and gradually came to realize that this girl was out of my league and beyond my grasp. Given the nature of our relationship, she, too, must have come to a similar conclusion, and so the idea of getting married never came up. But when she did get married, I was her number-one helper with all the arrangements.

I was not the first man in that girl's life, and her husband wasn't the last. Both were well aware of this. Not only were, but still are! Both are in a very good place indeed, and nowadays they own a large private clinic in the city where god knows how many doctors work. She's busy, I'm busy, so normally we end up seeing each other only in the no-man's-land of parties and social gatherings. Of course, I'm always hearing something about her. Not really news, more like gossip about what fellow she's taken up with and what woman her husband's chasing after. Gossip is a vital part of our lives, and it's not always untrue, its foundation erected atop fact, just like with my two imaginary characters, Zamir Ahmed Khan and Anisa. This couple is still happy, even after so many years, no matter the stories the world tells behind their backs. They don't care to know about or interfere in each other's affairs. The world around them is aflame with despair and greed, continuously generating its own smoke, but these two steer clear of the root causes of the fire.

There's me, and there's that girl. Even after going to a thousand fitness clubs, she's turned into a rotund woman. We call each other brother and sister even today, sometimes in earnest, sometimes in jest. Her marriage, then mine, meant that there was no chance for our relations to take a wrong turn, and we've never slipped up by mistake.

I still feel like saying a lot more—about the world, the country, the state, the city of Bhopal, and about myself—but I also feel that my inappropriate intrusion has become unnecessarily prolix. Although this novel takes place in an imaginary time and place with fictional characters, you will see a reflection inside of our time, world, country, city, and its inhabitants, despite my attempt to distort. I think some reality is needed to begin the act of imagining, even for a work that's beyond the realm of reflection and understanding. But I don't want to make the mistake of calling reality truth the way a writer friend of mine did. For days he'd been after me about reading his work. Because it was out of character for him to grab someone and read what he'd just written, it seemed he had some particular reason in mind. What he read to me was quite contrived, and I told him so in no uncertain terms. He thought for a moment, then said in a hurt voice, "But what I've just read is the truth."

This didn't sit right with me.

"First of all, Panditji," I began my lecture, as if I were a philosopher, "what you said doesn't change my opinion. Second, any work can be based on truth, but how can it be truth in and of itself? Even if a great writer like D. H. Lawrence, who understood a few aspects of truth and then wrote and lived without worrying about the ashes and the dust, abuses and invectives of the world—when did you begin to labor under the delusion that you could achieve something like that? Panditji! He who discovers or realizes a single sliver of truth, never mind all of it, will keep quiet for the rest of his life. He certainly won't write, and probably won't even speak to anyone either. History is full of names of such saints and seers and prophets."

Even as I'm still looking for it in my own writing, I'd like to present you with the proof that people and events in this novel I have attempted to write, despite being one hundred percent imaginary, are based on the truth.

In the Anisa-Zamir affair, at one point Anisa recites a line from a ghazal in order to give some weight to her words. "There are always more answers than questions." Zamir Ahmed Khan was familiar with the poem and knew the name of the poet. It's in the nature of this character of ours to remember hundreds of poems, whether good or bad, necessary or unnecessary. So the fact that he knew this particular poem was no surprise. What would be surprising is if either Anisa or Zamir knew a particular poem before it was even composed, before it came into the mind of the poet himself. In this case, though I grounded this novel in fact, I committed a small error: I wrongly used a poem the poet had written after 1970 to embellish a conversation that took place in 1967.

It's important for me to come clean about this since my characters are indeed fictive and can say or do anything at any time. The artist, whether poet or painter or writer, has their own fixed time and space, and there's a clearly defined history to their efforts. My writing is most certainly not about toying with historical truths or reality.

Having said this much, allow me to take leave, with apologies once again for this second intervention, and with the hope that the need will not arise again to provide details about what I want to say.

I thank you.

Part Three

Aziz aka Acchan:
A Trailer of the World in Pictures

Aziz wasn't merely an individual for Zamir Ahmed Khan but represented a series of indelible memories of the times back then, and of a particular phase in his life. A phase when, on the one hand, a stamp finally certified his indisputable incompetence and, on the other, he witnessed corruption in action, learning how much more virtuous it is to be dishonest than honest, never mind how the world is run and by what sort of characters. The memories of these six long years were condensed into a few major events, and the six years he'd spent with Aziz seemed more like six months. In the beginning as he gradually cut himself off from the world, he never imagined that he'd feel compelled to spend so much time with Aziz aka Acchan. Too much time on his hands and empty pockets are what delivered him to Aziz's doorstep, and it was no small comfort to find a person and a place to welcome him. Aziz never asked Zamir to take part in his wheeling and dealing. Amid the coterie that surrounded Aziz, Zamir Ahmed Khan held the status of guest of honor, a close family member of Aziz Pathan's, and even his dearmost pal at drunken mehfil gatherings. In addition, people saw him as the sole individual to whom Aziz told his deepest secrets. He dropped his most urgent work to sort out Zamir's affairs, even the most banal.

"Brother," Aziz responded to Zamir's question with a smile. "Have you ever seen my work suffer? It goes on just as I've planned it. Not working requires a completely different kind of skill, which I admit you have in spades! My work's never done, and all these hangers-on I look after, what use are they? Now that I've opened up this soup kitchen, I have to keep handing out damn alms. I'm getting along just fine, sure. But tell me, how will your work get done if I don't take care of it? That buddy of yours, Vivek, would he come and help?"

The hotel building wasn't Aziz's, but he exercised rights over it like a landlord. Along with the other staff of the hotel there was also a manager, but like the others he, too, was Aziz's employee, and deferred to Aziz regarding even the smallest details. The manager had been relegated to the front counter while the manager's rightful place to sit had been turned into Aziz's den for receiving visitors, and he used it like his business office. A long, broad glass table, high-backed swivel chair, and a few chairs strewn in front of the desk for visitors. The ceiling fan and lights, a red table lamp, an air cooler for summertime, a phone. The stuff of an office. Tasteful curtains hung in the doorway and linoleum covered the floor, making the room look more like a director's office than the office room of some hotel. A green lawn with tall guava trees and in the middle a fountain that spit out water surrounded the eighteen-room building. His was the kind of hotel that legally had both bar and restaurant amenities, but Aziz conducted all his business right out of that office. Providing girls to men of means, commissioning tenders and estimates from gambling and black-market partnerships, and cashing in big-time by using his muscle to have others do his bidding—the long list of Aziz's means of income was gradually revealed to Zamir Ahmed Khan. Then there was the high-stakes gambling on the side. And the legit real estate business Aziz ran with a partner. The entire operation was conducted using the hotel's address. Years earlier, Aziz had come here in search of work, and the hotel's elderly, childless Punjabi owner, Bare Miyan, must have seen some promise in him, so bit by bit he handed over responsibilities to Aziz. First he was promoted to manager, then an understanding was arrived at for two thousand a month with not so much as a contract or handshake, and then, finally, Aziz aka Acchan became the hotel's undisputed boss.

"The poor thing's been defeated by Urdu poetry," Aziz said about his benefactor, smiling. "Who says Urdu's the language of Muslims? After all, what have I done for Bare Miyan? I recited to him, or at his mehfil, whatever verse or two I remember of Sahir, Faiz, or Jigar whenever he wanted to hear some poetry in his spare time. And then there was the time that famous poet kept on blathering after having had too much to drink at the bar and I just sat there listening quietly to his cursing and cussing. He had more drink than money but wouldn't admit it. I let him leave with his dignity intact and made up the difference from my own pocket. Bare Miyan observed all of this and was impressed. He said, 'Reading and appreciating poetry is one thing, but showing respect to a living poet like you just did is a far nobler thing.' He began to choke up and gave me a teary-eyed hug. Whatever I have I owe to that man's favor, his generosity, and the magic in his heart, the earnings from those poetry readings!"

Though Aziz talked like this, he otherwise looked after and cared for that old man and his wife as if he were their son. Aziz's own parents had died when he was very young and Zamir Ahmed Khan was surprised to learn that Aziz, along with running the hotel and tending to innumerable other tasks, had long ago completed his B.Sc. at a local college and wanted to continue his studies until he'd earned an M.Sc. or at least an M.A.

Aziz hadn't studied English in any formal way and hadn't studied at a public school, but his felicity with the language was so impressive that Zamir Ahmed Khan was jealous. His amazing self-confidence and impressive way of speaking, no matter in which language and on what topic, were miracles in themselves. Whether dealings with gamblers, a fleeting display of love for a woman, or his praise of literature and appreciation of poetry, Aziz aka Acchan's face radiated a peaceful expression, with the red glow of the rising sun, as if the man had no other work to do in the world.

"Well, you know, people who worry all the time are the ones who think they won't get their work done," he explained when Zamir Ahmed Khan asked what his secret was. "Is there anyone in the world I have to answer to? I came here to work, it seems like yesterday, and the worst that can happen is I'm fired from my job as a contractor. You're worrying about me for no reason. If the law decides to come after me, brother, just think what'll be the fate of the ones who pocket money from the government with one hand and with the other make many times more than that by giving me and the likes of me protection from the law. You can't even believe how many people are in this boat. All they care about, brother, is their own bellies and securing a bright future for their kids. So why complicate things for no reason with the people who feed them? And the government? It's not as if the government were like their kids and would remember to repay its favors tomorrow. It's not as if the country were like their bedroom or living room where they could find rest and repose. Everyone wants something, lickety-split! ASAP! You don't know how deeply the disease has spread. But I know it all too well, and there's no cure for it on the horizon."

Bhopali businessmen, scrappers, gangsters, poets, rich men, fakirs, people with high hopes to make a quick buck, doctors, engineers, small-fry spiritual leaders greedy to ply their wares in the name of religion, singers, politicians, people who wanted to get a quick transfer, or avoid one, low- and midlevel bureaucrats, generally high- but sometimes low-level government officers invited to enjoy flesh for free that served as advance payment, policemen, commission men, bellboys: all these characters were part of the crowd that surrounded Aziz. He also had a huge soft spot in his heart for the pretty girls, poets, singers, writers, teachers, all who were beyond reproach, sober or drunk. Aziz ignored even their most egregious shenanigans.

"These people and their well-being are an indicator of the well-being of any great country or nation," he said with great earnestness. "Really, how can any nation turn its back on their kindness?"

In light of the opportunities presented as the city of Bhopal expanded, Aziz started a legal business, along with a partner, to buy farmland on the outskirts of the city, build residential colonies, and sell the development for a tidy sum. Aziz relied on his own network of middlemen in various interconnected departments to obtain information about the farmland, which didn't fall under the government's private development projects. They helped him complete the long and arduous formalities to transform the land into residential developments. These middlemen, in exchange for their services, not only got whatever amount they sought but also were treated to all sorts of special pleasure perks. By then some people were awakening to the quickly changing contours of the state capital, but only a handful had the long-term perspective. The great influx of newcomers was yet to come, and longtime residents continued with their belief that the city had already expanded to the degree it should, and would no more. Some must have had the vision and wisdom to see beyond this, but because of a lack of means they were probably powerless to put ideas into action. So that's how Aziz aka Acchan and his partner became leaders pushing for the development of the city. Here was the deal: the business partner put in the money, and Aziz did all the hard work. Profit was split fifty-fifty.

Small-time hustlers called him "Aziz Pathan," while the ones who mattered addressed him as "Khan Sahib." Still others called him "Don Aziz" or "Aziz Pahalwan" behind his back, even though he didn't bear the slightest resemblance in body shape or manners to a Pathan or a don or a wrestler. He wore stylish, expensive, English-style tailored clothing, dabbed himself with expensive cologne according to the season and occasion—and probably no one ever saw so much as a speck of dust on his shiny, polished shoes. Along with appreciating Aziz's refined taste, Zamir Ahmed Khan also witnessed other incidents and strange circumstances. Such as when Aziz aka Acchan, concealing a knife and club and gun, refused to back down from some principle he held dear. Zamir almost died as he watched a gun fire, the bullet striking Aziz a few inches from his heart, but not a wrinkle creased his forehead. Yes, blood was flowing, but he'd won the brawl that had led to the shooting. He scoffed at people who suggested that he file a report with the police, and then had the wound dressed by a doctor. This wasn't an isolated incident, something like this happened all the time. But no one ever saw him lose his cool, even when circumstances were far worse. He pretty much had the same body type as Zamir Ahmed Khan. But because he was a little shorter, Aziz aka Acchan was also a little less heavy. God only knows how much courage and strength he had bottled inside.

Sabbah's Paradise

Aziz lived and slept in a room right there in the hotel and furnished it with all creature comforts, but Zamir Ahmed Khan didn't learn of the secret of its existence until a good while later. On the surface, the room was decorated with stylish furniture and a wardrobe and drawers in the sleeping area, in addition to containing an unusual bed. In the sitting area, a magnificent glass-topped center table and other, smaller side tables in front of a velvet couch. Then there was the divan Zamir Ahmed Khan always saw draped with a tiger skin, about which Aziz aka Acchan kept a detailed file that contained everything from the permission to hunt it to tanning its skin and whatnot. "There's no glory in fudging the truth about such tiny things," he said, seriously or in jest, it was hard to say. "It'd be just as sinful and shameful as stealing the water jug from the mosque!"

There was the long bookshelf in Aziz's sitting room. Along with lots of expensive books, it was adorned by a complete set of *Encyclopedia Britannica* volumes. Plus all the books from the Time Life world series, piles of *National Geographic* magazines, and as far as fiction went, a trove of his favorite cowboy novels. He had some books of Urdu poetry, most of them signed by the poet, while the lone representative of Hindi fiction was *The God of Sin*.

"Have you read it?" Zamir Ahmed Khan asked.

"You make it sound as if I've read all these other books!" Acchan said by way of an answer. Then he added, "By coincidence I've actually read this one. I don't know what literary types think of it, but there's something in the book we all want to see happen. As we fill our bags with disappointment and misfortune, we can't let go of the, 'Oh, god, if only . . .' Have you read it? Maybe you're better equipped to appreciate it, it's more in line with your personality. I have this friend in Bombay who bankrolls movies, and I've been after him for years to make it into a film."

This conversation took place a long time after Zamir Ahmed Khan had met Aziz, a year or two after, and by then he'd fully understood that he was focused on using the money he made through his various lines of work to go abroad, no regard to profit or loss. One of the foreigners he saw Aziz flirting with in the New Market was an American girl who was waiting for him in the U.S. and whose photo Aziz always kept in his wallet. She'd met Aziz when she was living in Bhopal working for the Peace Corps, and their encounters quickly developed into a deep and intimate love. Two years before Aziz left the country, the girl once again came to India. This time, Aziz aka Acchan introduced her to Zamir. She stayed in Bhopal for only a couple of days and then returned to the States, after a sightseeing trip with Aziz to Kashmir, Goa, Bombay, and a few other places. These events came later, much later, when Zamir Ahmed Khan, in a Bhopali manner of saying, was just hanging out on the stoop, nowhere to go—and thought to himself, "The caravan passed on, I watch the dust settle in its wake." By the time he incanted this, he'd already become part of the dust and dirt that rose from the streets, covering houses, shops, shop windows, rooftops, leaves and plants, making it hard to breathe. Aziz owned an old Hillman that the two used to drive around on outings to nearby places or for fun to Indore or Ujjain, or nearby Sanchi, Sehore, or Raisen. In his mental state of suffocating boredom, when Zamir Ahmed Khan had no hope whatsoever of making a single penny, Aziz showered him with the sort of kindness that, were it the sole kindness he ever experienced, he wouldn't be able to forget for the rest of his life.

Other attractive features of Aziz's room included the bar and fridge, which contained both local and foreign liquor, ice trays, club soda, still water, and a couple of things to eat like fruit and cheese. He had a huge variety of expensive glasses and cups in all shapes and sizes. In short, his room in the hotel contained an abundance of creature comforts that you barely came across in even the poshest households at the time. The room also had a back door that opened out to a graveyard that was gradually being taken over by the living. Makeshift homes dotted a number of the graveyard plots, along with a few basic shops, but most of it remained empty. Crossing a little distance in the cemetery, anyone could come and go to the room through the back door without anyone in the hotel being the wiser.

A spacious bathroom with a bathtub and shower with hot water that ran twenty-four hours a day was attached to the room.

Chief among these amenities was a single bed that could be raised or lowered or the various sections adjusted according to one's fancy. What Zamir Ahmed Khan found even more peculiar was the full-length mirror on the wall at the foot of the bed, and a variety of adjustable lights focused on it. When Zamir Ahmed Khan asked Aziz aka Acchan to let him in on the secret, Aziz smiled at him the way a guru might regard a dim disciple.

"Brother, do you know what the most precious thing about you is?" he said, teasing a little. " 'Curiosity' in Urdu, 'inquisitiveness' in Hindi. In other words, your desire to know and understand the world and everything else.

And, by the by, do you know what your greatest flaw is? It's that even after someone explains something to you, you're still incapable of getting it! *You are incorrigibly dumb.* If you'll allow me, I'll explain. The factory up there that manufactures saints has ceased operations. I believe that its last batch of saints was the one that produced Gandhiji. So down below in today's world there's neither any demand for them nor a supply from above. But the demand for dimwits and idiots is timeless, and therefore they are produced in great numbers. You are the eternal, living example of this fact, and, if you decided to follow a few of my recommendations, in other words, if you learn how to stand before the world and pull a pigeon out of your hat, I wouldn't be surprised if within a few generations, people would mistake you for a saint or fakir!"

"People always think in the beginning that a saint's actually a scoundrel," Zamir Ahmed Khan replied in the playful spirit of what Acchan was saying.

"Wonderful! You imagine this your beginning! Now that you've done your namaz, darling, it's time to lift your hands in prayer for the dead. At any rate, it's your own life, and no one has the right to interfere, but if you're truly destined to be a rough-and-ready mahatma for our times, then don't forget how the world treated that truly great soul. In gratitude for his services rendered, they riddled his chest with lead! And as for the rest of the people who loved him, they made statues of him using their favorite metals and installed them on roadsides, in intersections, and parks. You know, with the plain dhoti, the wooden sandals, glasses, the thick walking stick in his hand. Now the statue is at the mercy of the world. It endures hot, beating sun, bone-chilling cold, and torrential rain right out in the open. And his pose makes it look like he's heading off somewhere, supported by his stick, but what he actually does is just stand there. Doesn't move an inch. His followers have extracted him from their hearts and handed him over to the rest of their compatriots, while they got busy making money for air-conditioned cars, big offices, swanky homes, and fancy clothes. This mahatma started using a lovely name to refer to a huge part of the downtrodden population, 'Harijan', in order to restore their self-esteem and self-confidence. Know what? His acolytes then adopted this new custom of giving beautiful, nice-sounding names to despicable, ugly realities, thus absolving themselves of any and all responsibility! Now tell me this. If under these circumstances, a kind of youish-like, second-rate mahatma were to come along, what would he do? Drink booze after taking drugs for fear of an allergic reaction? Wax sentimental and tell the woeful tale of his failed love? Recall all the good and sweet things of his childhood friend as if he'd been a lover while other times he gets upset and lists all his faults? Tell me, is there any joy in being this kind of mahatma?"

"Mahatmas are above considerations of joy or sorrow." It was imperative for Zamir Ahmed Khan to say something, so he did.

"Correct!" Aziz aka Acchan avidly patted him on the back. "So listen. The truth is this room of mine is not for mahatmas. It's for those mahatma followers who've freed themselves from any and all responsibility, who now simply wish to indulge. It's also a hub for wheeling and dealing. When your turn comes, you can make all your dreams come true. Everything that happens in this room stays in this room, and, believe it or not, even when it's my turn I get to spend only a few nights. Are you following me? You're still not getting it. Come, let me show you a few things." He walked over to the bookshelf and took one of the *Encyclopedia Britannica* volumes, which he handed to Zamir Ahmed Khan. "Please, take a good close look."

He cradled the volume, leafed through it, and opened it up to the middle. He breathed in the pleasing fragrance that emerged from its pages as he thoroughly examined its contents. "Amazing!" he said, full of praise. "The full set must have really cost you something!"

"Sure, it wasn't cheap, that's obvious. It's not some printed-in-Moscow translation done by a bunch of Russians. But you still don't get what I'm saying!" In Aziz's voice was the sting of a priori disappointment in Zamir.

"So what are you trying to say?" He was flummoxed.

"My dear, look how old this edition is! Here, it's on this page. Anything getting through now? It's not the most recent edition. *Encyclopedia Britannica* has already issued two newer editions that contain more up-to-date information. This old thing may be pretty to look at, and serve its purpose to a certain extent, but the truth is that it's an echo of a bygone age. I bought the set from a family that had seen better days but no longer had any use for books, and no means to keep them. And they needed the money. Obviously I got it for a good price. They got what they were looking for, and, yaar, I wanted the books to help create the right ambience in the room. Looking at it this way, they're worth their weight in gold. And it's the same story with most of the other furnishings. This carpet? Bought at an auction. The chandelier hanging from the ceiling was ripped out from some similar ceiling that wouldn't have supported its weight much longer. This bed? Any guess? It's imported, and the frame, headboard, and foot of the bed are all mahogany, and the mattress is the kind that rajas and maharajas and rich men slept on in the old days. The hearts of those who lie on it are usually anxious and filled with fear and terror when they think about the changing times. Some people, though they praise its many virtues, still complain of a feeling of an unknown fear. It's the same tale with the bathtub. And the story behind this sofa is even more pitiable than the rest. I bought it from the kind of newly rich guy who thought that the first step toward success was the final one.

He was like the drunk guy who insisted on buying Akbar's elephant and was humiliated as a result. A few clothes and shoes and books are mine. But otherwise, brother, you should think of it as a quatrain by Omar Khayyam! A screen, cover, curtain, mirage. But the thing is I'm not Omar Khayyam, I'm his childhood friend Hasan bin Sabbah who cast magic on his followers, made them carry out the work, and built a fake paradise right here on earth. If not a quatrain by Khayyam, you can call this room Sabbah's Paradise if you like!"

Zamir Ahmed Khan was indeed taken aback at what came out of Aziz aka Acchan's mouth on that day, but it was nothing in comparison with the kind of astonishment he would later feel as he came to understand the trade of Junkman Sharafat at the Treasure Trove. The same trade of making the rounds of princely estates and palaces and black markets in the big cities, buying expensive items on the cheap, then selling them for whatever price he named to the new rich on whose door good fortune had knocked. Zamir Ahmed Khan spent an important future chapter amid expensive chandeliers, vases, engraved vessels, carpets, furniture, and paintings like these, seeing how money came and went, and coming to understand how counterfeit was turned into the genuine article. The interval between these two periods of his life wasn't all that long, no more than eight or ten years. How could two totally different characters from two completely distinct periods of his life take on essentially the same meaning? Observing Sharafat Miyan's skillful dealings with his own eyes, Aziz aka Acchan came to mind. At the same time, the difference between the two was clear to see. The room Aziz aka Acchan called Sabbah's Paradise was one of his countless gambles and risky deals that were not an end in themselves but a means to get somewhere, while pious and abstemious Junkman Sharafat's furniture store was a kind of final destination that put an end to all journeys, and one that was reached after a long chain of doings and dealings.

Zamir Ahmed Khan smiled to himself in admiration of Aziz's words. "But you haven't answered my question," he said, pointing to the bed, mirror, and adjustable lights.

"I've already given my statement in a way you could understand, but have it in writing if you want." There was more anger than uncertainty in his voice. "Oof, can't you even grasp why people come here to spend a few moments in private together to do what they want to do? So they do it, and while they're at it, they want to look at themselves in various poses and positions! When a man takes a woman here, it's not just to give her flowers! Maullaham passion potion is flowing through his veins instead of hot blood, and he wants to enjoy a few moments of relaxation and pleasure to release the tension. There are some whose capability has long since vanished, but whose lust will never leave their hearts. All of this is a separate topic in and of itself, my dear innocent friend! Call it normal or abnormal. Politicians may be skilled in the art of serving their own purposes and making people into little fools by turning a bitter truth into a sweet pill. But even their bodies can't be tricked into making the little fool take a stand. Zamir, you're not playing a joke on me by pretending to be dumb? How is it possible at your age? I mean, I can understand if you haven't done it physically, but to still be an untouched virgin in your mind?!"

"When did I ever tell you to believe what I say?" Zamir Ahmed Khan said, wanting to display some daring. "The fact that I haven't done it doesn't mean I'm completely in the dark. I've seen those decks of cards, and books, and every once in a while looked at *Playboy*. I've also read some Japanese writers in English, and I'm sure you know they have their own wild ways in Japan when it comes to sex. I've also read a few of Alberto Moravia's books."

Aziz looked at him, intrigued. "Tell me, do you want to be experienced?" he asked solemnly, intimately. "Tell me all your desires, don't hold back. Why, even your ears are turning red!"

During the many hours the two of them spent together, Aziz aka Acchan asked this question many times and in many different ways. Sometimes seriously, sometimes sarcastically, sometimes in jest. The question turned into a private joke between the two. The kind that, had Zamir Ahmed Khan requested later on for his heart's desire to be fulfilled, he wouldn't have been able to do it, since he felt that taking the joke seriously would be proof of stupidity and having no sense of humor. Aziz's role was to ask the question and Zamir Ahmed Khan's to turn up his nose and tell him to go to hell.

"No, it's not like that," he explained himself after sending Aziz to hell for his suggestion once again. "I've figured it all out on my own," he lied, pointing to the bed. "And now that I've asked, I understand things even better."

"So if I were to affectionately call you the playboy, how would that work?" Aziz said mischievously.

"Don't be an idiot," Zamir Ahmed Khan said, again embarrassed. "Then I'd have to call you Hugh Hefner!"

"Just think of how few people who read his magazine know the poor guy. People here have copies of *Playboy* just to show off. And in that respect, you're no slouch either. As the poet says, 'You may look beautiful...'"

"...They may look nice, but not a whiff of sincerity!"

Zamir Ahmed Khan completed what was in some sense one of Aziz's lines.

An odd change that occurred as he spent more time with Aziz was that his allergy to alcohol disappeared. In other words, he was liberated from that particular incarnation of his three-faced Trimurti existence that, until then, had maintained the difference between halal and haram, and that always mounted spirited opposition against his drinking, and threatened to go on strike. If drinking always brought joy and comfort to his mind, there was no limit to the joy and comfort attainable. The good news was that the inner rebel imprisoned in his body was set free, but the bad news was Zamir Ahmed Khan's drinking grew more serious every day.

"Watch out!" he'd often chide himself when drunk. "Booze is as far as it goes! No gambling, no women. That's the limit!"

The Degree Dilemma

Aside from his spending time with Aziz, Zamir's daily life was like a kind of gentle slope. It was hard to say whether the scenes he saw all around were because of his movement, or whether he was actually standing still and the changes he saw were because of the world moving in its own direction. After completing his B.Sc., Vivek was busy trying to establish his business. Despite the bitterness of the past, their friendship had now returned to normal. Asim was Vivek's business partner, and they were trying to find a third partner with whom they could join forces and stake claim to Bhopal's rapidly developing industrial sector.

"Get yourself a degree, one way or another. Just do it," Vivek told Zamir time and again. "It doesn't matter how well you do since there's no need for you to find a job. It's all about taking advantage of state benefits for unemployed engineers. Once the three of us combine forces, there won't be any more clashes or drama."

So began a series of regular meetings with Vivek and Asim, sometimes at Aziz's hotel, sometimes at Vivek's house or somewhere else. Vivek liked to gamble. Zamir Ahmed Khan saw him both win and lose playing high-stakes cards at Aziz's. It didn't seem right to give him a hard time about it. There's a strange magic to this thing called age. Even the closest of relationships seem on the surface to be just like before, when in fact they change constantly with the slow rhythm of the seasons, and people go along with it as a matter of course. Then comes the moment when you notice the change, just like with the seasons, and you're taken aback. The glory that emanates from house and home, earth and sky, animals and man, stream and mountain, water and field—one day, it all dissipates. Things that were soft and smooth become hard and rough, and most of the time you don't even notice.

It's not as if not doing a degree had been a conscious decision. But the probability of it happening diminished by the day. He kept up the routine of going to classes, however irregularly, but was already convinced that where he'd wasted one year in Aligarh, five or six years studying here would produce the same result. The mood at home wasn't a happy one, and hadn't been since Anisa. Things worsened with the news of his spending more and more time with Aziz aka Acchan, which also meant coming home late at night, and with the rumors of his drinking. The other family members didn't like Zamir spending time with Aziz because Aziz aka Acchan hadn't forgotten the way they'd behaved with him when he was a nobody—and this despite his being close family—and Aziz never let a chance to rub their noses in it slip.

"So what's the issue with you finishing your degree?" Aziz once asked him very affectionately in the presence of Vivek and Asim. "Just take the exam. The rest will work itself out."

"How's that?" Zamir Ahmed Khan pricked up his ears.

"What you do, yaar, is complete whatever formalities need to be completed so you can sit in the exam hall for three hours each day. I'll take care of the rest. You'll find the answer book filled out when you get there."

"That's cheating!" Zamir Ahmed Khan let out a sarcastic laugh.

"You want a degree or not?" Aziz shot him an angry glance. "Both the fourth and the final years will be taken care of."

"And the practical exams and orals?" Now it was Zamir who was examining Aziz.

"Also taken care of, don't worry. Anything else?"

"So if all this is true," Zamir Ahmed Khan said in a bitter tone, "why haven't you taken an engineering degree or two for yourself?"

An awkward silence fell.

"I've said it before, and I'll say it again for the last time," he himself broke the silence. "Please listen to me. I can't cheat and I don't need any help cheating. Where is it written that everyone who goes to engineering school, talented or not, has to leave with a degree? If I don't manage, I'll most certainly leave without one."

"That's the spirit," Aziz had changed his tone. "But as the poet says, and not just any poet, the great Allama Iqbal, 'Better be a human than an angel, though it's much more work and toil.'"

"To hell with poetry about angels and humans!" Zamir Ahmed Khan lashed out. "When did I take an oath of honesty? Ask me to be dishonest about something I'm comfortable with, and then just watch! But this business about cheating on exams? I've never been able to pull it off, I don't know why. Do you really think I don't see all the cheating going on everywhere? That I don't have a clue? I do. Perfectly well. But I also know that I don't have what it takes to cheat."

"Let it go, yaar!" Aziz lifted his glass and said cheers. "Anyway, you may have discovered the path of righteousness, but I've only been kidding. Is changing answer books easy to pull off? If it were, like you said, wouldn't I have a degree or two? The fact that I didn't get a degree is like halvah on

Shab-e Barat. You make it whatever way you want, and you share it with whoever you want."

The fact that Aziz aka Acchan had suggested that he get a degree was a puzzle that Zamir Ahmed Khan had never been able to figure out. Sometimes he thought Aziz had brought up the whole thing as a joke, but he kept returning to the suspicion that the offer was very real, given the crowd that hung around Aziz and the contacts he kept. And if Zamir Ahmed Khan had taken him up on the offer, sincere or not, he'd be a degreed engineer today. But then, the splendid buildings on campus, the hallowed hallways and classrooms, the open spaces, fields, the faces of the professors and lecturers who taught there and the staff who worked in the offices came before his eyes, and a question welled up from deep down: how could such a thing have been possible with all the honest, upstanding, and good people who worked there? Anyway, after college there's this thing called university, and maybe this kind of cheating was possible there. But how would it work with practical exams and the oral defense? How could another person show up in place of the one supposed to be taking the exam? The disgruntled voice in his heart blurted out to remind him, *Don't you know? Compared with the written exams, orals are just a formality. It's been known to happen that students who don't know a thing about anything pass their orals simply because someone likes their looks.* This had played no small role in exams he'd passed himself!

In any case, he'd told Aziz to go jump in the lake. As was his nature, Aziz never brought it up again.

Mayaprasad and Trying to
Stand on Your Own Feet

He began spending most of his time in college with people who had no use for a degree. One gentleman wrote Urdu poems, and another, a typist by trade, wrote verse in Hindi. Yet another, who went by the name of Maya-prasad, was the chief of the staff workers' union. He barely scraped by with what he made each month, and had a big family to support.

Humble by nature, short in stature, dark-skinned: Mayaprasad was an ordinary individual with an extraordinary fondness for living creatures. It still baffled Zamir Ahmed Khan when he thought about him now. Maya-prasad took care of countless pigeons that had taken shelter under the tall roofs of the workshop, and there was so much love in his heart for them that he fed them each day without fail. That fateful Monday was seared in Zamir Ahmed Khan's mind when he found Mayaprasad sobbing in the college canteen. Asking what had happened, he learned that the workshop super-visor had sealed off the workshop on Saturday night and, together with his friends, had finished off the whole flock of pigeons with air guns the next day. They tore off the feathers and plucked them clean. When Mayaprasad set foot in the workshop the next morning, he was welcomed by a storm of pigeon feathers. This incident was a grave blow to the heart, but it didn't diminish his love for living things. He was angry, sad, and kept to himself for a few days. But before too long Zamir Ahmed Khan saw him bring new pigeons into the workshop in place of the old ones, and with the same devo-tion he fed them grain brought from home every day.

A man who takes more interest in Mayaprasad and his pigeons than in his engineering studies has no hope to lead a practical life.

After some time, he ran out of spending money from his family. On the advice of a tenderhearted professor, he tried to stand on his own feet—but this attempt was in no way a success. When he set off for his first tutoring session with the kind professor in the hope of putting some money in his pocket, he hadn't the slightest idea who and what awaited him. He was to give private lessons to a girl for a couple of months who was in her first year of a B.Sc. in chemistry, for which she had to do a lot of cramming. A lot of work in a little time. In other words the hope of big money.

They navigated their way through the narrow, labyrinthine lanes. The threshold they found themselves before was the tin door of a ramshackle house with mud walls and an old tile roof—exactly the kind of lower-middle-class home described in countless stories. Down to the sackcloth curtains and chicken coop. On the mud floor of the small veranda, boxes and boards had been arranged to form a desk of sorts for the girl, and a couple of tin chairs had been brought out. A white-bearded, drab, coarse-kurta-pajama-wearing elderly man with a muslin cap leapt to his feet and welcomed them. So did the chickens locked in the coop, clucking and crowing in excitement as soon as they entered the house. Professor Sahib introduced Zamir as the new teacher and the elderly miyan looked him over with doubt and suspicion. Maybe he was trying to get to the bottom of what kind of teacher this well-fed, well-dressed young man was. Well-to-do people come up with all sorts of shams to satisfy their various desires, playing games with the honor of innocent girls. The Professor Sahib in any case was a firm guarantee against these dangers, and therefore the girl was summoned, in whose fate it was written to become his pupil. A very simple, ordinary, insignificant little thing. The terms of the agreement were settled and from the next afternoon, he began the lessons. It was early in the rainy season and because the neighborhood was a fifteen- to twenty-minute walk from his house, Zamir Ahmed Khan went there every day, umbrella in hand.

The old man kept nearby like a watchman when he was giving his lessons to the girl, who, unfortunately, turned out to be extraordinarily pea-brained in her studies. In spite of his vigilance, the girl, given the natural demands of her age, tried to attract Zamir Ahmed Khan's attention, sometimes with romantic verse written in her notebook, sometimes by mixing Bollywood-style love talk in her notes. He matter-of-factly ignored her overtures. A week or two passed like this. Then one evening when he arrived at the house, umbrella in hand, the old man was waiting for him outside the house.

"Please come in, miyan." The old man leapt up as soon as he saw him, opened the door, and drew aside the curtain for him. Inside, everything was different. The chickens were eerily silent, and a clean tablecloth embroidered with flower patterns had been tastefully spread over the table. A cushion had been added with great solicitude to his normal chair.

"The young gentleman has arrived," the old man meekly informed his old wife, and the woman who had heretofore remained in purdah showed her face that day. Zamir found all these changes unsettling, and had no idea what lay behind. Though offered tea every time he'd come, he understood it to be a formality on their part, and had politely declined. But today the tea arrived even before he'd begun the lesson—the water had probably already been boiling in expectation of his arrival. He'd only caught a quick, flashing glance of the girl, while her parents stood there like servants, hands clasped, ready to do his bidding.

"Miyan, we have a serious complaint to lodge," the old man said with a sigh, watching him drink his tea. "Why didn't you tell us?"

Without understanding a thing, he glanced back and forth at the old man and his wife, bewildered.

"Miyan, who doesn't know Maulvi Muhammad Ahmed Khan and his family! We have been blessed to be the recipients of his great beneficence and mercy. All these days you've been bestowing your kindness to the poor, teaching our daughter, and we aren't able to treat you in a way that befits your eminence."

"Not at all." Who knows how many things he wanted to say, but immediately realizing the meaninglessness of it, that was all he said. "Father is Father, I've come here on my own account."

"Subhan Allah, god be praised!" the old man exclaimed, raising his hands in a gesture of blessing. "Sir, this is exactly the spirit inherited by one's honorable family elders. Your average so-and-so isn't born with this trait. Now masha'allah, as god has willed, he has provided your family with everything anyone might need. But you possess, what do you call it, the spirit of service and the desire to help those less fortunate. You would not waste your precious time for petty earnings—never! If, sir, we have unwittingly erred in our behavior toward you in the past days, then please forgive us. If we have wronged you, we have wronged god. How can we ever be able to express our gratitude for what you have done for us? We are indebted to your forefathers and will remain beholden to you as well."

And that's how Zamir Ahmed Khan's plan of "little time, big money" came to naught. After giving lessons to the girl for the prescribed period, he took leave from her family, showered with praise and prayers from her parents.

"It worked out for the best," said Aziz in his sarcastic way after listening to his pitiable tale. "Who gets blessings in today's world! What you're harvesting today is the sowing of your elders. Who among the likes of us would do all of the work on our own, plow the field, sow the crops, and then wait for the harvest! What's money compared with blessings?"

"But," Zamir Ahmed Khan said in a griping tone, "I didn't go and teach in order to receive blessings!"

"Well, try going somewhere with the hope of receiving blessings, and maybe you'll be paid in cash! There's no sure bet in today's world. What's money, my dear? It's nothing, like dust that comes off your hands."

"My hands have been scrubbed thoroughly clean, thank you!" That's what Zamir Ahmed Khan wanted to say, but he kept it to himself.

Aziz, About to Take Off

Normally he took the city bus to Tin Shed on his way to campus. From there, he crossed the Mata temple, the poultry farm, and, nearby, a mosque taking shape over the years, getting off at the first stop on the long, winding street, then climbing the hill, alone, or talking with someone he knew, then walking the rest of the way to campus. During this daily journey, he caught glimpses of the rapidly changing landscape that cast its shadow over his inner world like a strange silence. In no time at all, trees that looked different according to the rhythm of the seasons were disappearing from fields stretching out near and far, while rocky hills were being leveled to flatten the land for future settlements of the new city. The proud mountain that stood in between the island of the college and the Birla temple was being flattened, bit by bit, turned into gravel, loaded onto trucks, and hauled to the sites where construction work was in full steam. And it was the same story on the other sides of the college island—to one side BHEL, on another the Arera colony, on another the boundaries and settlements of the Kolar project, all slowly but surely closing in and choking the college island as the surrounding town was tightening its grip.

"So doesn't all this political topsy-turvy affect your business?" he asked Aziz aka Acchan one day, bewildered. "First there was the Congress government, then the coalition was in power, and now it's Congress again, all in the blink of an eye."

"It's not like I have to join a political party and fight elections or aspire to a minister's post," Aziz said nonchalantly. "You've been watching the circus around me for years. Why would an innocent fellow from some party see me as a rival? They care only about their own interests no matter the cost."

"What, don't you think that everyone wants to work in the interest of their own people, no matter which group they belong to? That they'll give priority to their own people rather than to others? Doesn't this get in the way of your business?"

"Business, yaar, is just another word for getting snags out of my way." Aziz's voice was full of sharp sarcasm as he repeated the same line he'd said to Zamir Ahmed Khan countless times before. "And you don't perform sacrifices and havan rituals for the soul's liberation while the person's still alive. Everyone wants money. If you can give more money than me, then I'm out and the job's yours."

"Really, is it that easy?" Zamir Ahmed Khan had no reason to believe Acchan at this point. "You mean, the country's ideals and idealists have been cooked from the beginning? And it's hardly been forty or fifty years since independence!"

"No!" Aziz laughed sarcastically. "There's no need to lose heart, the country still has a fair number of idealists. The thing is they've become irrelevant to today's way of life. They're sitting somewhere all alone, or probably sulking, or pulling their hair out. Or, if they have a bit more piss and vinegar, they're probably consoling themselves by writing an autobiography or the tale of the country's struggle for independence."

"Do you ever feel that you and the people like you are responsible for this sad state of affairs? You, who, forget about everything else, just sat around your hotel, and can count the number of times you attended college classes on one hand, but then managed an M.Sc. somehow, top of your class?"

"I'm no social reformer, missionary, or politician!" Aziz said, brushing it off. "Nothing could've stopped me from becoming whoever I am today and achieving whatever I've achieved. I've got so much moxie in me, sweetie, that even if I'd lived a different kind of life, I'd still lead a life of luxury. The M.Sc. and all the rest are small potatoes. I knew how to survive from the get-go and had enough sense to figure out this one thing. That the water I've had to swim in was teeming with sharks, and in order to survive, I had to become like them. What did my close family ever do for me? Even your own mother and father? Or the rest of the world, which I tried in vain to grace with honesty, love, and affection—like arranging mustard seeds in the palm of my hand?"

"But, really, is everything in such a sorry state as you make it out to be? Pointless and meaningless?"

"It's not that I made it out that way," Aziz said, leaning into his statement. "It's what you have chosen to hear."

"So what is it you're trying to say?"

"One thing is clear. The way life's realities set the tone for your success raga today is very different from how the struggle for independence was fought using ideals as weapons. And it's also very different from what people venerated in independent India from Nehru's to Shastri's times. The political parties aren't the same, and neither are the problems the country is facing. The rest of the world's changed, too. Before, we had to beg others for wheat, but now, the green revolution has solved the problem, in spite of the fact that the country's population keeps growing fast. Along with this, although I'm not an accredited economist, mark my words, any time a country's currency is devalued, it's not just about the money, truth be told, it's the devaluation of the country's people and society. You may find plenty of reasons for this, but it won't cure the fatal disease that has spread to the country's economy like spinal cancer. Even though the currency was devalued and the rupee's devaluation was nominally brought under control in the rest of the world some years back, if you look at the situation today, it will turn out to be no more than a temporary cosmetic fix. Want me to go into detail about anything else? You yourself have seen all the theatrics that swirl around me, and for quite some time. I just don't have it in me to withdraw from the world or do the saint-prophet thing. Sure, every imaginable kind of illegal activity goes on in this hotel, but it's not as if I were the one going into the good people's homes to lure them onto the path of the wicked. I don't force girls to sleep with strangers, and I don't try to convince men that debauchery is important or needed. Even if you'll have to make the kind of compromise that will finally lead to your conscience dying a slow death because of it. Or you'll have to strangle it. I told you long ago that this is Sabbah's Paradise. People are so under its spell that they can be goaded to do anything and everything in the craze to return. I really don't want to go into detail with you about all of this because then you'll start looking at my life, too, and tally up rights and wrongs. If someone manages to make it through life without moments of cynicism, what can I say? At most, I'll be jealous. In any case, I'm just a guest in your city and country now. I'll soon be gone! And once you're gone you don't look back."

And, in 1972, it truly did come to pass that Aziz aka Acchan, very quietly, flew off to his destination—America. Before he left, he'd handed over the reins of the hotel to an individual whom he regarded as honest and capable, introduced him to the former owner of the hotel, reminded him to pay the rent on time each month, had a new lease written up, and, only after he was reassured that all was in order, did he set his date of departure. A few days before he left he sat with Zamir Ahmed Khan on the hotel lawn in his favorite spot. There was whiskey, Black Knight, Aziz's first love, which he preferred to any scotch. There was also scotch for Zamir Ahmed Khan, which he refused to drink since he was so emotional, the whole time drinking Aziz's brand instead.

Sailor on Horseback

"Come on, yaar, there's really no reason to draw a long face or pout," Aziz said, trying to sound cheerful. "It's not as if I were leaving Bhopal tomorrow. Remember the good times, and be merry."

It wasn't easy to be merry. Given his circumstances, even thinking about Aziz not being there made Zamir Ahmed Khan feel a bit like an orphan. As they drank a couple of rounds, conversation limped along, despite Aziz's best efforts—but how long would that last? Alcohol works its magic and speaks its own voice in the end. Just before the magic began to bestir Zamir Ahmed Khan, Aziz asked him very guardedly, "Zamir, I'd guess you're probably three or four years younger than me?"

He looked at Aziz, surprised. "I don't know," he told Aziz. "Anyway, I assumed the two of us must be more or less the same age."

Aziz asked him which year he was born.

"So I was right," he said after doing the math. "About four years. You have no idea all the places I hung out as a kid. If we'd bumped into each other back then even by accident we would've thought that we were the same age judging from each other's heights. In any case, a chapter of our lives is about to conclude, and our future lives, both yours and mine, will be very different from what they used to be. In the future, the most we can do is want the best for each other just like we do now. To expect more is unrealistic. Listening to me you must've felt many times that my heart is full of animosity toward the world, especially toward my relatives, and that I hate them. It's probably fair to say I am angry, but I neither hate anyone nor hold grudges. Look, when it's just you and me sitting and talking, there's no room for lies or cheating or showing off. When I think about it, I feel I ought to be grateful to everyone who in some way helped Acchan aka Aziz to become Aziz aka Acchan. What would have happened if one of them had gone ahead and taken responsibility instead of leaving me to my own devices? Either I'd be working in their fields or factories or managing their households. And deep down I'd keep a running list of favors, wondering how to ever free myself from the burden of obligation and pay it all back. When I look at it like this, I'm really grateful that they didn't lift a finger for me."

"Maybe you're right," Zamir Ahmed Khan concurred, carried along in the stream of emotions and drink. "And this gratitude, believe me, is what distinguishes you as an elder."

"To hell with being an elder!" he snapped back. "Elder, younger, who cares? And though you're a shining example of middle-class culture, sometimes even you don't follow these conventions. Just think, Nasrat is the same age as me, Kamal is younger than me, but behind their backs and in front of me you respectfully refer to them as Nasrat Bhai and Kamal Bhai, whereas I'm only Aziz to you, while sometimes calling me Acchan does the job. Why do you think that is? Is it only because for a long time now I've been forced to stay away from your crowd? Under conditions that dictate that anyone who considers me family would put their honor in jeopardy?"

Zamir Ahmed Khan didn't answer.

"It's not because of that," Aziz's voice suddenly clouded over. "It's because you and I have turned our backs on family history and tradition and have come to a neutral space that was neither yours nor mine. Remember that day ages ago when we met in New Market and the last time we met before that when we'd run into each other after god knows how many years? You didn't call me Aziz but Acchan! This was actually the beginning of our friendship. If you'd called me Acchan Bhai or Aziz Bhai then the relationship would have stopped right then and there. Forget about the details and look at the heart of the matter. I never considered you as family, but as a friend. So asserting my rights as your friend, there are two things I'd like to entrust you with tonight, and you have to accept them without objection or fanfare. Yes?"

Aziz went to his room and came back with a black leather bag.

He put the bag down on Zamir Ahmed Khan's lap. "First, a novel about Jack London's life called *Sailor on Horseback*, which turned out to be the greatest teacher and most important thing I ever got in my life. It's a strange story about one man's life struggles, and just like any classic it comes with a tragic ending. I've been wanting to give you this to read ever since the day we met, but I kept making one excuse after the other to put it off. Now there's no time left to put it off, so keep it with you and read it lovingly and earnestly, and keep in mind that the very stones the mason thinks useless and discards sometimes turn out to be more important than the entire building. You'll get the gist of what I'm saying when you read the book, and maybe you'll even like it. Jack London wrote his own epitaph on his tombstone. It reads, "The Stone the Builders Rejected.""

Aziz sat down and poured another glass.

"So what else is in the bag?" Zamir Ahmed Khan asked, more afraid of dewy sentimentality than drowning in drink.

"I could have given you even more," Aziz merely said as if talking to himself. "There's ten thousand rupees in the bag. Zamir, I want you to take it. Do whatever you want with it. No excuses, no second thoughts. Give it as alms to someone if you want, it's all yours now. End of discussion. Because I can't plan your future or use the money to make more. Do with it what you can, whether you make it work for you, or waste it. Just take it and don't make a fuss."

"But," Zamir Ahmed Khan wasn't capable of hiding his surprise. He could not but politely object. "But you're the one who's going abroad. Won't you need the money?

"I have enough," Aziz said with great humility. "More than I need, and that's why I'm giving it to you."

"One more thing," he added. "I need you to agree to one more thing. There're only a couple of people who know why I'm leaving Bhopal and going to the U.S. You can't tell anyone that I gave you money, not even Khala Biya and Khalu Miyan at home. Never ever. And of course," he stopped and laughed, "I'm well aware of your soft spot for Vivek Sahib. If you just can't help it after a while, go ahead and tell him. But no one else!"

When Aziz aka Acchan left Bhopal, even those near and dear to him had assumed—just as Aziz had told them—that he was going to Bombay in order to expand his business. And so one fine day, Aziz set off for Bombay as if going out for a morning walk, and from there to that city in America he had secretly longed to reach for who knows how many years as he'd gone about his daily life in Bhopal. Among the few people who knew the real story aside from Zamir Ahmed Khan was Aziz aka Acchan's business partner in the housing colony construction project. But Aziz had warned him that if people got wind that he'd left town, many in the business would start to act on their own and do as they pleased. So he kept it a secret. And in the long stretch of time since he left, aside from a greeting card or two, Zamir hadn't received so much as a hi or how are you—no letter, no photo.

That is, even if he'd wanted to, contacting Aziz aka Acchan wouldn't be possible today. *Sailor on Horseback* was far out of his reach.

With Aapa—at Ease

Aapa was relaxing in her easy chair, the glass of sherbet on the side table next to her sweating with condensation. The high roof with its old tiles, the thick whitewashed adobe walls, the lime floor, and the arched doorways were alive and present, still exuding the smells and fragrances of a bygone era. Aside from this room, which served as both living room and bedroom, with its almirahs and arched wall niches, the entire house exuded a feeling of spaciousness that was rapidly disappearing from the world. The large courtyard, greenery, all sorts of potted flowers, two guava and a pomegranate tree with ripe and half-ripe fruits dangling from their branches, red-and-white buds blooming and then lying scattered on the ground like a colorful carpet. Even in the most sweltering heat, the house was inhabited by a particular feeling of relief and coolness. It stood in a small lane some distance from the main road, so even traffic noise was dampened and diffused by the time it reached the house. Whenever Zamir Ahmed Khan came to Aapa's house—a couple of times each year—he didn't feel in a hurry to leave, despite the fact that his relationship with Dulhabhai, Aapa's husband, was not exactly a close one. Aside from his government job, Dulhabhai was interested in only two things: chess and his religion, namaz, fasting, prayers. Or, if he was in a really good mood, he did the cooking. He wasn't much of a talker or a listener. In the beginning this is how he acted with Aapa as well, but with age, and with their children growing up, he began to listen to what she had to say, and very attentively at that.

There was a reflection of the ceiling fan spinning in Aapa's glasses.

"It's so peaceful in here," Zamir Ahmed Khan said while sipping his sherbet. "You wouldn't think that it's infernally hot outside."

"Yes," Aapa said in a soft voice. "But it's only like this during the hot season. During the rains, you never know where to start with the leaks. If it's not leaking here, it's leaking there. We live like refugees in our own home. Things are in such a sorry state that we don't even know how to look after them. And then to find someone to fix the roof, it's almost impossible. Cats run all over the roof fighting and mess up the tiles. I've given up trying to tell your Dulhabhai to have a proper, modern house built like they build them today, but he doesn't have time to take away from his little diversions. We haven't even managed to install a WC in the bathroom—we still have to rely on the latrine cleaners!"

Zamir Ahmed Khan sighed deeply. "There's no peace of mind for anyone, anywhere."

"The thing is we've spent more than half our life in these ruins," Aapa said, trying to find a glint of hope in her gloom. "It's up to our children to do whatever it takes to make things better."

"Don't call this place a ruin, Aapa," he objected, laughing. "It was a beautiful house in its own time, and still is."

"It's the passage of time that marks the difference between a house and a ruin. Your Abba was always ahead of his time, so you can't even imagine how hard it is to live in this kind of old house. Back then he built his own house in a way that it had all the necessities of modern life. Just think how difficult it was for him to scrape together each and every penny, make the plans, and supervise construction all by himself. You probably don't remember much, you were very little at the time."

It was true that he had only a very faint memory of the house being built, even though he remembered many other things from that time in great detail. Zamir Ahmed Khan would never dare to contradict whatever Aapa might say about Abba. It was writ. The life that Abba had lived and how he'd lived it, despite his limited means and abilities, was no doubt an achievement in and of itself.

"Do you remember Phaphu Biya's bungalow?" Zamir Ahmed Khan asked Aapa in order to relive his childhood memories. "Whenever I come here, I remember her house."

"May Allah Miyan save this house from the sad fate that befell the bungalow!" Aapa heaved a heavy sigh; she didn't like her house being compared to Phaphu Biya's bungalow. "Just a few days ago Bhai Miyan came over, and we found out from him that you're unwell again," Aapa said in order to change the subject. "I wanted to visit you myself, but my blood pressure gives me such a worry I don't dare venture out. Also, something important has come up and I wanted to seek your advice about it, so that's why I asked you to come."

"Well, these dizzy spells are now a daily thing for me," Zamir Ahmed Khan said, laughing, resigned to the fact that his illness had become a part of his life. "I've lost track of how many years have passed like this. It feels like playing hide-and-seek."

"The same kinds of dizzy spells?"

"Exactly. Who knows what it really is, but calling it dizzy spells is probably a good enough name for it. The same old ailment. And the doctors still claim that it's not an illness at all."

"Are you working in the shop these days?"

The shop—that is, Junkman Sharafat's the Treasure Trove.

Zamir Ahmed Khan snorted.

"If you already talked with Bhai Miyan, you probably know all the details," he said in a level voice. "Number one, I'm not working in the shop, and number two, Rahat Biya is staying at her family's with the girls. Now that this is clear, let's talk about something else, shall we?"

"This is not good, Zamir," Aapa took a little sip of her sherbet. Her glasses continued to reflect the ceiling fan spinning dutifully. "Well, you're a better judge of the Sharafat Miyan situation than I, but you shouldn't have let Rahat leave just like that. If she left because of something you said, you should've gone to her house and brought her back."

"Just like you," Zamir Ahmed Khan teased Aapa, "when you used to sulk and storm off to our house and Dulhabhai came begging like a wet cat and sweet-talked you into going back home."

"Hmph!" Aapa sounded a little irritated despite enjoying their talk. "As if he's ever sweet-talked anyone! He doesn't know the first thing about honey-coated words."

"How would he? The poor man is always running back and forth. And now he must be nearing retirement. So! Then he'll be at your beck and call twenty-four hours a day and you'll get fed up. And as for Rahat, Aapa. Did you really call me over here just to chide me? Didn't you just say that you also wanted to seek my advice about something?"

Aapa wasn't capable of telling even the whitest of lies.

"Yes, true. I've invited you here because we've received a marriage proposal for Bitiya. I need your advice about this. Especially since you know these people quite well."

"Since when do I count as one of the family elders?" he said with a chuckle. "When it comes to matters like this, you should ask advice from people who've not only ingested the world but have digested it, too. As for me, I've just tasted a little bit of it with the unfortunate result that I have to be in attendance at the doctors', at their service all the time."

"What elder is left?" Aapa reminded Zamir Ahmed Khan of the sad truth. "Abba, Amma, Bare Abba, Bhai Jaan—all of them are gone, one after the other. There're some old people left in the family, but would any of them qualify as an elder? They're all caught up in the ways of the world and have made enemies of one another. You may ask them as a formality or bring the matter up, but the final decision has to be made by you people, whether Bhai Miyan or your Dulhabhai."

"In today's world, Aapa, the final decision ought to be made by the boy and girl themselves. That time is long gone when matches were made in heaven."

"I agree with you one hundred percent. People can give a little guidance by virtue of being older, but it's up to the boy and the girl to choose their own path."

Aapa's personality was an odd confluence of Abba's and Amma's characters. Amma's practical nature and realistic outlook and Abba's love of the spiritual, Sufi side of things all came together in her. She kept her distance from the day-to-day quarrels of the extended family and busied herself with the responsibilities of her own home, in which the education of two boys and one girl, and decisions related to their futures, took priority. After that came being the first to lend support and share in the joys and sorrows, big and small, of all the other relatives, near and far. All of this was an integral part of her daily life. She had brilliantly mastered the challenge of providing her children with a good and decent upbringing on her husband's limited income. As a result, her oldest son had finished his degree and since last year was earning a good salary in the Middle East, while his younger brother and sister were studying at college. The fact that Amma was no longer there certainly caused Aapa some sorrow and grief, but after Amma was gone she also developed a kind of maturity that in many ways made her whole and complete, as if after having been the crown princess for a very long time, she had truly become the queen. Despite the ups and downs of her health, she kept abreast of all the goings-on of the extended family in great detail.

It sometimes surprised him that despite the deep love and affection between Aapa and him, they didn't enjoy the same kind of informality that existed between her and Bhai Miyan. One possible reason was their difference in age. Aapa was barely one or two years younger than Bhai Miyan, while a gulf of ten years separated her from Zamir Ahmed Khan. He was barely six or seven when Aapa was married and went to live with her in-laws. After that it wasn't possible to achieve the kind of intimacy that can come from living in the same house, as had developed between Bhai Miyan and Zamir Ahmed Khan.

"So, who's the boy?" he asked, finally acceding to Aapa's train of thought.

"You know him," Aapa said matter-of-factly. "It's Karim, Idris Miyan's eldest son. He just graduated and a few months ago found a job in Kuwait. His family wants to do a simple engagement ceremony before he leaves."

"Which Idris Miyan?" he said, a little surprised. "Not that contractor who used to live in Ibrahimpur and just built a house at the Idgah?"

"One and the same," she confirmed. "You know him, right?"

"The Idris I know," Zamir Ahmed Khan said, suppressing the unbecoming anger in his voice, "is a first-class fraud! You know he cheated me, don't you?"

Trimming betel nut onto the plate, Aapa became lost in thought.

Things Happen for the Best

Actually, it was none other than Contractor Idris who facilitated the squandering of the ten thousand given to Zamir Ahmed Khan by Aziz aka Acchan and the five thousand from Abba, for a total of fifteen thousand. It happened long ago, just a little while after Aziz left.

The first thing Zamir Ahmed Khan did with the money Aziz had given him was to go straight to Vivek to ask him for advice about what to do with it, perhaps with the secret hope that Vivek would grab him and his money right away and say, great, why don't you become my partner? In hindsight this hope seemed foolish, ludicrous. Even if he was worth ten thousand more back then than today, how far would it have gone? Ten thousand is a drop in the bucket for someone who's trying to start a business that requires millions.

"Where did this come from?" Vivek asked about the money right away, and Zamir Ahmed Khan told him the whole story.

"I can't figure out for the life of me what to do with it," he said, presenting the problem to Vivek.

"Indeed," Vivek said as if to himself, understanding the gravity of the matter. "The things that can be done with this kind of money? You just don't have it in you. I mean, either start a small-time business yourself, or partner with someone who has the skills for it. It would be better if you . . . Look, there's no harm done yet, you still have the money, so finish your degree. Otherwise you won't be able to do anything with it anyway."

"What if I wanted to work in your office?" He deliberately used the phrase "in your office" instead of "with you." "All I'm saying is, work in your office, no more than that, forget about the ten thousand."

"Give it some more thought," Vivek said candidly. "This idea isn't good for your future, as I see it. You know where my business stands at the moment. I have high hopes, but nothing much has happened yet. The building for the factory is ready, we have machines on order, and employees drawing salaries without any work to do. So what would you actually do if you started working with me right now? And look, what would your status be with the other partners? Even though I can vouch for you to a certain degree, would you be able to handle disagreements with one of the others? Thinking about it, I wouldn't be happy if . . ."

"It's not like I'm already on the payroll!" Zamir Ahmed Khan tried to put a light touch to a serious matter, although Vivek's blunt but truthful words had actually made him lose heart. He'd expected that even if Vivek didn't give him the sweet prize, he'd at least offer some sweet talk, something Vivek was unable to do in the moment. "I just brought this up to test the waters."

"If you want to test the waters," Vivek said in a practical manner, "then keep on coming to my place. You know it's yours as much as mine. This is not the first time I'm telling you and I'm sure it won't be the last."

"I know, yaar," he said, affectionately patting Vivek's hand. "I hope it doesn't come to that, otherwise things will inevitably be awkward between us again. Given the advantages we've enjoyed so far, we've had the luxury of not needing to know what's yours and what's mine. And as for the future, maybe at some point we'll have to determine first who's the owner of a particular thing. When your life changes from individual concerns to future responsibilities, you automatically begin to understand the need for the law and how useful record keeping, contracts, and agreements can be. I get what you're saying."

After Aziz had left, Vivek once again became Zamir Ahmed Khan's one and only support. Their quarrels subsided by the day, and a maturity and sense of purpose entered their conversations. In the moment, he'd said all these things to Vivek just to say something, as if he'd already developed a sound grasp of life, the proof of which would be manifest in his future achievements. Like learning about the harsh truths that stem from the change from individual concerns to future responsibilities. Like understanding the importance of the law, record keeping, contracts, agreements. But when the time came for him to act on these facts, he ignored them.

He retrieved his riches from Vivek and took them to Amma.

"What's this?" Amma said wide-eyed, regarding the stack of rupees.

"Keep it and spend it on things you need." Zamir Ahmed Khan had turned into the embodiment of propriety, obedience, humility.

"What am I supposed to do with all this money?" The surprise grew stronger in Amma's voice. "And tell me, where did it come from?"

Zamir Ahmed Khan had no choice but to tell the story, and so tell the story he did. How he had amassed four thousand rupees working incredibly hard for months on end, how all the tutoring that'd forced him to come home late at night and had enraged Amma so, and then how in partnership with an honest contractor the four had turned into ten thousand rupees within months!

Amma's reaction after seeing the money and hearing Zamir Ahmed Khan's story was a prime example of the extent to which parents, as they search for signs of success in their progeny, can sometimes overlook all other manifest facts. She took the money for safekeeping. God knows why, but a big burden was lifted off Zamir Ahmed Khan's shoulders. Until the moment years later when he was summoned before Abba.

"I'm happy that you're doing something," was the gist of what Abba said. "You don't need to complete a degree, just lead a purposeful life. We don't need the money you've earned," he said as he gave back Zamir Ahmed Khan's ten thousand, and added five from his own pocket. "If the work is profitable, then go ahead. We'll pray to Allah Ta'ala for even greater prosperity."

So, Zamir Ahmed Khan sought out Contractor Idris, who was often seen hovering in the orbit of Acchan. Idris did contract work for the Public Works Department and had been tight on cash for some time. He went to him with the fifteen thousand, and without as much as putting anything into writing, became his business partner.

"You know me well," Zamir said, as if addressing someone he was well acquainted with when in fact he didn't know him at all. "And I know you. You're the registered contractor, so the work should be done in your name. We'll split the profits. Written contracts are one way to do things when the parties don't trust one another. Why don't you start the job? Anyway, I have no experience at all in this line of work. You should look after the building site and so on. Of course I'll come and sit in the office every day."

The money went down the drain the very instant he placed it into Contractor Idris's hands, but the public announcement of this and his severing of ties with Idris would happen only in 1975, when Zamir Ahmed Khan was already married, Abba had quietly departed from the world of sights and sounds, and the game of light and shadows in his mind had only just begun—and just a few months before he was taken to Doctor Crocodile's the first time.

As Zamir spoke with Aapa, he suddenly realized the delicacy of the matter. "I'm not one of those people who take grown-ups' fights to the children's doorstep. No, never. It was just that when you mentioned the name of that man, it immediately put a bad taste in my mouth. Now let me have a little bit more sherbet to cleanse my palate!"

Aapa breathed a sigh of relief and, with a smile on her face, went to fetch the sherbet. He'd regained his composure by the time she returned.

"The main thing is the boy," Zamir said. "Let's take a look at his education, whether he's good-looking and, of course most important, what he's actually doing with himself. God forbid that the relationship between Bitiya and this boy, what's his name again—Karim?—turns out like Zamir and Rahat's. Let's just pray for this."

"Did Idris Miyan do something bad when you worked together?" Maybe Aapa wanted a fuller picture. "Look, the point of asking your advice is that we haven't taken a final decision yet. Now's the time to speak up if you have any ill will against those people."

"Why would I harbor ill will against the kid?" he said in order to cut things short. "And as for Contractor Idris, it's such an old story. If he's forgotten it by now, I'm also ready to let it go. The world has moved on in the meantime, and so has he, just look where he is now! My story with him goes back to the days when he was going through a rough patch. Also, I was the one who made the basic mistake of not getting anything in writing. And I may also be wrong in assuming that he cheated me. It's entirely possible that our joint business ran at a loss as he claims, and the money really did go down the drain. His son, in any case, has nothing to do with any of this."

"Brother, we look at the parents and see the child. And Idris Miyan went out of his way to mention to your Dulhabhai that Zamir Miyan is angry with me and won't even say salaam when he sees me."

"And that's because he doesn't deserve my salaams!" Zamir Ahmed Khan wanted to smash the glass of sherbet onto the floor. But instead sat there sipping away.

Given the manner Contractor Idris had fleeced him, there was no room for doubt that he had indeed done so. However, from Zamir Ahmed Khan's point of view, the loss of the money was less important and troublesome than the delicate point in time when it happened. Entrusting the money to Idris Miyan had given him the kind of relief one experiences when putting money into a savings account that will accumulate a certain amount of interest after a fixed period. After he lost everything, Zamir subjected himself and the world around him to deep scrutiny and arrived at the conclusion that in this changed world the Zamir Ahmed Khan who'd been devalued in each and every way would have to build entirely new bridges and discover new roads in order to continue living life. Maybe for the first time, he experienced failure at a practical level and learned what it's like to find yourself alone. Despite the fact that he'd invested fifteen thousand into the "business," the intensifying feeling of the meaninglessness of life ultimately oriented him toward the road that leads to death. It felt like a noose around his neck, tightening day by day, and to free himself he announced that he wished to get married and suggested Rahat's name to Amma himself. Amma didn't trust him, and placed the matter before Abba, who was even less convinced than Amma. However much of Zamir Ahmed Khan's veneer may have come off by then, he still seemed a person from another world and different background.

"I always feared that one day he'd grab any old girl by the hand, turn up, and say, 'meet your daughter-in-law,'" Abba said frankly to Amma.

The family's joy knew no bounds. Although he didn't have a red cent of income after his failed investment—even for spending money he had to turn to Amma or Bhai Miyan—his "not working," under the circumstances, didn't create an obstacle in finalizing the marriage to Rahat. He had already proved to his family that he was capable of doing something. Things had been a little tight recently, but it was just the nature of contracting work, where there's always ups and downs.

Vivek was the lone individual who opposed the marriage, but perhaps it was written in Abba's fate to experience this final joy, for hardly four months after Zamir Ahmed Khan and Rahat's wedding, he was afflicted with an illness that neither hakim nor doctor could figure out right until the end. And then the day arrived when Abba left this world, leaving behind a great void.

"What I think," he said, explaining to Aapa, "is we should forget about whatever happened in the past with the old generation and look at things with the children's future in mind. I don't want to dig up old dirt and risk more resentment, but the biggest complaint I have against the contractor is that I wasn't able to pitch in even one paisa from my own pocket when Abba was dying. Bhai Miyan did, you did, other relatives must have, but I just watched the entire spectacle from the corner, like a helpless pauper. Who'd want to give their salaams to such a man? So, fine. If Bitiya marries into that family, I'll start saying my salaams to the bastard!"

The words flowed easily from his lips, but Aapa knew this would never happen. Zamir Ahmed Khan wasn't stubborn, but in certain matters he could prove to be quite headstrong. This she knew all about.

"I have no ulterior motives in asking," Aapa said. "But are you certain that Idris Miyan defrauded you on purpose?"

See! The marriage proposal had just come and Aapa was already trying to view the dealings of Contractor Idris the same way that inquisitive historians want to trumpet new and shocking findings to the world, rediscovered after a long time, to add to what's been written in the history books. Her actions made it easy to guess what could, and what would, happen next. This question was posed by none other than Aapa, Zamir Ahmed Khan's blood sister, who'd witnessed how helpless he had been during Abba's illness, and even before that, who could testify to Zamir Ahmed Khan's utter penury on his wedding day. Eager to share in Abba and Amma's happiness, people helped out with the expenses without saying a word. Or maybe it was on account of Bhai Miyan's generosity that a cotton rug suddenly made its appearance in Zamir Ahmed Khan's room, a ceiling fan was installed, and curtains, nicely covered by pelmets, were hung on the doors and windows, plus the electrical system was rewired, all in the blink of an eye—most of the things that made all the difference to his room, even now. The other things were what a girl from a middle-class family brings to her new home for which the husband's expectant family leaves a wide swath of space: a bed, a steel almirah, a sofa-cum-bed, a namaz chawki, a dressing table, and so on. This despite the protestations of taking no dowry. He shamelessly watched others take care of everything, first for his own wedding and then during Abba's illness. A chief bystander during all of this was Aapa herself, who now so innocently asked about the honesty or dishonesty of Contractor Idris.

Zamir Ahmed Khan's heart suddenly filled with self-loathing. What was he trying to prove? That his life had been ruined because of Contractor Idris? That not one paisa of the fifteen thousand—ten from Aziz, five from Abba—had been earned by him, that it was the kind of sum that once squandered would make you hang your head in shame for the rest of your life? The example of Bhai Miyan came to mind. He'd suffered countless setbacks with his business, yet today was leading a perfectly good life. And it wasn't even the full fifteen thousand. Zamir had now and again helped himself to Idris Miyan's money—a sum that eventually added up to four or five thousand.

"I'm not in a position to say for sure," he said, giving in to Aapa's reasoning. "But am I hearing you suggest that I'm the one who committed fraud?"

"But Idris Miyan hasn't accused you of anything," Aapa said, innocently. It was now clear to Zamir Ahmed Khan that her asking him for advice was a mere formality. Aapa and the elders had already agreed to the match between Bitiya and the son of Contractor Idris, and all that remained was to go through with the ceremony. He'd at least hoped Aapa wouldn't subject him to this kind of treatment, or, rather, ill-treatment, helpless and powerless as he was. "What he says," Aapa continued, "is that it wasn't just your money. His went down the drain, too, along with the business. And he wasn't the one who severed ties, it was you who stopped seeing him and even stopped your salaams."

"He didn't bitch and moan about the typewriter thing, did he?" Zamir Ahmed Khan said with a soft sadistic laugh.

"What typewriter thing?" Aapa had no idea.

"If you wanted to translate it literally from English to Hindi, it would be something like a 'parting kick.' When I left the office for good I took his typewriter and sold it to a junkman for a song! This was after Abba had passed away, when it began to look like Rahat was going to be a mother, and after I'd begun to suffer from my spells."

"He never said anything," Aapa said with dismay.

"Okay," Zamir Ahmed Khan said matter-of-factly in order to be done with it. "The fact is that to do business you need a particular mindset that I don't have. If it had been only Idris Miyan, we can agree he acted dishonorably. What finally did me in, though, was the mess with Sharafat Miyan. But setting all that aside, as far as Rahat's concerned, even I wouldn't call her dishonest."

Aapa didn't say a word. Trying to interpret her silence, he also remained quiet. When the hot summer afternoon spreads over the clay-tiled roofs, and in its final throes wilts into evening, a faint daze enters even birdsong and each phrase that's being sung seems no more than an effort to sing—a failed attempt to say something, anything at all.

"Well, take a good look at the boy," he said, shifting in the chair and trying to get up. "There's Bhai Miyan, Dulhabhai, and the rest of the elders. Ask them for advice, and, bismillah, make the decision, and then be done with whatever kind of ceremony you want. I have no right to make a decision, good or bad, since who could be worse than I to judge common standards of good or bad, Sahib? Just as you and I have discussed, the main thing is that the boy and the girl like each other. You must've found out by now, and if not, please find out. After that, whatever remains to be done, let me know, and I'll do whatever I can."

"Why are you leaving?"

"It's getting dark, and I should be heading home."

"What's the hurry?" she said trying to stop him. "Bua must have sprinkled the courtyard by now, let's go and sit outside. Have dinner before you go, and by the way I've prepared your favorite dish, watermelon-rind curry and channa dal."

Proximity and distance in and of themselves render the ordinary extraordinary and the significant insignificant—the fact that Aapa remembered was a testimony to this. She knew that as a child Zamir Ahmed Khan relished his watermelon-rind curry mixed with channa dal. What she didn't know was that for a long time now he'd found the dish tasteless. In the same way, she felt justified concluding that he had no objections to her daughter marrying the son of Contractor Idris in light of what he'd revealed.

"You're right, what's the hurry," he said to Aapa, stretching. "Sometimes too much free time can rob a man of his tranquility. This isn't the case with me, so if you say the word, I'll stay for dinner."

After the courtyard had been sprinkled, cane chairs were brought out. It'd been such a long time since he'd inhaled the fragrant scent of the damp earth of the courtyard, he thought, as he bid farewell to the evening sun setting behind the tall roofs. What kind of change was this? Devastating city after city in the name of new residential developments? Rise in population? It wasn't population but devastation!

After instructing Bua to prepare dinner, Aapa turned the pedestal fan on the veranda toward the chairs and turned it on. Wiping the sweat from her face with her head scarf, she sat down next to him. "There's no breeze," she said, gazing from behind her glasses at the motionless leaves on the trees. "It's the same unbearably hot weather you chose for your wedding."

"I chose?" he said absentmindedly. "It was Abba's decision. It's a good thing he did, since if we'd waited for better weather, he wouldn't have been able to take part. I truly believe things happen for the best."

"When did you start to see things like this?" Aapa said, trying to make light of a serious topic. "You never even let a fly land on your nose, always had to have things your own way. And you'd argue for hours about the difference between being and doing."

"What kind of a proverb is that, Aapa," he said, trying to cover his embarrassment. "If you don't have a nose, a fly has no place to land!" Even before Aapa responded, he started laughing.

The more he thought about the grudge he held against Contractor Idris, the more he hung his head in shame. What virtue had he seen in Contractor Idris that inclined him to work with him? Honesty? Certainly not! Idris had hovered around Aziz aka Acchan, flattering him in order to get his problems solved, but those weren't an honest contractor's problems. Nor did they share the kind of bond where Zamir Ahmed Khan might do something for cash-strapped Idris, expecting that Idris might do something for him in return—not at all! Did Zamir Ahmed Khan even have an interest in the kind of work that Idris was contracting for? If he did, then instead of wasting his time chatting in the office, he would've gone out with Idris on the job and cultivated relationships with people who were useful to the contracting business. He considered Idris's ten-by-fifteen room to be a kind of convenient base camp where he could stay put. Out of sight from the family and "keeping busy," Zamir weighed, examined, and discussed the whole wide world over cups of tea with all the fine and not-so-fine local poets, journalists, small-time politicians, and teachers. Things were cheap back then.

Close to the "office" was the maulana's hotel, where even though the salty tea was considered expensive, it ran only a quarter rupee per glass. And cigarettes, paan, and bidis were about the same price. Yet somehow the daily "office" tab for chai-paan came to around ten rupees. As long as Zamir Ahmed Khan had money in his pocket, he'd generously take care of the expenses, but when his pockets ran dry, he had the maulana enter it into his ledger. The credit was in Zamir's name, but when it came time to settle the tab, Idris Miyan was the one who the maulana asked to pay up, and he had to whether he wanted to or not. For a long time the "office" was also furnished with the convenience of a phone, which was utilized liberally by whoever dropped by. The bill kept increasing month after month, so Idris Miyan finally had the number transferred to his house. When an accountant showed up two or three times a week in the evening to help Idris Miyan do his books, Zamir Ahmed Khan, along with his companions, spent his time somewhere else. The biggest complaint Idris had against him was he didn't spend his days with people useful to business. Aziz aka Acchan truly respected every artist with all his heart, while Idris, without denying their importance, wanted to put them to use as the need arose. He never pressured Zamir Ahmed Khan to do so, and only tried to explain by way of dropping hints at first, but later made clear his disappointment by the way he acted. Zamir Ahmed Khan couldn't pretend he didn't get the hints. He understood them all too well, but chose to ignore them.

Then why work with Contractor Idris? What was his motivation? Maybe Zamir Ahmed Khan assumed that after he'd received a little support during tough times Idris would prove a successful entrepreneur and, with his help, the business would take off. The people who flocked to Aziz in the name of success corroborated with their actions something that Aziz himself had said: the world's changed, the standard to measure life has changed, and lies have become an integral part of our lives. That success and dishonesty have become synonymous. So in the moment, he'd viewed Contractor Idris as having the potential of being a successful fraud, a quality that Zamir Ahmed Khan himself lacked entirely, and he'd put his money on him like gamblers at the races bet on the winning horse—forgetting that Contractor Idris was not a horse but a man, who was capable of cheating the whole world and his so-called partner along with it. So why complain and rebuke him? He should be pleased that his initial impression of Idris turned out to be correct, and that today Idris was one of the people in town who had really made it. He had it all—bungalow, cars, educated children. It was a real point of pride that a man like him would want a child of his to marry a close relative of a good-for-nothing like Zamir Ahmed Khan.

The first instance of discord between Zamir Ahmed Khan and Idris happened when Zamir brought some of his friends to the office to drink despite Idris's having forbidden him to do so. Zamir took responsibility for his misstep and was able to brush it off adroitly. Idris himself didn't drink. During the time he worked with him, if Zamir Ahmed Khan considered anything as an achievement it was that his drinking was curbed to a great degree. He rarely drank, and that in a hotel or at a bar with Vivek or a few other friends.

Meanwhile Idris also began to keep his distance from Zamir because of his repeated demands for money—first for his own wedding and later when Abba fell ill. Then one day they came face-to-face after Abba had passed away, and Idris threw up his hands. Enough.

"What do you need money for now? I don't know what you're talking about." Instead of beating around the bush, Idris attacked Zamir straight-away. "Partnership means that profit and loss, both are shared equally. It's not like you lent me the money on interest and I have to give it back no matter what."

"Is business that bad? My whole fifteen thousand's gone down the drain?" he said cynically, demanding a detailed explanation from Idris.

"No, actually I'm lying!"

"So what you're saying is that you've also lost fifteen thousand of your own money? And the two of us kissed thirty thousand good-bye in the hope of a little profit?"

"I'm not in the mood to argue, take a look at the books yourself!" Idris maneuvered Zamir Ahmed Khan into a corner. "While you, miyan, worry about your fifteen, I'm trying to stomach the loss of a hundred thousand all by myself. Who can I go cry to about that? It's no secret how things have been ever since Emergency was declared. Relentless."

Zamir Ahmed Khan was prepared to settle accounts with Contractor Idris. "It seems that this Emergency has given your dealings something like a death sentence!"

"Mind your own business!" Idris flew off the handle. "I never would have guessed you'd turn out to be completely useless, when you're such a close buddy of strongman Aziz's! I agreed to our partnership because I thought that you'd be making the rounds as well and bring into the business contacts you'd made on account of him. But you're a man of no substance. Taking you on has not been one ounce of help, Zamir Khan. What's worse is you're a backbreaking liability. Let's forget about the money I gave you again and again. I also forgive you for the way you criticized me and made fun of me, calling me an idiot behind my back. But with this I declare that our partnership ends right here and now! Finished!"

Contractor Idris became so agitated that he completely forgot that the office where he was sitting and uttering all these words was legally his, and he got up and walked out after he was done. After he left, Zamir Ahmed Khan cast a regretful look around until his gaze came to rest on the type-writer that stood on the side table. He wrapped the typewriter with old newspaper, locked the door behind him, and, as usual, handed over the key to the maulana from the hotel. He set off on his way, one that until today's conversation with Aapa never again intersected with Contractor Idris's.

So much so that even Contractor Idris had deemed it wise to write off the typewriter, an entry in the book of errors.

As the curtain came down on his dealings with Idris his health troubles had begun to manifest. Rahat was now expecting and after some time was to give birth to Sana. How quickly Father had shuffled off this mortal coil after a very short illness was beyond comprehension. Abba's demise was extremely dramatic. Until his very last breath he kept recognizing and talking with Amma, Bhai Miyan, Aapa, all the children of the household, and even distant relatives, addressing everyone by name. But during the final hours before he closed his eyes for good only one question was on his lips: where is Zamir? He saw him, refused to recognize him, and asked, "Where is Zamir?" He called out to him saying, "Abba, I'm here, Zamir, right in front of you." And Abba, shaking his head in despair, kept repeating, "Zamir? Where is Zamir?" Each and every one, from Amma to Bare Abba and Phaphu Amma and whoever else had gathered during those fateful hours, tried to convince and reassure him that Zamir was really there, but for Abba it was as if he had become invisible and nonexistent, someone who he could not see, hear, or feel. With the exception of Zamir, everyone else was present who he could give counsel to, who he could listen to, whose hand he could hold on to to make the pain of death more tolerable. Zamir Ahmed Khan was the sole person with whom Abba's connection had been severed while still alive, and about whom he was very worried, asking again and again, where is Zamir, where is Zamir?

The way that life and death are closely intertwined: little Sana arrived after Abba had departed. He found this experience unsettling in the sense that he didn't feel any of the things he'd read and heard about during the course of his life, like a parent's affection for their children, and so on. He had a hunch that if his daughter were dropped in the middle of a group of other kids, he wouldn't be able to tell her apart. In the end he concluded that the love you feel for a child is proportional to how much time you spend with them, and how well you get to know them. If some nurse in the hospital were to switch our baby right after birth in a way that we never found out about, then maybe we'd spend our whole life with the child of another just as we would with our own. In one baby we'd find characteristics of the mother, and in another likeness to the father. And if not, we might say the kid has turned out a disappointment. Who knows, it's entirely possible a hospital nurse had been playing this game with our children for a long time!

It was only a little while after Father's death and Sana's birth that Zamir Ahmed Khan's health deteriorated to the extent that he was taken to Doctor Crocodile's clinic for the first time.

This happened some ten years ago.

Junkman Sharafat

Zamir Ahmed Khan was still in bed the morning he received word that Sharafat Miyan was at the house. After quickly realizing that this wasn't the end of some bad dream but reality itself, he smoothed out the wrinkles in his clothes and stepped outside. The heat was stifling, as if the sun had never set the night before. The air was a furnace and the sky the color of dull ash.

Outside, Junkman Sharafat was sitting in his red Maruti leafing through some papers. When he saw Zamir, he got out of the car.

"We need to talk." He adopted a businesslike tone from the outset, not even bothering with the customary salaam. "I thought it would be best to pay you a visit in the morning."

With all the hustle and bustle of the traffic, it was hard to imagine that it was still morning. The road was packed with minibuses, three-wheelers, handcart pushers, and pedestrians. There seemed to be a competition between the heat of the sun and the movement of people, and it was only bound to intensify.

Zamir Ahmed Khan stood silent without concealing his displeasure.

"Did I wake you up?" Whether Sharafat Miyan was being sarcastic or not was a subtle distinction Zamir didn't feel the need to know. "Anyway, with this weather, you may as well call early morning afternoon."

"It's not like you can change my daily routine by lecturing me in the street!" he said, irked. Sharafat Miyan's turning up was an unwelcome surprise Zamir Ahmed Khan was in no way prepared for. The idea of inviting him in was unpleasant enough, never mind sitting down and having a chat. What could he do? Sharafat Miyan stood before him as if all means of escape were blocked. "Come in," Zamir finally said, giving up.

"Anyway, what right do I have to change your thinking," Sharafat Miyan said with false humility as he climbed the stairs, surreptitiously giving the first floor a once-over. To keep vigilant and inspect everything in exacting detail wherever he went was one of his hallmark traits. "You educated people have your own ways of seeing the world. We're ignoramuses! How could anything I say be of use to you?"

"It would have saved us a lot of trouble if you'd thought along these lines nine years ago," Zamir Ahmed Khan said, turning up the fan and making space for Sharafat Miyan to sit on the divan. "Would you like tea or something cold?"

"Thanks, I just had breakfast," Sharafat Miyan took a deep breath as he subjected the room to a detailed examination. "But I'd be happy to have a cup of tea with you. Take your time, wash up, and then come sit with me. Is Rahat Biya downstairs?"

Zamir Ahmed Khan didn't respond but scurried into the bathroom. Why the hell did that bastard show up? He couldn't let go of the question. After having vanished without a trace for so long, what could possibly be the reason for Sharafat to suddenly turn up like this? It was idiotic to think that the man would do anything without his self-interest in mind—Zamir had already made that mistake in the past. Surely there was some hidden agenda or ulterior motive in his visit, just as there had been nine years ago when the Treasure Trove wasn't yet a reality but still a hazy scheme in Sharafat Miyan's mind. The kind of scheme that according to Bhai Miyan had enabled Sharafat Miyan to lead Zamir Ahmed Khan up the garden path.

After Abba's death, Sana's birth, and the first time Zamir Ahmed Khan had been taken to the doctor, a period came when he did little and thought a lot. He thought about the light and shadows that played in his head, expanding and contracting, he thought about the void growing in his being, he ruminated about the possibility of whirling around in confusion and plummeting into an abyss. He wanted to once again comprehend the place of man, paradise, and god in his life. Rahat, Bhai Miyan, and Vivek had urged him to finish his degree, and, after giving serious thought to it, he'd even taken some concrete steps in that direction. But it was all for show, and he knew that the unfinished chapter of the engineering degree was already closed to him forever. It was during that time, and before the Treasure Trove really took off, that Sharafat Miyan for his part had begun to rope him in for his future project. What happened was that Sharafat Miyan descended on the house every few days under the pretext of asking about his health, sometimes bringing fruit, sweets, or a toy for little Sana. He sat and chatted for hours about his plans, repeatedly urging and insisting that Zamir Ahmed Khan join him in all of this.

"You must understand," he repeated his proposal, with fervent enthusiasm, "I'm thinking of this line of work with your potential in mind. The honest truth is that old furniture and junk has allowed me to prosper. By the grace of Allah, you can make a living even out of this. But the times are changing, Sahib, and we have to be inventive. There's plenty of scope for progress, and scope to really do something in the city nowadays. Those who don't take advantage of this are unlucky indeed. And here you are, still chasing after this degree business, when the fun you could be having working with me is worth more than a hundred degrees."

Without understanding the ins and outs of business, Zamir Ahmed Khan, simply by observing Sharafat Miyan's earnestness, began to convince himself at some point that he was entering into the messy world of business only on account of Sharafat's shining example.

Then one day, along with sweets, Sharafat brought the happy news that a deal was as good as done for a shop in the market, and it was time for Zamir Ahmed Khan to take the final step.

"I've told you from the beginning that I don't have any business experience or the right disposition," he said to Sharafat Miyan after congratulating him on the shop. "Do you think it's a smart move to put faith in me and to make plans and invest money?"

"Leave that to me," Sharafat Miyan beamed, and then put to good use one of the few English sayings he repeated by rote like the Kalma. "*No risk, no play!* Not every business is created equal. Some people are destined for the small time, while others are meant for bigger and better things. I'm here for the little jobs and odds and ends while you shall accept the responsibility of being the boss."

Zamir Ahmed Khan realized full well that these sweet words were designed to flatter, but, absent any proof, why consider Sharafat Miyan guilty? It's also possible that by then Zamir Ahmed Khan was already operating under the assumption that he'd been born in the world destined not for the small time but for bigger and better things. The only thing was that the opportunity hadn't yet presented itself.

"Will I really be able to do something?" he asked Sharafat Miyan in earnest, sharing the doubts and fears that had been growing inside. "Leave aside everything else, but considering the mental state I'm in?"

"It's far more difficult to mount the elephant than to ride it!" Sharafat Miyan said to Zamir Ahmed Khan, using the sales pitch skills that had helped him prosper as a seller of junk. "The elephant is waiting for your 'yes' and your humble servant here is eager to be the ladder that helps you mount it. What are you afraid of? Once you really dig into the work, the thought of being ill will vanish from your mind."

Still undecided, he went with Sharafat Miyan to see the shop, although as far as he was concerned, it didn't matter whether he saw it or not. The most important thing about the shop was that, besides being quite spacious, it was close to his house, and could easily be reached on foot. Then, bit by bit, he developed an interest in the decorations and design of the store, so much so that he truly did forget about his illness. Then, after working day and night for months, came the grand opening of the Treasure Trove—it was after the Emergency had been lifted, after Congress had been swept away in the elections, and the Janata Dal had come into power at both the central and state levels. Some state minister acquaintance of Sharafat Miyan's officiated the grand opening, sometime in the middle of 1978. A full nine years ago . . .

When Zamir returned to the room carrying the tea tray, Sharafat Miyan had put on his glasses and was busy leafing through the files he'd brought.

"Thank you," he said, taking a cup and peering at Zamir Ahmed Khan over the frame of his glasses. "Can it get any hotter, Sahib? It's been like a furnace since early morning. Oh, yes, I was inquiring about Rahat Biya," he said, taking in the spicy aroma of the tea as if it held the answer to her whereabouts.

"If you'd let me know beforehand that you were coming, I would've asked her to be here. For now, allow me to be of service to you!"

"May your enemies be of service!" Sharafat Miyan said, pinching his earlobes in a little performance of humility. "Actually, given what I've come for, I was hoping she would join us."

"To begin with," Zamir Ahmed Khan sounded put off, "I don't know your intentions in paying me a visit today. And as for Rahat, she's definitely not here."

Junkman Sharafat quietly sipped his tea. After all these years, his physical appearance hadn't changed. He had begun to wear safari suits made from expensive fabric. And now he was smoking cigarettes, not just bidis. The same oil-slathered hair, kajal around the eyes, and the same neglectfully cultivated three-day stubble. True, in the meantime his family had flourished and his holdings increased—he'd bought a plot of land here and a house there, and he'd traded in his old scooter for a new Maruti. But the real transformation was seen in his son Salamat, who in no time at all began to outdo young aristocrats in giving attention to everything from clothing to shoes to cologne. He tried to improve his accent by watching English and American movies on the VCR, he played Western music, and behind closed doors practiced dancing. The day was not far off when he would offer his opinions on literature and poetry, only in order to impress customers of the Treasure Trove! Salamat, to be honest, had attained this sophistication by taking Zamir Ahmed Khan as his guru and role model—but soon far surpassed the guru. And maybe what appeared artificial and false to Zamir Ahmed Khan today might seem real and true to the world tomorrow. Zamir Ahmed Khan might become the lie, and Junkman Sharafat and son the truth!

"I'd prefer there to be a third party to witness whatever the two of us end up discussing, someone who can decide who's right and who's wrong," Sharafat Miyan said, dropping the chatty tone and getting down to business. "After all, how long can things go on like this!"

"What things?" Zamir Ahmed Khan said, angrily putting the cup of tea down on the table. "Excuse me, yaar, but I'm not some lackey of yours you can come whining to about your work whenever you want and then make threats."

"Talk about the pot calling the kettle black!" Sharafat Miyan said sarcastically, "I just want to settle this whole business once and for all."

"Settle what?" Zamir Ahmed Khan's irritation grew by the second. "Look, yaar, my health's not good, so don't make it worse. I don't need to settle anything! If you're so fond of witnesses, where were they before? What's the point now?"

"One mistake can hardly be remedied by another," Sharafat Miyan said in a controlled tone. "If we have a witness this time, at least you won't complain about our discussion."

"And what's there to discuss?" Zamir Ahmed Khan asked in anger and surprise. "Is there anything left to say?"

"You may have said everything you wanted to say," Sharafat Miyan said tensely. "But I should also be given the chance to present my case before others."

"What do you mean?" Zamir Ahmed Khan's surprise and anger both grew. "First you tell me to not come to work for a few days and then you disappear just like that as if we'd never known each other! Then you go around complaining to all and sundry about how useless I am, what time I get up in the morning, what time I go to bed at night, how I work, how I behave, only to prove that I'm the most worthless human being in the whole wide world! Have I ever said anything to anyone?"

"It's not just you, your older brother also goes around telling anyone who'll listen that Sharafat Miyan ruined Zamir. That Sharafat Miyan made his fortune on Zamir's back and didn't give a damn about him. Can you give me one example of something I did that could be construed as harming you? I've always given preference to you over my own son Salamat and even over myself, so much so that I made you the undisputed, black-and-white master of the store."

"Sure!" Zamir Ahmed Khan said, vexed. "Now it's my fault that I only got the black parts."

"Whatever you chose, it was your choice!" Sharafat Miyan said sarcastically. "In any case, there's no difference between black and white when you're not even conscious."

Zamir Ahmed Khan grew silent.

"I've told you before not to interfere with my personal life," Zamir Ahmed Khan said meekly.

"That's always been the problem with you," Sharafat Miyan said, feeling he was getting the upper hand by keeping up the attack. "You had no idea where the work ended and where your personal life began."

Sharafat Miyan continued to talk, and as he listened to the undulations of his voice, a face began to take shape before him—the face of Vasima Begum.

Vasima Begum

She was a beautiful woman, about Zamir Ahmed Khan's age, and she first came to the Treasure Trove to browse and buy some furniture some one and a half years after it had opened. She asked him to visit her house because she wanted to have wall-to-wall carpeting installed, and was also interested in wallpaper. The house was a big bungalow right beside the lake, surrounded by spacious lawns and guarded by various breeds of barking, biting dogs—this he found out when he arrived. He also found out that Vasima Begum was a widow and that her only son was studying in an out-of-town boarding school. She lived alone with her servants in the bungalow.

After one or two visits to her place, Zamir Ahmed Khan came to understand that Vasima Begum wasn't half as interested in buying things at the Treasure Trove as she was in using them to sell off some of her expensive items and belongings. She was getting ready to emigrate to the U.S., where other relatives of hers had settled. She was an educated, intelligent, and attractive woman, aside from being a grieving widow. Zamir Ahmed Khan had entrusted Sharafat Miyan with the responsibility of conducting business with Vasima Begum, while he had taken it upon himself to lend her sympathy and love.

His relationship with Vasima Begum was the kind that people from average middle-class families—to which Zamir Ahmed Khan certainly belonged—dream of all their lives, and one they perhaps bequeath to their offspring after they're gone. The Shoreline was the name of the bungalow where Vasima Begum sat sadly and made plans to settle in the U.S. after her heart had been shipwrecked. Zamir Ahmed Khan was actively involved in these plans for a full year. Vasima Begum, who had a degree in psychology, concluded after her first analysis of Zamir Ahmed Khan that he wasn't happy with his wife. He thought it wise to neither confirm nor deny this assessment. Rather, as he listened, he encouraged with meek and hollow laughter her misconception that she wasn't on the wrong track at all and that truly he suffered at the hands of his wife. Why? It was the first time the body of a woman other than his wife appeared to be within his grasp. And such a shapely body at that.

And that's how Zamir Ahmed Khan innocently gave Vasima Begum the chance to think as she wished, as he regularly spent most evenings at the Shoreline, despite being well aware of the danger that gradually she'd begun to include him in all her plans.

"I have a degree," she reassured him. "There are sponsors in the U.S. You have no idea of the opportunities that'll come your way once you leave this kind of environment behind. Show some courage and make up your mind."

While it is true that he never made any promises to Vasima Begum, it was equally true that he didn't disabuse her of her assumptions. Sometimes he played along with her plans for the future, while at other times he thought it best to sigh or keep quiet or give a little laugh, whatever was most convenient. While Zamir Ahmed Khan had started a ledger of love and allure with Vasima Begum, Sharafat Miyan was busy drawing up a list of the valuable items in her bungalow and looking for potential clients he could haggle with. These two different kinds of risk and speculation were accompanied by a growing physical attraction between Zamir and Vasima. Teased and tormented, Zamir Ahmed Khan expected something to happen very soon.

Until that winter evening, slowly fading into night. Zamir Ahmed Khan had waited for this moment, this instant, without knowing what the next one would have in store. It was a Sunday night when he arrived at the Shoreline, and Vasima Begum summoned him upstairs to her quarters. It wasn't as if Zamir Ahmed Khan and Vasima Begum hadn't had any physical contact before that evening, but it'd been of a different kind. Up until then, what had happened was that after some flirting with Vasima Begum, petting in some secluded corner, Zamir Ahmed Khan would reach home with a deep, fiery urge that he'd extinguish with Rahat, impatiently waiting for the moment when he'd be able to do the same with Vasima Begum. As he climbed the stairs to the second floor that night, he had no idea that the moment he'd been waiting for lay only a few steps ahead. He saw Vasima Begum standing in the dim light of the veranda, dressed in black, staring at the fog over the pond. He went up to her. Instead of the usual perfume, there was the scent of amber and incense coming from where she stood. Zamir Ahmed Khan asked her how she was and Vasima Begum cordially invited him to sit down on the deck chair and again began to look for something in the sulfury mist wafting over the surface of the pond.

She turned around and sat down in the other chair. "Exactly three years ago today," she said in a solemn voice, "my husband's plane crashed . . ."

Zamir Ahmed Khan was at a loss for words.

"You must have loved him deeply," he said after a moment's silence.

"What is love, anyway?" Vasima Begum was briefly caught off guard, and then said with a sober smile, "For god's sake, don't give me the *Love Story* answer, 'Love means never having to say you're sorry.' I'm sad enough as it is."

"Why?"

"Because we'd had a fight before he got on the flight he never returned from, and I'd made up my mind to ask him for forgiveness when he came back."

"Maybe you wouldn't have done so if he'd come back."

"What would that prove? That I loved him? That's not what I meant to say, I merely asked, what is love."

"Did your parents arrange the marriage?" Until then Zamir Ahmed Khan had never talked with Vasima Begum about her married life.

"I would still have gone along with it," Vasima Begum said with resignation. "But the marriage was my choice, call it a love marriage if you like. During these three lonely years, I've unsuccessfully tried to understand how a feeling like love that's bound up with passion can become like a prison and lose all meaning."

Why, then, this black attire, this burning of amber and incense, and atmosphere of mourning? An irritated Zamir Ahmed Khan wanted to ask Vasima Begum but remained silent. There was much to like about Vasima Begum from what he knew about her so far. While her habit of analyzing things occasionally put him off, it was still tolerable. In any case, Zamir Ahmed Khan wasn't in the mood to go down memory lane with Vasima Begum any further. Despite all her attractiveness, this was one of those moments when Vasima Begum came off as artificial and contrived. He ignored this thought and decided to just have a good time.

"Did you become disillusioned with your husband for some particular reason? Or did it just happen of its own accord, over time?" he found himself asking though he wasn't really interested.

"Both are true," Vasima Begum sighed. "He did have ties to Bhopal, but I met him in Bombay at my sister's. Her husband is a famous architect, and now they both live in the U.S. We saw each other for a little while and went out to dinner in hotels, and then we became engaged. I wanted to tell my future husband several times before we got married about the life I'd lived so far, because something had happened I didn't want to keep secret from him. A love affair that ended with scandal. Despite my insistence, he always brushed off the topic saying he was interested in our future, not my past. This made me respect him even more, since he never gave me a chance to tell him what I had to say, despite my pleas. After our engagement and a courtship of two and a half months, we were married. And then, can you guess what happened after the wedding?" Vasima Begum continued sourly.

"Your husband objected to your not being a virgin? He called you names? He wanted to know the name of the man you'd been with?" Zamir Ahmed Khan replied wearily as if he'd heard the story many times before.

"No!" Vasima Begum laughed coarsely, "the first thing he told me in private after the wedding was that he knew every last little thing about my past. He recounted the scandal to me in detail and emphasized that while some people continued to doubt whether it was true or false, he knew his information was correct. Before we started our physical relationship, he warned me that from now on I'd have to be very cautious and careful. The threatening words he used and the moment he'd chosen to raise the issue seemed like blackmail to me. We were married, sure, but after what he said it wasn't possible to start a normal husband-wife relationship, and we never did. I did as I pleased in order to make him jealous and try his patience, and that started an endless series of arguments. Time went on, a child was born, then three years ago on this very day, he died in a plane crash. I was left behind to pick up the pieces of my life and ask god for forgiveness."

As Vasima Begum went on, Zamir Ahmed Khan began to wonder how thick the fog was by now on the pond and how much moonlight he'd be able to see. He was getting a little peeved. He was interested in Vasima Begum for one reason, but right now she was sitting in front of him, the personification of gloom. Did he have to spend his whole life figuring out her secrets? A photo album was lying open on the coffee table, and the face of her husband, a stranger to Zamir, examined the surroundings. A stranger to Zamir Ahmed Khan, true, but known to the bungalow's walls and ceilings and servants and dogs, who would have been well acquainted with the sound of his footsteps, the tone of his voice, and the way he breathed in his sleep.

"What do you even call such a relationship?" Vasima Begum got up from her chair. "Sometimes I'm amazed I stayed with him so many years. Why didn't I try for a divorce? Maybe I thought other men wouldn't be any different. And then I have my own limitations that not everyone understands. This whole country doesn't suit me and neither does the way of life here."

"So you think men and women in other countries are any different?" Zamir Ahmed Khan said halfheartedly.

"You and I are not like them," Vasima Begum took his hand and got up. "We can make a fresh start together."

Holding his hand, Vasima Begum led him to her bedroom. She disappeared and soon reappeared wearing a baby doll and sat down next to him on the bed. Then she suddenly got up and went to the large picture on the wall, turned it to face the wall, and came back to the bed. Zamir Ahmed Khan's guess that it was a picture of her late husband would prove correct in the coming days as he was able to spend more memorable time with Vasima Begum there in her bedroom.

And this first experience of being with a woman who wasn't his wife! How should he remember it? A sense of boredom? Suffocation? Or the kind of pain felt when a scab covering a half-healed wound is torn off? The entire time Zamir Ahmed Khan couldn't shake the feeling that the husband lay captive in the room, bound by rope, and everything Zamir Ahmed Khan and Vasima Begum did was intended to cause him the utmost torment. Or that the husband hovered over them, whip in hand, directing them what to do. Or even that Zamir Ahmed Khan, hidden in a corner of Vasima Begum's spacious bedroom, was masturbating as he watched her and the dead husband have intercourse. But even in these uncomfortable moments he could tell the difference between Rahat's and Vasima Begum's bodies and their way of making love. He knew Rahat's each and every move like the palm of his hand, while Vasima Begum's remained mysterious like the inside of a closed fist. Rahat had let her body go after getting married and giving birth to Sana. Spending a little time with her husband, and usually at his request, had simply become one of Rahat's many domestic chores from which no novelty or variety could be expected. In contrast, Vasima Begum's body was one of the most soft and supple things Zamir Ahmed Khan had ever had the chance to touch in his life. And she had insight into the fine points of male anatomy that could never be expected from Rahat. She was uninhibited in a way that suggested a life lived differently. But Zamir Ahmed Khan would get a detailed sense of these facts only in the days and nights to come. This first time, an irritation and anger took hold of him, and in this fever he had tried to wrest and break Vasima Begum's body, while somewhere deep inside a voice warned him that this woman was a fraud and a fake, so don't ever come under her spell. He lay in Vasima Begum's arms, ashamed of himself, tried to catch his breath, and finally, leaving all his joy and relief in her care, he returned home, into Rahat's arms.

"Look," Zamir Ahmed Khan turned to Sharafat Miyan, returning to the moment. "There's a misunderstanding from your side. I haven't complained about you to anyone, justified or not. I don't regret that our association is over and I don't demand anything from you. Have it in writing if you want!"

"What would be the point of that?" Sharafat Miyan said in a business-like tone. "Actually, your friends and family should already be aware of this, whether it's your older brother or your dear Vivek. I also enjoy a measure of respect in this bazaar where we're sitting. If Rahat Sahiba isn't at home, you'll have to inconvenience Bhai Sahib a little, but let's get this over and done with one way or another!"

"Don't waste your time pushing me." Another wave of anger ran through Zamir Ahmed Khan's body from head to toe. "Just because that's what you want doesn't mean your dirty deeds can be sorted out. My not wanting to deal with you doesn't mean I'm weak. You're the one who'll end up in dire straits."

"If I considered you weak," Sharafat Miyan sighed, controlling his voice, "why would I have come all the way here? I came here thinking that if there's a misunderstanding between us, we'd sort it out. Forget about the business, you can start something on your own tomorrow, you don't need me for it. In any case, our association isn't restricted to business. Even if we part ways, we can still wish each other well."

"I couldn't care less what you do in the future," Zamir Ahmed Khan said in a harsh though weary tone, "and I'm not holding my breath that we'll wish each other well. Whatever we could have done for each other we've already done. And I don't want an angry me to take any actions that might harm you and that I'd regret later."

"I hear what you're saying," Sharafat Miyan said in a practiced voice. "And I appreciate your feelings. But for my own information I'd like to ask, what kind of harm could a person do to me, a person who until yesterday was my well-wisher and companion? You're near and dear to me, you're threatening me because you're angry, but it's not like we need more ene-mies in the world. May I please be apprised of my own weaknesses so I can face them when the time comes?"

As far as Zamir Ahmed Khan was concerned, every single word uttered by Sharafat Miyan oozed with contempt.

"I don't know about the rest of the world," he said with venom. "But if I felt like it, I could have your store shut down. All I have to do is send a list of clients and artifacts to a few government departments and you'll get caught up in a never-ending legal headache."

Sharafat Miyan sat, patiently tilting his head back and forth.

"You'll recall," Sharafat said sarcastically, "that when you began, you were taken on as a partner."

"What do you mean, taken on? You just said a few words, and that made me partner."

"Are you threatening to punish me for my mistake?"

"Nothing of the sort." Zamir fanned himself with the bottom flap of his kurta. "All I'm saying is that if you're trying to harass me, it won't turn out well for you. If you're operating under the false assumption that you can ruin me by revealing my relations with Vasima Begum, then forget about it! My wife knows all about my affairs and so do all the other people who have an interest in whether I live or die."

It was a bald-faced lie that must have escaped Zamir Ahmed Khan's lips in the heat of the moment. Whether Vasima Begum or any of the other women who would come and go from his life, he tried his best to hide them all from Rahat. The main reason, as he saw it, was not wanting to hurt Rahat or cause her pain.

"It's none of my business how far and wide the fame of your activities has spread!" Sharafat Miyan said, irritated. "But, miyan, I've also had to pay the price for your dalliances. And I almost lost my reputation on account of this Vasima Begum of yours!"

After this first painful experience with Vasima Begum, he settled into a routine of gaining pleasure by inflicting pain on himself, going along with her proposal to migrate to America and leave his wife and young daughter behind. Without having said a definitive yes or no, Zamir Ahmed Khan kept spending his evenings at the Shoreline. It was then that Rahat, out of the blue, became pregnant. As the birth of their younger daughter, Saba, drew near, Zamir Ahmed Khan began to panic at the thought that his lie might be exposed. How could he possibly face Vasima Begum after the birth of his child! When speaking to her about Rahat, he'd suggested he no longer touched his wife or even looked at her! How would Vasima Begum react?

After Saba was born, they encountered each other only once. Vasima Begum, who in the meantime had cried her heart out to Sharafat Miyan behind his back and had even threatened to kill Zamir Ahmed Khan, treated him like a complete stranger. She had come to the Treasure Trove to settle her accounts with Sharafat Miyan. Before her visit, Sharafat Miyan, who had kept Zamir Ahmed Khan fully apprised of Vasima Begum's anger, had implored him to leave the store for a little while, but he'd been stubborn and refused. He'd made a mistake, so he would face up to it, he declared valiantly. If this woman was able to shoot him, then let her go ahead! Amid this tense situation, Vasima Begum had stepped into the shop, ignored him completely, and had gone straight up to Sharafat Miyan. For about an hour she discussed her accounts with him, chatting and laughing, while Zamir Ahmed Khan, with all kinds of thoughts running through his head, anxiously paced the shop trying to find a pretext to talk with her. After her conversation with Sharafat Miyan, Vasima Begum very casually stood up, cast a farewell glance at the items throughout the store, and was on her way. Sharafat Miyan trailed behind, escorting her out.

Vasima Begum's indifference had dealt a great blow to Zamir Ahmed Khan. Relationships have to follow a certain cadence—if not friendship, then certainly enmity, he thought dejectedly. He had never expected this woman to act like a total stranger. In a way, his inkling that she was a fraud and a fake was bound to come true. The thought of seeing her or talking to her on the phone crossed his mind a few times, but his good judgment told him that this wasn't free of risk. After a while he heard, or rather Junkman Sharafat informed him, that Vasima Begum had sold her bungalow and moved to Bombay, and, in keeping with her plans, had then sold her estate and possessions and vanished to the U.S. It was nearly five years since all of this had happened.

A little later, Sharafat Miyan had left after handing over to Zamir Ahmed Khan the papers that formally detailed his dealings with the Treasure Trove. The calculation included all the various amounts that Zamir Ahmed Khan had deliberately taken out of the store's till, without Sharafat Miyan's knowledge, to cover his expenses. And the price of all the things he'd given Vasima Begum as presents from the shop while they were still seeing each other. The list included the small eleven-hundred-rupee antimony container that Zamir Ahmed Khan had given her as a present—after an unsuccessful search for it, it had ended up in the lost-items ledger. Later, Sharafat Miyan had drawn up a list of all the gifts, either by guessing or by taking advantage of Vasima Begum's anger and asking her directly. Within nine years he had amassed some two hundred thousand rupees in cash and kind from the Treasure Trove, which by all accounts was more than Sharafat Miyan or his son Salamat had earned from the store. After making him ride the elephant's back, Sharafat Miyan had paid the debt in full. If Zamir now had to walk on foot, so be it.

He spent hours trying to figure out to what extent the accounting was correct and how much incorrect. Could the price of this antimony container, which was very beautiful, no doubt, and god knows how old and made from god knows what kind of metal, really be eleven hundred rupees? It sure looked expensive, precisely the reason Zamir Ahmed Khan had decided to give it to Vasima Begum—but that expensive? And had he really helped himself to that much money from the Treasure Trove?

And yet, he realized on second thought, there was no way all the luxuries he'd indulged in back then would have come for free.

There was no way to win: whether the account was true or fabricated, he wasn't in a position to disprove Sharafat Miyan.

He collected the empty cups. When he came downstairs, Bhabhi had a message from Rahat—come to the house and see her.

Face-to-Face with Rahat

"What is it you want? Can you at least spell it out?"

"What's so complicated about what I'm saying that is so hard to understand?"

Zamir Ahmed Khan, in strange foolish straits, sat opposite Rahat. Once again it seemed impossible for him to grasp that no one had control over their fate. It was foolish to feel detached from the stream of destiny: you remain part of it, no matter what. Staying put at home was an existence just as much as trying to change the world. While nonexistence is also a form of existence. He sat across from Rahat at his in-laws' after such a long time, amazed that her health had improved instead of getting worse in the mean-time, or, as the saying goes, she looked as fresh as a daisy—yet another link in the chain of existence and nonexistence. Sana and Saba, who he'd been with moments earlier, were also happy here, sweet and loving toward their father, and busy doing their own thing. It was possible his in-laws had felt a similar way when they saw Zamir Ahmed Khan. Whether they did or not, nobody had said a word.

"I've never denied you anything," Zamir Ahmed Khan said with difficulty, "But . . ."

"But you also didn't do anything for us either!" Rahat's voice was sharp, dripping with sarcasm. "Better not go into detail now, since what had to happen, happened. What's to gain from rehashing the bitter past?"

"But," Zamir Ahmed Khan tried to finish his earlier sentence, "it's such a big and consequential decision. Have you really thought it through? Have you thought about the consequences for yourself and the girls?"

"Thought it through? I've spent my whole life thinking things through. In fact, wasted it," Rahat said in a tone filled with sorrow and spite. "Now maybe I'll get somewhere."

"But what about the girls . . . ?"

Zamir Ahmed Khan's question hovered over the silence like a shadow.

"Think about it," Rahat said. "What would be better than you assuming responsibility for the girls? They are your daughters, talk to them and see for yourself if you want."

"Me, just on my own . . ." He didn't finish the sentence. Silence again.

"Do you really think," after a brief respite Zamir Ahmed Khan resumed, now scowling, on the attack, "that I'm living the good life and have forgotten you and the girls? That I got rich and opened a bank account behind your back?'

"That's not what I said," Rahat's voice was now calm and collected. "And it's not because of us that this dream of yours didn't come true. You've lived your life the way you wanted, so why complain now?"

"You're the one who should complain, not me," Zamir Ahmed Khan conceded. "There's a lot I should have done but never managed, and it's all on display now right before your eyes. You must also be thinking that despite his good intentions this good-for-nothing hasn't really achieved anything. If you want to call me useless, I won't object. Still, I think your decision to divorce me is wrong and unjust."

"I have always done you wrong!" There was a threat in Rahat's tone filled with a postdecision coldness. "In asking you for forgiveness I want to take the path that leaves no room for complaints about each other, from either me or you."

"I don't have any complaints and don't have any right to complain!" Zamir Ahmed Khan made an angry gesture telling Rahat to shut up. "I can't believe you're serious when I listen to you! This talk of divorce sounds like a joke you came up with just because you're so angry."

"So my decision will reach you through legal means," Rahat said firmly. "I want us to reach an agreement without making a spectacle of ourselves. The rest is up to you."

Zamir Ahmed Khan sat there, stunned into silence.

The small barsati-like room on the third floor where they sat was covered by a roof made from asbestos sheets. On the open terrace in front of them an assortment of pots with dried and wilting plants was arranged haphazardly. The room hadn't been built the last time Zamir Ahmed Khan had come to the house, a long time ago. He used to come to the house regularly, alone or with Rahat, for many years after their wedding.

Gradually these visits were reduced to Eid, Bakra Eid, or other occasions of celebration and mourning, until finally, without any conscious decision, they stopped altogether. It wasn't as if he had any complaints or bones to pick with his in-laws, it was simply that this house, like ninety percent of places, was so different from the world of imagination Zamir Ahmed Khan inhabited that he'd almost forgotten all about its existence. The family elders certainly kept up regular visits to one another, whether Rahat's parents or Abba and Amma, and now Aapa, Bhai Miyan, and others. Rahat, for her part, had not forgotten her parents' place despite her responsibilities for her own family and in-laws, and regularly took part in everything that happened there, good or bad. Whenever Rahat had complained that Zamir Ahmed Khan didn't visit her parents' place, and she'd done so innumerable times, he would readily admit his guilt and assure her he'd visit in the near future. It was his way of putting things off. Over the past ten years, time and again he'd heard all the details from Rahat: which brother or sister had been married, how many children had been born, what they looked like, and what they were doing. And yet Zamir Ahmed Khan remained oblivious to it all. So when he arrived today at the house, and in light of the circumstances, he'd been given no more than a lukewarm welcome and then, led by Sana and Saba, found himself seated in that same room where he was now sitting face-to-face with Rahat, stunned and troubled. He'd arrived at sunset; he guessed it must be half past nine or ten by now. Geckos chased insects in the milky light of the fluorescent tubes. The pedestal fan's whirring filled his ears like the sound of a breeze.

Sana, carrying a tray with food, and Saba, with a glass and pitcher of water, entered the room.

"What's this?" he asked, surprised and irritated.

"Grandma sent this." The girls were frightened. "Please, Abba, have something to eat," Sana insisted.

"I'm sorry, beti," Zamir Ahmed Khan said softly, controlling his temper, "I have an upset stomach and can't eat right now."

His daughters stood there, one holding the tray, the other the glass and pitcher.

"I'm not going to eat, beti," he repeated firmly. "Take it back."

"Put it on the table," Rahat instructed the girls. "And I'll take the glass. Why don't you go back inside. What videotape did Uncle bring for you?"

"*Mr. India,*" Saba said eagerly, repeating the famous line from the movie, "'Mogambo khush hua!'"

"Amma, the tape isn't playing right," Sana said, making a face. "It's jumpy and blurry."

"Did you see the film at the cinema hall?" Zamir Ahmed Khan asked, trying to take part in the conversation.

"Yes, we did," Sana replied in a cool, formal tone. Perhaps she was angry at her father's sharp words a couple of minutes ago.

"See, I kept meaning to see it, but then it wasn't playing anymore," he said in an endearing way, trying to win over the girls. "So, what other good films are showing these days? Let's go and see one together."

Children never give up hope, no matter how many times they've been let down. Maybe because forgetting and forgiving come naturally to them. If they do remember, it's not to lay blame or take revenge but simply because their memory works well and because it hasn't yet recorded everything the world has added and subtracted. This state of being is the first incarnation of memory, and who would know better than Zamir Ahmed Khan how many different incarnations memory assumes as you grow older. In the future, his two daughters would come up with their own explanations of their father's behavior, sometimes in jest, sometimes judging him, but they'd never be able to fully grasp the complex reality of things. Maybe that's why the world chooses the path of least resistance, and reveres and worships this path under the guise of honesty and faith. Children have faith in adults up to a certain age and unquestioningly treat them as their gods. How else to explain that children trust what adults say despite having the rug pulled out from under them time and again?

His two daughters stood there silent, pensive.

"Have you ever taken them to the movies in your whole life?" Rahat shot him a biting remark. She turned to the girls. "Do you remember your father ever taking you to the movies?"

A gloomy pall spread over the girls' innocent faces.

"Well, I have," Zamir Ahmed Khan said, trying to hide from his predicament. "I'm not totally sure about Saba, but I've certainly taken Sana. I don't remember the name of the film. Anyway, you go and see movies with your grandma all the time. Tell me the name of a good film, and we'll go see it."

"Let them go downstairs," Rahat interrupted him again. "Everyone must be waiting for them to start the film."

"Actually, Abba, they aren't showing any good films these days," Sana said, trying to boost his morale, "but *Mr. India* is still up. Who told you it's not showing anymore?"

"Really? It's still running?" Zamir Ahmed Khan said with fake surprise. "Somehow I had the impression it was gone."

"We'll let you know as soon as something good is playing." This time his younger daughter, Saba, reassured him.

The girls left and he was again alone with Rahat.

"Why didn't you tell them to take the food back?" he snapped at her. "I'm not going to eat."

"Let it sit there," the anger that'd flared up in Rahat's voice while the children were there was gone now. "I'll take it back later."

"Have you really thought about this from each and every angle?" Returning to their earlier conversation, Zamir Ahmed Khan sounded even more resentful. "About not only living separately but also getting a divorce?"

"Yes, I've tried to."

"But how am I going to pay back your meher?"

"It's not you asking for the divorce, I'm the one asking for it. There's not the slightest need for you to worry about paying back the meher you owe me."

"Even if that's what the law says, I don't agree!"

"That's up to you."

"I'll tell Bhai Miyan that the part of the house that belongs to me should be given to you as your meher."

"It'd be better if you kept the other family members out of this. I didn't mention it even to my own parents."

"You must be out of your mind!" Zamir Ahmed Khan's anger rose. "It's divorce we're talking about, not some stroll in the park you can keep from your parents."

"I've asked for only one thing," Rahat's voice was controlled. "The rest I leave up to you. I've already told you about the meher. Since I'm the one asking for the divorce, I'm not entitled to it, and I'm not asking you for it."

"It's difficult as it is to labor under the burden of your kindness," Zamir Ahmed Khan said brusquely. "Enough. But can I ask you something?"

Rahat didn't respond.

"This idea of a divorce," Zamir Ahmed Khan tried to sound casual, "is there someone else you want to marry?"

She didn't answer, but despite all her efforts to keep her composure, Zamir Ahmed Khan could see how the expression on her face slowly changed, like wax being heated by a flame.

"Is that any of your business?" she replied in a now-meek voice that broke the silence. "I'm asking you for a divorce. In the future I'll do as I please. I'll try to fully carry out the responsibility for the girls as best I can, whatever hard work and effort it'll take. I'll tend to the family elders. And as for the rest, I'll try to find some purpose in life."

"Why do you need a divorce for that?" Zamir Ahmed Khan interrupted her. "You can do that anyway."

"Yes, I do need a divorce," Rahat was almost screaming at him. "I won't have to answer to anyone no matter what I do. And as for all the duties people expect me to fulfill, you won't be one of them since I can't get along with you anymore!"

"I can withdraw from your life," Zamir Ahmed Khan said in a supplicating tone. "Believe me, I won't get in your way at all."

"Who knows?" Rahat said, irritated. "Maybe I'll think about getting married again! Not only think about it, but do it!'

"That's a different story, and you have my word that if you come to that decision I will happily agree to a divorce. But not now, please! Please don't insist, if not for my sake, then for the children's. Children are so sensitive at this age and the slightest thing can totally throw their life out of whack. What's left for the two of us anymore? And I mean the two of us, even though I admit full responsibility for messing things up. The most precious years of our lives are already over. Why should the children be punished for the things we did? Whatever you say, I swear, whether you stay here or come back home, I won't do anything against your will. I won't even touch you, I won't even talk to you."

"Oh, really?" Rahat said mockingly, "as if you're conscious of what you're doing in the state you're in when you come home at night. You're not even aware that the girls have grown up, and here you are pleading on their behalf."

"It was different back then," Zamir Ahmed Khan implored. "You hadn't made a decision. Now I'll do whatever you want me to."

"Won't even touch me?" Rahat muttered in a venomous voice. "Is there any lack of women in the world to fool around with? Why the hypocrisy and pretense now? Just to keep up appearances? It's no secret how hollow and fake our relationship is. And since Abba and Amma are no longer with us, I don't have to pretend fearing I'll cause them pain."

"I'm not forcing you to do anything," Zamir Ahmed Khan said helplessly. "And I never wanted to cause you pain. I'll formally ask you for forgiveness for everything that happened if that's what you want."

"What's the point? You can't fix what's broken. Hell, you weren't even with your family the terrible night of the gas leak. While we were all out in the streets trying to save our lives, you couldn't even pry yourself away from your affairs. Had it been up to you, we all could have died that December night!"

This was true. But so were all of Rahat's complaints.

That December night, when a cloud of death hung over the city, Zamir Ahmed Khan's absence from home was proof of his indifference toward his family, and everyone who cared to know knew about it. He'd come up with an excuse for the sake of saying something, and in the pandemonium of the moment no deeper meaning had been assigned to his absence. But he had a hunch that sooner or later it would come out with full fury, and would lead to grave consequences.

Where was he and what was he doing on the night of December 2, some two and a half years ago?

December 2, 1984

It was a Sunday night, and he'd gone for a stroll and arrived at the home of a college friend. He was from Delhi and had come to Bhopal following a job transfer, and for the past five or six months had been living on his own in a small rented house. Zamir Ahmed Khan often spent his evenings there. The friend had left his family behind in Delhi with the hope that he'd be transferred back very soon. He'd found the rental with the help of Zamir Ahmed Khan, and the two reminisced about their college days whenever they got together in the evening. When on occasion a girl could be arranged, that particular kind of entertainment was also enjoyed. The friend was stunned when he realized the reach of Zamir Ahmed Khan's influence. He couldn't have imagined in his wildest dreams that the shy and bashful college lad who used to proclaim lofty ideals could be such a bad boy. The friend was awestruck at Zamir Ahmed Khan's accomplishments—the booze, the girls, the thriving business at the Treasure Trove—and time and again felt the need to curse his own useless degree, job, fate. Zamir Ahmed Khan in no time had become his role model and object of envy.

They'd made arrangements for hard liquor that night as well, and awaited the arrival of a new girl at half past eight. The pimp had nothing but praise for the lass—she was beautiful, young, from a good family, only in the business for fun, and on and on. Zamir Ahmed Khan and the friend waited for this mistress of virtues to arrive, their glasses full of liquor while the TV played in the background. The two friends talked about the assassination of Indira Gandhi and the anti-Sikh riots erupting all over the country. The friend had just come back from Delhi and was describing the scenes he'd witnessed there.

After things had ended with Vasima Begum, the fire burning in Zamir Ahmed Khan's heart for women other than his wife hadn't been extinguished. Time and experience had augmented his hope and desire that he might be able to experience an ecstasy and release with some woman, perhaps—a pleasant fantasy he associated with the act of sex, and the delights of which he'd heard people talk about and had read about extensively. This journey had led him to meet women of all shades of color, beauty, and character, sometimes in run-down houses and rooms in narrow alleyways, sometimes in the unfamiliar and strange yet less-sordid location of a hotel. In sum, this journey was a bitter and disappointing experience that he still couldn't make sense of. He'd well and truly tried as hard as he could to find some kind of meaning in his encounters with women, and had adopted all the "best practices" put forward by those in the know. As a result, drinking and spending part of the night with female strangers had become part of a routine since he'd parted ways with Vasima Begum. Up until that fateful night on December 2, 1984. He was drinking and talking with his friend as they waited for the girl to show up. It was almost nine. He began to worry. There was no need to worry for long: the pimp arrived with a healthy-looking woman wrapped in a warm shawl, and left saying he'd pick her up at midnight.

As it turned out, the young, beautiful girl from a good family they'd been waiting for had metamorphosed into a stout, middle-aged matron—this was enough for Zamir Ahmed Khan and the friend to lose all enthusiasm.

She's only for one night, Zamir Ahmed Khan silently consoled himself, we'll deal with it one way or another. He tried with glances to get this message across to the friend, who seemed terrified by the woman's physique. The buxom lady casually relieved herself of all unnecessary garments, lay down on the bed, and in spite of the cold, covered herself with no more than a thin sheet. She ignored the men's superfluous attempts at conversation and asked for a drink, then avoided their gaze as she put the bottle of straight whiskey to her lips and gulped half of it down. Half an hour later she was drunk—maybe she'd had something to drink earlier—and commenced with singing film songs at the top of her lungs. Zamir Ahmed Khan and the friend immediately wrote the night off and turned their attention to what the landlord and neighbors might think about the noise. They implored her to stop singing and to please speak softly while trying to think of a way to get rid of her. The friend ran off to fetch her an auto rickshaw while Zamir Ahmed Khan, with a mixture of pleading and threats, finally got her to put her clothes back on. The agreed-upon sum was paid to the lady and rickshaw driver, and it was about a quarter to eleven by the time this divine calamity departed with a "Ta-ta! See you soon," oblivious to their expletives.

The two men's high had long since vanished. By chance, there was more liquor in the house. The friend poured two more glasses and recited a couplet: "Why is the world of my heart forlorn, has someone gone and left it behind?" They made light of their embarrassment, went over what had happened, kept on drinking and cracking each other up so much that they lost track of time and how much they'd drunk. After eating the meal the friend had cooked, it was finally time for Zamir Ahmed Khan to head home. It was past one. The friend was concerned about the cold and the unlikeliness of finding an auto rickshaw and insisted he stay the night; Zamir Ahmed Khan for some reason accepted his suggestion without a fuss. Who could have known that night that a calamity even more deadly than the stout, middle-aged fiasco awaited them, batting her eyelashes in welcome? They'd barely shut their eyes when the landlord banged on the door and told them a gas tank had exploded at Union Carbide and that everyone's life was in danger and that they must run for their lives. Zamir didn't believe it, but there was an acrid, pungent smell in the air. The friend hurriedly fetched his scooter and told Zamir to hop on the back. The scene in the streets was enough to convince anyone: countless people, hundreds, thousands, poured forth like a raging river, coughing with a lifeless voice. Most were on foot while others crammed on and into any kind of vehicle imaginable. Home and family flashed before Zamir Ahmed Khan's eyes—Amma, Rahat, Sana, Saba, Bhai Miyan, Bhabhi, the nephews—like the vision of paradise must have flashed in front of Adam's after he'd been banished from the garden. While Zamir Ahmed Khan thought about his family, the friend gestured to the mass of people fleeing. In a split second, seated behind the friend, he tried to get as far away from the city as possible to save his own life.

What took place in the city later on is a history unto itself.

"You were the one who told me not to dredge up old stories," a shame-faced Zamir Ahmed Khan said, unable to look Rahat in the eye. "I ran away that night to save my life like you and everyone else. I simply didn't have a scooter to come and rescue you. Even if I did, I don't think I was brave or strong enough to make it all the way home in the chaos. How many times have I declared to you how ashamed I am! And after that night I haven't spent a single night away from home."

This wasn't entirely true. In many ways, the night of December 2, 1984, signaled the end of the chapter titled "My Experiments with Other Women" in Zamir Ahmed Khan's life, whether as a consequence of the gas leak or some other reason. Yet he went on believing that Rahat was completely unaware of his doings from beginning to end. Was he wrong? The way Rahat was talking to him now: if she knew, then how much?

"I'll say it again," Zamir Ahmed Khan was growing weary of the conversation dragging on for no reason. "I won't force you to change your mind. The most ironic thing is that our family elders arranged our wedding date on the tenth of May. It was on that same day in 1857 that the revolt that is now considered the first war of independence began in the Meerut cantonment. It's no surprise that a wedding taking place on that day should turn into such a debacle! Anyway, getting divorced at our age will make people laugh at us rather than be shocked. Here's my friendly advice, don't let the world turn you into a laughingstock!"

"Enough," Rahat replied firmly. "No more. I can't bear any more and I'm not ready to give up and die. For the sake of our daughters if nothing else. And I don't want to go back to that house either. If you care about the children at all, listen to what I'm about to say. They are your children, after all. You've got everything you need and you can have whatever you want. People like me are the truly powerless ones. I can't leave this relationship up in the air. Divorce means divorce. You shouldn't doubt my intentions when I talk about divorce and admit that I'm helpless."

"You say I often come home at night stumbling and half conscious and even act rudely. That's only half the truth. Have I never tried to make you and the girls laugh, make you happy? How many times have I fallen at your feet and asked for forgiveness? I would've tried to quit if you'd objected more strongly to the drinking. It's not so difficult to stop."

"Well, you wanted me to start, too!" Rahat sneered. "I tried to forbid whatever I could and as much as I could, whether drinking or the other business. I carried on with the hope that you'd change your ways. In the long time we've spent together I've had plenty of time to make sense of things, take a step back, forget certain episodes, or think things over. I haven't made this decision because of some particular event or something you said, and therefore it's impossible for me to change my mind."

"You can't be serious."

"That's what you think."

"Nothing I say might change your mind?"

Rahat shook her head.

"Still," Zamir Ahmed Khan said in a conciliatory manner, "think about what I've proposed for a couple of days. There's still the saying, 'No one's seen water coming out of a stone.' The mere existence of the proverb suggests there's always hope, that the impossible might become possible. Try to consider what I've said with an open heart and don't dwell on my failings. Perhaps there's still some way for Zamir Ahmed Khan to be saved. I'm not going to force you, I'll accept whatever decision you make. Let's see each other again . . ."

He stood up. Rahat remained seated and didn't respond.

"Okay," Zamir Ahmed Khan swallowed hard. "I'm off."

"Here, have some food," Rahat said softly.

"No, I'm not hungry at all," Zamir Ahmed Khan said, his voice sounding to him as if it were coming from a far-off place. "Give my salaams to Amma, I'm in no state to meet with anyone right now. Please show me out."

Rahat switched on the staircase light on the other side of the rooftop terrace and slowly began descending the stairs. Zamir Ahmed Khan followed behind and came to the outer door of the house. He felt for an instant that with the next step he might lose his balance and fall. Then slowly he stepped out of the house.

July 1987

Zamir Ahmed Khan was sitting at an elevation from where he could easily see the land stretching out in front of him far and wide. To his left and farther in the distance was flat land and a range of rocky hills, while some hundred feet beyond lay the shore of the lake still brimming with water even after it'd endured the cold and the heat.

"That's the deepest part of the lake over there."

Vivek had arrived at sunset and pointed this out to him after quickly taking in the surroundings. "Obviously, there's less water now than during the rainy season, but there's still plenty. It's actually very good for the land. Anyway, we don't need it since now with the three tube wells we don't need to go down so deep for water. The people drilling the well were surprised how plentiful it is. Even if we didn't find water we'd still be able to use the lake for irrigation with a little know-how and wheeling and dealing."

"How much land is there?" he asked Vivek.

"Probably around eleven or twelve acres. I got a great price."

"How much?"

"After all the paperwork and legal stuff it came out to be twenty-two thousand per acre. It's barely been six months since I bought it and they're already willing to pay fifty thousand per acre in this area."

"How can that be?" Zamir Ahmed Khan sensed that Vivek was trying to impress him with the fake bragging. Every day now Vivek's behavior gave him that feeling.

"For one thing, we were the very first to buy land here," Vivek replied self-assuredly. "The other thing was that the seller needed money and was also involved in court battles that he didn't have the cash or connections to resolve. Also, six months ago no one, let alone me, had any idea how development might play out on this side of the city. The development project was finalized only four or five months ago. It hasn't even been formally announced by the government yet."

"So it was a gamble."

"A gamble?" Vivek asked, taken aback. "I didn't buy the land with the hope of making a buck. I certainly thought, though, that if I had to sell it in a pinch, I'd at least be able to recoup what I paid. I've always told you I don't want to spend my retirement cooped up in a room reading autobiographies, but instead want to be out in the open air, in the fields, on the threshing floor, digging into the soil, water, manure. Who knows, maybe these things are passed on from generation to generation. Whatever else you may say, it's the blood of Punjab that flows through my veins."

"Sure," Zamir Ahmed Khan's voice hardened. "Just like all these Afghani Khan Sahibs in the city who grace the paan shops, from kings to paupers from one generation to the next, you never know."

"I don't agree," Vivek said, laughing in order to change the topic. "It's not like you can pin everything on past generations."

Zamir Ahmed Khan felt the strong urge right then and there to share the matter of selling his part of Abba and Amma's house. Give me only fifty thousand rupees, he wanted to say to Vivek, so that I can be free of the obligation of paying back Rahat's meher. The house may sell for slightly more, but I'm not interested in the extra money. Let's go, I'll sign all the paperwork in the presence of Bhai Miyan as early as tomorrow. He reckoned that Vivek would think of this whole divorce affair as a joke. Or if he took it seriously, he would advise him to come to some kind of understanding with Rahat and explain to him that his responsibility toward the two girls was a far more important obligation than Rahat's meher, and furthermore that Zamir Ahmed Khan couldn't just run away from the facts of life like this, and he shouldn't.

"Honestly," he said to Vivek in an animated voice, "I never imagined such a beautiful place so close to the city. There's such a feeling of openness even when it's really humid and muggy. What's the land like, and what do you plan to do with it?"

"Half of it is excellent farmland, the rest is uneven and rocky and there's a hillock. Once there's a chance to do something there seriously, I'll think about it, but for now I've marked the boundaries and put up a wire fence and left it to be looked after by some servants. These twenty-one tall trees are all mango, though it's a different matter that this year there was almost no fruit. There's also rose apple, kabeet, three wood-apple trees, and an orchard full of guava trees, some forty altogether. All this came with the land. We've also planted some new trees and will do even more in the coming days and we've ordered some rare fruit and flower shoots for grafting, we're just waiting for the right weather and time. There were no accommodations to speak of, so work's been going on to build a two-room house with a kitchen and bathroom and I hope the work will be done soon, provided the rains cooperate. Then you can come and stay for a couple of weeks, a month, however long you like, for a change of scenery. Oh, I forgot to mention the animals. I'm also planning to start a small dairy farm with Jersey cows."

Zamir Ahmed Khan was getting tired of Vivek's enthusiasm and having to listen to all the ins and outs. "Poultry farming is all the rage these days," he said. "As soon as you leave town, no matter which way you go, you come across poultry farms with fancy new names every step of the way. Just like during Emperor Ashoka's time, or so I've heard, when they used to plant shady trees everywhere for travelers to sit under."

"That's a different line of work," Vivek explained without picking up on the irony. "And, pardon me, it's not an idea I like at all. If you think along those lines, there's no end to the work. To be honest, I don't have time to do anything here myself, the servants will be in charge of everything. I'll look in on things whenever I have time."

The sun was about to set when they'd arrived, and a few listless clouds scattered throughout the sky looking sad and forlorn. Vivek had reminded him that it was a full-moon night and that they'd soon be sitting and talking under the moonlight. His servants had set up a table and chairs, food and drink had been fetched from the car and laid out on the table, and on Vivek's instructions bottles of beer had been put into a tin bucket filled with ice. Vivek had gone off to pay the servants and inspect the progress on the building, leaving Zamir Ahmed Khan to himself. Sitting there, he tried to guess how far his home was and in which direction. It had barely taken them twenty minutes by car to arrive, but the landscape on this side of town had turned out to be totally unfamiliar and disorienting. He'd definitely passed through here a couple of times on the highway, but he'd had no idea of what he'd find ten minutes after getting off. He could say with certainty he'd never been here before.

As one light faded from the sky, another emerged, and with it a profound silence enveloping them. What he found most distinctive about the place was that in spite of being so high up the shimmering lights of the city weren't visible from every spot, and the expanse of the lake wasn't either, so long as you didn't climb up and stand on the top of the hillock, where it seemed as if all the dazzling light of the city was only a couple of steps away. Driving up the hill, Vivek had pointed out a dry, deserted well, where pigeons lived, according to him. To prove his point he threw a little stone into the well, and sure enough, there was a fluttering of wings and pigeons flew out.

"I've heard about and have even seen pigeons living up in domes or abandoned havelis," said Vivek, "but this is the first time I'm seeing pigeons live in a well."

"These are dark times, brother," Zamir Ahmed Khan sighed. "It sounds like another version of 'The swan gets the crumbs, while the crow eats the pearls.'"

As he said these words Zamir Ahmed Khan remembered something and burst out laughing.

"What is it?" Vivek asked. "Are you thinking of that poem about a letter box you wrote? 'Kept in this box are countless white-winged doves, at daybreak they'll fly off in the sky north, south, east, and west. To meet their destiny, the place they belong.' Remember?"

Zamir Ahmed Khan silently thought of something for a moment, then smiled again.

"Maybe the real pleasure of life is this," he said solemnly. "You never know what might slip away, and when. How naturally everything happens. It's surprising, and something worth pausing and thinking about for a moment. But who has the time for moments of reflection like this nowadays? We're wrongly imprisoned in the world in which we live. Sometimes I wish, as the poet says, we could take our footprints with us."

"But a person's nature doesn't change," Vivek said. "You were reciting poetry before, and you're still doing it."

"If only! Simply rearranging words grammatically can hardly be called poetry. Anyway, I was laughing about something else: remember Amma's parrot?"

"The 'assalam alaikum' one?"

"It's not like Amma kept so many different parrots that you'd have to tell them apart by name." A tinge of irritation crept into Zamir Ahmed Khan's voice. "If your thoughts are somewhere else, why are you wasting your time with me?"

Vivek let out a laugh. "I'm right here with you," he said reassuringly. "So what about Amma's parrot?"

"Amma and that parrot developed an odd kind of bond," Zamir Ahmed Khan said, lost in thought. "At first they were strangers, and everything she said was answered with gibberish. Then all of a sudden they became so close that even Amma's own children didn't stand a chance. After her death that poor creature became an object of scorn, possibly because there was no room or need for him in anyone's life like there had been in Amma's. No one to clean the birdcage, no one to feed him. He'd greet everyone without needing to be prodded or praised, he'd welcome people and invite them to sit down. He'd start squawking right from the dawn prayer and try to wake everyone up. I witnessed the whole performance for weeks, for months. One morning the moment the bird began reciting the confession of faith, I took it up to the roof terrace and opened the door of its cage. For a moment he seemed undecided, but then flapped his wings and flew off into the sky."

"You set the parrot free?" Vivek was incredulous.

"No, I didn't," Zamir Ahmed Khan replied, emphasizing the "no." "What I did was release a living, speaking, hearing, and seeing creature from captivity, whose only crime was our desire to keep him captive—a desire that didn't exist in him, but only inside our minds. It may have counted as a good deed while Amma was still alive, but after she passed away it became a sin."

"The other family members must have been upset?"

"What do I know," Zamir Ahmed Khan said with indifference. "Everyone's interested in raising their own parrot these days, people couldn't care less about Amma's."

Moonlight filled the sky. Vivek set out a salad he'd made himself. There was no breeze whatsoever. In the deep silence Zamir Ahmed Khan felt the air rush in as he breathed in through his nose, the whoosh down his windpipe flooding his lungs, oxygen absorbed into the bloodstream, and then the spent breath exiting through his nose. He could hear the whole process in his ears from beginning to end. He marveled how the flow of his breath went in and out, uninterrupted, one intertwined with the next, for an entire lifetime—twenty-five years, fifty, a hundred. Wasn't this a miracle?

"This beer isn't doing the trick," he said taking a big sip from his glass. "I feel like there's a short circuit somewhere and it's not hitting my brain. On top of that, it's expensive."

"We've also got whiskey and rum," Vivek offered. "You can have that if you want."

"That would be an insult to you," Zamir Ahmed Khan mocked. "I thought that the well-to-do and twice-born drink beer as a rule when it's hot."

"Why are you so grumpy?" Vivek said, lighting a cigarette. "You're feeling okay these days, aren't you?"

"Deluded! Suspicious! Driveling!" Zamir Ahmed Khan grew more querulous. "The doctors, my wife and children, my relatives, friends and acquaintances all agree on this. Even those who didn't at first have now begun to think so and, I trust, only want what's best for me. I'm sure you're also one of them, so what's the point in asking and pretending you don't know?"

"Well, I can't sit by and listen to you talk like this without doing something about it." Vivek sat up, summoned the servant, and instructed him to switch on the tape recorder. "It's a recording of a Ghulam Ali concert, just came out. Someone brought it for me from Dubai. Let's listen and give it due praise!"

"Isn't this Ghulam Ali Sahib of yours also a Punjabi?" he said sarcastically.

"He is indeed," Vivek didn't take it the wrong way. "And so is the poet who wrote the lyrics."

"And going on about the same old things, clouds, an overcast sky, and wine," Zamir Ahmed Khan teased. "Things irrelevant to poetry today, and to the country and the world." He took a gulp of beer and said in an emotional voice, "Don't you see? The signs of drought didn't come out of nowhere. I'm telling you, no more thick clouds gathering in the skies. No blessing of rain from Allah. Everything will shrivel up in the heat just like that and wait for its end to come, thanks to our actions. People will tell stories of the old days when the rains came and the ashen-colored earth turned green overnight. Flowers, fragrances, color, beauty, all will vanish from the earth and people will listen to old folks' tales of these bygone things, drunk, just like we are now. Tell your man to turn off the music, I'm really not in the mood!"

"Wow, you've really put on quite a curse." Vivek got up and switched off the tape. "All my plans are in limbo waiting for the monsoon. Grass has to spread, flowers need to grow, new plants planted. Besides, my friend, who can imagine life without rain? 'Charged with the warm imagination of what it will be like to sing, I am a bird of paradise yet unsprung.'"

"Ghalib?"

"Who'd know better than you! Even the 'I' of the poem is you."

"Yet unsprung?"

"Which hasn't been born yet. Glad I can be of service to someone who's not a fan of Urdu."

They were silent.

By then, the moonlight had spread throughout the dome of the sky and outshone the rest of the stars. It seemed as if the place where they sat were gradually being drawn upward into the illuminated sky by the moonlight like some flying saucer.

"And how's Asim's business going these days?" Zamir Ahmed Khan asked a straightforward question to keep his thoughts from wandering off.

"It's going well," Vivek replied without offering any detail. "It's never easy in the beginning, but now it has really taken off."

"So there were no more hard feelings and disagreement when you two went your separate ways?" Although he already knew everything, Zamir Ahmed Khan asked for the sake of asking.

"Nothing major," Vivek brushed it off. "You know about the problems we had in the beginning. Some were resolved, the rest written off as a loss. In any case, Asim's very busy these days with that 'Free the birthplace of Shri Ram' movement."

"According to my sources," Zamir Ahmed Khan said as if lifting the veil of secrecy, "so are you."

"I'm not doing anything out of enmity."

"So to defend your religion then?"

"Is it so important for you that your sources are right?"

"Well then, prove that I'm wrong."

"Whether you believe it or not doesn't make any difference. Let it go and tell me, did you meet with Sharafat Miyan again or not?"

"I did not," Zamir Ahmed Khan lied with great aplomb. "But I'm thinking I should meet him soon."

"So you'll go to his place?"

"Yes. If he feels it improper and hesitates to come and see me, I'll go and see him myself. It'll take a little shamelessness, yaar, since it's a dicey enough matter as it is. After years of hard work, nothing's going to get done sitting sulking at home. And then my own responsibilities, my wife, the kids. How long can I avoid facing those? Something or other has to be done in this life. If I don't have to answer to Sharafat Miyan it'll be somebody else. Better to stick with Sharafat Miyan than to start anew with a total stranger. For better or for worse, I've had more than enough time to know him inside and out. What do you think?"

Vivek was silent, perplexed. "It doesn't matter what I think," he said. "But will you have the guts to go? It's easy to say, but will it be as easy to do? To make peace and settle things once and for all? And will Sharafat Miyan be able to appreciate your noble intentions?"

"It's not as if we'd gone to war," Zamir Ahmed said with magnanimity. "How long can you keep on paying someone who just sits around at home, bhai? In a way, he didn't do anything wrong. I was the one who made the world despair of me by calling this fantasy of mine illness. It's really nothing, our quarrel is simply a case of 'an idle mind is the devil's workshop.' If I really put my mind to something I won't even think about it. Keeping yourself busy is the cure for a hundred diseases. As for Rahat, she's staying at her parents' with the girls, pouting. Her complaints are also justified in their own way. It won't be hard to bring her around if I find something to do with myself. There's a limit to what a human being can tolerate, and this is something I also need to understand. I've been thinking of turning over a new leaf and making a fresh start . . ."

"If you manage to pull that off," Vivek said, voice full of doubt, "what could be better?"

"I have no choice," said Zamir Ahmed Khan, emphasizing each and every word. "No more giving in to pointless worry or doubt. Cheers!" He raised his glass and emptied it in one go. "Starting tomorrow . . ."

"Cheers," Vivek said with a mixture of doubt and enthusiasm as he finished his drink.

"Now tell this Bande Ali Khan servant of yours to put on some music," Zamir Ahmed Khan said, stretching out his legs and arms. "But not this tape, let's have some of your Jagjit Hasan or Mehndi Singh or whatever their names are. Old or new, it doesn't matter."

Vivek stood up to go look for the cassette.

"Oh, by the way," Zamir Ahmed Khan said, remembering something. "I forgot to tell you some news. Remember Aapa's daughter Banno? Her marriage's been arranged, the engagement's going to take place in a couple of days."

"Wow, she grew up so fast," Vivek said, surprised.

"That's what girls do," Zamir Ahmed Khan said in a weary voice, opening another bottle. "They grow up as fast as men grow old!"

"That's great news," Vivek paused for a moment after putting in the tape. "Who's the boy? Some relative?"

"Do you remember Idris Miyan who used to be my business partner, back in the day? It's his son. He's working somewhere in the same place your well-wishers got that Ghulam Ali tape for you."

Vivek didn't consider it necessary to explore the matter or inquire about Zamir Ahmed Khan's troubled relations with Idris Miyan from way back when.

"It's wonderful news." He turned on the music and sat down in his chair again.

Zamir Ahmed Khan sat and stared into the bright expanse of the sky. When he was little and the house had a big inner courtyard, during summer nights they'd sprinkle water over the ground and arrange the bedding under the stars. He'd lie on his cot and in the fading light of the sky count flocks of birds as they flew from one end of the sky to the other. On one side of the house was the settled part of town, while on the other, gardens of various names—Umrao Dulha, Farhat Afza, and who knows how many others. They were dense with mango trees. Parrots, herons, geese, finally free from the day's hustle and bustle, returned in flocks to their respective places of rest. As darkness fell, Amma would come and lie next to him and point out a constellation of shimmering stars in the night sky that, if you connected them in a particular sequence, spelled the name Muhammad in Arabic script. He soon became adept at it and was able to trace the name in the sky without Amma's help. As the night wore on, the name appeared in different parts of the sky. When he tried to find these stars again much later, he couldn't. If Amma were there to help, he thought to himself—but meanwhile Amma herself had joined the stars in the sky. When he asked another elder of the family where the constellation was, the elder replied with a mix of laughter and sarcasm, "As if I could see that far at my age!"

Zamir Ahmed Khan had gone off for a walk and came to the edge of the plateau beyond which lay the lake a hundred feet below. The city's flickering lights extended their arms toward where he stood, embraced him, and the moonlit sky and the lake had merged into one. From behind, the music bumped up against his ears, and in the distance Vivek was reclining in his chair, legs stretched out, on a speck of land that rose like a hillock to the sky. Though the air was still, he could hear the quiet melody of waves lapping against the rocks somewhere below. He looked around him and leaned forward to study the waves as they touched the rocks.

Hopefully it's not too late, he thought.

Bhai Jaan appeared before his eyes, driving the jeep in his peculiar way through the foggy valley. He wore the same high-collared camouflage coat and beret he used to wear while hunting. He smiled his trademark solemn smile that was his character made manifest and that set him apart from everyone else. Someone sitting at the back of the jeep, with its top off and windows rolled down, deftly trained the searchlight into the fog. Bhai Jaan drove the jeep fast on dirt roads, over potholes, or off road in the jungle with such dexterity that the other passengers on the hunt didn't get jostled. He sat at the steering wheel at a little angle. When he drove out of the city, the police posted at the crossroads saluted him, to which Bhai Jaan responded with his smile and a slight nod of the head. The searchlight moved about the fog as Bhai Jaan slowly drove the jeep. He saw that while Bhai Jaan was indeed driving a jeep, this one was much bigger and more roomy than a normal one. He was startled as his gaze suddenly fell on the other people sitting inside: Bare Abba, Phaphu Amma, Phaphu Miyan, Amma and Abba—all of them! And others—relatives, acquaintances, people who'd worked for the family. Murshad, Phaphu Biya, and Dulhan Chachi, too. So far no one had discovered the spot where he was hiding.

"Are you sure we'll find him here?" Abba Miyan asked Bhai Jaan.

"Yes," Bhai Jaan replied curtly. "What's going on, Harun Miyan?" he said, laughing at the person sitting at the back. "Have you forgotten how to use a searchlight?"

Bhai Jaan's hunting friend Harun Miyan began to cast the light about more intently. The jeep traversed cloudy mountains, foggy valleys, and silent rivers.

"Maybe this isn't the right time," Abba said, stroking his beard.

"Have a little patience," Amma admonished him.

There were colorful strips of fabric lying in Phaphu Biya's lap, which she was busy weaving together. "Let me know when you find him," she said in her faint voice, "I forgot my glasses."

"Do you ever remember what you're supposed to in life?" Phupha Miyan teased her and broke down in tears.

"Allah have mercy," Phaphu Biya groaned.

"The Sang-e Aswad, covered in spit!" Dulhan Chachi was overcome by a fit of laughter.

"Allah save us from all misfortune and calamity, Allah!" Murshad echoed.

All of a sudden the searchlight came to rest on him.

"It's him." Bhai Jaan's smile came to life, and he drove the jeep toward him and stopped right in front.

He greeted everyone with great respect.

"We're not too late, are we?" Bhai Jaan asked.

"His health is better, Allah be praised," Abba Miyan said with a smile of relief.

"Who is it?" asked Phaphu Amma.

"Zamir," Abba and Amma said simultaneously. "It's good that you're here. All of us were worried sick about you."

They made room for him in the jeep and he sat down timidly between Amma and Abba. Bhai Jaan turned on the engine, and Harun Miyan again began to cast the searchlight.

Heading into the steamlike haze of the clouds all around, the jeep he rode in slowly disappeared from Zamir Ahmed Khan's view.

Epilogue

December 1992.

Silence all around. Silence and the sound of police cars in the streets. And along with your heart beating, a fear that expands and contracts: something is going to happen.

Lamenting faces on the TV expressing condolences. *It was awful, really awful,* everyone says. *Who can control the honeybees! Who can reign in the buzzing honeycomb? Everyone's equal, but under some circumstances, some are even more equal. What's happening is or can be the exception. Their intentions are not bad. The miscreants will be apprehended. They'll pay for what they did.*

Voices of policemen talking in the streets. At the crossing, a whistle responding to other inquiring whistles, a reassurance that all is well. A chill lies languid all around. A police van, sirens blaring, pulls up near the house. Indistinct muttering curses the silence.

"See anything?" Bhai Miyan has come upstairs.

"Just because the police are outside doesn't mean we're safe inside. If two people shove up against the front door, it'll collapse, along with the wall!"

He asks about Abba's canes. Abba was fond of collecting all sorts of walking sticks to lean on. No one knows where they're kept. "At least they'll give us some sense of security," he mumbles. "The way things are, even geckos and mice in the house are giving us a fright."

Outside behind the trees in the graveyard the red glow of fire is spreading. Silence and voices mingle.

"Someone's set fire to something," Bhai Miyan's voice is full of vigilance and worry. "They can show or hide whatever they want on TV, but BBC radio is saying that the whole country's on fire. Hundreds have already been killed."

Bhai Miyan returns downstairs. Trapped between sleep and terror, I begin to doze off. God knows when I'll see Rahat, Saba, and Sana again, but I will. Who knows why I'm so sure, but the question is, when? Maybe the curfew will last a long time, maybe a lifetime will go by before it's lifted. Rahat will be an old woman by the time I see her, and Saba and Sana middle-aged. How will we recognize one another? Will we ask, what did you do during the curfew?

The sight of a crowd advancing from all sides toward the city's Lal Parade Ground. All are in deep mourning. Most are dressed in white. They wear skullcaps out of respect. "Prayers for the missing, prayers for the missing, prayers for the missing," the entreaty echoes like a funeral lament from the crowd. There's a heavy police presence, but out of respect they've all lowered their rifles. I remember when I was little, some important person died somewhere far away and they weren't able to bring the bier. I attended the funeral prayer for the missing together with Abba. As I'm walking toward the Maidan, carried along by the crowd, I see people of all faiths among the faces of the mourners, not just Muslims. Some are friends and acquaintances. The mourners are told to form prayer lines, and those who've come to lead the prayers assemble accordingly. Others move back to the side. I also want to join them, but someone pulls me in. "But I don't know how to say namaz," I whisper. Someone puts a finger to his lips telling me to be silent and whispers in my ear, just do what everyone else is doing! When they fold their hands, fold your hands, when they salaam, you salaam. Don't argue with me, the prayers are about to start.

I see the Maidan is already full of people who've gathered to say the funeral prayer for the missing, or express their condolences. I still want to run away from those praying namaz and join those who've come in sympathy. As shouts of "Allahu akbar!" fill the air, my hands automatically rise to my ears and fold atop my chest. Immersed in the moment, I'm now part of the funeral prayer for the missing.

I wake up with a start. The night is still young. I sense the growing cold, darkness, and dread, so I get up and turn on all the lights in the house, one by one.

Bhopal would have been a more fitting location, but in the dastan tradition of encounters in strange and unlikely places, it was in an arrival lounge at Chicago's O'Hare Airport that we first met the author who is known as one of the most significant Muslim voices in contemporary South Asian literature. It was 2009. For Hindi writer Manzoor Ahtesham, it was his first visit to the United States. For one of us it was a much-awaited, first face-to-face meeting with the author whose work she had studied and written about for many years. For the other, it was the first encounter with the creator of the unforgettable fictional character of the Lost Bhopali.

Born in Bhopal in 1948, Manzoor Ahtesham has been writing fiction in Hindi for more than four decades. His rich and varied oeuvre includes five novels, four collections of short stories, and several plays. Known for his nuanced psychological portraits of Indian Muslims in postcolonial India, Ahtesham depicts the social and historical experience of India's largest minority community in all its complexity. Much of his writing explores the unspectacular territory of everyday life. The characters populating his fictional world are ordinary and eccentric, familiar and strange. He gives us intimate, authentic, and evocative portraits of real human beings; even his secondary characters are fully fleshed out and rarely just stock figures. His descriptions of Muslim family life capture the small joys, conflicts, struggles, and ironies that inform daily existence. While his writing keeps coming back to the extended family as a primary source of identity and belonging, the themes of loss, struggle, and failure loom large in the lives of his characters. The recurring theme of family disruption and decline serves as a powerful symbol of the threats to Muslim identity in the rapidly transforming social, economic, and political landscape of contemporary India. In portraying individual lives reacting to the forces of history and tradition, Ahtesham's writing engages larger political issues and raises timely questions about Hindu-Muslim relations, minority politics, communal violence, and the Indian nation's commitment to secularism. These are large questions, for which he offers neither easy explanations nor ready solutions. His commitment to the craft of writing comes with a deeply humanistic and pluralistic vision. A profound interest in the complexity of human relationships and a staunch refusal to view individual choices through a sentimental or moralistic lens are characteristic features of his writing.

What first attracted us to *The Tale of the Missing Man* was its playful narrative mode and refreshing irony. The novel marks a significant departure from the still-dominant mode of social realism in modern Hindi fiction. We enjoyed the author's subversive and sardonic stance and were intrigued by the novel's unusual and seriously flawed hero, who is urbane, witty, and thoroughly disaffected with himself. But there's more than this. While *The Tale of the Missing Man* continues to explore the themes of Muslim family life and middle-class existence, it also functions as a writer's quizzical and profoundly self-ironic commentary on the process of writing autobiography. *The Tale of the Missing Man* is a novel of a heroic quest gone awry. Ahtesham playfully twists the conventions of the Urdu romance, or dastan, where heroes engage in brave exploits and where heroic actions are invariably rewarded by love. The hero of this modern dastan suffers an identity crisis of epic proportions: he is lost, missing, and unknown to himself and to others. *The Tale of the Missing Man* weaves a twofold narrative, in which the protagonist's and the writer's fate become inextricably linked: the lost hero sets out in search of himself, while the author goes in search of the lost hero, his fictionalized alter ego. In addition to raising questions about Muslim identity, Ahtesham offers a funny, dark, and thoroughly self-reflective take on the modern author's engagement with the genre of autobiography.

Zamir Ahmed Khan, the novel's unlikely hero, suffers from a mental condition that resists diagnosis, a murky mix of alienation, guilt, and postmodern anxiety. As his doctor flippantly, though aptly, puts it, "The world goes from *A* to *Z*, but you go from *Z* to *A*. Fascinating!" As Zamir wanders through life and the streets of Bhopal, he strikes up a series of ill-fated love relationships, manages to alienate his wife, family, and friends, loses his job, and fails in his aspirations as a poet. He is a total nonachiever. Yet unlike many characters in modern Hindi fiction, Zamir is not the typical victim of societal forces. Rather, Ahtesham has created a fascinatingly devious antihero, "by nature an underground man." Dostoevsky, along with André Gide and E. M. Forster, provides a rich intertextual canvas for the narrative's mingling of fictional selves and fictional others. Even as Zamir loses his innocence he is, as the reader soon discovers, a deceptive character and an unreliable teller of his tale. His many white lies are as much a cynical comment on Indian social reality as they are a metaphor for the author's reinvention of his own self in the autobiographical process.

The novel's other protagonist is Bhopal, the city where Ahtesham was born and raised and where he continues to live as an independent writer. Bhopal is not only the setting in much of his writing but also a living presence—alluring, multifaceted, and elusive. As an urban cultural landscape, the city reveals its rich Muslim past in its architecture, lakes, parks, and graveyards. But Ahtesham's Bhopal is not merely a site of nostalgia and memories of bygone days. Rather, the city encapsulates a bewildering urban modernity, with its sprawling cityscape, social dynamism, and its man-made tragedies, epitomized in the Union Carbide disaster of 1984.

A word on language is in order here. As an author who has chosen Hindi as his medium of expression, Manzoor Ahtesham is a versatile stylist who uses a wide range of linguistic registers and has many styles in his repertoire. Like his other novels, *The Tale of the Missing Man* delights in blurring the boundaries between Hindi and Urdu. Ahtesham easily switches from the Persianized vocabulary of refined Urdu to the Sanskritized idiom of choice Hindi, while he never shuns the earthy flavor of the colloquial. Commenting on the elegance and wit of Ahtesham's style, eminent literary scholar and critic Harish Trivedi has called it "so fluent and idiomatic, and so subtly and variously flavoured, as to be a source of constant relish." Trivedi's provocative suggestion that Ahtesham is "basically an Urdu writer writing in Hindi" may have been made in jest, but it captures the richness of a style that defies categorization along established linguistic boundaries between Hindi and Urdu. In this, and in many other respects, Ahtesham's voice is a significant complement and counterpoint to the more familiar English-language fiction that originates in South Asia and in the writers of the South Asian diaspora.

A master storyteller, Manzoor Ahtesham has won many of the top literary prizes in India and has received the Padma Shri, the fourth-highest civilian award of the Indian government. Yet, as with many modern Hindi authors, little of his work has been translated into English. Published in 1986, Ahtesham's second novel and most widely acclaimed work to date, *Sukha Bargad*, has been translated by Kuldip Singh as *A Dying Banyan* (New Delhi, 2005). A complex portrait of growing up Muslim in postcolonial India, the novel may well be called a modern classic in Hindi. *The Tale of the Missing Man* is the first translation of Ahtesham's third novel, *Dastan-e Lapata*. First published in 1995, the novel was shortlisted for the Sahitya Akademi Award, one of India's highest literary awards, and received the Madhya Pradesh government's Vir Singh Deo Award.

Why did the two of you decide to translate the book together, and how did it work logistically? We're asked these questions often, particularly since our partnership as translators deviates from more familiar duos where one cotranslator is closer to the source language and the other the target. We had already cotranslated an early anticolonial satire piece from Hindi and were very happy with the process and outcome. Being contacted by *New York* magazine about a feature on the world's best yet-to-be-translated novels was the catalyst—and we began translating *The Tale of the Missing Man* together, sentence by sentence.

Literary writing is rarely easy, even if there is only one person involved: the meanderings, negotiations, gestations, editing, rewriting all take time, even if it's one person signing off on the final edit. And we were, in a sense, three. Two, often in the same place, sometimes spending hours disentangling a single sentence, shaping and reshaping the sentence until we were both happy with it. And a third person, the author, occasionally physically with us in Chicago or Bhopal, at other times virtually proximate via email or WhatsApp.

Translating from Hindi or other South Asian languages into English means thinking about English in a way that translators of Japanese or Finnish don't have to. South Asia is home to an estimated two hundred fifty million English speakers, and potential readers, of their English translations, and this English has its own history, different in meaningful ways from North American and British English idioms. Is our reader in Delhi or Dallas? If in Delhi, we as translators could render our English as more Indian and assume a closer cultural proximity to the original. This might mean a little less translation, leaving more words in the original Hindi. If in Dallas, we might choose an English more American in flavor and feel the need for more careful recontextualization.

Our general approach was to translate *The Tale of the Missing Man* with a non–South Asian readership in mind. The reason is that the literature of Hindi, despite its status as the world's second-most spoken language, is virtually unknown outside South Asia—and even within, few Hindi authors are known in English. With the goal of gaining a wider readership for both Manzoor Ahtesham in particular and Hindi literature in general, we wanted to make sure that the translation would be approachable by the largest possible audience. We wished to offer a novel translated enough for our reader of serious literature in Dallas but not too much so that our reader in Delhi might feel that they're being served tasteless flat bread instead of piping-hot roti.

Though we kept a non–South Asian reader in mind while translating, there were still many occasions when we felt it was justified, even necessary, to retain Hindi words in our English. Our approach was to try to gloss these words within the text, providing the reader with the necessary context and clues to figure out meaning on their own. We felt that italicizing Hindi words would unnecessarily call attention to them as "foreign," and this in a book that depicts a world that will likely already be quite different for most readers. We decided to avoid footnotes as there are none in the Hindi, and footnotes can give a misleading and undesirable air of academic writing to a work of pure literature. Similarly, we decided against using a glossary, since glossaries divide the readership into those who know and those who don't. We felt confident in our "stealth glossing" of terms within the text itself, and, if necessary, a reader can always Google a word. And despite our general orientation toward a North American readership, we were quite happy to use expressions and idioms from Indian English or British English often and as needed. Indeed, a major aspect of the art of translation from any language is drawing from many different registers and Englishes.

As a novel is re-created, rewritten, and translated, the final arbiter of the English is often the "ear" of the translator. Does it sound right? Are there desired or undesired associations and connotations? In our case, one translator, a native speaker of North American English, was tuned to one frequency, while the other, with deep roots in British English, was tuned to a slightly different one. For the most part, our divergent English "ears" allowed us to generate a greater number of possible solutions to various translation challenges. But it was not uncommon for the two of us, hearing the English differently, to enter into lengthy discussions when one of us felt that a possible choice was either too American or too British. We hope that readers will join us in celebrating the joys of the translators' quest.

ACKNOWLEDGMENTS

This book is the outcome of an amazing shared journey over three continents. We are first and foremost indebted to Manzoor Ahtesham for his enthusiasm for the project since the very beginning, and for his unwavering patience and generosity of spirit through the years, fielding our seemingly endless queries with great dedication and a steady dose of humor. We are also deeply indebted to Manzoor and his family for the warm hospitality with which they received us on numerous occasions in Bhopal: Aijaz and Tasneem Ghafoor and their family, including Ayaz and Navera, who opened up their beautiful lakeside home, and Sarwar, Sadaf, and Sahil, who made us feel part of the family and supported our project in countless ways. Immense thanks to Kathleen Schneider and Martin Stark for sharing their incomparable lakeside refuge in Porto Ronco, Ticino, with us, where we worked on parts of this translation and enjoyed their hospitality *al Lago*. Special thanks go to C. M. Naim for helping translate the book's epigraph, and further thanks go to Timsal Masood for reading our translation with the Hindi by his side. We are lucky to have profited from the insights of our colleagues and students at the University of Chicago. We are indebted to and humbled by the award committee of Northwestern University's Global Humanities Initiative for selecting this project as one of the winners of the inaugural Global Humanities Translation Prize. We would like to gratefully acknowledge the generous support of the National Endowment for the Arts Literature Fellowship in Literary Translation to support this book. A special thanks to Becka McKay, and to friends from the Third Coast Translators Collective for their keen editorial attention to earlier drafts of this book. We are grateful to the editors of *Pratilipi*, where an earlier version of the first chapter of this book appeared. We are indebted to Jennifer Lyons for her steadfast support of this project and for her unparalleled commitment to the world of literary translation. Finally, thanks to our editors and everyone else at Northwestern University Press—and in particular Gianna Mosser, Anne Gendler, Greta Bennion, JD Wilson, and Mike Ashby.